IMPERIAL VENGEANCE

IAN ROSS has been researching and writing about the later Roman world and its army for over a decade. He lives in Bath. Visit his website: www.ianjamesross.com

TWILIGHT OF EMPIRE

War at the Edge of the World
Swords Around the Throne
Battle for Rome
The Mask of Command
Imperial Vengeance

IMPERIAL VENGEANCE

IAN ROSS

HEAD ZEUS

First published in the UK in 2018 by Head of Zeus Ltd
This paperback edition first published in 2018 by Head of Zeus Ltd

Copyright © Ian Ross, 2018

The moral right of Ian Ross to be identified as the author
of this work has been asserted in accordance with the
Copyright, Designs and Patents Act of 1988.

9 7 5 3 1 2 4 6 8

A CIP catalogue record for this book is available
from the British Library.

ISBN (PB) 9781784975319
ISBN (E) 9781784975289

Typeset by Ben Cracknell Studios

Printed and bound by CPI Group (UK) Ltd, Croydon, CR0 4YY

Head of Zeus Ltd
First Floor East
5–8 Hardwick Street
London EC1R 4RG

www.headofzeus.com

IMPERIAL VENGEANCE

Ipse audiam omnia; ipse cognoscam et se fuerit comprobatum, ipse me vindicabo.

I myself will hear everything; I myself will judge. And if it is proven, I myself will avenge.

Emperor Constantine, *Codex Theodosianus*

THE CENTRAL PROVINCES OF THE ROMAN EMPIRE
A.D. 323–326

ATIANS

GOTHS

DANUBE

EUXINE

NAISSUS

THRACIA

BOSPHORUS

SERDICA

PONTICA

MOESIA

ADRIANOPLE

BYZANTIUM

NICOMEDIA

PROPONTIS

NICAEA

THESSALONICA

IMBROS

HELLESPONT

ASIANA

AEGEAN

ATHENS

HISTORICAL NOTE

After a decade of civil war, the Roman world remains divided between two rival emperors. Constantine controls Rome itself and the western provinces, while Licinius rules Thrace, the east and Egypt. For now, a fragile truce holds between them.

Both men have promoted their sons to be Caesars – junior emperors. In the west, Constantine's eldest son Crispus rules in Gaul. Aided by capable military commanders, he has already won a series of victories against the barbarians beyond the Rhine. Loved by the troops and the citizens of the provinces, the young man's prestige and influence grows.

But all know that Constantine and Licinius are ambitious for sole power, and their mutual hostility must soon ignite once again into open war. The prize of battle will be supreme mastery of the Roman Empire.

PROLOGUE

Pannonia, April AD *323*

Fausta was trying not to listen to the screams of the burning men.

Smoke wreathed the three pyres on the riverbank, shot through with spitting flames, and the victims bound to the upright stakes were almost obscured. From the raised imperial tribunal where Fausta was sitting, two hundred paces from the execution ground, the screams sounded almost like the cries of scavenging birds. The smoke rose, three long black smudges against the grey sky, and streamed away across the Danube.

'How long does it usually take them to die?' Fausta asked. She inhaled slowly, nervously, wondering if she might catch the reek of roasting flesh. She thought of the rich meal she had eaten earlier, and her stomach tightened. But all she could make out was the familiar aroma of woodsmoke.

'It depends on the construction of the pyre, domina,' said Rutilius Palladius, the *primicerius* of the Corps of Notaries. 'Sometimes death can take an hour, sometimes much longer...'

'Too much green wood on those pyres,' the emperor broke in loudly. 'They'll choke on the fumes before the flames kill them.' He stifled a cough, and pressed his jaw down against his chest.

Fausta glanced at her husband. Constantine sat in a high-backed ivory chair, his heavy jaw sternly set, his muscular face in profile looking more than usually hawkish. His deep-set eyes glared at the distant pyres, and he held a gold cup of wine in one hand, balanced on the arm of his throne. Fausta wondered if he was already slightly drunk. He wore a plain brown soldier's cloak flung around his shoulders, covering his embroidered tunic and mantle; he had picked up a cold during his campaign against the barbarians earlier in the spring.

'But perhaps, majesty,' one of the eunuchs said lightly, 'this is not a display suited to ladies?'

Constantine snorted, as if the idea amused him, then rolled his head to glance at Fausta. He smiled sourly. 'My wife is made of stronger stuff than most,' he declared.

Fausta merely nodded, sitting upright on her cushioned chair. In fact she found the sight of the pyres slightly revolting. She had never enjoyed the spectacle of death, not even the sight of gladiators in the arena or criminals being mauled by beasts, which most people seemed to find so entertaining. Burning in particular unnerved her; she had recurring nightmares of death by fire, or of being roasted or suffocated in an oven. But she was determined not to show any sign of weakness.

'So she may be, but I am not,' said the old woman beside her, gathering her white mantle around her bony shoulders. Fausta and Helena, her mother-in-law, were seated close together, as if they were the best of friends. 'At my age such things are not to my taste.'

Hypocrite, Fausta thought. She had seen the relish on the woman's face as the prisoners were led out and bound to the stakes, and the fires lit beneath them.

'But perhaps you enjoy the sight, Fausta dear?' Helena asked in a cold dry whisper, leaning closer still so no others could hear. 'Don't the gods you worship – the *demons*, I should say – enjoy *burnt offerings*? They eat the smoke as their sustenance, isn't that right?'

4

Fausta turned to meet the old woman's creased brown face and flinty gaze. Helena's voice still carried the sibilant accent of her native Bithynia. She was an innkeeper's daughter, raised from the dung of the stables by Constantine's father. How old was she anyway, Fausta thought with distaste, seventy, eighty? Why wasn't she dead?

With the embroidered silk hem of her shawl Fausta covered her lips. 'At least my gods do not murder their own sons,' she whispered, and managed a smile.

Helena grinned tightly, and a spark of light winked from her eye. To anyone watching, the two women would appear to be sharing a private joke. 'Perhaps you should try living on smoke yourself for a while?' Helena said, laying a thin hand on Fausta's sleeve. Her fingers tightened to a pinch. 'You are looking somewhat plump these days!'

Fausta's smile was a glazed mask. She refused to rise to the bait.

The emperor's mother had first appeared at court only a year or two previously. Since her arrival in the palace, Flavia Julia Helena had insinuated herself into the emperor's confidence. She was a Christian too, of course, even more fanatical in her piety than Constantine himself. She had surrounded herself with priests and religious teachers, and had built a personal retinue, a court within the court, of officials and eunuchs who wished for her patronage and the access she could grant them to her son's favour.

Fausta had never managed anything as clever. Her marriage to Constantine might not be happy, but at least it was stable. She had given him three children so far, and he allowed her considerable freedom. But now she had been outflanked, and her hatred of Helena was all the purer for being reciprocated. Decades before, Constantine's father had divorced Helena to marry Fausta's own much older half-sister; now the old woman was determined to wreak a long cold vengeance for that insult, and she was savouring every moment of it.

'Well, I will leave you to your amusements, my dear,' the old woman said, then got up, pausing to distribute a few low-value coins to the attendants. Fausta did not turn to watch her depart. She suppressed a shudder of loathing.

Down on the riverbank the pyres were burning more fiercely; Fausta could hear the snap and hiss as the flames rose. If she narrowed her eyes the fires resembled torches, raised against the great grey barbarian wilderness on the far side of the river. A cold sweat was forming on her brow as the familiar night terrors filled her mind. She tried not to think of the bursting flesh, the charring bones.

'Remind me,' she asked in a loud steady voice, 'what crimes those men have committed?'

'Remind her, Palladius,' the emperor said in a weary tone.

'They have been found guilty of conspiring with the barbarians in their recent depredations, domina,' Palladius said. 'Two of them are decurions of the towns of Gorsium and Margum, while the third is the sub-prefect of the Pannonian river fleet. Our Augustus, in his sacred wisdom, has decreed that anyone found to have collaborated with barbarians, or shared in the plunder of their infamous attacks, should suffer death by fire. A ruling perfectly in keeping with the traditional ancestral virtue of the Roman people, and the revived moral spirit of our age!'

'I see,' Fausta replied. She frowned lightly; it often amused her to feign the sort of simplicity expected of women in these matters. There was nothing very traditional about the execution method, she knew; crucifixion would have been usual once, but these days nailing people to crosses was thought problematic by those of the Christian faith.

'And these barbarians would be the Sarmatians that my glorious husband defeated in battle last month? The ones led by... Rampsy Mondus?'

'Rausimodus, domina,' Palladius said, with a condescending shrug. 'The Goths and Sarmatians, yes. The guilty men conspired to allow them across our border, and shared in the spoils of their pillaging. For that they must be punished!'

'No doubt my brother in the east had a hand in it too,' Constantine said from his throne. 'At least one of them was in the pay of Licinius, maybe all three. Weakening our frontiers works to his benefit. Those smoke trails are a clear enough message to him, I'd say.' He waved his cup in the direction of the pyres.

'And now he claims that our troops violated his borders in pursuing the barbarian filth,' Palladius said, his voice rising in outrage. 'He claims that we seized provisions from citizens within his domains!'

'If Licinius wants another war,' the emperor declared gravely, 'he can have one. On my terms.'

The assembled men – military officers, ministers and secretaries – gave a collective rumble of agreement.

Fausta gazed at the burning pyres, and thought about guilt, about punishment. She had never believed in justice; life was dictated by chance, and by struggle. Everywhere the weak and the innocent suffered while the powerful and unscrupulous grew wealthy. If the gods existed, they were too divinely content to care. But Fausta understood power. The power of men, at least: she had been surrounded by it since she was born. Both her father and her brother had been emperors, until Constantine had ended their lives. Now her husband was the greatest emperor of them all.

Casting her gaze across the scene in front of her, she took in the gorgeously patterned tunics of the courtiers and the ministers, the cordon of white-uniformed Protectores standing around the tribunal, the ranks of household troops beyond, the eagles of the Lanciarii and the Third and Sixth Herculia legions, and the banners of the horse guard units. Even here, with the executions in progress, there was a crowd of petitioners waiting to speak to the emperor, to assail him with their pleas. And beyond them all, the three pyres still sending their smoke up towards the clouds. All of it was a demonstration of her husband's power: a power so immense that he could cause those who displeased him to die screaming in the flames.

Yes, Fausta understood power. She understood vengeance too, and that at least she could believe in. Staring at the pyres, she wondered idly who the victims might be, if she had the power to dictate these things.

First, of course, would be Helena. Fausta did not think of herself as a malicious person, but it gave her a sharp satisfaction to imagine the old woman perishing in the blaze. No doubt Helena would return the compliment, if she ever got the chance.

The second pyre, though, would be reserved for Flavius Julius Crispus, Fausta's stepson. That thought gave her less pleasure. Crispus was her husband's eldest child, by an earlier union of dubious legitimacy, but he was his father's pride. Six years had passed since Constantine made Crispus Caesar and sent him off to govern the western provinces, and in that time the fame of the young hero had spread throughout the empire. Crispus had smashed the invading army of the Franks on the plains of northern Gaul, campaigned across the Rhine against the Alamannic tribes, forced treaties of submission or alliance on almost all the Germanic peoples of the frontier, and returned the west to peace and prosperity. And he was just twenty years old.

Twenty. Fausta herself was only a decade older. She was closer in age to Crispus than to her husband, who was over fifty

8

now. She remembered the wedding at Serdica two years before, when Crispus had returned, triumphant, from his victories on the Rhine to marry some plain little grand-niece of Helena's. That too had been the old woman's doing; another tactical move. Once the boy had been a gangling spot-faced adolescent, but when Fausta saw him at Serdica he had looked like a young god, so gloriously handsome it was disturbing.

And now he had a wife, and that wife had already given him a son of his own. Crispus was the anointed successor to the throne, and when that day came Fausta and her own children would be left dangerously isolated. Helena would have her victory.

Fausta had already made several covert attempts to end the young man's career, and his life. Those attempts had failed. Vainly she had wished that some Frankish spear, some Alamannic javelin, might rid her of her young rival. But he was still alive, back in Gaul and flourishing. In fact, Fausta knew that most of Crispus's victories were the work of his military officers: her eunuch, Luxorius, maintained a very efficient intelligence network. But the young Caesar took all the credit, of course.

No, Crispus might be a hero, and a divinely beautiful one too, but he was still her adversary and a danger to her and her children. *The enemy of my blood*; she must destroy him.

And who should die on the third pyre? Fausta considered the question, raising her hand to her mouth and biting at the carnelian ring she wore on her smallest finger. One of those military officers that had made Crispus such a success, perhaps? She only knew the name of one: Aurelius Castus. For a moment she placed him there, in the heart of the fire.

But she had known Castus, long before, and although many years had passed since she last saw him, she still thought of the man as an ally. Perhaps, in a strange way, as something approaching a friend. He could be useful to her, at least. No – the third pyre would not be for him.

She was distracted from her fantasy by two men riding up from the execution ground towards the tribunal. They had been the ones supervising the burnings; both of them wore the belts and insignia of the *agentes in rebus*. They dismounted and approached the emperor, the cordon of guards parting before them. One was a bow-legged, balding man with a dour expression and a stubbly black beard. The other was younger, blond and curly-haired; he could almost have been handsome, Fausta thought, were it not for the fixed intensity of his gaze and the smirk that flickered across his face like a nervous tic.

The younger agent bowed as he stepped up to the tribunal, then knelt.

'Majesty,' he announced, 'the sentences have been carried out. All three guilty men confessed their crimes before the end. They begged your sacred mercy that their families should be spared a like punishment.'

He glanced up as he spoke, and Fausta caught the gleam of enthusiasm in the man's eyes. Just for a moment she pictured children burning, and cold nausea rose in her throat.

'They shall be spared,' Constantine said, with a lazy circling motion of his hand, then turned to Palladius. 'Reward these men for their exemplary service,' he told the official.

The two agents backed away, with a slight air of disappointment. Fausta fought down her repulsion. The third pyre, she thought – the third pyre should be for the smirking executioner himself.

But the man had only been following orders. He was a tool, an appendage of a greater power. It was her husband

Constantine who had ordered the deaths and watched as the sentences were carried out. Just as it had been Constantine who decreed the deaths of Fausta's own father and brother, years before.

The third pyre, surely, was for her husband.

Just for a moment, a heartbeat, the thrill of that thought illuminated Fausta's mind. Then the fear gripped her, a sense of horror so deep she clenched her back teeth. She felt the pulse quicken in her throat; if anyone had even guessed that she had these thoughts... Enough, she told herself. She banished her treasonous fantasies.

She was tired, weary of this imperial cavalcade. Soon it would all be over, and they would travel the twenty miles south to the palace at Sirmium. The thought of a hot bath was almost overwhelmingly pleasant. Would the emperor come to her bed again that night? He often did, after returning from campaign. Fausta felt no pleasure at the prospect. She was almost certain that she was pregnant again; over a year had passed since the birth of her last child, her daughter Constantina. And this was her role in life, she thought: a mill for producing imperial offspring...

'Majesty!' one of the eunuchs said. 'The wind is changing, we should retire...'

A low roll of thunder came from the north; the clouds were dark across the river, where the country of the barbarians stretched to the horizon. Before anyone could move, a gust of damp breeze swept over the tribunal, bringing the unmistakable reek of burning.

Fausta got up, coughing, her maids fussing around her. Constantine was on his feet as well; the entire imperial household stirred into motion. Above them, the long trails of smoke had backed and arched, trailing southwards. The canopy over the tribunal billowed and cracked in the breeze.

'I think we've seen enough here,' Constantine announced. Beyond the cordon of bodyguards the petitioners were already pressing forward, calling out their acclamations even as the smoke gusted around them.

As Fausta turned to her husband, she saw a single black smut whirl down from the air and fall upon his cheek. Constantine raised his hand, brushing at it irritably. A smear of dark grease remained upon his skin.

Moments later, the first heavy raindrops struck the canopy overhead. In the distance, the rain was already damping the fires on the riverbank. As the flames sank into hissing vapour, Fausta could see the charred stumps of the stakes and the blackened bodies bound to each one. In the haze of smoke and steam they appeared to be writhing still.

PART ONE

FOUR MONTHS LATER

CHAPTER I

Germania, August AD *323*

The first sun was just touching the fortifications on the hill crest when the Roman war trumpets sounded from the valley below. The brassy notes echoed, one blending into the next, and birds rose in clattering flocks from the misty beech forests that covered the slopes.

As the last trumpet blast faded, Castus shook the reins and urged his horse forward from the dense gloom beneath the trees. He looked up into the pale glowing blue of the dawn sky. Still cool, but the coming day would be hot. Tipping back his head, he touched his brow and muttered a prayer. *Sol Invictus, Unconquered Sun, Lord of Daybreak, grant us victory...* By the time the sun had climbed halfway to its zenith, he knew, the hill fort must be taken.

Reaching a low rise clear of the treeline where he could survey the slopes ahead, Castus hauled back on the reins. His mount was a big dark gelding named Ajax, restive and ill tempered but strong enough to bear his weight. Castus still missed his old horse, the well-trained mare he had ridden for years, but she was back in Treveris now, in the pastures of a well-deserved retirement. Raising himself in the saddle as the horse blew and kicked at the turf, Castus peered up at the fortification lining the crest of the hill. He lifted his mutilated left hand, the three remaining fingers held stiff to block the low sun, and scanned the enemy ramparts.

No sign of the defenders at first, except for the fading haze of their night fires; then he caught the glint of metal. Speartips along the rampart. Cries of defiance came rolling down the slope towards him, and the dull roar of a Germanic horn from somewhere inside the fortress.

Castus nodded to himself, satisfied. Two months before, the Brisigavi tribe had broken their treaties with Rome and raided both their neighbours, and the settled lands inside the frontier; the Roman troops advancing from the Rhine bridgehead at Brisiacum had already laid waste to their villages and crops. Now only their hilltop fortress, the seat of their king, remained. Soon enough the barbarians would learn the futility of defying the empire.

'Looks strong enough on this side,' one of the staff tribunes said, riding up alongside. The other eight men of Castus's mounted staff followed, forming around him with the long purple tail of the draco standard stirring the air above them. 'The gods grant the scouts were right about the eastern approach.'

Castus grunted in agreement. This was his first view of the fort, but the scouts had prepared a detailed report. At the top of the wooded slope that climbed from the valley there was a cleared expanse of rising ground, cattle pasture in times of peace. A ditch and fence marked the boundary of the fortification, but that was a minor obstacle. The slope beyond was studded with spiked pits and staked with sharpened branches. A hundred paces further were the real ramparts: a deeper ditch, backed with a palisade, and behind that a massive wall of heavy stones dug into the hillside, with a strong wooden bulwark lining the top. Anyone advancing against the fortress would be caught in the killing ground between the two ditches, exposed to the defenders' slingshot and javelins.

But to the east, so the scouts had reported, the hill dropped steeply from the rear of the fortress, and there were no ditches or stakes. Thick woodland clung to the slopes, tangled with thorny bushes. Were the paths that threaded up the hillside really as navigable as the scouts claimed? Castus refused to think about that.

From his left he could hear the troops advancing from the valley. He turned in the saddle, looking back as the first column marched out of the dawn mist onto the open pastureland. The sun caught their standards, glowing on the gold eagles and the streaming draco banners, the images of the gods and the portraits of the emperors. Then the ranks of shields appeared, the big white ovals of the Octavani and the red of the Divitenses. Castus heard the familiar stamp of studded boots, the clash of arms and armour and the low growls of the centurions marshalling their men, and was filled with a profound sense of pride.

Castus had served in the ranks himself for many years. In his heart he was still an infantryman. When he heard the trumpet calls, the sounds of the marching troops, he felt an instinctive response: a surge of energy in his muscles and his blood. But his youth was far behind him; he was forty-seven years old, heavily built, his broad tanned face stippled with scars and his short-cropped hair grey at the temples. With his mutilated left hand he could never again grip a shield properly and stand in the line of battle. He was no common soldier now; he was a senior commander, *comes rei militaris*, companion in military affairs to Crispus, Caesar of the West.

Another wail of horns, then Castus heard the massed clatter as the troops deployed into their assault columns. He had four thousand men under his command: four strong legionary detachments backed up with Frankish *auxilia* and a force of cavalry. Enough to make the barbarians think the killing blow would come from this direction. And perhaps, he thought, they would be right.

'Signal to the tribunes,' he said over his shoulder. 'Let's announce ourselves.'

The hornblower behind him cleared his throat, spat, then lifted his curved horn and sounded the command. The call repeated down the line, and a moment later the front ranks raised a shout. A volley of noise rolled along the slope from the infantry formations, the percussive clash of spears against shields gathering to an echoing din. Birds wheeled in panic in the dawn sky. Castus smiled tightly. That was more like it. He could see the motion along the enemy ramparts, the barbarians thronging to oppose them. Many of the fort's defenders would have been up all night around their fires, drinking and boasting; they would be weary now, but still full of fight.

Every few moments, Castus flicked a glance across the eastern hills behind the fort. The stacked forests were still deep in blue shadow. No wink of light. Every man of the command party was doing the same. Castus was beginning to sweat: should he give the order to attack? How much longer could he delay? The knotted scar on his jaw itched and he scratched at it, rubbing his fingers through the grey stubble of his beard. *Calm*, he told himself. *Wait...*

A rider was approaching from the right, galloping fast with his cloak billowing behind him. Castus recognised him as he drew closer: Aelius Saturninus, a square-headed and soldierly-looking officer, tribune of the guard cavalry, the Schola Prima Scutariorum.

Saturninus saluted as he reined to a halt. 'Excellency, all my men are in position. I've kept them well back, out of sight.'

18

Castus nodded briefly. 'Make sure they stay that way. You'll know when they're needed. No sign of the signal yet?'

Saturninus rode a little closer. 'Nothing. I've got scouts posted all around our perimeter.' He peered at Castus, squinting. 'You could have held him back,' he said quietly. 'He'd have listened to you, if nobody else.'

'You think so?'

Saturninus grinned. 'Our Caesar holds you in high regard! Everyone knows it.'

'I tried my best.'

'No man here would blame you if something happened to him...'

'It's not the men here I'm worried about.' Castus made a sign against bad luck. He remembered the conference in the command tent the evening before, the young Caesar Crispus poring over the sketch map the scouts had prepared, tracing the routes of attack with a fingertip.

'Tell me again about the fort in Britain,' Crispus had said. 'It was like this, wasn't it?'

'Similar, majesty. Not as big, I think.' Castus had told the young man all about the attack he had led on the Pictish hill fort many years ago when he was only a centurion in a frontier legion. He could hardly have refused; Constantine had been in that fight too, and Crispus already knew the basics. Castus regretted it now.

'But you made your attack up the rear face of the hill, yes? You scaled the ramparts on the blind side?'

'We had artillery then, and incendiaries. And it was at night...'

'And we'll scale the slope here by night! Under cover of darkness. I shall lead the assault party, with a thousand men of the Lanciarii Gallicani in light order, and the auxilia of the Bucinobantes...'

'Majesty, with respect, the hill on that side's thick with trees and undergrowth. If they've got any sentries at all over there you'll be spotted and pinned down...'

'But they won't be watching that side!' Crispus had declared with an eager grin. 'Because you'll have assembled the main army over here, to the west, ready to launch a feint attack on the ramparts as soon as my force is in position. While they mass on the western wall to repel you, my troops will scale the defences to the east, burn the palisade and take the fortress from the rear.'

Castus had frowned deeply, peering at the plan, the teardrop shape of the hill fort scribed with charcoal. It was a classic stratagem, and not a bad one. The only problem lay in Crispus's desire to lead the surprise assault himself. Years before, Castus would have insisted on leading it, but clambering up steep wooded slopes in the dark was hazardous even for a man half his age. Besides, Crispus wanted the glory. He wanted to be first across the enemy wall. And that desire for valour unnerved Castus more than anything.

In the last six years, Crispus had changed almost beyond recognition. When he first arrived in Gaul to take up the position of Caesar, ruling in his father's name, he had been a boy of fourteen, gangling and soft. His interests had extended only to poetry and the teachings of his Christian tutor, and nothing had suggested that he had any aptitude for command, certainly not for war.

Since then, Castus could not deny, the young man had proved himself. Crispus had put aside his poetry and philosophy; now he studied only books of strategy and tactics, the *Commentaries* of the deified Julius and the *Dacica* of the deified Trajan, the exploits of Alexander the Great. He had led men into war, and fought on the field of battle. He surely did not realise the extent to which his officers guided him and shielded him, keeping him from the worst perils. Just as his capable civilian bureaucrats ran his empire, Crispus's military officers had run his wars. Until now.

'Caesar,' Castus had told him in the command tent. 'I have to ask you to reconsider. This attack isn't for you, it's too dangerous. Let me appoint one of the senior tribunes to lead it…'

'No!' Crispus had declared with a petulant snap, banging the flat of his hand down on the tabletop. 'I shall lead it myself. My mind's made up.'

Had Castus gone too far? Could he have gone further? He had clasped the young man by the shoulders, urging him to think again, and Crispus had shoved him roughly aside. Knocking back the rest of his cup of wine, the Caesar had paced from the tent. The conference was over, and Castus would have been risking open mutiny to try and change anything now.

So be it, he thought. Somewhere to the east the young Caesar would be getting his troops into position. The only hope of success, of Crispus's safety, lay in driving a frontal assault against the western defences so hard and so fast that the enemy were overwhelmed. It would be costly, but the risk was too great otherwise. If Crispus were injured, if he fell in his vainglorious assault, Castus would be blamed. And whatever Saturninus and the other officers might think, the penalties would be harsh. Even thinking about that sent a prickle of dread up Castus's neck.

A single assault, then, to take the fort. That, and a last-moment act of duplicity that he felt ashamed even thinking about. Guile had never been in his nature.

'Excellency!' one of the Protectores cried. He did not point, but only nodded to the east. Castus swung his gaze, blinking. A moment later and he saw the flash of light from the far hill, the sun reflected off a polished blade. One flash, then a second, repeated. The signal.

'That's it,' Saturninus said through his teeth. He grinned. 'Now – let's hear some battle music!'

Castus nodded and motioned to the hornblower. 'Sound *general advance.*'

Before the ringing notes had relayed along the front lines, the standards at the head of each column dipped and swayed and the troops broke into motion. The trumpet calls were drowned out by the thunderous crash of four thousand shields slamming into formation, the stamp of four thousand pairs of studded boots. Dawn mist still clung to the tussocked grass of the pastures, and streamed like smoke around the flanks of each advancing column.

Castus raised himself in the saddle. Sweat broke at the top of his spine and coursed down his back. His horse felt his agitation and began to toss its head, stamping and pulling at the reins. Fierce cheering rolled down the slopes from the enemy wall; there were men up on the ramparts now, yelling defiance and shaking their spears. A few of them hurled javelins, far too soon.

The columns closed in on the fort from the west and north-west, like the fingers of a clenching fist. To the south the ground was clear. Down there, at the narrowest point of the fort's teardrop, where the main gate lay, Castus had ordered no attack. *Always leave your enemy a way to flee.* At least, so it might appear to them. Saturninus had already ridden back to join his men, the thousand cavalry troopers concealed in the wooded dip.

Now the head of each column had reached the first ditch. They flowed across it, barely slackening the speed of their advance, the rows of bright oval shields sinking and then rising again on the far side like the scales on the back of a huge snake.

22

As the legionaries pushed on into the killing ground, smashing aside the first lines of stakes, their formations tightened into wedges. Shields rose and butted together into a carapace at the head of each column. They were in range of the missiles from the ramparts now, and already the first javelins and slingstones were arcing down at them.

'Excellency, the eastern wall!' one of the staff tribunes cried, pointing. Castus tore his gaze from the advancing troops and looked towards the far side of the fort. Dark smoke was uncoiling against the morning sky, and when Castus turned his head slightly he could make out the distant shouts of the sentries, the cries of battle. He cursed beneath his breath. Crispus's assault had already begun.

No time for delay now. No crafty stratagems; any pause in the advance and the enemy would muster to hurl back the men from the eastern wall. Nothing left now but immediate attack, hard and fast and carrying all before it.

'Double time,' he growled to the trumpeter.

The horns picked up the signal, and a moment later the advancing troops surged forward, the men behind the locked shields breaking into a crashing jog as they approached the enemy defences. Castus stared after them, his teeth clenched and the reins wrapped tight around his fists. He knew what the men in those columns would be feeling now: the rush of fear and the thunder of blood, the darkness behind the shield wall punctured by blades of light, the rattle of missiles overhead, the weight of armoured bodies pressing on all sides; the sweat and the sheer driving exhilaration of combat.

Men were running forward from the columns, engineers hefting picks and mattocks, and they hacked and gouged at the stakes to clear a path to the enemy wall, while the javelins and slingstones rained around them. Castus saw the columns buckle

23

as men fell, the bodies tumbling between the stamping feet of their comrades. Still the advance ground closer, but it was slowing now. The barbarians packed the wall above every point of approach, screaming as they hurled their spears, some of them heaving down rocks at the advancing Romans. Archers moved up between the assault columns, shooting volleys of arrows up at the defenders. But too few to make a difference. If only they had artillery… Even a dozen *ballistae*, Castus thought, would be enough to sweep the ramparts clear for long enough to gain a foothold.

'Send the auxilia forward,' he said through his teeth. The trumpet cried, and at once the mass of allied Germanic troops waiting in reserve raised a bellowing yell and began to charge up the slope in the wake of the legionary columns. At their head Castus could make out the red tunic and blond hair of Bonitus, the Frankish chief who had led his people across the frontier five years before to fight for Rome. Many of Bonitus's warriors wore Roman equipment now, mail shirts and helmets, but their barbaric glee in warfare was undiminished.

Castus eased his right hand from the knotted reins, and drew the long broad-bladed *spatha* from his scabbard. 'We're moving closer,' he said. 'Ursio – guard my left.'

The Protector behind him saluted and moved into position. Flavius Ursio was a big man, almost as heavily built as Castus himself; despite his Roman name, his high cheekbones and almond-shaped eyes clearly showed his origins among the eastern Sarmatian peoples. Not a great talker, but he was a ferocious fighter and Castus needed a good sword on his undefended flank.

With the purple draco banner streaming out above them, the men of the command party cantered forward with the mounted escort of horse archers close behind them. Ahead, the first assault column had reached the deeper inner ditch;

as he rode, Castus watched the leading men drop down the slope, raising their shields above them to form a bridge. Their discipline was formidable, months of training on the drill fields of Treveris paying off. When the bridge was secure, the next party of men surged across, supported on the shields of their comrades, and threw themselves at the palisade on the far side.

At the brink of the outer ditch Castus slowed his horse and waited for the command group to form around him. Slaves were carrying the wounded and dying back from the track of the advance. At the palisade, a fury of axes. The sky above the fort was black with smoke now, the eastern wall burning. Had the assault party managed to break through? No way of telling from here. A cheer went up from the men of the Octavani as the palisade ahead of them collapsed; already they were dragging the heavy timbers back to form a solid bridge across the ditch, others pressing forward through the breach and wrestling the scaling ladders into position. All of it beneath a hail of barbed iron and whirling stone.

The first ladders went up and the leading men began to climb, shields gripped before them. Further along the wall, the advance party of the Divitenses had formed a ramp of interlocking shields for the Franks coming up behind. Castus saw Bonitus leading his warriors up the shield ramp against the wooden bulwarks lining the brink. Arrows cut the air and thudded against the timbers, but the ramparts were boiling with defenders. Men fell tumbling, screaming, their shields cast aside.

They won't make it, Castus thought, icy dread rising through his body. He longed to leap from the saddle, run at the wall himself. His horse pranced, pawing at the turf along the lip of the ditch.

'The gates!' somebody called. Castus swung his head and saw one of the staff tribunes pointing away to the south. 'Excellency – they've opened the gates!'

Sure enough, the massive wooden portals of the main gate had been swung wide, and a tide of people was surging out through them and scattering across the open ground to the south. Most were civilians, women and children, some carrying bundles of possessions. But there were plenty of warriors fleeing among them too: whatever sub-chief had been ordered to hold the gates had deserted his post. Castus's breath caught in his throat; he had hoped for this, leaving the southern approaches clear as an encouragement, but had not expected it so soon.

'Ride to Saturninus,' Castus called to one of the mounted messengers. 'Tell him to bring his cavalry up, cut through those fugitives and take the gate!' Pulling on his helmet, lacing the straps beneath his jaw, he glanced back at the gateway: there was a pack of bodies in the opening now, some of the defenders trying to stem the tide of fugitives and close the gates again. Only moments remained to act, and the closest mounted Roman force was Castus himself and his bodyguard.

'After me!' he shouted, kicking his horse forward to vault the ditch. 'We're taking the gate ourselves!'

One of the tribunes grabbed at his horse's bridle. 'Excellency! You risk too much...'

'My men are dying up there!' Castus shouted, stabbing a finger at the ramparts. 'Get your hands off my fucking horse and *obey orders*!'

As he crossed the ditch and rode clear, the irony of the situation brought a savage grin to his face. Only the night before he had been trying to persuade Crispus not to throw himself recklessly into combat; now his own officers were doing the same to him. For a moment he realised the danger; he thought of his wife and children, back home in Treveris: could they ever forgive him if he were injured, slain...? Then the speed of the charge and the pulse of his blood blanked his mind, and all he felt was the thunder of the hooves beneath him as his powerful gelding stretched out into a gallop.

One of the fleeing warriors turned to confront him; Castus raised his sword, but before he could strike, Ajax's flying hooves had kicked the man down and trampled him. Others scattered before the charge. From the corner of his eye he could see Ursio closing on his left, the rest of the command group coming up fast behind him. The draco standard let out a whining howl as it flew. A running figure veered across Castus's path, and he caught the flash of a woman's face, grey with fear, before she fell beneath the hooves.

Men were streaming along the rampart walkway, trying to reach the gates. This was a race now; to his left Castus saw Ursio blast through a pair of warriors at a flat gallop, his sword wheeling, drops of blood flashing in the sunlight. He chanced a look to his right, and saw the leading horsemen of Saturninus's Scutarii powering up the slope from the woods. The mounted archers behind him were already shooting from the saddle, picking off the men on the ramparts and on the gallery above the gateway. And the gates were still open.

Closing the distance fast, Castus sawed at the reins and swerved his horse towards the stone ramp that climbed to the gates. Warriors blocked the path, shields and spears raised. They shrank back from the fury of his attack, but the big wooden portals were closing. Another moment and they would be sealed, Castus and his men trapped in the narrow funnel of the gateway, exposed to the missiles of the defenders above. A javelin darted down, raking Ajax across the haunch. The horse screamed and reared, Castus clinging to the saddle as he fought to regain control. For a moment he feared he would tumble backwards and fall beneath the hooves of the riders behind him. Something struck his helmet, and another javelin deflected off the gilded metal shoulder of his cuirass.

Then Ursio was riding past him, spurring his horse up the ramp with his shield held above his head. The horse rammed against one of the gates, pushing it back, then the big Sarmatian was through the gap, his sword hacking at the defenders.

Castus leaned forward over the saddle horns, bringing Ajax under control and kicking his heels. The horse bucked, and then bolted forward, shoving aside one of the barbarians still blocking the ramp, lashing out at another with bared teeth. A warrior with a flaring red-dyed beard aimed a spear-thrust at him, and Castus smashed it aside. He swung a backhand blow from the saddle, cutting down the last opponent; then he was riding on through the gates after Ursio with a tribune and two archers at his back.

The ground beyond the gate was spattered with blood, and the hooves kicked it into a churned mess as the riders pushed through into the fort. The mounted archers were riding in by twos, turning in the saddle to loft their arrows back at the men on the ramparts. Saturninus's armoured horsemen followed close behind them, and everywhere the defenders were in flight.

Castus blinked. Blood in his eye, and he felt a sharp ache in his shoulder. He was in a lower compound of the fortress, another stone wall to his left. But it was only a raised terrace, with no palisade, and above it Castus could see the thatched roofs of the settlement inside the circuit of ramparts. To the east, flames rose from the far palisade. Cheers from the western wall as the defenders fell back, rushing to protect their wives and families from the horsemen piling in through the gate. Any moment now the first attackers would be across the rampart.

'The gods are good!' Saturninus cried, slowing as he rode past. 'You must be the first man in living memory to storm a hill fort with a cavalry charge!'

Castus shrugged, grimacing. His shoulder hurt, and there was blood on his face and a hot stinging pain above his left eye. The Scutarii had formed into a rough wedge and were pushing on into the heart of the fortress, driving the barbarians before them, warriors and civilians alike. For a moment Castus remembered the woman he had ridden down as he raced for the gate. Was it fate that had thrown her before him? Was it the will of the gods? Smoke eddied in the clear morning air as the riders fired the first of the huts.

'A glorious victory!' Crispus declared in a hoarse shout, picking his way between the corpses lying on the bloodied turf. 'Have we managed to capture their king?'

'He fell in the fighting at the western wall, Caesar,' Castus replied, swinging from the saddle. 'Bonitus took his head, I believe.'

Crispus was grinning, still dazed, his dark blond curls plastered to his scalp with sweat. He held a sword in his hand, and there was a smear of blood on his cheek.

'You came over the eastern wall with the assault party?' Castus asked warily, avoiding the young man's eye.

Crispus's grin slipped for a moment. 'No,' he said. 'Not in the first wave anyway... I would have done, I wanted to... But my fool of an orderly managed to mislay my helmet in the darkness. I didn't want to take one from another man, and I had to order the assault before it was found.'

'Very wise,' Castus said, nodding, with a tight frown. 'Shouldn't go attacking walls without head protection.'

Crispus glanced at him, a flicker of doubt crossing his face. Then he threw back his head and laughed. All around him men were shouting his name, lifting their hands in salute. He raised his sword in the sunlight, acknowledging their acclamation.

As the young man strode away, Castus noticed the orderly lingering some distance behind him, the Caesar's plumed golden helmet cradled in his hands. He caught the man's eye, nodded, and raised his hand slightly. Doubtless the orderly would be punished for losing the helmet at a vital moment, but Castus would see that he was recompensed. The man had only been following his orders, after all.

The fight inside the fortress had lasted only a brief time after the gate was taken and the ramparts breached. With their king slain, the Brisigavi warriors had retreated to a redoubt at the centre of the fort, but they could not have hoped to hold out for long. Surrounded on all sides by disciplined Roman troops, most had thrown down their weapons after a short and demoralised defence. Now all that remained was the chaos that followed every battle. Castus scanned the burning huts, the reeling bodies, the Frankish auxiliaries running wildly in search of plunder. The legionaries were rounding up the surviving barbarians, civilians and disarmed warriors, and herding them into cattle pens in the southern compound. Soon those ragged survivors would be sent to the slave markets of Treveris and the cities of Gaul. Rome had enacted her vengeance.

Through the smoke that hung in a reeking fog across the inner compound, Castus saw the Frankish chieftain, Bonitus, with the warriors of his retinue. The Frank called out to him, pumping his spear in the air, and Castus raised a hand in response. Pulling himself back into the saddle, he rode up towards the fallen redoubt.

He was familiar with the numbed disgust that followed victory. It was different for the soldiers – for them, there was only celebration, fierce pride, the chance of plunder. But for the commander, Castus had learned, there was little joy in a battle won. His brief foray into combat, and the realisation

30

of the risks he had taken, had left him cold and shaken. Once he could have taken pleasure in it, but no longer. He forced himself to look at the corpses on the ground around him. Many of them women, even children, slain on the thresholds of their own homes. Such was war; he had known it all his life. But inevitably now he thought of his own wife, his own children. All that he could have lost, and so easily.

Over by the rough stone wall of the redoubt, a band of Frankish auxilia had formed a ring around a huddle of surviving Brisigavi. Castus peered at them, mystified: for some reason the soldiers were hanging back, raising their shields, although none of the barbarian prisoners appeared to be armed. As he turned his horse and rode closer he spotted an officer among the auxilia, dressed in a Roman scale cuirass and plumed helmet.

'What's happening here?' Castus called. 'Get those prisoners down into the pens with the rest!'

The officer punched the side of his helmet in a rough approximation of a salute. 'There's a witch woman among them! My men fear she'll curse them if they go near...'

Castus spurred his horse forward, the ring of auxilia parting to let him through. Other horsemen were coming up behind him, drawn by the suggestion of trouble.

The knot of barbarians was pressed back against the stones of the redoubt, huddling together behind an old woman in a tattered dirt-brown robe. Castus felt a nervous prickle of superstitious dread, a queasy sensation in his gut. The old woman's long unbound hair was matted with what looked like dried blood, and she wore a necklace of bones and amulets around her withered neck.

'Your king is dead,' Castus called to the barbarians. 'Your fort is ours. Obey our orders, and Rome will be merciful!' He had no idea if any of them understood his words.

As he urged his horse forward again, the old woman threw up one bare corded arm, fingers spread. Castus flinched instinctively, clenching his thumb into his fist as a ward against evil magic. He was careful not to meet the woman's gaze.

'I know you!' the woman cried, in cracked Latin. Fumbling with her necklace, she drew forth a circular amulet of misted amber glass and held it up to one eye. She peered at Castus through the glass, the fingers of her raised hand flexing. Castus heard the men around him gasp and shuffle backwards.

'I know you – a killer!' the witch said, squinting through her glass. 'A taker of innocent lives! You are a man of *blood* – the spirits see it!'

Castus opened his mouth to speak, to command, but his voice was gone. His scalp crawled, and fingers of dread itched his spine. All he wanted to do was snatch out his sword and cut the woman down. He felt his horse shiver and try to turn away.

'Many more you will kill!' the woman declared. 'Much more blood you will spill... Innocent blood... And you also will kill your own king!'

Something snapped in the air just behind Castus, and he swayed in the saddle. When he glanced back at the old woman, he saw the arrow had struck her through the throat. She made no sound, no cry. For a moment more she stood, then her body seemed to fold beneath her and she collapsed to the ground.

Castus turned and saw Saturninus lowering his bow. 'Best be rid of such people,' the tribune said with a shrug. 'They only cause trouble!'

The Frankish soldiers paused barely a moment before rushing forward, stepping around the ragged corpse of the witch as they seized the remaining prisoners. Castus tugged at the reins and let Ajax carry him a short distance back down the slope away from the redoubt. *It meant nothing*, he thought. The rantings of a mad old woman. *It meant nothing.* But the strange cold sensation did not leave his body, and he was fighting hard not to shudder.

Who had heard her words? Few of the Franks understood Latin, and the officer commanding them had been standing well back. Then Saturninus came riding up alongside him. There was no need to ask the question.

'I didn't really catch what she was saying, did you?' Saturninus said with a slight, conspiratorial smile. 'Who knows what the old hag meant, eh?'

Castus drew a long breath, pulling himself up straight in the saddle. He should forget it, but he could not. The old woman's cracked voice ran through his mind.

And you also will kill your own king...

CHAPTER II

The doors closed behind him, cutting off the sounds of the street. In the gloom of the entrance vestibule Castus waved away the slaves who rushed to attend him. He removed his own boots and cloak, and splashed his face with water from the basin on the bench. For a moment he stood still and relished the cool and quiet. Nearly two months had passed since he had left Treveris to join Crispus and his army on the campaign against the Brisigavi. He did not like to admit it to himself, but he was glad to be home.

A strange noise was coming from the garden court, a staccato gabbling squawk. As Castus emerged into the sunlight of the colonnade he saw the two girls, his stepdaughters, sitting on the low wall between the pillars and peering down into the garden. At the sound of his footsteps they both turned, surprised.

'Oh, you're back already!' cried the older girl, Dulcitia. For a moment she rose, as if to run and greet him, then regained her self-possession. 'We didn't expect you until the end of the month...'

Castus crossed the tiled floor in three long strides and enfolded both of them in a hug. 'Nor did I,' he said. 'Thought I'd slip in quietly and not disturb anybody...'

Stooping, he planted a rough kiss on the crown of each head, and the girls flinched away from him, laughing. Dulcitia was fifteen now, and liked to affect a superior air. Within the year she would be married; let her play at being an adult, Castus thought, while she was still a child. Castus had known her and her younger sister Maiana for over five years; at first they had been wary of him, finding his size and scarred ugliness disturbing. But now they were a part of his life. How surprising, he often thought, that his love for them should feel so uncomplicated, so freely given and received.

'Who are the slaves outside the front door?' he asked. 'I didn't recognise them.'

'They belong to the man who's come to see Mother,' said Maiana, then wrinkled her nose. 'He's a *Christian*.'

'Actually, he's the new *bishop*,' Dulcitia said with a pious air.

'Is that so?' Castus said, low in his throat. He had known for some time about his wife Marcellina's growing enthusiasm for the Christian cult.

'Well, anyway, he's talking with Mother in the library room,' Maiana said, then switched her attention back to the garden. 'Have you seen our new goose?'

Frowning, Castus glanced at the large grey-white bird strutting and flexing its neck over by the pond. Grain was sprinkled on the gravel in a spiralling pattern, but the goose was ignoring it.

'We're trying to teach him to dance,' Maiana said. 'But the silly thing won't follow instructions!'

'Not surprised,' Castus said under his breath. As he watched, the goose let out another gargle of squawking noises, then launched itself upwards and managed to flutter the short distance into the pond. Its clipped wings beat the water into a fountain of spray.

'Diogenes said that a goose saved Rome, back in the ancient days,' Maiana said. 'It warned everyone when the barbarians were attacking the Capitol!'

'Did it?' Castus mused, raising his eyebrows. He often wondered if it had really been a good idea to have Diogenes, his military secretary, educate the girls in Roman history. Diogenes had been a teacher once, but he had some baffling ideas. Castus was often unsure when the man was joking... But Marcellina had insisted on it. 'The girls should learn of their ancestors,' she had told him. Castus was amused by that: she had never been to Rome herself, and her own ancestors were Spanish and British tribal nobility. Castus's forefathers were Pannonian peasants from the Danube. Rome was something of the mind and the heart, not the blood.

'The barbarians wouldn't ever come here to Treveris, would they?' Maiana asked, narrowing her eyes speculatively. 'I don't know if our goose would be much good at warning us if they did.'

'Don't worry about that,' Castus told her. 'The only barbarians around here are serving in the young Caesar's bodyguard.' A shadow passed across his mind, a brief memory of the slaughter after the fall of the hill fort. He dispelled it. 'Where's Sabinus?'

'In the bathhouse yard,' Dulcitia said. 'He's *training*...'

Leaving the girls to their new pet, Castus circled the garden court towards the passageway that led to the yard at the back of the house. He wanted to see Marcellina, wanted to see her more than anything, but he would wait until she was finished with her guest.

This house had been his home since he was promoted to the Caesar's retinue, although he spent little enough time here. It was a grand structure, taking up half a city block adjacent to the palace, with a double-storey central courtyard, garden and fountain courts, a private bath suite, faded wall paintings and polychrome mosaics. Pacing along the corridor, Castus was reminded once more that he was a wealthy man now. It was an unsettling thought. He had never been comfortable with luxury or riches, or with the privilege and formality of high rank, and while he was glad that he could provide a good home for his wife and the children, he had never felt he truly belonged in these surroundings.

How strange it was, after spending most of his life in the all-male world of the legions, to find himself in this new domestic environment, surrounded by females. Once he might have found it intolerable and longed for the sour fug of the barracks hut and the centurion's quarters that had been his home for so long when he was a younger man. But, stranger still, he found that he had come to enjoy these brief intervals of domestic tranquillity, and the company of women.

'Dominus!' a voice said. 'They told me you were back...' Castus turned to see Eumolpius hurrying down the stairs from the upper floor. Eumolpius had long been his orderly and armour-bearer; he was no longer a slave, but still a part of the household, a freedman steward now. He clasped Castus by the hand in greeting. Castus had always thought of him as a young man, if an unnaturally grave and sombre one. Now he noticed the steward's greying hair and the lines on his face as he smiled. *Gods, we're all getting old...*

'Have the bath heated, will you?' Castus said. 'And send a message to my wife that I'm back. Otherwise I'll need nothing else before dinner.'

Eumolpius went to make the arrangements, and Castus continued along the passage towards the sunlight of the yard. There was another sound now, a familiar one: the smack of arrows into wicker and straw.

To one side of the yard were the whitewashed apses of the baths, to the other was the wooden portico fronting the kitchen and carriage shed. In between, before the gates that led to the street, was a large bale of straw painted with a target and bristling with arrows. Aurelius Sabinus, Castus's son by his first wife, stood at the centre of the yard with a bow in his hand. He lifted it, drew, and took careful aim; for a heartbeat he held the arrow, then loosed. It struck the target with a powerful *whack*, a little off centre.

Castus stood for a moment, leaning in the doorway and watching. Sabinus was twelve years old now, and the boy's resemblance to his mother was striking. But he was growing well, and quickly; the long hours of exercise, horse-riding and training had paid off. The boy was naturally gifted, fast and dextrous. Castus felt a glow of pride and love as he watched. He had never demanded such attention to arms, had not even encouraged it. Either the boy enjoyed it, or he felt he had something to prove.

Three heartbeats later, the archery trainer noticed Castus leaning in the shadow of the doorway and cleared his throat, saluting.

'Father!' Sabinus cried, turning abruptly as he lowered the bow. Just for a moment Castus saw the boy's look of genuine pleasure at his appearance. Then Sabinus's eyes clouded. 'You're here,' he said. 'Is the war over then?'

'That one is,' Castus said, shoving himself away from the door. 'For now, at least.' He crossed the yard, dropped to one knee and gathered his son in a firm embrace. Sabinus stiffened at first, embarrassed, then Castus felt the flex of the boy's body as he relaxed and returned the hug.

'You're hurt,' Sabinus said, pulling away with a concerned frown.

'Just a small cut,' Castus told him, touching the stitched welt above his left eye. 'From my helmet rim. Should have worn more padding under it, eh?' His shoulder was still heavily bruised as well, and his hip ached, but he did not want the boy to be concerned.

'Was the Caesar hurt too?'

Castus grinned, shaking his head, and scruffed the boy's fine black hair. Ever since his first introduction to Crispus, years before, his son had nurtured an abiding fascination for the young ruler of the west. Castus had often found it troubling. Partly, he knew, because his own relations with his son were strained at times. The boy's mother had died over six years before, but her shade still lingered, and Castus's frequent absences on campaign or on military business had left Sabinus alone in a household of women and slaves. Did his son still feel neglected? Did he somehow blame Castus for his mother's death? Castus himself had never been confident in emotional matters. He knew he was clumsy with the feelings of others, and while he tried to show his love for his son he found it difficult to communicate with him. Perhaps, in time, things would change.

'Back to your practice!' he said, straightening up with a grunt. 'I need to speak to your stepmother.'

Sabinus shrugged, turning away at once, and plucked a new arrow from the quiver at his feet. Castus felt the skip of his heart; again he'd made a mistake. He clasped the boy by the shoulders for a moment, then released him. One day, he thought; one day they would understand each other.

Back in the garden court, he almost collided with a figure hurrying from the further passageway. The man stepped back neatly, bobbing his head in apology. Castus saw the grey beard, the patterned robes: this, he realised, must be the Christian priest, the new Bishop of Treveris. What was his name? Agrinius? Agricolanus?

'My apologies, excellency, I was just leaving,' the priest said, glancing at Castus with an awkward smile and an expansive gesture. Two of his own liveried slaves hurried along behind him. 'I should stay to congratulate you further on the glorious victory granted to our blessed Caesar, but duties compel me...'

'Hmm,' Castus grunted, with a curt nod. He stepped aside to let the priest and his slaves pass, then watched as they stalked quickly through the vestibule to the front doors.

Trying not to let the encounter darken his mood, Castus continued along the passage towards the library room, his wife's favourite chamber. She had always loved books; Castus had been illiterate for most of his life, and only recently had he managed to gain any appreciation for the written word. Even so, the library was his wife's domain, not his own. Ahead of him, one of the house slaves opened the panelled doors and announced him.

Sunlight spilled through the window that opened onto the fountain court at the far end of the room. It fell across the grey mosaic floor and the shelves of scrolls and codices, and illuminated the couch where Marcellina sat waiting. She had tinted her hair with henna, and the light made it glow like burnished copper. As Castus entered the room she got up, gathering her pale green shawl around her shoulders.

'Husband!' she said, blushing slightly as she fought to hide her smile. The pair of slaves that attended her were gazing at the floor. 'I didn't expect you so soon, I'm sorry, I...'

'No matter,' Castus said, a warm grin breaking over his face. He had longed for this woman all the time he had been away. Not with the aggrieved hungry longing he had felt for his first wife, but with a love far deeper and truer than anything he had known in his life. Marcellina ran to him, and he met her in the middle of the room, pulling her into an embrace.

For a few long heartbeats they remained locked together, heedless of the slaves. Castus breathed in her scent, the soft warmth of her body. Marcellina was thirty-five years old, but she still had the vivacity of youth; she appeared more beautiful now than when Castus had first met her, a seventeen-year-old, at her father's villa in the north of Britain.

Then, all too swiftly, she drew away from him again, composing herself.

'If I'd known you were returning so soon I would never have invited Bishop Agricius—'

'I said it *doesn't matter*,' Castus broke in, a little too firmly. He did not want to talk about Bishop Agricius; not now, perhaps not ever. Marcellina caught his eye, a flinch in her gaze, and then looked away. Castus noticed the cane chair drawn up to face the couch, the circular table with its two cups. Wine, not water. Was the Christian god supposed to turn wine into water, or was it the other way around? Then he noticed the amulet that his wife was wearing, suspended on a necklace of coral beads. The interlinked X and P, the same symbol that Constantine had ordered his troops to inscribe on their shields before the battle of Milvian Bridge. The Christian sign. A sudden flush of anger tightened his jaw.

'But I invited him, as I say,' Marcellina went on, returning to sit on the couch. She was speaking lightly, but her voice betrayed her. 'We were speaking about poetry, as it happens. Virgil. The bishop's a very educated man! He has a fascinating theory about the *Aeneid*...'

'Educated,' Castus grunted. *More educated than me*. He was struggling to hold back his annoyance, and not let this unexpected development sour their reunion. But it felt too late now, all of a sudden. Marcellina could always read his moods perfectly.

'He comes here often then?' he said, unable to restrain the bitterness in his voice. 'To talk about *poetry*?'

'Castus, please...'

'I know what's happening. He wants you to join his cult!'

'His *cult*,' Marcellina declared, sitting upright on the couch in a blaze of indignation, 'is the faith of your emperor! And your Caesar, and most of the officials you call friends!'

'Not *my* friends!' Castus said. He was pacing across the room and back, his shoulders bunched.

'And yes, since you mention it. I've decided that I want to be baptised into the faith. I was going to tell you later, but why not now?'

'*Baptised?*' Castus cried, appalled, and smacked his fist into his palm. He knew the word, and what it meant. 'Not even the emperor himself's gone that far! And then... what? You'd deny the gods of your ancestors, the gods of Rome? For a heap of old bones and the chanting of old men?'

He recognised the anger now, and knew that it had been building in him for months, maybe for years. All that time he had concealed his unease and his misgivings, his confusion at the way the world around him was changing. It was all too fast, too foreign to him. And now this new alien idea had invaded his own house, his own family, the woman he loved.

Marcellina stared at him, taut with frustration and anger. With a gesture she dismissed the slaves. After the doors closed there was silence, broken only by the spattering of the fountain in the courtyard outside.

'I deny nothing,' Marcellina said. 'I merely admit a possibility, that's all. A possibility of *hope*... Why can't you understand that?'

Castus dropped his gaze to the floor, trying to hide his fury, and the mosaic pattern of birds and foliage was a grey blur

42

before his eyes. 'Your father despised the Christians,' he said. 'He laughed at their ideas.'

'My father was completely ignorant of them!'

For a heartbeat the anger peaked between them, charging the room. Then Marcellina let out a cry and dropped her head into her hands. Castus winced with guilt. He should not have spoken of her father in that way.

'That's just it,' Marcellina said, her voice quiet and broken. 'Don't you understand? I've lost so much... My father and mother, my brother, my first husband. Since I was barely more than a child I've been surrounded by death.' She looked up at him, her eyes wet with tears, her hands open and imploring. 'Isn't it better to believe there's something beyond this life? Something more than shadow and forgetting? To believe that we can be reunited with those we loved, after death? That the world wasn't just created by chance, and ruled by violent beings that wish us harm... Castus, Christianity is a religion of love, of forgiveness! Can't you accept that?'

Castus bit back his words. He knew the stories. He had heard them at the palace: the Christians said that all who did not believe in their ideas would be punished after death, burned for an eternity. What sort of love was that? Would Marcellina really sentence the souls of her family to such a fate, or did she think she could save them with her devotion?

But when he looked at his wife, and saw the intense anguish that racked her, the rage died inside him. With an effort of will he eased his clenched fists and lowered his shoulders. A deep groan rose from inside him, and he crossed the room and knelt before Marcellina, taking her hands.

'I'm sorry,' he said, letting his head drop to her shoulder. The words were a rough grunt, but they were enough. She rubbed at the bunched muscles at the back of his neck. 'You can believe whatever you like,' he said. 'I'm sorry... There are many things in this world I don't understand.'

'There are so many things you do understand as well, my love. More than you know. And I would never ask you to change.'

He felt her lips against the scar on his brow, her slender fingers tighten in his grip. The tension flowed from his body. Then a burst of rueful laughter rocked her back onto the couch.

'You stink of horse sweat, husband!' she said, grinning. He saw the light in her eyes, and smiled back at her.

'I told Eumolpius to heat the bath,' he said. 'Want to join me?'

For a moment she considered it, smiling as she bit her lip. 'Later,' she said.

Castus stood up, drawing Marcellina to her feet. A thought struck him. 'There's a banquet at the palace tomorrow night. To celebrate the victory...'

'The victory, of course!' she said, eyes wide. 'I'm sorry, I should have congratulated you already. You must tell me all about it.'

Castus frowned, tightening his lips. He told his wife little about what happened on campaign; with all that she had suffered, all that she had seen, he thought it best to say as little as possible.

'Another time,' he said. 'If you like. And you can tell me all about Virgil and his fascinating theories.'

'The bishop, you mean, and *his* theories?'

Castus shrugged, unable to stifle his smile. *I would do anything for this woman*, he thought. *This woman, my son, my family... Anything but deny my gods and the faith of my ancestors.*

Only as he was pacing back down the corridor towards the garden court did his mood of pleasurable reconciliation shift.

The memory of the burning fort returned to him, bringing the cracked voice of the old Alamannic woman, the witch. Her prophecy. He paused in the darkness of the corridor and fought down a shudder, feeling the dance of shadows at the back of his mind.

Then the sound of the children's voices came to him, distant birdsong, the squawk of the goose. Castus gave a dismissive grunt, cleared his thoughts, and marched on towards the baths.

CHAPTER III

'This Roman civilisation grows on me, heh!' Bonitus declared, flourishing his cup towards the painted ceiling high overhead. Spiced wine slopped and spattered on the silk dining couch. 'If my people back in Germania could see this place, they would think only the gods lived in such a way!'

'Would they still make war on us?' Saturninus asked with a wry smile.

'Of course!' the Frank replied, his voice loud over the surrounding noise of the banquet. 'They are warriors! But they would wonder, I think, why you make war on *them*! When you have all this, what else could you desire?'

The other six men reclining on the semi-circular couch laughed. All of them were soldiers, officers of rank, and all had fought in the campaign against the Brisigavi. They had earned the right to take such things lightly. They laughed, drank, and helped themselves to slices of roast boar in pepper sauce from the silver platters laid before them.

Castus, reclining in the place of honour at the end of the couch, gave a lopsided smile. He remembered the days, long before, when he had fought beside Bonitus against the Saxons on the Rhine. Almost fought against him, too; Bonitus was a friend, but he could easily have become an enemy. The Frankish chieftain had changed a lot since those days. Now Flavius

Bonitus was a Roman citizen, holder of high imperial rank, and his people farmed the lands of northern Belgica, paid taxes to the state and provided military service. He had a son too, with a Roman name: Silvanus, the boy was called.

The lean and dangerous-looking young warrior that Castus had known years before was long gone; Bonitus was still a staunch fighter, but he was getting fat on Roman luxuries. He still wore his blond hair past his ears and a moustache covered his top lip, but now he was dressed in fine embroidered wool and linen, and at his throat he wore a chunky gold torque set with portraits of the Augustus and the Caesars.

'In my country,' Bonitus went on, flinging out his arm at the hall full of banqueting guests, 'we would not have such a scene! Just a wooden house, thatch on the roof and in the cups, beer. And after the eating – fighting!'

'What, you watch gladiators after dinner?' Saturninus asked, frowning.

'No! *We* fight. Everyone together. Much beer, much fighting!' Bonitus threw back his head and roared with laughter, then banged his cup down on the table.

Castus grinned again. He was enjoying himself, although the rich food was not to his taste, and he had never liked reclining to eat. The scent of aromatic oil and burning spices filled the air, and at the centre of the room a chorus of male slaves intoned a melody to the accompaniment of tambourines and a water organ. The music was almost drowned out by the echoing roar of voices: there were nearly sixty guests at the tables, and with the slaves, the choir and the bodyguards the huge chamber was packed.

Long ago, when he served in the Corps of Protectores, Castus had stood guard at banquets in this same hall of the palace. In those days it had been Constantine himself reclining at the high table in the central apse. Now Crispus sat there instead, together with Bishop Agricius and the members of his inner council, but a statue of the Invincible Augustus, gilded bronze and twice life-size, loomed over them all. And in the statue's raised hand was not an orb or a sceptre, but the interlinked X and P, the Christ-monogram, the same symbol that Marcellina now wore on her necklace.

Castus glanced back across the hall towards the far table where his wife sat with the imperial ladies. Marcellina was dressed in silk, her hair plaited and bound in a gold net in the fashionable style. She noticed Castus's attention and looked back at him with a brief wry smile. The woman beside her, the wife of one of the higher ministers, did not stop talking. Crispus's own wife had taken the place of honour on the ladies' table. She sat quietly, plain and abashed-looking. Only sixteen, but she had already given the Caesar a son. Amazing to consider, Castus thought, that her fat red baby might one day sit on the throne of empire...

Time has moved on. Another generation is set to supplant us. Ah well, he told himself, *let them*. The gods had been good, none could deny. And yet, beneath the evening's amusements and Castus's good humour, there was a current of unease. He had been feeling it ever since he had returned from campaign. Before that too, most likely, although he had been unaware of it. He had never put much faith in imagination, but instinct was something else.

He stifled a belch and covered his mouth with his mauled left hand. Ridiculous, he thought, to be mulling on such things. The present was all that mattered; the future could look after itself.

The banquet was over, the lower tables already cleared and the more senior guests beginning to file from the hall, still laughing and talking loudly. Castus sat up blearily on his couch, waving to Marcellina as she made her way towards the doors. He was just about to rise and join her when a figure appeared beside him, one of the Protectores.

'Ursio,' said Castus, glancing up. The big Sarmatian nodded a greeting, then flicked his eyes to the right, indicating the raised table in the apse where Crispus was still lingering.

'Caesar?' Castus asked, and Ursio nodded again. Castus let out a low sigh and wiped his hands. He motioned to Marcellina to leave without him, then got up and followed the Protector towards the apse.

As Castus joined him, Crispus took the flower garland from his head and tossed it on the floor, wiping a few stray petals from his hair. He shrugged his heavy purple cape over his shoulders, then gestured towards a smaller door beside the apse.

'Walk with me, brother,' he said.

The door led, via a dogleg passage, to a wide corridor giving access to the private wing of the palace. Castus knew it well from his days in the bodyguard. He paced slowly beside Crispus, and the young emperor remained silent until they were halfway along the corridor and the noise of the banqueting hall had died away behind them.

'A good feast, wasn't it?' Crispus said. 'I think the city officials enjoyed it. And the delegations from the provinces too!'

'Yes, majesty,' Castus replied. What did the Caesar want of him? He was trying not to feel apprehensive. They paced in silence for a few more moments.

'You know,' Crispus went on, in a different tone, 'I was well aware of that ruse you played with the helmet, back at the fort.'

Castus felt his throat contract slightly. No point in denying anything now. 'Apologies, majesty,' he said with a sniff. 'I thought it best.'

Crispus laughed, and in the gloom he sounded very youthful. 'I'm sure you did!' he said, and clasped Castus's shoulder. 'Well, I can't blame you, I suppose.'

'The safety of the Caesar is the prime concern of the army,' Castus said stiffly.

Crispus tightened his grip for a moment, then let his hand fall with a sigh. 'But the Caesar must be a man,' he said. 'The Caesar must be a leader of men – yes? I forgive you, Castus. But please, do not do that again. If the troops thought for one moment that I was holding back deliberately, letting them fight in my place...'

'I understand.' *Next time,* Castus thought, *I'll let you kill yourself.* But he was impressed all the same. There was a maturity in this young man that he often overlooked.

'Good, good...' Crispus said, nodding. He paused suddenly, turning on his heel to confront Castus. 'They say you dragged my father out of the battle at Verona! He blamed you for it, I hear.'

'Sometimes we don't think too clearly in the heat of battle, majesty.'

Crispus grinned. 'Oh, I think *you* were thinking clearly enough... It's easy to feel invulnerable, when you have men saluting you and acclaiming you all day. But don't concern yourself on my account. I lack your years and long experience, brother, but I'm not as stupid as I might seem!'

Castus tensed, drawing a quick breath, and then relaxed. He had been close to power for long enough to distrust the feigned friendship of the powerful. But Crispus was still smiling, and as they began to walk once more he realised that the young emperor had implied no criticism. Quite the opposite, in fact.

The corridor had led them to a colonnaded terrace over-looking the gardens. There were torches moving in the darkness below them, guests from the banquet still making their way from the palace grounds. Here and there knots of figures wandered randomly; some of the provincial city councillors, Castus guessed, getting lost on purpose. Laughter drifted on the night breeze, and somewhere a man shouted as he fell into a flowerbed.

Crispus seated himself on the balustrade between the pillars, gazing out. Castus remained standing, legs braced, thumbs in his belt, the old military stance second nature to him after all these years.

'I'll be leaving for the east before winter,' Crispus said. 'I'm to join my father at Sirmium. You may not know this yet, but Licinius has indicated that he's set on another war. He's begun persecuting the Christians in his domain: seizing wealth from the churches, forcing bishops to attend traditional sacrifices, even sending them into exile!'

Castus raised an eyebrow. It sounded like a fairly inconsequential sort of persecution. Not exactly savage beasts and red-hot pincers... And the Christians themselves seemed eager enough to persecute one another these days. But he said nothing. Causes for war were seldom as just as men liked to pretend.

'This time there can be no holding back, no more treaties,' Crispus said firmly. Something of his father in his tone, Castus thought. A steely certainty. 'This will be a war like few have ever known. Even you – and you've seen more wars than most, eh?'

Castus just inclined his head.

'Preparations have begun already,' Crispus went on in a musing tone, staring into the darkness. 'All in complete secrecy of course. Licinius has spies everywhere, so they say. But my father wants every man that can be spared. We'll need to send the entire field army of Gaul east, and all the barbarian levies too.'

'That leaves the provinces very weak,' Castus said.

Crispus nodded. 'It can't be helped. I've decided to leave the western territories under the control of my Praetorian Prefect, with Hypatius as supreme military commander. My father's appointed me to lead the Gallic expeditionary force. I want you, Castus, to accompany me and act as my chief military commander.'

Castus straightened, squaring his shoulders. He would not have dared ask for it, but as soon as the young man had started speaking he knew he wanted a part in what was to come. 'I would be honoured, majesty,' he said.

'Good,' Crispus said, and Castus saw his smile in the torchlight from the gardens. 'You'll follow me east then, as soon as you can. My father will base himself at Thessalonica, so if you join me at Sirmium we can travel together from there...'

Crispus's words trailed away into the night. He was waiting before he spoke again, and Castus realised that the revelations about the war had been a mere preamble.

'God willing,' Crispus said, 'by this time next year my father will be master of the entire empire.' He kissed his fingers and raised them to the sky. Castus did the same, although he was praying to a different god. 'And within two years,' the young man went on, 'he will have completed his *Vicennalia*. The twentieth anniversary of his rule. Do you remember what old Diocletian did on his twentieth anniversary?'

'He announced his abdication, majesty.'

'Yes... He abdicated, he and Maximian together, and handed power on to the Caesars. My grandfather, and Galerius. You were serving in the legions then, is that right?'

'I was,' Castus said. He well remembered the day he had been called to the praetorium in Eboracum and told the news of the forthcoming change of rule. The shock of the men in

52

his century when, much later, they heard the news. It had been something that none of them had ever known, or believed possible. A god stepping down from the heavens, and turning into a man once more.

'How did they react – the troops, I mean?' Crispus asked. 'Did they accept the change easily?'

'Not easily, majesty,' Castus said. A knot of apprehension tightened in his gut, and he felt a chill up the nape of his neck. 'You've spoken of this? To your father?'

'No,' Crispus said. 'No, not yet. But I will, in time...'

'Majesty,' Castus broke in with a choke of dismay. 'This is a dangerous thing to consider. To speak of, even. Only the Augustus himself can decide these things.'

'Of course.' Crispus smiled, then got up and laid a palm on Castus's shoulder. 'And I have told nobody about it but you. For now. Treat it as a thought, a confidential thought, that's all. I believe I can trust you with that.' He drew in a long breath, shrugged lightly, and turned as if to depart.

'May I advise you to mention this thought to nobody else?' Castus said abruptly.

Crispus peered at him in the darkness, frowning. 'You're saying this as my military commander?'

'I'm saying this as your friend, I think,' Castus told him. And he found, to his surprise, that he meant it.

'So,' Marcellina said, 'are you allowed to tell me what our glorious Caesar wanted to talk about?' She lay beside him in bed, settling herself against the bunched muscle of his shoulder, and he drew her closer with one arm.

'Some of it,' Castus replied. He rolled slightly, and she stretched her leg across his hips. 'There's going to be another war with Licinius, and Crispus wants me to lead his troops.'

Marcellina stirred, stifling a quiet groan. 'No surprise there. You're his best commander by far. Everyone knows it. Except you, maybe...' He could tell that she was displeased, but she would not show it. 'When do you leave?'

'Soon. In a month, two at most. I need to get across the Alps before the snow seals the passes.'

'You'll miss the wedding!'

'Wedding?' Castus said.

Marcellina raised herself on one arm, and punched his chest. 'Dulcitia's wedding! Your stepdaughter! It's in December, if you recall.'

Castus exhaled loudly. He had forgotten the wedding, it was true. With a sigh of resignation, Marcellina rested her head against his shoulder again, and for a long while neither spoke.

'It's going to be bad, isn't it?' she said quietly. 'This war.'

'Civil wars are never pretty. But I'll be careful. My days in the front ranks are over anyway.'

'Not what I heard. Your friend Saturninus has been telling everyone you took that fort single-handed. But I fear for you, husband,' she said with sudden urgency. 'I fear that you're going to go off and die in some battle and I won't even know of it. For *them* – the emperors. Their victory, their glory. Don't risk your life for them – promise me that? For my sake.'

'I promise.' He kissed her brow, and felt a shudder run through her. Marcellina knew war; she had seen it herself, in Britain and in Belgica. She had seen death, and had taken lives herself. Castus did not doubt her courage, or the strength of her faith in him. He understood her fear of what neither of them could control or influence.

'And when it's over...' she said, pressing her spread hand against the muscles of his chest. He knew what she was about to ask; she did not need to speak the words. 'You've served more than your time,' she said.

Castus said nothing. They had talked before about him leaving the army, but it was not a subject he enjoyed. If he gave up the military life, the world he had known since his youth would come to an end.

'Consider it, at least,' she said, rubbing his creased brow with her thumb.

Why not? he thought. Only the demands of duty, the draw of the imperial court. The conflicts that beckoned from beyond the eastern horizon.

The lamp had burned down, and the chamber was filling with shadows.

'Well,' she said, after a long pause, and he heard the smile in her voice. 'If you're going away again so soon, I ought to make the most of you while you're still here.'

She snuffed the lamp, then pulled off her sleeping tunic and stretched herself across him.

CHAPTER IV

The day was fading, and the wind was flurrying sleet across the bleak hills of Dardania. The column of riders was strung out along the road, each man heavily armed and wrapped in a dun-coloured military cloak, a fur cap pulled down to his eyebrows against the piercing cold. They had ridden for many days in this winter season, and now it was late February. The Danube was two days north, and the city of Naissus more than twenty miles to the south-east.

Reining his horse in near the head of the column, Castus bared his teeth to the icy wind and peered up the road in the fading light. Specks of blackness whirled against the low grey sky: ravens, he realised. They seemed an ill omen, and he tensed his shoulders as a shudder ran through him. The sleet was gathering into cold rain.

'How much further to the next posting station?'

'From what I remember of the itinerary, dominus,' Diogenes said, stammering slightly as his teeth chattered, 'Praesidium Pompei should be about three miles ahead of us. There's a *mansio* there, I believe.'

Castus nodded, satisfied. They could make it before darkness fell, although the rain was already turning the frozen rutted road surface to liquid mud. He ordered one of the scouts to ride on ahead and warn the superintendent of the mansio of their approach; another to take the message back to Crispus that they would be halting for the night. He guessed that the Caesar would be glad of it; they had set a good pace so far, but the rigours of many days on horseback were beginning to tell on the young man.

Ursio, the big Sarmatian Protector, was leaning from the saddle, oblivious to the rain as he studied the mounds of fresh dung in the centre of the road.

'I noticed that too,' Castus said, riding to join him. 'Mules, I think, and horses. And those narrower wheel-ruts mean carriages. There's a convoy ahead of us. They'll be at the posting station by now.'

Ursio shrugged, straightening in his saddle.

'Looks like some of us could be sleeping on straw tonight, brothers!' Castus called to the men behind him. 'But unless it's the emperor himself up there, we should be able to kick a few people out of their beds!'

As the men laughed, Castus raised himself in the saddle and stared back along the column: Crispus was riding with the light baggage carts, Saturninus and two troops of his Scutarii escorting him as a bodyguard. Castus saw the scout he had sent with the message waving back at him. He gave the signal, and the men of his advance party spurred their horses and cantered onwards.

The rain was coming down hard by the time they sighted the village and posting station ahead of them. Praesidium Pompei was a meagre scattering of houses ringed with a ditch and palisade, a few larger buildings – workshops and taverns – surrounding the more substantial enclosure of the mansio. It was a relief to see the glint of lamplight and smell the woodsmoke on the damp evening air, but as they approached Castus could already make out the vehicles filling the wagon park, a large carriage with sodden purple drapes among them. Perhaps, he thought with a frown, it really was Constantine and his retinue at the mansio? But the emperor had left Sirmium before they arrived; he should be well to the south by now, at Serdica or even Thessalonica.

Riding his mud-spattered horse up to the gate in the wall, he swung from the saddle and marched into the yard of the mansio. The superintendent was already running towards him, a cloak pulled over his head against the rain.

'Excellency!' the man cried. 'Greetings! This is a surprise… A surprise, I'm afraid. Your scout tells me that the Caesar Crispus follows with your party?'

'That's right,' Castus said curtly. 'We'll need beds and fodder for sixty riders, and whatever you can provide in the way of food. You have other guests?' He was eyeing the smoke coiling from the vents of the bathhouse and the sentries at the doors of the main building.

'Indeed, excellency!' The superintendent dropped his voice to a reverent whisper. 'We are graced with the presence of the *nobilissima femina*, Flavia Maxima Fausta, wife of our Sacred Augustus!'

'*Fausta?*' Castus said beneath his breath. He had not seen the emperor's wife for many years, and the memory of her stirred something in his chest. He had not even known that she too would be travelling this same road. Quelling the unexpected mood of trepidation, he gestured the superintendent forward and then followed him across the yard through the rain-dashed puddles. Ursio and the other men of his guard came striding after him.

The guards beneath the wooden portico – men of the Lanciarii in waxed rain capes and hoods – stamped to attention as they recognised his rank. Castus nodded to them, then stepped gratefully into the dim lamplight of the stone-flagged entrance lobby. He unlaced his dripping cloak and tossed it to the door slave.

Another slave was pulling off his muddy boots when a figure appeared from the inner doorway. Castus glanced up briefly, taking in the dark complexion and the perfectly shaven head that shone like polished wood. As the slave slipped clean shoes onto his feet, he remembered where he had seen that face before.

'I know you,' Castus said. *Luxorius*, he remembered: a eunuch who had served as chamberlain to the Praetorian Prefect, many years ago in Gaul.

'Ah, yes, we've met!' Luxorius said. 'And how surprising to see you again, excellency...'

Castus was still staring at him. He had not expected to encounter this eunuch again, but he remembered all too clearly what had happened when they last met. He had no proof, but he was convinced that Luxorius had made several attempts to murder the Caesar Crispus. The eunuch had almost admitted as much, but he had left Treveris soon afterwards; Castus had hoped that Luxorius was gone for good. And yet here he was, alive and well...

Standing, Castus paced across the lobby, and the eunuch backed up a step closer to the wall. 'My mistress, the nobilissima femina, is currently bathing,' the eunuch said, 'but she's been told of your arrival. You and the, ah, young Caesar...'

Castus grunted tightly, staring at the eunuch a moment longer and then striding past him. The superintendent was gesturing for Castus to follow him along the covered passageway that circled the inner court.

A few steps, and then cold realisation struck him so hard he almost gasped.

'Dominus?' Diogenes said, coming up behind him. 'Is everything all right?'

'*I've been a fool*,' Castus whispered through his teeth. He turned and spoke quickly, urgently, to Ursio. 'Find that bald eunuch we just passed,' he told the big Sarmatian. 'Find him and stick close to him. Don't let him out of your sight, understand?'

Ursio gave a brisk nod, then stalked back down the passage towards the lobby.

Ignoring Diogenes' concerned frown, Castus forced himself to walk on after the superintendent. With every step he struggled to keep the anger and dread from showing on his features.

'Through here, excellency,' the superintendent said, bowing almost double as he drew aside the curtain from the doorway at the end of the passage. The mansio was not a large building, but it had a wing of heated rooms; Castus stepped through the curtain and entered the scented warmth of one of the larger chambers.

In the lamplight he saw two or three women turning from their conversation, a group of slave maids and another eunuch waiting attendance upon them. One of the slaves, a tall young woman in a yellow tunic with very dark skin and braided hair – Aethiopian, Castus guessed – was arranging goblets on a tray in the centre of the room. She straightened, facing him with lowered gaze.

'My mistress is still dressing after her bath, dominus,' the slave said, with a slight lisp to her voice. 'She asks that you take some wine, and she'll join you shortly.' She looked up quickly, the flash of a smile in her eyes.

Clearing his throat, squaring his shoulders, Castus hooked his thumbs in his belt and remained standing, trying to appear oblivious to the probing glances of the women on the couches at the far end of the room. Fausta's companions, he guessed; his first wife would have been among their number once. For a few long moments nobody spoke, everyone frozen like actors in a stage tableau.

Then the curtain covering the far doorway parted, and the emperor's wife entered the room. She was dressed in a tunic of dark blue patterned silk, her hair still wrapped in the shawl she had worn in the bath, but pendants of pearl and gold hung from her ears, and she wore a heavy gold medallion suspended from a neck ring, embossed with a portrait of her husband Constantine. Castus caught her scent as she approached him. Musky myrrh and roses. *That perfume alone must cost a purse of gold.*

'Aurelius Castus!' Fausta said, smiling. 'It's been years. Too long!'

'Domina,' Castus said, swallowing the knot in his throat as he dropped to one knee. He had known Fausta since she was a girl, a plump newly-wed lost in the treacherous currents of court intrigue. She must be over thirty now, he thought. Mother to the emperor's children. But there was something instantly captivating about her, troublingly so, and Castus realised with a pulse of consternation that she too must remember the connection there had once been between them. He had managed successfully to quell the memory, almost to forget about it, until now. *Some things are too dangerous to remember.*

'Oh, stand up, please,' she said. 'In this barbaric place there's no point in protocols! Tomorrow we'll be at Naissus and can resume our courtly functions, but for now we can be free citizens together, I'd say. Hasn't Niobe given you wine?'

'I...' the dark girl said, widening her eyes.

'I'd prefer to wait until the Caesar Crispus joins us,' Castus said stiffly. 'He should be here at any moment. I must apologise if our arrival has... inconvenienced you.'

'Not at all! It's a relief to have some familiar old faces around. This journey's been so tiring. We can dine together, yes? I'm sure this crude establishment can scrape together some porridge and beans, or whatever they have... And you'll be travelling on with us towards Serdica?'

'No, domina. We travel south from Naissus, direct to Thessalonica. We'll be leaving early, and moving fast.'

'Ah yes,' Fausta said, with a light shrug, 'the usual military haste, I suppose.'

For all her casual attitude, Castus knew that the strain in their words must be obvious. He was trying to appear unmoved by her presence, but the shock of his realisation about Luxorius was still rioting in his body.

He had assumed, back in Gaul seven years before, that the eunuch must have been taking his orders from the rival emperor Licinius, or some other enemy of Constantine. But now the eunuch had reappeared, in Fausta's retinue. Could it be that he was her servant all along? And if so – the thought was monstrous, incredible – could Fausta have plotted her stepson's murder? With every moment Castus found the idea more plausible. It made a terrible sense, after all: Crispus stood between Fausta's own children and their father's favour; between them and the throne itself.

But he could still hardly bring himself to believe it. How, if she had planned such a thing, could she appear so oblivious of it now, so languorously unconcerned? Castus felt another swell of cold nausea rise from his stomach.

'Niobe,' Fausta said, turning to the Aethiopian slave, 'tell the nurses to bring the children in here. They'll be eager to meet their renowned big brother, I'm sure!'

Voices came from the passage as the slave left, footsteps on the tiled floor, then the curtain was swept aside and Crispus strode into the chamber. His hair was wet and clinging to his head, and he scrubbed his fingers through it before flicking his hand at the floor, exhaling loudly.

'Warmth!' he cried. 'Dry warmth!'

Then he caught sight of Fausta, and stopped short. For a couple of heartbeats they stared at each other, clearly uncertain how to behave.

'The hero of Gaul!' Fausta said with a tight smile. 'Greetings, stepson.'

'Nobilissima femina,' Crispus said, a shy catch in his voice. He paced forward and the two of them embraced, slightly awkwardly, Crispus kissing Fausta on both cheeks.

'This is an unexpected meeting in such a drab place,' Fausta said. Castus sensed the haughtiness creeping into her voice, the ceremonial stiffness into her posture. 'I don't believe I've see you since...'

'My wedding, domina,' Crispus told her. 'Serdica, nearly three years ago.'

'Quite so. Your dear wife is well, I hope? And I hear you have a child now?'

'A son,' Crispus said with a grin. He appeared, Castus thought, very young and unsure of himself in Fausta's presence. There was barely a decade between them, even so; Castus himself felt like an old man by comparison.

But now Niobe was returning, three children and a nursemaid carrying a baby following her. The children, two boys and a small girl, were already dressed in their linen sleeping tunics; they shuffled into a line, glancing suspiciously at Crispus.

'Constantine Junior, Constantius, Constantina and baby Constans,' Fausta said. 'My husband is hardly inventive with his names, as you can tell. Salute your noble brother, children!' she commanded.

'Greetings, noble brother,' the three children dutifully intoned.

Castus backed away from the group slightly as Crispus greeted each child in turn, stooping to kiss them, then touching the baby Constans lightly on the brow. The older boy, Constantine Junior, was Caesar too, he remembered. It had always seemed absurd to Castus that such a young child should hold the title. Seeing the boy now, eight years old and half asleep, it seemed almost laughable. He glanced at Fausta instead: she appeared nervous, biting her lip and twisting the carnelian ring on her smallest finger. *She would have murdered her stepson for these children.*

'She's an impressive woman, don't you think, my stepmother?' Crispus said later, as they sat soaking in the warm pool of the mansio baths. 'Very assured, for a female. Very intelligent too, I believe, with an independent mind.'

'True enough,' Castus replied, trying to keep his tone neutral. If he let the slightest hint of his suspicions slip out, he knew that Crispus would notice and demand to know more. If only, he thought, Marcellina were here with him; he could confide in her, and she would know what to do. His wife had a cool sense of reason that he had come to rely upon. He had missed her badly ever since leaving Treveris; he needed her counsel now.

'I've never really spoken with Fausta before, you know,' Crispus went on, spreading his arms along the stone rim of the basin. 'We've only met at court, with my father present. Would you say she's... quite attractive?'

'Quite,' Castus said with gathering discomfort. He stood up quickly, showering water, and grabbed one of the coarse linen towels from the bath slave.

'I can tell she likes you, actually,' Crispus said, smiling. 'You've met before, I think?'

'Once, and long ago.' Castus flung the towel around his shoulders, turning his back to hide his unease.

They ate in the gloomy main chamber, Fausta and Crispus sharing one of the old-fashioned couches and Castus and Saturninus another. Fausta's three lady companions reclined in silence on the third couch. Protectores stood guard at the doorways, and the kitchen slaves dashed rapidly in and out of the room with lowered heads, bringing stewed meats and coarse bread, pickled olives and flagons of acidic white wine flavoured with herbs.

'You must tell me all about your exploits in Gaul, Crispus,' Fausta said as she picked at her food. 'We've all heard stories of your victories over the barbarians!'

'Oh, you should ask Castus really,' Crispus replied, smiling across the table. 'He's been in command most of the time – he's kept me from anything like real fighting!'

For a moment Castus feared that the story of the lost helmet would come up; he could do without that duplicity becoming common knowledge. Fausta was gazing at him with that slightly mocking look of enquiry he knew well, her large eyes heavy-lidded, her full lips just suggesting a smile. He shrugged, stuffing his mouth with bread and meat.

'Ah, these military men are so commendably modest,' Fausta said with a sigh. 'And now you're both going off to fight a war against Licinius? Good thing too – I never liked him. I only saw him once, at Mediolanum, but he seemed a lumpish sort of man, not at all an emperor. He smells sour, like stale wine dregs, and his eyes are too close together.'

'Hardly a reason to fight him, domina!' Crispus laughed. He assumed a pious air. 'He's also been persecuting the Christians in his territories, of course.'

'Well, I couldn't fault him for that,' Fausta said.

'Really? I...' Crispus had an expression of bemused incomprehension. Could it be, Castus wondered, that the young man thought everyone at court was a fellow Christian? Crispus was still watching Fausta, puzzled, as if waiting for some further explanation. Then a slow and knowing smile crept over his face, and he looked away.

The furnace was pumping heat up through the tiled floor, and the air in the room was close and perfumed. Castus was trying not to watch Fausta too obviously, but now and again she caught his eye. A quick tremor in her expression, mingled fear and challenge. *She knows*, he thought. *She knows that I suspect her.*

Wiping his mouth and throwing down his napkin, he stood up from the table. 'Majesty,' he said to Crispus, 'we have an early start tomorrow. If you'll excuse me?'

Crispus waved his dismissal, and Fausta gave a slow nod of accord.

Diogenes was waiting in the passage outside. 'Pass an order to Ursio,' Castus told him quietly. 'He's to stand guard outside the eunuch's door tonight. If the eunuch leaves his chamber for any reason, tell Ursio to follow him closely. He can use any force necessary.'

Castus's own chambers lay at the far end of the building, opening off the passageway. He set the lamp down on the side table and closed the door behind him with a deep gasp of relief. Unbuckling his belts, he sat on the edge of the bed and pulled off his boots and tunic. The cold air felt good against his skin. Kneeling beside the low table, he reached into his belt pouch and drew out a small linen bag.

From the bag he took a bronze figurine, a horse with a large head and a flaring mane. His son had given it to him when he left Treveris; Sabinus had owned the little statuette for many years, and Castus had assumed that he had grown too old for such toys and trinkets. It had surprised him when the boy had pressed it into his hand at the moment of departure. He remembered the look on his son's face, the solemn unspoken desire. *Come back to us.*

Raising the statuette to his lips, he kissed it lightly and then set it on the table in the circle of lamplight. *Yes*, he thought, *I promise.*

He took a second memento from the bag. A silver amulet, embossed with linked dolphins. Another gift, from Marcellina this time. She had claimed that her priest, Agricius, had blessed it; Castus had not been pleased by the idea at the time, but he found that he did not care so much now. It was a reminder of her, and precious because of that alone. He kissed the amulet, too, and laid it beside the horse figurine. Closing his eyes, he muttered a brief prayer. *To the gods of the hearth, the protecting deities: watch over those I love and keep them safe until I return.*

Taking a pinch of incense from the dish on the table, he sprinkled it over the lamp flame. Then he took his sword and propped it against the wall beside the bed, and concealed his military dagger beneath the bolster. This was surely the most heavily guarded mansio in the Danube provinces, but he had learned not to trust in apparent security. Pulling off his breeches, pulling on his sleeping tunic, he shivered in the cold draught for a moment and then snuffed out the lamp. Stretched on the narrow straw mattress, he pulled the musty quilt and blankets over himself.

It seemed only moments before he was awake again, but his instincts told him it was the dead of night. Already his hand was beneath the bolster, gripping the hilt of the dagger; he knew from experience that a shorter blade was more effective in the dark.

The click of the latch had woken him. Now he saw the figure entering the room, dimly lit by a covered lantern. As the door closed he caught the lingering trace of her perfume.

'I need to speak to you alone,' Fausta said as she set the lantern down on the table and uncovered the flame. 'This seemed the best way. You should be more careful – your guards are easily bribed.'

Ursio would not have proved so tractable, Castus thought, and cursed himself for sending the Protector elsewhere; then cursed himself again as he realised how incriminating it would appear if this meeting were ever discovered. He eased his hand away from the dagger and he shoved himself upright until he could sit with his back against the wall.

'You're the wife of my emperor,' he said quietly. 'How could I refuse you? But this is dangerous, domina.'

There was a stool beside the table, but Fausta remained standing. She was dressed in a long linen tunic, a plain shawl draped across her unbound hair.

'Dangerous, yes,' she said. She took a step towards the bed. Castus felt even more strongly than he had in the chamber earlier the force of memory upon him: the recollection of that shameful night when he had lain with her unawares. They had both been fooled then, both used by powers that cared nothing for their security. Things were different now. They had nobody else to blame.

'I know you suspect me of... certain plots. Certain actions,' she said.

'You sent your eunuch to Gaul to attempt the murder of your stepson, I know that.'

He heard Fausta take a long breath. He half expected her to deny it, but she did not. Not exactly. 'I've made certain errors in the past,' she said. 'All my life I've felt my way forward, like someone walking in a dark room. I've feared for my life – did you know that? The lives of my children, too. So, yes, I have made mistakes. But I am surer of myself now.'

'And this is what you came to tell me?'

Fausta shuddered slightly, then took another step and sank down to sit on the edge of the bed beside him. She seemed very human now, very far from the regal figure, the emperor's wife, to whom Castus had grown accustomed.

'I came to ask your forgiveness,' she said. 'And to promise you that those... *events* will not happen again. I mean Crispus no harm. If I did in the past, it was because I did not know him. He was far away, a name, a threat. Not a person. But now I've seen him as a man I understand why so many other men respect him. He has a real virtue about him. One day he will be a good emperor. The sort of emperor that his father could never have become.'

Castus was very tense, his back pressed hard to the cracked wall plaster. He felt the cold of the night soaking through the bricks behind him, and sensed the dark rain-drenched country beyond, miles of emptiness surrounding them. Truly they were alone here.

'What do you mean?' he asked, his throat tight.

Fausta laughed under her breath. 'You haven't seen Constantine lately, have you? Oh, he still has the power, the force of will. But he has never had grace. Never a true sensibility. Can you understand such things, I wonder?'

'Don't underestimate me, domina.'

'I never would,' she said in a whisper, then smiled. 'My husband doesn't want this war because Licinius is annoying the

Christians. He wants it because the notion that another man might rule over any part of the world *offends* him. Possibly, one day, Crispus might be a better sort of tyrant.'

She paused a moment, as if expecting a response. He said nothing, and she continued, 'I said I mean Crispus no harm. I mean you no harm either, Aurelius Castus. And I thank you for keeping certain things secret all these years. Not only what happened in Gaul.'

'That secret could kill us both. I've tried my best to wipe it from my mind.' *And you're not helping with that.*

'It could indeed. But listen to me carefully now – there are others at court that have no love for your young Caesar. They dissemble, but they would rejoice to see him fall. Such a young man, rising so far and so fast... You must guard Crispus well. Guard yourself, too.'

'Tell me their names then.'

She shook her head quickly, her hair falling across her face. 'No, better you do not know. I can't be certain of their identities myself. But I just wanted to be sure that you would not suspect me. I give you my solemn oath. I'm not an evil woman, Aurelius Castus. And if I can aid you further, I will.'

'Very well,' he said.

She was sitting very close to him now, her ringed fingers catching the light as she brushed the hair from her face. Castus was uncomfortably aware that she was naked beneath her thin tunic.

'You've been injured again,' she said, taking his mutilated left hand.

Castus flinched at her touch. 'Somebody tried to chop off my arm with a knife,' he said. 'They missed.' Her fingers closed around his hand, and he felt a deep warmth and pressure growing in his chest, the heavy beat of his blood.

'Clumsy of them,' she said.

Breathing in, Castus glanced across the room towards the table in its pool of lamplight. He saw Marcellina's amulet, the bronze horse his son had given him.

'You should leave now,' he managed to say, his voice rough and deep in his chest.

'I know I should. But I get so few opportunities to speak freely. Just... know that I am your friend.' She lifted his hand, and kissed the scar where his finger had been cut away.

Castus felt the strain in his body, almost painful as he fought to keep himself pressed against the wall. He realised now the attraction he had always felt for this woman; he could scarcely believe that she felt anything similar for him.

'Yes, I should go,' she said, drawing away from him. 'You know,' she added, the hint of sly mockery returning to her voice, 'my slave Niobe rather likes you. I can send her to you, if you want pleasure...'

Castus drew a hissing breath between his teeth, pulling his hand back from her. 'You know how to use people, don't you?'

'Oh?' Fausta said, in a lilting tone. 'You *don't* want pleasure?'

'You know what I want.'

She laughed then, a sudden involuntary giggle. Composing herself, she pulled the shawl tighter across her hair. 'Maybe I want the same,' she said. 'But we are prisoners of our fate, aren't we?'

With a single lithe motion she stood up and moved away from the bed, taking the lantern from the table. 'Remember what I told you,' she said. Then she turned to the door, and a moment later she was gone.

Castus subsided onto the bed with a long, aggrieved sigh of frustration. His mood of arousal was veering abruptly to anger and remorse. What had he been thinking? How had she

71

managed so easily to draw him in? He lay still for a moment in the cold darkness, listening to the rain beating against the wall beside him. Then he shoved himself up off the bed, pulled on his breeches and rekindled a flame in the lamp. There was a cup of watered wine on the table, almost freezing; he relished the shock of the cold as he drank it back.

Sitting on the stool, he thought back over everything that Fausta had said. What was her aim? Had she only intended to reassure him that Crispus was safe from her, and from Luxorius, or did she just want to divert his suspicions? Then again, her tale of other unnamed plotters seemed plausible enough. Cursing her, cursing himself, Castus picked up the silver dolphin amulet and turned it in his fingers, then pressed it to his brow.

He had been sitting like that for only a short time when he heard a light tapping on the door. Castus opened his mouth to call a challenge, but said nothing. The latch clicked, the door swung open and the woman slipped into the room. Only then did he realise that he had been expecting her.

'My mistress sent me,' the slave said. She was still wearing her yellow tunic, and in the low lamplight her skin was black as jet.

'I guessed that,' Castus said. 'But you don't need to be here. Go back to your quarters.'

Niobe remained beside the door. There was a nervous smile on her face, and her eyes gleamed. Perhaps she really had wanted to come to him? But no, Castus thought – slaves have no control over what happens to them.

'Please,' she said. 'It's cold.'

Just for a moment Castus felt the stirring of the desire he had experienced when Fausta was with him. There was no risk here – and perhaps it was what he needed, after all? Temptation flowed through him. For five years he had lain with no woman but Marcellina; almost absurd for a married man to be so faithful. But he had wanted nobody else. He still held the amulet gripped in his hand.

'Get into bed then,' he said gruffly. 'Get warm. In the morning you can tell your mistress anything you like.'

Niobe shivered, stepped over to the bed and pulled off her tunic in a single quick motion, then slipped beneath the covers. Castus could see her watching him from the shadows, the quilt pulled up to her nose.

'Sleep if you can,' he told her, and managed a smile that he hoped appeared reassuring.

With a feigned yawn, he snuffed the lamp once more and slid from the stool. Sitting on the floor with his back to the wall, he pulled a dry cloak from his travelling case and wrapped it around his shoulders. He could sense the woman in the bed still watching him, perhaps expecting him to change his mind. As he felt the cold of the floor beneath him, Castus wondered if he might do just that. Only to sleep, he thought, smiling to himself. Or just to lie there. And perhaps if Venus compelled him…

The sound of a scream jerked him upright. At once he threw the cloak away from him and lunged across the room, seizing his sword from beside the bed. Niobe had sat up with a gasp, and he hissed at her to stay where she was. He could hear other cries now, shouts of alarm from somewhere along the passageway outside. Barefoot, sword in hand, he flung open the door and charged out through the vestibule.

Weaving lamplight and rushing figures met him. Castus shouldered aside a panicked slave, then yelled to one of the sentries to follow him. The scream had come from the chambers occupied by Crispus, and at the far end of the passage Castus could see a knot of people, slaves and guards and women mingled, thronging around the door to the Caesar's rooms.

'Get back, get away,' he shouted, his voice ringing. The sword was naked in his hand.

As he approached, the crowd around the doorway split suddenly and fell back. A woman screamed. A man paced slowly from the dimly lit chamber, one of the mansio slaves, holding something before him. Castus stared, his breath caught. With outstretched arms the slave was holding a stick with a long mottled snake looped across the end.

'It was on the Caesar's bed,' the slave said in a trembling voice. 'I saw it when I woke – it was lying coiled on his chest!'

'Gods protect us!' somebody cried. 'Is the Caesar unharmed?' a man's voice demanded.

'I'm here. I'm unharmed.' Crispus walked from the chamber, still dazed from sleep, his hair matted and sticking up. He had a glazed look on his face. Several people dropped to their knees before him, raising their hands as if in prayer.

'Horned viper,' said Saturninus, striding along the far passage with two of his Scutarii at his heels. 'Throw it in the yard and kill it before it bites somebody!'

'Domini, forgive me!' the superintendent was saying, clasping his hands before his face. 'This is a terrible occurrence! But these snakes... they sleep, you see, in the winter. This one must have got into the hypocaust and been wakened by the heat of the furnace!'

Saturninus flung open the door to the inner yard, and the slave leaned through the gap and gingerly slid the snake from the stick.

'Castus!' Crispus said, seeing him in the crowd. 'The snake was right there, in front of my eyes. But it made no move to strike me. I was watching it, and it was watching me. Like it was... trying to tell me something...'

'An omen!' announced the supervisor. 'It's said that a similar thing happened to the deified Severus! Yes, it's true – an omen of greatness!'

'Kill it anyway,' Saturninus grunted, and gestured to one of his men.

Castus sheathed his sword and gripped Crispus by the shoulders, staring into the young man's eyes. He seemed almost blissful, like a drinker lost in the fumes of wine, unmoved by what had happened. Then the crowd around them shifted again, and Fausta came hurrying down the passageway. She was still dressed in her light sleeping tunic, barefoot, with her unbound hair hanging loose. She rushed up to Crispus and took his face between her hands.

'You're truly not hurt?' she demanded. 'Speak to me!'

'I'm well,' Crispus said. 'It was a shock, but nothing more…'

Fausta glanced at Castus then, and he saw the stark terror in her eyes. He had believed at first that this was her doing, that she had lied to him back in his chamber. But her expression was unfeigned, her relief palpable. Before the eyes of everyone she hugged her stepson, letting out a sobbing cry.

Castus spotted the eunuch Luxorius at the back of the crowd in the passage. Ursio was following dutifully behind him, and Castus motioned the Sarmatian to his side.

'Have a bed made up for the Caesar in the middle of the dining room,' he ordered. 'Station guards around it and have them watch him while he sleeps. I don't want anything like this happening again.'

Ursio nodded, and then frowned towards the eunuch.

'Forget him for now,' Castus said.

Already the crowd was beginning to disperse, Crispus's slaves leading him away. In his mind, Castus heard the cold echo of the supervisor's words. *An omen of greatness.* He remembered what Crispus had told him, that night back in Treveris. The young man's wish for power. *Dreams of greatness can be dangerous, when you are not yet great.* Fausta lingered, watching Castus from the corner of her eye until she could speak to him in privacy.

'This was none of my doing,' she whispered. 'You must believe that.'

'I believe it,' Castus said, moving closer until he felt the warmth of her body in the dimness. 'But if you're wise you'll make all your people swear never to mention what happened here tonight. Omen or accident, none should hear of it.'

'I understand,' she said. For a moment she held his gaze, then she turned curtly and paced back towards her rooms, taking a shawl from one of her lady companions to wrap around herself.

Peace settled slowly, the light of the lamps fading as the doors closed along the passageway. Castus waited, leaning on his sheathed sword. Fatigue rushed through him. From the dining room came low voices, the grunt of shifted furniture. With a long sigh Castus winged his shoulders, feeling the stiffness of his muscles. Then he returned to his room.

Closing the door behind him he crossed to the bed and threw aside the covers without thinking. The Aethiopian girl sat up quickly, and he gave a grunt of surprise before he remembered what she was doing there.

'What's happened?' she said, her voice lisping quietly in the darkness.

'It's nothing. All finished now.'

She drew him by the hand, and he heard her shifting aside on the mattress to make room for him. Lazy desire rose through his fatigue. Then he shook his head, and pulled his hand away.

'Go back to sleep,' he told her.

Reaching in the darkness he found his fallen cloak, and spread it on the floor. Lying down on the cold hard tiles, he pulled the cloak over him. The girl's arm trailed from the bed, her fingers stroking his arm and then falling slack. A moment later he heard her quiet snore.

Castus lay still, then rolled onto his side. He needed to sleep, but the thought would not leave his mind. Had Fausta really sent her slave to his room to distract him? All that he knew for sure was that the events of this night must be kept secret, for all their sakes.

CHAPTER V

'Many of you gathered here today,' the emperor said, his voice booming beneath the soaring dome of the hall, 'have witnessed battles, or been spectators of a war, in which Divine Providence has granted victory. When men commend my triumphs, which owe their origin to the inspiration of heaven, do they not see that *God* is truly the cause of all that I have achieved?'

Flavius Valerius Constantinus, Invincible Augustus, Triumphant Victor, Conqueror of the Goths and Sarmatians, Conqueror of the Germans and the Britons, Father of his Country, stood upon the dais before the tall central apse of the Octagon Hall in the imperial palace of Thessalonica, dressed in his full court regalia, his cloak stiff with gold embroidery.

Arrayed in the hall before him, over a hundred members of the imperial retinue, the ministers of the *consistorium*, military officers, ladies and priests of the household sat in stiffly attentive silence. At least, Castus thought, they had been given folding stools; he had stood through many an imperial address in his time, but several of the older civilians present were finding the ordeal far more strenuous. He noticed the man in front of him sagging in his seat, his chin dropping to his chest and then jerking up again. The hall was warm, heavy with the smell of incense and fresh sweat. Glancing at the position of the sun through the high arched windows, Castus estimated that the emperor had been speaking for over an hour already. Up on the dais, Crispus sat behind his father on a low throne, immaculately composed, his face stony and without expression.

'Now, once again,' Constantine declared, 'we hear the cries of the oppressed, who in their ardent longing for liberty implore the help of God to remove the evils under which they groan. Once again the cruelty of ungodly men, raging like a devouring fire, maintains a furious, cruel and implacable war against Piety...!'

Tightening his jaw, Castus inhaled slowly, stifling a yawn. Already the emperor had told them of the Christian God's endless mercy and charity, the prophecies of his greatness and certainty of his victory. Even Virgil had crept into it somehow – Castus was reminded of that awkward exchange with Marcellina, six months before. Did the emperor even understand what he was saying, or was he just repeating what his priests had told him?

Castus would have ignored the oration entirely, but Constantine had chosen to deliver it in a gruff shout, as if he were haranguing a legion on the eve of battle. Now the emperor was growing hoarse, his heavy-boned face reddened and sheened with sweat. He paced upon the dais, his golden robe swaying behind him, jutting out a hand to point fiercely at the dome above.

'What do these servants of tyranny, these most impious of men, hope to gain by their atrocious deeds? What is the cause of their insane fury? Do they say these acts are done in honour of the gods? *What gods are these?*'

Castus dropped his gaze to the red and white marble tiles beneath his feet. Annoyance tightened his stomach, and he felt himself blushing darkly.

'Do they say,' the emperor went on, with a shout of laughter, 'that the customs of our ancestors are the cause of this conduct? Those very customs proceed from the same folly! Can they truly believe that some special power resides in images formed and fashioned by human hands? Why else obey the commands of these mighty and highly exalted so-called *gods*, when they urge the unrighteous slaughter of innocent men?'

Breathing in, Castus raised his head again. His shoulders were bunched tightly, and he knew that his anger must be evident to all around him. How many of them were Christians? If they were not, how many felt his shame and outrage at the slandering of the traditional deities of Rome?

'Compare their erroneous faith with our true religion,' Constantine said, fanning his jewelled hand in the air. 'Is not ours a life of simplicity, which disdains to cover evil beneath the mask of fraud and hypocrisy? Do we not humbly acknowledge the true God, and his undivided sovereignty? Truly, ours is a religion sincere and undefiled. Those that follow this life of wisdom are travellers on a noble road, and shall receive the reward of everlasting life, while the wicked shall receive the punishment due to their crimes!'

Ignore the taunts, Castus told himself. This was politics. The artful maintenance of a suitable cause for war against Licinius. And yet, when he gazed around the room at the figures seated ahead of him, only the small conclave of Christian priests near the dais appeared to be enjoying themselves. They sat forward on their stools, avid for the emperor's every word, like excited spectators at the games watching their favoured driver race for the victory palm.

Soon, Castus thought, this would be over and they would be permitted to leave. He had been in Thessalonica for over a month, preparing for the arrival of the campaign army, and the atmosphere of the court was stifling. He made an effort to relax, and his stool creaked and squealed on the marble tiles. A plump official seated to his left turned with an expression of pique, making a hushing gesture. As Castus glanced away, he caught sight of the group of women seated to one side of the hall. Fausta was sitting with them, and she turned at that same moment and peered back at him.

The moment lasted a heartbeat. Then Fausta dropped her jaw in the very slightest impression of a yawn, and rolled her eyes towards the domed ceiling.

Castus coughed back an involuntary laugh; the man to his left turned quickly with a furious hiss. The sound was lost in the vast echo of the emperor's voice, booming out across the hall as he reached the climax of his oration.

'And so, as we face once more the stern demands of war, let all pious persons render thanks to the Saviour! Let us entreat the favour of Christ with holy prayers and constant supplications. For He alone is the invincible ally and protector of the righteous! He alone is the supreme judge of all things, the prince of immortality, the giver of everlasting life!'

The last echo died into the marble hush. Then the assembled listeners rose to their feet as one and raised their hands in salute, crying out the acclamation in a single voice. '*Constantine Augustus! May the Divine Spirit preserve you for us! Your salvation is our salvation!*' Again and again they cried, until the noise of their shouts became a roar that filled the domed hall.

Over, thanks to the gods... Castus paced through the doorway into the vestibule, the noise of the milling throng at his back. Ursio was waiting between the pillars; Castus signalled to him, and the Sarmatian followed him into the fresh air of the peristyle courtyard.

The crying of gulls came from the seashore, only a few

hundred paces away beyond the southern wall of the palace precinct. All Castus wanted to do now was to lose himself in his work; it would be another month or more until the first detachments of the field army marched into the holding camps outside Thessalonica, but mustering an army tens of thousands strong needed preparation.

'So eager to make your escape?'

The voice halted him. Composing his face, Castus turned slowly. Fausta was strolling behind him, flanked by her slaves and eunuchs. The sunlight slanted between the pillars and threw bars of shadow across the mosaic floor.

'You seem to have made a prompt exit yourself, domina.'

Fausta smiled, nodding in acknowledgement. She must have left the Octagon Hall by a side door before the last acclamations had faded. Now she dropped into step beside him, and they walked together along the colonnade.

'They say,' Fausta told him in a low breathy voice, 'that the Emperor Nero used to make his courtiers sit through his own musical performances. He played the lyre, apparently. Anyone who failed to be enthralled paid a harsh penalty, of course!'

Castus snorted a laugh, although he was more perplexed than amused. He glanced at her, and saw the glow of intimacy in her hooded eyes.

'Domina,' he said, gruffly awkward, 'I have duties I must attend to.'

'Ah yes, duties,' she said with a distracted air. She shook her head slightly, and her pearl-drop earrings swung. 'Well, we all have those. But I think you won't be going off to mingle with your soldiers just yet. My husband wishes to speak with you.'

'Domina?'

She gave him a light smile, enjoying his discomfort. 'Or so I hear. No doubt he has some weighty military matters he wishes to discuss. I expect he'll ask you about Crispus too. Be careful what you tell him.'

She was still smiling, but there was a sharper note in her voice. Her attendants had dropped back, and Ursio was gazing intently between the pillars at the courtyard garden.

Castus sniffed, unsure whether he should be offended by her tone. Even now, after years of navigating the subtle currents of the imperial household and imperial protocol, he felt disarmed by this woman's company. The recent memory of what had happened at the mansio stood between them too.

'Why should I be careful?' he said. 'I have nothing to hide from the emperor. Nor does the Caesar Crispus.'

Fausta made a very slight tutting sound between pursed lips. With a cold stab of premonition, Castus remembered the omen of the snake, and what the young man had told him the previous autumn in the palace at Treveris.

'Just be careful,' Fausta said quietly, moving a step closer. 'And remember, it is seldom the great who suffer by their own faults.'

She moved briskly away from him then, without a parting glance.

'Aurelius Castus!' the emperor declared. 'Good to see you, brother. Sit! Take some wine...'

Castus would rather have remained standing. He had been expecting a formal audience, with all the rituals of kneeling and cape-kissing. The Protectores that had summoned him from the courtyard and conducted him to this upper room of the palace had suggested nothing less. But Constantine was in a relaxed mood after his lengthy oration, it seemed; he had thrown off his gold-embroidered robe and lounged back in a chair, dressed in his purple tunic and white breeches, plain sandals on his feet.

There was something pale caked around his jaw and hairline: the remains of face powder, Castus realised, which the emperor had wiped off after leaving the Octagon Hall.

He sat, and slaves brought a golden tray with cups of wine. The Protectores had withdrawn from the room and closed the doors behind them, but the window shutters were open, framing a view over the tiled roofs of the palace to the broad blue expanse of the Thermaic Gulf and the white-capped peak of Mount Olympos in the far distance.

'You enjoyed my speech, eh? My oration?' the emperor said briskly. 'Endured it, I should say!' He took a heavy swig from his cup. 'Not the kind of thing we soldiers are apt to discuss, I know, but these things must be stated, I find. One must be seen and heard to rule, hmm?'

Castus said nothing; a reply did not seem necessary. He sipped wine, and kept his expression neutral.

'I hope you were not offended by my references to the old religion?' Constantine asked.

'No, majesty,' Castus lied.

'Good! I know you are not yet a believer, brother... I was myself confused for a long time, I confess. But now things are clearer to me, and I – well, I find I cannot remain silent. God's truth illuminates us all, you know.'

Castus forced himself to nod. In all the years he had known Constantine, watching him scale to the summit of power, he had never seen the emperor so informal, so relaxed. Perhaps, he thought, this new religion had truly opened something in Constantine's mind or heart, some locked chamber of ambition and fury? But no – all of that was still there, in the steady gleam of the man's eyes, the muscular tension in his body. Constantine might act as if he had found a greater spiritual peace, but in this mortal world he was still a warrior, still hungering for power. This was as much a show as the performance he had given on the dais of the Octagon Hall.

'You, I take it, still hold to the old religion? To Sol Invictus, Mars, Jupiter...?' The emperor scraped at the residue of powder caking his jaw, then frowned as he rubbed it between his thumb and forefinger.

'I do,' Castus replied. It was not hard to admit. All his life he had followed the traditional ways; he had never thought to believe otherwise. The gods had been all around him, their rituals governing and patterning his world. Never, until the recent rise of the Christian cult, had this seemed worthy of debate or question. Only now did it come to appear a conscious choice.

'Sol, you know, I still revere,' Constantine said, glancing towards the daylight through the open window. 'Although I suspect that what we call the Unconquered Sun is no more or less than God, the Christian God. An avatar of that greater divinity... I came to see this – and I hope that one day you will see it too. I shall pray for that day, brother, for the sake of your immortal soul.'

Sitting very stiffly in his chair, Castus fought to assume the correct expression of gratitude. For all the emperor's appearance of friendly concern, Castus reminded himself of the power that lay between them. He tried not to let the insult of those words register in his expression.

'But enough of religion!' Constantine said. 'How are matters with the troops? Is everything prepared for the muster?'

'Everything that can be done, majesty. We have camping grounds prepared for thirty thousand men from the Pannonian and Moesian armies at Pella, and for the auxilia at Tauriana. They'll be arriving next month, and the troops from Gaul should be here soon afterwards, in early May. When the transports come in we'll have supplies, draught animals and fodder sufficient to keep sixty thousand men in the field for up to five months.'

'Excellent,' the emperor said gravely. 'No doubt our enemy has already had word that we're mustering our forces. We must be ready to advance as soon as all our troops are assembled. Make sure the contractors play us no tricks – corruption follows an army like the plague. If any give you trouble, the usual punishments apply.'

Constantine meshed his fingers beneath his chin; his broad face took on a ponderous expression. 'I selected you personally for this role, you know,' he said. 'I heard of your exploits in the west. You've done well to guide my son, to show him the ways of war. Protect him from the worst danger too – I know all about that. He's impetuous, I grant you, but he's still a youth. I need you to be as assiduous in the coming campaign.'

'Certainly, majesty,' Castus said.

Constantine raised his eyes, glaring at him with a look of stern command. 'Crispus will want to throw himself into combat. He wants to impress me, and to impress the troops. He has a lust for acclaim – he inherits it from me, of course. You must see that he proves himself, but not allow him too great a share of the glory, do you understand me?'

Castus nodded, trying to keep the look of consternation from his face. There was something more here than a father's concern for his child, he realised.

'Has Crispus said anything to you,' Constantine went on, 'that suggests he might have... desires beyond his current situation?'

'He wishes for greater responsibility,' Castus said carefully, weighing his words. 'And hopes, I think, one day to... prove himself worthy of power.'

'*One day?*' Constantine said sharply. There was nothing

86

relaxed about him now; his voice was tight and hard, and his fists were clenched on the arms of his chair. 'Or some time sooner, perhaps? Has he said anything of that sort to you?'

Castus paused, feeling the sweat gathering at his hairline. He tried not to glance away from the emperor's questioning gaze. His throat felt tight; he knew he had to lie. 'No, majesty,' he said.

Constantine gave one brisk nod, settling himself back in his chair, as if the answer had satisfied him. 'Good, good. I believe you, Aurelius Castus. You, of all my officers, I trust in this matter. But you'll remember to report anything of that sort that you happen to hear. Your rank and position come from me, understand?'

'You are the Augustus,' Castus said, lowering his eyes.

'Crispus is a brave boy; I love him dearly and I would not want him to come to harm. But he must keep his ambitions within the bounds I decree.'

But Castus was remembering a night many years ago, a rainy night in Eboracum in the north of Britain. An emperor newly made by his troops, clothed in the purple and raised on a shield as the mob of soldiers bayed his name, in defiance of imperial protocols. There had been no bounds to Constantine's ambitions back then.

'I'm placing Crispus in command of the naval division of the expeditionary force,' the emperor went on. 'I've ordered a fleet of ships constructed at Athens, to supplement the vessels we can gather from the western flotillas. Crispus will be going to Athens to view the work in a few days, and I want you to go with him. You'll need to make a study of the new fleet and gauge what we'll need in terms of marines and supplies. You will, of course, be taking an active role in the command of the troops we embark.'

'Understood, majesty,' Castus said with a curt nod. The trip to Athens and back would mean more days on the road, but already he was glad of the opportunity to escape the imperial court.

There was a noise from outside the room, an exchange of voices, and then the doors swung open.

'Majesty,' one of the Protectores said, stepping through from the hallway. 'The domina Helena...'

Another figure followed the guard, brushing him aside. An old woman with a dry brown face, dressed in gold-embroidered white. Constantine got to his feet at once, and Castus stood and bowed from the waist. The emperor's mother, he realised: he had seen the old woman several times at court.

'I wanted to congratulate you on your speech, my dear,' Helena said, her face lifting as she smiled. 'Exemplary! Now none can doubt your faith...' She glanced at Castus, then stared more intently at him. 'And who is this?'

'His excellency Aurelius Castus, Mother,' Constantine said. There was the slightest trace of annoyance in his voice; the emperor did not care to be so abruptly interrupted.

'Ah, yes!' Helena exclaimed. She assessed Castus with a cold eye. 'You are the soldier who's been keeping my grandson safe in Gaul? Good. No doubt you will continue to do so – be his shield, so to speak, against the rage of our enemies. We would be most displeased if any evil should befall the most blessed Caesar!'

Castus opened his mouth to speak, then thought better of it. He kept his eyes downcast, and the old woman seemed pleased by his deferential air.

'But now I have matters I must discuss with my son,' she said.

Constantine made the slightest gesture of dismissal. Suppressing a shudder of irritation, Castus saluted and paced towards the door.

'Remember my words, soldier,' Helena said without a backward glance. 'Make sure the Caesar remains safe, or you shall answer for it.'

Castus turned on his heel at the threshold, saluted again, then marched past the Protectores and made his escape.

Gods, he thought, his hands curling into fists at his side. Bad enough to be lectured on his duty by the emperor himself, let alone his mother. And the implied threat of those closing words brought a hot swell of rage. *As if I'm some glorified bodyguard, some hired gladiator...*

The anger stayed with him as he rode westwards towards the newly constructed docks, along the broad colonnaded main street of the city. The carriage rattled and jogged on the uneven paving, stopping and starting as the crowds parted before it, and Castus stared with unseeing fury at the faces under the colonnades, his teeth clenched in sour frustration.

A beggar approached the carriage, and he reached into his belt pouch for a coin. He glanced down at the copper in the palm of his hand: the reverse showed the figure of the sun god, with words stamped into the metal around him: *soli invicto comiti*. Unconquered Sun, companion of the emperor. *For how much longer?*

He tossed the coin, and the beggar snatched it from the air.

CHAPTER VI

'Athena Parthenos, bright-eyed goddess, guardian of the city!' Crispus cried, raising his arms to the glowing sky. 'Sprung from the head of Zeus! Companion of heroes, and mistress of the arts of war! Hail, goddess, and give us good fortune!' Turning slowly to face the massive hulk of the ruined temple, he let his arms fall. He closed his eyes and breathed in, filling his lungs with clean thyme-scented air. 'Ah,' he said, smiling as he exhaled. 'For so long I've dreamed of this place!'

Several of the officers and bodyguards waiting in the lee of the temple inclined their heads and made polite sounds of agreement. Castus just shrugged, squinting as he peered at the mass of broken stone capping the hill. It was only April, and early in the day too, but the sun was hot on the exposed summit, glaring back off the dusty marble. The huge pillars of the temple threw hard black shadows.

'That's a very great hall,' Bonitus said, gazing up at the ruin. 'But so dirty! These Greeks are a lazy people to leave their halls so unclean.' The Frankish leader had joined the Caesar's party only the day before, after riding hard from Treveris.

'Burned, by the look of it,' Castus said, kicking at the litter of marble fragments covering the ground. The stones gave a dry rattle. 'More than a few years ago, I reckon.' He gestured at the blackened pillars, the marks of old smoke and flame now smudged and freckled with moss. Tufts of wiry yellow grass had sprouted from the broken pediment. The inside of the temple was an overgrown mass of rubble and mossy roof timbers.

'Once this was the greatest temple in the Hellenic world,' Crispus said, shaking his head sadly as he approached the group of officers. 'The Parthenon, it was called. It was burned when my grandfather was a young man. Even the great statue of the goddess was lost to the flames.'

'They never wanted to repair it?' Castus asked. He tipped his head back to peer up at the blackened frieze of figures below the pediment. The thought of a conflagration ripping through a building this size, the flames bringing down the high roof, consuming and melting all within, made him shudder. Just for a moment he seemed to feel the heat of the fire upon his face, and smell the smoke and the burning.

'No,' Crispus said. 'No, they never did.'

Grit crunched beneath the studded soles of Castus's boots. Scorpions scuttled among the broken slabs of the temple precinct, and a thin brown snake slithered away through the weeds. Shading his eyes, he stared out across the plain towards the distant hills. A placid view in the soft light, beneath the hot dome of the sky. Cocks crowed from the surrounding countryside, and somewhere a dog was barking. Castus had little conception of history, but he knew that Athens had been a mighty place once, centuries ago; now it resembled a small town, dwarfed by the ruins of the past.

Casting his travelling cloak back over his shoulder, Crispus had climbed the steps to the base of one of the huge pillars, placing his palm against the stone and gazing upwards. For a moment he stood in thought. 'One day,' he declared, 'if, God willing, I am Augustus, I will rebuild this place.' He turned, squaring his shoulders, and the sun gleamed off the gold embroidery of his tunic and the jewelled hilt of his sword. 'I'll rebuild this whole city, and restore it to its ancient glory!'

'You'd do that?' Castus asked, frowning, as the Caesar came back down the steps. 'Restore the temple of the goddess? As a Christian, you'd do that?'

'Yes, of course,' Crispus said, bemused, as if he saw no contradiction in his ideas. 'The gods of our ancestors – Athena, Apollo, Zeus – they're not actually gods, of course, not divine beings to be worshipped. They're ideas – ideals, perhaps. But they shaped our civilisation, and we should pay them reverence!'

Castus wondered if the Christian tutors who had schooled the young emperor for so many years would agree. Or his father Constantine, for that matter. But the thought gladdened his heart nevertheless. *If I am Augustus* – no, he would not think about that.

'And those,' Diogenes declared, gesturing at the tumbled mounds, overgrown with grass and scrub, that lined the road down to Piraeus, 'must be the famous Long Walls! Or what's left of them...'

'Barbarians destroyed them too, eh?' Castus said. He frowned: surely these old fortifications had fallen many centuries ago, before the time of the Heruli invasion?

'Oh no, it was us that did that!' Diogenes said. 'Romans, I mean. The army of Sulla, back in the great days of the Republic.'

Castus turned in the saddle, peering back at his secretary. 'Do you just *know* all this?' he asked, quizzical. 'Or do you... read it in books, or something?' Diogenes's ability to identify every random chunk of old masonry along their route was baffling.

'The siege of Athens is quite well known, dominus,' Diogenes said, raising his eyebrows. 'Although I've just spent a very pleasant few hours at the Library of Hadrian in the agora, while you were up on the Acropolis. Some extraordinary works, even if much was lost to the fire when the barbarians sacked the city...'

'Truly,' said Bonitus, stroking his moustaches with his thumb, 'your man here knows very many useless things!'

Castus shrugged, grunting. He had become used to his secretary's antiquarian enthusiasms over the years. Even now, dressed once more in an approximation of military dress, Musius Diogenes did not look much like a soldier. With his wild scrub of grey hair, his bald pate and his permanently startled expression, the little man resembled some sort of philosopher, or perhaps the schoolteacher he had been many years ago, before he was conscripted into the legions in Britain. But Castus had learned to overlook the man's eccentricities; he was a thorough and efficient secretary, understood Castus's needs without too much prompting, and he had proved himself in many a tough situation. Castus respected him, even if he seldom understood him.

The road they were following led from the city to the port. They rode in a loose column, an armed cavalry escort ahead of the Caesar's retinue and a trail of secretaries and Protectores bringing up the rear. All of them had been travelling together for many days since leaving Thessalonica at the beginning of the month, and there was little sense of formality or protocol between them now. The few other travellers on the road fell back to the verges to let the mounted men pass, farm-workers in sleeveless tunics and straw huts, donkey-drovers and sailors alike lining the road and raising their arms in salute. Probably, Castus thought, these Greeks did not recognise Caesar Crispus; quite possibly they knew nothing of his existence, but all of them recognised Roman power when they saw it: the armed guards in their white uniforms, and the purple draco banners curling above the lead riders.

For all the ruins, and the armed escort, it was easy to forget that war was on the horizon. Greece seemed a country entirely at peace, the spring sunlight glowing with a warm clarity that Castus had hardly known anywhere else. He had to remind himself that this was a military expedition, not a sightseeing tour. Even now, twenty thousand troops of the Gallic field army were approaching Thessalonica; in only a few months' time he would be leading those men into war. He wished that the young emperor would remind himself of that same thing.

'It was a Roman emperor who rebuilt Athens,' Crispus declared, looking back towards the city and the Acropolis mount. 'The deified Hadrian... although of course he was only a *mortal man*,' he corrected himself quickly, piously. 'But a great ruler, despite his love of false religions. I admire him immensely!'

Saturninus coughed lightly. 'Your father, majesty, the Invincible Augustus, was quite rude about Hadrian, I believe. And Trajan too. Didn't he call Hadrian a *paintbrush* and Trajan *wall ivy*?'

Crispus's expression darkened, and he shook his head. 'My father was wrong to say such things,' he said. 'The great deeds of our ancestors should not be mocked!' He rode on a few more yards in silence, pondering. 'Although,' he said, 'I've never understood the comment. Trajan carved his name on a lot of walls and monuments and things, certainly. But why would Hadrian be called a *paintbrush*?'

'I believe, majesty,' Saturninus said, coughing again – it was quite dusty on the road, 'that the name was a subtle reference to the emperor's, uh, sexual tastes. His liking for boys and so on. The word *paintbrush* being a slang term for, uh...'

'Oh,' Crispus said, and blushed visibly. He turned away. For all his confidence, Castus thought with a sly smile, the young man was still a prude.

It was an hour's ride from Athens to Piraeus. While the city had subsided into part-ruined slumber, its port was filled with rough and vigorous life. Warehouses covered the flat ground at the edge of town, and the smell of the sea mingled with the scents of drains, pitch and warm, festering rubbish. The main street was lined with taverns and brothels, the wooden porticos packed with curious onlookers, many of them crying out acclamations as the Caesar and his entourage rode by. But Castus noticed many closed faces among them, even a few hostile glances. He reminded himself that this port, this whole country, had been part of Licinius's domain until recently.

At the gates of the military harbour the crowd was much thicker. Word had spread of the young emperor's arrival, and the roadway was packed on both sides. Castus looked down and saw a forest of arms stretching up into the sunlight, a jostle of open mouths crying out. He felt the reins stiffen in his hands, his big war-trained horse alert to the threat, the possibility of combat. It had been easy, in these recent days of relaxed travel, to forget that the young man riding beside him was Caesar, the son of the Augustus, the master of the west. The *Autokrator Kaisar*, in the Greek tongue. He knew enough of the language to understand the crowd's shouts. '*The blessings of the gods upon our emperor! By the fortune of Caesar we are granted liberty...! By the fortune of Caesar we are free!*'

All it would take, Castus thought, would be a single man with a knife, a bow or sling. Even a well-aimed rock, and Crispus would be dead. He called to the commander of the mounted escort, then stabbed his fingers downward. The commander gave an order at once, and his men turned their horses and began pressing the crowd back from the gateway, some of them slipping from the saddle with spears gripped in both hands to force a lane through the mob. Castus kept his hand on the hilt of his sword until the party was through the gates.

Down on the quays the sun was hot, glaring back off the oily slop of the water in the circular harbour basin. Standing on the worn stone, Castus gazed out at the ships moored in the harbour. Six big war galleys, and twice as many transports and smaller craft. Another galley was just coming in between the fortified moles that divided the harbour from the sea; many more had been hauled up into the circuit of huge ship sheds at the top of the slipways. One of the biggest galleys, a blue-painted bireme with a gilded eagle at her prow, was backing towards a slipway under oars, gangs of men already waiting in the shallows with the big hauling cables to drag her out of the water.

'The *Aquila*,' said the squat, squinting naval commander, Hierax. 'Just came in from Ravenna yesterday evening. Most of the bigger ships are from the Italian fleets, but we'll have every war vessel in the western Mediterranean here soon enough.'

'Impressive,' Castus said. It was true enough. He had seen plenty of ships before, but never in these numbers. There must be over fifty in the sheds alone.

'Indeed it is, *strategos*!' Hierax said. He was a bearded Sicilian, tough and blunt-featured, and Castus had liked him at once. 'Piraeus hasn't seen a muster like this for many a generation. The old port's not got the facilities to handle these numbers; half the ships are over in the commercial docks. But once it's assembled...' He blew out a breath, his eyes vanishing into the creases of his face. 'There hasn't been a fleet this great since the battle of Actium. And that was over three hundred years ago!'

Actium. Castus recognised the name – had Marcellina once read him a poem about that battle? Perhaps, he thought, poets would one day write about this campaign... But no – the days of poetry were long gone.

He followed Hierax down off the quay and along the shore past the slipways, leaving Crispus and the other officers to admire the ships in the harbour. Diogenes trailed behind him, already scratching notes onto a wax tablet – names of vessels, numbers of transports, crew rosters. All around them was the activity of the dockyard, the shouts and curses of half-naked men working in hot sun and salt water. Ropes dragged, mallets banged, beams swayed, and steadily the big galleys were hauled up the ramps into the covered sheds.

'There should be nearly two hundred warships, once all are assembled,' Hierax said, stepping over a stack of beached spars and rigging. 'Though more than half are lighter vessels, triaconters. And four hundred transport ships, if the weather doesn't break.'

Castus whistled below his breath. A fleet like that could carry many thousands of men across to Asia. He paused beside one of the slipways and looked up at the prow of the ship beneath the shed at the top of the ramp, the heavy bow timbers and the bronze-plated ram. Over five years before, he had led a naval expedition into the marshy estuary at the mouth of the Rhine; that was his only experience of fighting on a ship's deck. But the open sea, the turbulent Aegean, would present a greater challenge than those sheltered waters.

Careful of his footing, Castus climbed over the slipway and walked on along the shore. Now that he was looking at the ships more closely, he began to notice the signs of age. Even with his untrained eye he could make out the recent repairs, the patched timbers that the fresh new paintwork could not hide, the joints held together with crude bronze nails. He guessed that most of these big old ships had been laid up for decades, and barely made seaworthy enough to make the voyage around to Piraeus.

'From what we hear,' Hierax said in a hushed rumble, 'the enemy has a larger fleet by far. He's pulling together all the ships from the Euxine to Egypt. Could be several hundred of them. Powerful vessels too. Triremes, many of them.'

'How many triremes do we have?'

'Between you and me and the sea, strategos, not one. We don't have the timber or the skilled shipwrights to build any, neither. Our yards here can build liburnians and monoreme triaconters, but that's all. Licinius has got the best ships from Alexandria and Rhodes, and they still build them the old way down there!'

Castus made a sound in his throat, nodding. With any luck, he thought, there would be no need to fight a sea battle. The warships would be sufficient to guard the transports that would carry the troops and supplies along the coast, then if required they could make a landing on the Asian shore and fight on dry land. A far more pleasing concept.

Passing through another gateway, they moved from the confined harbour onto the open seafront. Here too was activity: the expanse of sand and mud sloping down to the sea was covered with wooden slips and heaps of timber, where gangs of workmen laboured with adze and mallet. Twenty or more vessels stood on the stocks, with more beyond them. The air smelled of hot pitch, wax paint and the sweet resin aroma of fresh-cut pine. A good smell, Castus thought: here, some serious work was being done.

'Will these be finished in time?' he said, pointing to the construction yard.

Hierax nodded. 'Another month and we'll have them all ready for sea. We're building with green wood; all our stocks of seasoned timber are already gone. But these are triaconters, scout vessels. They won't be needed for any long service, if the gods are good.'

Pacing along the shore, Castus studied the new ships. They were all built to the same pattern: open-decked galleys with a single bank of oars, fifteen benches to a side. The more finished ones were brightly painted in red, blue and green. Very similar, he thought, to the light scout vessels he had seen on the Rhine and the Danube. Their prows were shaped like half-moons, from the raised keel spur to the curving stem post. Seeing them all lined up on the stocks, Castus was reminded of a phalanx of angry crabs, claws raised aggressively towards the lapping shore.

'They're fast, these boats?'

'Fast enough,' Hierax said. 'Nimble too, and shallow draught.'

'They'd outrun one of those triremes Licinius has got, then?'

The sea captain made a chuffing sound, and grinned. 'Not a chance! See, a bigger ship can carry a much greater press of oars than one of these little boats, no matter the draught or weight of the hull. There's nothing on the seas that can outpace a trireme at full pressure! Not much that can stand against one in battle either.'

'Then what's the purpose of these small galleys?' Castus asked, trying to keep the disdain from his voice. 'They can't run and they can't fight.'

'These? They're escorts and scouts for the main fleet, and light transports if we need them...' Hierax shrugged his head down into his shoulders; Castus could read his mood easily enough. 'Tell you the truth,' the naval commander went on, dropping his voice, 'for all our numbers, we don't have the timber for a naval battle. But there are spies all over Piraeus; better the enemy thinks we're prepared, even if we're not.'

Castus twisted his mouth and glanced away towards the

sea. Out beyond the crowded anchorage, a brace of the light triaconters were going through their paces. They looked fast enough, seen from dry land, the keel spurs throwing a fine spray as they cut through the gentle waves. But Castus knew now why the bigger ships had been brought to Piraeus. A façade of strength, without substance. Constantine's grand fleet was a collection of half-rotten old tubs and poorly constructed scout galleys, not fit to take on the might of the eastern flotillas.

But as he watched the ships, Castus was remembering the Frankish and Saxon boats he had seen on the Rhine. Could those light nimble vessels, he wondered, attack a larger galley on each beam, racing up over the oar banks just as the Saxons had done in the estuary years before? He had no idea – but soon enough he was going to have to find out.

'In this country my eyes feel young again!' Bonitus declared as they rode back towards the city. 'The air – so clear! I like it.' He breathed in, expanding his chest. Ahead of them the Acropolis was blazing in the early evening light.

Castus had spent the day at Piraeus, remaining there long after Crispus returned to Athens with Saturninus and his mounted guard. Of the officers only Bonitus accompanied him now, with Diogenes and the Protector Ursio. He gazed around him at the slumbering farms and vineyards, the overgrown tombs that lined the road; he needed no other escort here.

'Did you see those smaller ships, the triaconters?' Castus asked. Bonitus pursed his lips, then gave a curt nod. 'Do you think your Franks could handle a ship like that?' he asked.

'Of course!' Bonitus said. 'My people could handle anything that floats. Better than these Greeks, I think! They can row in a straight line, but they've forgotten anything their forefathers knew of fighting on the sea.'

That at least, Castus thought, gave them an edge. Many of the troops he was bringing down from Gaul had served in the galleys of the Rhine flotilla. But once again he reminded himself that the open sea was a different element. Out on the waves, with the wind and the deep-water currents at play, all of them would be foreigners.

They entered the city by the seaward gate and rode up through the suburbs, following a street that ran between the walls of orchards and gardens. Dust swam in the early evening light, and above them the grey limestone crags of the Acropolis still held the sun. Flights of birds were wheeling around the temple ruins on the summit. The villa where Castus and staff were billeted lay another half-mile further north-east, in the district called the Garden of the Muses. It had been a long day, and his skin felt clammy from the salt air of the harbour. He relished the prospect of a hot bath.

The sound of a dog barking broke him from his thoughts. Athens was full of dogs, or so it seemed, but this noise was different: urgent and aggressive. Castus shortened his reins, slowing his horse as he turned to peer up a narrower lane to his right. There was a house there – Castus could see the tiled roof through the surrounding trees. The barking cut off suddenly into a long whine, and then silence. Evening quiet, the distant notes of a flute, the chirring of insects.

Then a scream came from the house at the end of the lane. Castus tensed in the saddle, his hand going at once to his sword hilt. He knew the sound: a man in torment. The next moment he heard a woman's shriek.

The other riders around him had halted. A second scream, and the incoherent shouts of men. Castus saw a figure running down the lane towards him. A woman, cradling a child in her arms and crying out in Greek. Castus caught the words – he

101

knew the dialects of Greek spoken in the east, but this was pure Attic. And the meaning was clear enough. *Help me*.

One swift glance at the fleeing woman – she was young, well dressed, but her tunic was torn at the neck and her hair in disarray – and Castus switched his gaze to the four men who pursued her. All wore rough sleeveless tunics, military daggers at their belts, and two carried staves. They slowed as they caught sight of the horsemen waiting on the road.

The woman ran straight out from the mouth of the lane, the child in her arms beginning to kick and scream. Castus backed his horse as she approached, then swung Ajax forward to circle her, moving between the woman and her four pursuers. He kept his hand on his sword hilt. At the margins of his vision he saw Ursio moving up behind him, Diogenes shifting his mount to block the road ahead. Bonitus remained by the verge, leaning onto his saddle horns with a look of wry curiosity.

'*Kyrios*, please!' the woman cried. She ran to the far side of Castus's horse, still cradling the struggling child, and gripped the nearest horn of his saddle. She was talking fast, panicked, and Castus was only half listening. He caught something about the woman's husband, her child.

He nudged his horse a step forward, pulling away from the woman, then without looking back he pointed across the road to a weathered monument that stood on the far verge. The woman ran to it at once, pressing herself against the masonry. If there was going to be trouble, Castus needed her out of the way.

The four pursuers had halted at the mouth of the lane, gazing open-mouthed at the riders. One of them slung his stave across his shoulders, holding it braced in both hands. Castus saw another edging the dagger from his scabbard. But there were two more figures marching down the lane now, moving fast but slowing as they came out through the cordon of men onto the dust of the road.

Castus kept his knees tight against the leather of his saddle, the reins bunched in his left hand. He was ready to kick the big horse forward and draw his blade at the first hostile movement. Bonitus, for all his apparent calm, had a tensed focus in his gaze; he, too, was primed to fight. None of their party wore armour, and they carried only swords, but still they outclassed their opponents.

The two newcomers on the road both wore the patterned tunics and red leather belts of imperial officials. The younger one had curling blond hair and a broad smiling face; the other was older, balding, with bristling black stubble and a resentful glare.

'Greetings, brothers!' the younger man said with a self-assured smirk, hooking his thumbs into his belt. 'I thank you for apprehending our fugitive!'

Castus made no reply. He had no standard with him, but his uniform and equipment would mark him out as an officer of rank. With a quick glance back, he checked that the woman was still pressed against the monument on the far side of the road. She cried out in Greek, a panicked spill of words. Castus understood enough. *Torturers... My husband... They want to hurt my child!*

'Allow me to introduce myself,' the smirking man said. 'My name is Flavius Innocentius, *ducenarius* of the agentes in rebus. This,' he said, with a gesture to the bearded man at his side, 'is my associate, Gracilis. The woman there is in our custody. Her husband is a spy for the eastern tyrant, and we need to question her further about his... activities. If you'd care to move aside, my men will take her now.'

He signalled to the four *quaestionarii* flanking him. One man took a step forward; the others exchanged glances. Castus shifted in the saddle, and Ajax stamped at the dust and tossed his mane.

'The woman's under my protection now,' Castus growled. 'Take your torturers and get out of my sight.'

The agent was still glaring at him, his blue eyes unblinking. There was something hideous in the level intensity of his gaze, and the smirk that flickered across his face. From the far side of the road came the child's gasping cries.

'We have no wish to pick a quarrel with the army!' the agent said, raising a finger. 'Nor do we wish to cause a scene here... The last thing we want is some mob of outraged citizens interfering with our work.'

With a pang of distaste, Castus noticed the blood beneath the man's fingernails. One swing with the flat of his blade, he thought, and he could lay this primping torturer in the dust.

'But I must caution you,' Innocentius went on, 'that we carry a mandate to investigate enemy intelligence networks in this city to the utmost extent. That mandate comes from the very highest level – from his eminence Rutilius Palladius, Master of Offices. So, you see, legally we outrank you in this issue!'

Castus recognised the name: Palladius had recently been promoted from primicerius of notaries, and was now one of the most senior officials of Constantine's court. These agents had no connection with Crispus and his retinue.

'Don't quote laws at me,' he said. 'We carry swords.'

Turning his horse, he slid the long eagle-hilted spatha from his scabbard and laid the blade flat against his leg. 'And your mandate extends precisely as far as the reach of my arm.'

The agent's fierce gaze did not slacken. The bearded man at his side was breathing quickly, his sallow face darkening with rage, but Flavius Innocentius showed no sign of agitation.

'You are making a poor choice, excellency,' Innocentius said through his smile, his words lilting.

Castus tapped his sword against his leg. He could see the four torturers shuffling out to either side, as if they meant to rush the horsemen, perhaps try and snatch the woman. But they knew they were the weaker party. Four men on horseback with long swords could cut them down in a few heartbeats. The moment for action approached; then it was passed.

Another slight gesture from the leading agent, and the quaestionarii began stepping backwards towards the mouth of the lane. Innocentius and his friend remained standing, holding their ground.

'You are Aurelius Castus, am I right?' the agent said.

Castus gave him a curt nod. There could not be too many senior commanders in the army who matched his description. He was fighting the urge to spur his horse forward and cut the smirking agent down. Instead, with an effort of will, he lifted his sword and slipped it back into the scabbard. He waved to Ursio, then pointed at the woman.

The big Sarmatian slid from his horse and led it across the road to the monument. The woman shrank back from him, alarmed by his size and his barbarian features. Ursio flashed a quick smile, then took the woman by the waist and lifted her, and the child in her arms, up onto the saddle of his horse.

'My master will hear of this infraction,' Innocentius said. 'I hope, for your sake, he does not take issue with your conduct today.'

'Do what you like,' Castus grunted. He glanced up the lane behind the cordon of torturers, wondering for a moment if he could press his advantage further. Lead his horsemen up to the house and liberate the woman's husband... But no. He could

105

not risk his own men like that. If the husband genuinely was a spy, Castus would have to let him suffer for it.

'I suspect our paths may cross again, Aurelius Castus,' the agent said, raising his palm in a brief mockery of a salute. 'I bid you farewell, for now...' Snapping a finger at his torturers, he turned and marched back up the lane towards the house. The bearded man gave a last sneer, then spat on the road at his feet before turning to follow.

Dust settled slowly. Castus saw Bonitus grinning. The woman perched on the back of Ursio's horse was weeping quietly, pressing her child to her breast. Castus hoped she had relatives in the city who would shelter her.

'Let's go,' he said, and nudged Ajax forward. The others moved off with him, Ursio on foot leading his own horse.

'Some *interesting* people your emperor keeps in his pay,' Bonitus said, shaking his head. He patted the hilt of his sword, clearly disappointed that he had missed the opportunity to use it.

They rode on in silence, and Castus tensed as he waited for the sound from behind him, the screams from the house at the end of the lane that would tell him the torturers had resumed their work. But the stillness of the evening was unbroken. High above in the bright clean air the birds were wheeling around the Acropolis mount. From away to the right, in the direction of the Olympieion, Castus could make out the sounds of chanting, the chime of cymbals. He knew that whatever was happening back in the house would never be disclosed. But he would see Flavius Innocentius again, he was sure of that. And next time, he thought, he would not be as civil.

CHAPTER VII

A stiff breeze from the north-east was raising choppy waves across the broad expanse of the Thermaic Gulf, and the bows of the fifty-oared liburnian galley *Artemisia* burst the water and flung spume back over the deck. Sunlight flashed on the double bank of oar-blades as they rose and fell. Perched on the curving rail below the stern, Castus squinted into the fierce reflected glare. Across the waves to leeward, he saw the squadron of smaller galleys, the bright-painted thirty-oared triaconters, pulling steadily against the headwind towards the shelter of the harbour at Thessalonica. He had an infantryman's instinctive disdain for the navy, but he had to admit that it was a beautiful sight.

The long hulls of the triaconters were riding low, barely clearing the wavetops, each craft burdened with twenty armed men crowded along the narrow central gangway. Many of the vessels mounted artillery as well, light ballistae and catapults. It had been a long and gruellingly hard day of training, but the sweating oarsmen, stripped almost naked, were pulling with gusto. The sound of raucous singing drifted across the waves, mingling with the cries of the gulls.

'Your barbarians are in fine voice,' Hierax said, joining Castus at the stern and handing him a flask of watered wine.

'They should be,' Castus said, taking a swig and passing the flask back. 'They did well today.'

Eight of the little warships carried bands of Bonitus's Salian Frankish warriors. As Castus expected, they had excelled at the shipboard manoeuvres; when the ships had rammed up against the barges towed behind the larger galleys the Franks had stormed forward over the bows without a pause. Their aim with bow and javelin from a pitching deck was better than that of the legionaries too.

'Still,' said Hierax, shrugging, 'attacking fully manned triremes is harder than boarding barges.'

'So you keep telling me,' Castus replied with a wry smile. 'That's why I want to use the larger galleys as targets next time. We'll see how they get on attacking some oared vessels.'

He heard Hierax sucking air through his teeth. 'Better hope they do well. Otherwise you'll be looking at a lot of broken timber. Lot of broken bones too. What was the score for today?'

'A few cuts and grazes, no serious injuries. I don't care about broken timber, or broken bones either. I want to make this fleet fit for war.' Castus took the flask again, and drank with relish.

'A commendable goal, excellency. But please don't destroy it in the process. Who was it who said you Romans treat your drills as bloodless battles? I always thought the *bloodless* part was the most important!'

'Nope,' Castus said with a grin. 'The battles are the most important part. And I intend to win ours. So tomorrow we do all this again, and we do it better.'

Yes, Castus thought: he would drill them like this, every ship in the fleet over and again, at any cost in oars, damaged ships, lost weapons and shields, even broken men. He would drill them until they could use these little scout galleys as proper fighting machines; only then would Crispus's makeshift navy stand a chance against the Licinian ships.

The triaconters were pulling ahead now, racing each other back to the shelter of the harbour. Hierax had trained his oarsmen well on their voyage up from Piraeus, against the first swells of the northern Etesian wind. Castus breathed deeply, and fresh sea air filled his lungs. He felt good; for the first time in months he felt everything was clear and working to a purpose.

From his perch on the stern rail of the *Artemisia* he could see the network of military camps spreading across the broad plain to the west of Thessalonica. Smoke from the cooking fires hazed the air, blurring the mountains beyond. The men in those camps had marched enormous distances to be here. The Gallic units had covered well over a thousand miles of road in the last three months. Important, Castus knew, to keep them fit and disciplined. He had ordered constant training, frequent parades and regular exercise: wrestling, ball games and foot races. The spirit of competition, he hoped, would forge unity among them. Already there had been disputes and violence between different units. Many of them had fought on opposing sides in the last civil war; now all were serving under the banners of Constantine.

As the galley entered the bay, Castus saw the proud sea walls of the city ahead of him, lit up by the evening sun. Unlike Athens, Thessalonica had no monuments of antiquity or claims to ancient fame, but it was a vigorous place, seething with life. Seething with spies, too, if the rumours were true. At the left-hand end of the sea wall was the new military harbour, with its long curving moles. At the opposite end, to the south-east, Castus could make out the high vaulted arches of the circus, with the domes and roofs of the imperial palace alongside. He had managed to avoid the palace for most of the last month, and was glad of that. Crispus and his father spent the majority of their time hunting in the hills, and Castus had little desire to encounter Fausta again, or the emperor's aged mother either.

The *Artemisia* rowed between the harbour moles and into the expanse of enclosed water beyond. A forest of masts rose from the moored transport ships, and along the slipways slaves were already wading out into the water, ready to haul the galleys up into their sheds. Most of the slaves were Goths, Castus had learned, captured during the emperor's war on the Danube the year before. There were thousands of them working in the harbour alone.

With a last sweep of her oars, the liburnian galley turned her stern to the quay, and the boarding plank rattled across. Some of the smaller ships had berthed nearby, the legionaries and Frankish warriors already disembarking. As he strode up the plank onto the stone paving of the quay, Castus could make out a loud strained voice rising above the clatter of timbers and the noise of the milling soldiers.

'You there!' the voice cried. 'Are you in charge here? What's the meaning of this?'

Castus paused, planting his feet wide and hooking his thumbs into his belt. The man approaching him was barrel-bellied and bow-legged, with a clipped beard beneath his chin. He wore the round embroidered cap and decorated garments of an imperial official, although Castus had never seen him before, and he was flanked by attendants and a squad of bodyguards armed with staves.

'What's the problem?' Castus asked, squaring his shoulders.

'The problem is that my ships are filled with barbarians!' the well-dressed man said, his face dark with anger. 'I gave no such permission. Who are you, anyway?'

Castus was dressed in a plain old army tunic, stained with salt and sweat, and only the torque he wore around his neck and the fine spatha belted at his side showed his military standing. But he was not going to make this easy.

'Like you say, I'm in charge here,' he said.

'You will address the prefect correctly!' snarled one of the man's bodyguards, a swarthy soldier with a centurion's staff over his shoulder. Castus gave a crooked smile and raised one eyebrow. The soldiers from the *Artemisia* were trooping up the gangplank now, grounding their spears and shields on the quay paving and watching with stern interest. The other soldiers, the Franks among them, were massed across the quay behind them. The well-dressed official's bodyguards gripped their staves and exchanged nervous glances.

For a few heartbeats Castus and the official stared at each other in silence. Then the other man flinched slightly and glanced away. He gestured angrily to the centurion beside him.

'You are speaking,' the centurion announced, 'to the distinguished Flavius Theophilus, prefect of the fleet under the command of Crispus Caesar!'

Castus turned his head slowly and saw Hierax on the stern deck of the galley. The Sicilian shrugged back at him.

'Ah well, in that case,' Castus said. 'You're speaking to Flavius Aurelius Castus, comes rei militaris, senior commander of the soldiers of the expeditionary force under Crispus Caesar.'

'You?' Theophilus gasped. He fingered his clipped beard. 'I... Strategos, we haven't yet been introduced. I didn't know...'

'Obviously,' Castus said, inclining his head slightly. 'As for the Franks, they're aboard the ships on my order, which was agreed by the Caesar himself. If you want to protest, tell him about it. But now you're keeping me from a cold bath, prefect.'

111

A clatter of laughter from the watching troops as Castus pushed past Theophilus's guards and strode along the quay, Ursio and the other members of his staff following him. Castus had not known that a prefect had been appointed over the fleet; clearly it was a recent decision. An irritating one as well; Hierax was more than capable of marshalling the naval side of the expedition, and this Theophilus looked capable only of making a nuisance of himself.

But the evening was fresh and warm, and the pleasure of being back on dry land and surrounded by the activity of the dockyard soon lifted Castus's mood. The house that had been assigned as his quarters, a former merchant's residence, lay only a block from the harbour. A short walk, and he had come to know it well. The air was heavy with the scents of tar and salt and timber, but Castus could smell the frying fish from the little stalls just outside the dock gates. He was walking with a fast clip to his stride; he knew that a letter had arrived from Marcellina that morning, and he had put off reading it until he returned.

As he entered the main street that led uphill from the docks, Castus noticed the words painted on the brick wall. 'CONSTANTINE THE OATHBREAKER'. They must have appeared the night before; already a gang of slaves were scrubbing at them, scouring the wall clean of its treasonous message. Castus had seen several notices like this around Thessalonica, painted or chalked or scratched into the plaster. The work of the enemy's agents, no doubt. But he tensed all the same, unable to avoid the swell of unease: Constantine had indeed sworn oaths of brotherhood and peace with Licinius, not so many years ago. Glancing away, he tried to rid his mind of the thought.

There was a group of men gathered at the doorway of his house, and they stepped back into the street as Castus turned the corner. Three of them were his own door slaves; the other two wore army tunics and cloaks, but it took him a few moments to recognise them. As he approached, they assumed the military stance, saluting.

'Claudius Modestus!' Castus called. 'And is that Felix with you there?'

'Present, dominus!' the wiry soldier said. But Castus was already throwing his arms around both of them.

'Heard you were billeted here,' Modestus said, buffeting Castus's shoulder. His creased slab of a face split into a fearsome grin. 'Senior commander now, isn't it? We got in with the Second yesterday; came down to find you, but everyone at the docks was saying some bearded Greek ape's in charge here. Guessed that couldn't be right!'

Modestus had always been an ugly man, and his sunburnt complexion gave him a particularly porcine look. Felix was doing his best to look agreeable, but his long jaw and muscular dangling arms appeared predatory; not surprisingly, the door slaves had refused them admittance.

'You're a *centurio campidoctor* now then, I hear?' Castus asked Modestus. 'A drillmaster? Not bad for a drunk and a shirker.'

Modestus screwed up his face even more. 'Twenty-five years under the standards, excellency,' he said solemnly. 'Felix here's only done half that number.'

'I remember it well,' Castus said. Valerius Felix had joined Legion II Britannica back in Gaul, shortly before Castus took command. A taciturn man of unusual talents; he had saved Castus's life more than once since then.

Looking at them now, Castus realised that he had known these men longer than almost anybody else in his life. Both were around the same age as himself, both moulded by the army, just as he had been. For a moment he felt the familiar nostalgia, almost a sense of loss, that came to him when he remembered the simpler life he had led in the legions.

'Come inside,' he said. 'Take a cup or two of wine.'

Modestus frowned, peering in through the doors, thrown open now at Castus's arrival. 'Generous of you, dominus,' he said with an evasive air. 'But it's not really our place… we're meeting a few others at a bar – low sort of dive, really – and we're late as it is…'

Castus understood, though it grieved him. Even after all these years, the barriers of rank separated them. 'Well, if you're sure,' he said. 'But I'll see you at the camp soon enough.'

They left him then, saluting with only the slightest trace of good-humoured mockery, and Castus entered the house. In the vestibule the crowd of petitioners pressed forward: slaves of higher officials, most of them, with a few lower-placed contractors and civilians. Castus waited while his bodyguards pushed a way between them, then marched through into the private area of the house. He was still thinking of the *low sort of dive* Modestus had mentioned – he would have much preferred to spend his evening in a place like that, drinking with a pack of scarred old soldiers.

'Anybody important in that mob out there?' he asked as he entered the chamber set aside as his office.

'No, dominus,' Diogenes said. 'I dealt with the more pressing cases myself. But some of the rest have been waiting since midday.'

'*Midday?* Let them come back tomorrow and wait at dawn, then we'll see if they're serious.'

He had tried to be scrupulous with his appointments, but it was an impossible task. So much needed doing: people to cajole and direct, judgements to make, documents to assess and clear, all the administration of a vast army flowing through his office, and he needed somehow to keep track of it. It was easy to become dismissive. Easier still, he knew, to fall into corruption.

The letter from Marcellina was waiting for him on the table. Castus had wanted to leave it until he was bathed, freshly dressed and relaxed, but he knew he could wait no longer.

'There's a note from your son enclosed with it,' Diogenes said. Castus had given him permission to check all his correspondence. 'I didn't read it, but I notice he has a very elegant hand for his age. Really quite talented with his letters.'

Castus snorted a laugh. Diogenes had personally appointed the boy's *paedagogus*, and both he and Marcellina had given Sabinus extra tuition themselves. But how strange it was, he thought, that a son of his could have a *very elegant hand*... Castus himself had been quite unable to read or write until he was in his thirties, and even now he often found it a trial.

Taking the letter, he walked into the shade of the colonnaded garden at the heart of the house, pulled up a chair and sat. Marcellina had inked her words onto five conjoined leaves of thin wood, with Sabinus's note folded between them. Frowning, he held the little wooden sliver in his big hands and began to read. The letters were certainly elegant, as if his son had copied then from a manual of calligraphy. *I salute you dear father. All is well here at Treveris and we are happy. Dulcitia has visited us many times since the wedding and she is happy too...*

Castus was smiling as he read, although there was little in the note but the usual polite formulas. He read it again, trying to imagine Sabinus speaking the words to him. But all he could imagine was his son's labour in writing, his determination to sound like an adult. The written word was so often like that, Castus thought: it concealed more than it communicated.

Next he read the letter from his wife. More rather stiff greetings and family news. Only at the end, on the last leaf, did some genuine feeling break through. *We all miss you more than I can say. Do you still think next year we might be reunited in Dalmatia? I long for new places, as I long for you.*

They had spoken of that before he left Treveris; for many years Castus had owned a villa on the Dalmatian coast, inherited from his first wife, although he had never seen it. The place had become almost a joke between him and Marcellina, but now it seemed she was serious about the family moving there. Castus pondered the idea for a moment, shrugged, then read on.

There are rumours here of some prophecy or curse you encountered on campaign last summer. I do not believe in such things, of course, but people will always speak ill of those who have risen by merit rather than wealth or favour. I shall pray for you, and pray to see you victorious soon. Your loving wife, A. M.

Castus read the words again, and felt a chill up his spine. He had spoken to nobody about the Alamannic witch and her strange declaration. Only Saturninus had overheard, or so he had thought... Leaning back in the chair he gazed into the slanting afternoon sunlight. So many people had been warning him lately – what did they know that he did not? Was this some test, or the nudgings of a deity? More than anything he wished that Marcellina were here with him, and not a thousand miles away in Belgica. He should have spoken to her before about his doubts, his fears...

'Dominus!' a voice called from the passageway. Eumolpius, his orderly, emerged from the shadows. 'A message, dominus, from the palace!'

'Another message?' Castus mumbled. This one was less likely to please him. But already his pulse had quickened. 'Read it,' he ordered.

Eumolpius broke the seal and scanned the words. 'All military officers of senior tribune rank or above are to present themselves at the audience hall of the sacred palace, at the first hour of the night,' he said. 'That's all.'

All officers, Castus thought. This could mean only one thing. They were ready to sound the trumpets at last.

'Eumolpius,' he said, standing up quickly, 'I need a cold bath immediately. And my best clothes and clean kit. And I need them *fast*!'

CHAPTER VIII

The vestibule of the imperial audience hall was already crowded by the time Castus arrived. Some of the men waiting there had come straight from the camp, unshaven and stinking of sweat; others were finely dressed and freshly scrubbed, some of them even wearing perfume. Castus moved between them, acknowledging salutes and wordless greetings. The doors of the hall were still closed and guarded, but there was a charge of anticipation in the air.

Bonitus appeared from the crowd and clasped Castus by the shoulder. His cloak was thrown back, revealing the glitter of his gold belt buckles and sword fittings. He was keeping his distance from Hrodomarus, the chief of the Alamannic Bucinobantes, who had fought in Constantine's army for over a decade. There were other Germanic tribal leaders in the gathering too, mingled in uncomfortable proximity with the Roman officers.

Glancing around, Castus saw other men he recognised. Gratianus, the young tribune of the Moesiaci, was a tall muscular man with corded arms, renown for his strength as a wrestler. Then there was Evander, the general who had led Constantine's army during the Italian campaign. Theophilus was there too; the naval prefect pursed his lips and bobbed his head in a sour greeting.

118

Saturninus came striding in from the courtyard, and Castus moved quickly to intercept him. With a gesture, he drew the cavalry officer to an alcove on one side of the doorway. No time for lengthy speeches or oblique questions now.

'In Germania last year, when we took the Brisigavi fort,' Castus said, low and urgent. 'You remember the old woman, the witch? You remember what she said?'

Saturninus nodded. No trace of guilt on his face.

'My wife says they're talking about it in Treveris. Did you speak of it to anybody?'

'Not I!' Saturninus said. 'But you know how these things get about, brother. Somebody else must have overheard... Think no more of it. Idle gossip.'

Castus frowned, nodding. Surely the man was right, but the thought troubled him. Just then there was a noise from behind them, the exhalation of air as the great doors swung open. With a slap on the shoulder, Castus led Saturninus back into the waiting throng as they began to file into the hall.

The huge space was in darkness, illuminated only by tall lamps set at the far end near the dais. As the officers assembled they fell into rank order; Castus moved to the front and joined the other senior commanders. From there he could see the wooden trestle standing on the lowest step of the dais, a long painted panel set upon it. Turning his head, he tried to make out the pattern on the panel, but at first he could distinguish nothing but curling lines of blue and brown. Then the shape became clear: it was a painted itinerary, he realised, an illustrated route map. He had seen maps before, but nothing this elaborate.

At the left-hand end of the panel was the city of Thessalonica, depicted as a cluster of domes and towers inside a wall. Immediately to the right was the bulging peninsula of Chalcidice, with its three long promontories like the crooked fingers of a mutilated hand reaching out into the blue Aegean. To the right of the peninsula was the Strymonian Gulf, then the island of Thasos, and from there the coast ran straight to the far end of the panel, where the blue curl of the Hebrus River met the sea. Following the coast, a little inland, was a black line: the Via Egnatia, marked along its length with the names of towns and road stations.

Castus was distracted from his absorbed scrutiny of the map by the voice of a herald. A horn sounded, and every man in the hall stood stiffly to attention as the emperor entered by a side door and ascended the dais, his son Crispus following him. Both were dressed in rich purple robes embroidered with golden palm fronds. When they stood upon the dais, the assembled men raised their hands in salute and cried out the acclamation. '*Constantinus Augustus! Crispus Caesar! May the gods preserve you for us! Your salvation is our salvation…!*'

The shouts died into a hush, the men in the hall dropping to one knee as their emperor seated himself upon the tall ivory throne. Crispus took a seat just behind and to the left of him. They would preside over the meeting, but it was Acilius Severus, the Praetorian Prefect, who moved to address the assembly as the officers stood up once more.

'Brothers,' he announced in a tone of aristocratic gravity. 'The hour approaches when we will commence our advance against the tyrant Licinius. All of you here know the just causes for this war, which we undertake with the mandate of heaven. It falls to me now to divulge the plan of our operation, which will lead the loyal troops of our Sacred Augustus to certain victory.'

He gestured towards the wooden panel, and at once two imperial slaves lifted the trestle supporting it and moved it forward into the glow of the lamps. The officers behind Castus shuffled, craning their necks for a better view.

'You see here the illustrated itinerary of our eastward advance,' the prefect said. 'Four days from now, on the kalends of June, the main force of our army, under the command of the Sacred Augustus himself, aided by the *comites* Flavius Polemius and Flavius Aurelius Evander, will march east from Thessalonica to the Strymonian Gulf. Meanwhile, the fleet of galleys and transports under the command of the most blessed Caesar, aided by the *comes* Flavius Aurelius Castus and the distinguished Flavius Theophilus, will put to sea and circumnavigate the promontories of Chalcidice, to meet the land forces at Amphipolis and Neapolis.'

As the prefect spoke, Castus glanced up at the emperors upon the dais. Both sat perfectly still, expressionless as ivory statues.

'Once the fleet has arrived,' the prefect said, 'a general advance will commence. The main army will proceed by the Via Egnatia, while the fleet follows their progress along the coast, establishing supply points at regular intervals. The galleys of the fleet must ensure that no enemy cruisers fall upon our transport ships, or gain intelligence of our overall numbers.

'Should we meet the enemy in force,' the prefect went on, 'the troops carried on the ships will be landed on the right flank of the main army. If we do not, the advance will proceed to the mouth of the Hebrus. From here we will prepare a further advance against the enemy, wherever he may be, to pin his army and crush him in battle.'

A stir of muttered words came from the assembled officers. It seemed a good enough plan, Castus thought, although his own role would be no more than a guard over the seaborne supply convoy.

Acilius Severus cleared his throat lightly, appearing suddenly evasive and a little unsure of himself. 'There's another matter,' he said.

After a pause, he continued. 'It is the desire of the Sacred Augustus that this campaign be conducted under the sole guidance of Almighty God, and Christ His Son. Accordingly, there will be no prayers or sacrifices to any other deities or spirits by our army, nor will auspices or omens be sought.'

A moment of silence, then a vast collective intake of breath, and a harsh rumble of muttering. The prefect raised his voice to speak over the noise.

'Just as this is a war between light and darkness, and of truth against falsehood, so our army will take as its standard the conquering symbol of the true God. This standard, the Sacred Labarum, will precede our army, as the images of the false gods once did, and all soldiers will revere it as they revere the persons of their emperors.'

At his gesture, three men in the white uniforms of the Protectores marched from one side of the hall into the light. Two carried silvered spears, while the third carried a tall military standard. But at the top of the pole, where an eagle or the statue of a god would once have been displayed, there was a large gilded symbol: the conjoined X and P, set within a circular wreath of golden laurel. The sign of the Christian faith.

Voices broke from the chorus of gasps and cries. Castus heard the word *sacrilege*. Somebody behind him whispered: '*The troops will never accept this! They'll mutiny!*'

'Silence!' cried the herald, then repeated the order.

Castus stared, disbelieving, at the standard. He felt a dull pressure in his chest, a swelling in his neck. Behind him now was a breathless hush. He glanced at Evander, but the senior commander would not meet his eye; clearly, some men had known of this decision in advance. He was unable to hide his expression of anguish.

'Aurelius Castus.' The voice boomed from the dais, amplified by the tall apse behind it. The emperor had dropped his blank mask and was leaning forward from his throne. 'You have something you wish to say?'

Castus felt a jolt of naked terror run through him. The other officers were shuffling back, leaving him exposed at the front of the hall. Why had he alone been picked out? He did not know, but he knew he must speak for them all now.

'Majesty,' he said, almost choking as he spoke. He tried to clear his mind, to find the right phrases. His words echoed in the darkness. 'Majesty, I have served over thirty years in the army. I have fought in twenty campaigns, over fifteen pitched battles. Many under your own command. The legions have always carried the images of the gods into battle. They have always made sacrifice and given prayers to the divine spirits before going to war. This is our way... But this change, this new rule...'

The words clotted in his mouth, and he felt the pressure all around him: expectation, guilt, fear. He could say no more, and the silence stretched long.

'And so, what?' Constantine declared. 'You think the troops would not fight bravely without these empty symbols and rituals? You think their courage would fail them? You think they would no longer be loyal?'

Castus said nothing. In his mind, he saw temples burning.

The emperor got up suddenly. Standing tall, he appeared to tower over the assembled men below him. 'You, yourself,' he said, pointing at Castus, 'fought at the glorious battle of Milvian Bridge! Did I not order this same sign, this holy sign of the Almighty God, painted on the shields of our troops? Were we not victorious then?'

His voice had risen. He was almost shouting now, his words rolling like thunder in the vast space of the hall. 'Why should our soldiers not recognise and revere the God that brings them victory? Why should they cling to the false idols that bring only defeat for our enemies? With this standard before us, there is no way that we can fail to conquer – this has been revealed to me! Go now, all of you – go to your junior officers and your men and tell them what you have heard here. Go joyously! But tell them this: any man who refuses to serve loyally will be branded a deserter and a traitor to his sacred oath!'

With that, the emperor turned on his heel and stalked from the dais. The crowd of men in the hall stood motionless for a moment, then began to break up. None seemed willing to comment, or even to look another in the eye, as they filed out of the hall.

In the warm night air Castus stood on the steps and felt the rage and humiliation pouring through him. He could not bear to speak to any of the others that passed him, for fear of uttering some treasonous outburst. It took him several long moments to notice that the men gathering in the courtyard were peering towards the rooftops, some of them pointing. He caught a strange smell on the night breeze. Smoke and distant burning, as if the fevered images from his mind had taken form.

Then he glanced up, and saw the sky to the north-west lit murky orange. A horseman came galloping into the courtyard, sliding in the saddle as he reined to a halt.

'Domini!' the messenger cried. 'Domini, the docks are on fire!'

By the time Castus arrived, riding hard down the broad avenue of the city with Ursio behind him, the flames were clearly visible above the roofs of the warehouses. Smoke filled the air, boiling from the dockyard gates as Castus turned his horse and forced a path through the mob of panicked people. He leaned from the saddle, seizing a fleeing figure by the neck of his tunic and spinning him around.

'Get back there!' he shouted. 'Get back and fight the fire, you bastards!'

Inside the gates, the quays were hazed with flame-lit smoke, figures reeling and running in the fog. Castus saw that the fire had not yet reached the nearer ship sheds; as he watched, a sheet of flame peeled upward from a warehouse roof, scattering sparks and streamers of fire out across the black basin of the harbour. Men were in the water, stripped to their loincloths as they hauled up buckets and kegs to fling on the blaze. Others were labouring at the slipways, trying to get as many of the ships as possible down into the water and out of reach of the fire.

'Not like that!' a voice bellowed. 'You clumsy beggars, you'll break her keel!'

Castus saw Hierax down by the shore, and rode to join him. Leaping from the saddle, he grabbed the Sicilian by the arm. 'What's happened here?' he demanded.

'You see it plain!' Hierax said, gesturing at the burning sheds. His face and the front of his tunic were black with smuts. 'The fire started in the ropewalk behind the western sheds – with this warm breeze it's spreading fast and far. Maybe a dropped lamp, an accident...'

'Sabotage?'

'Well, I wasn't going to suggest it,' Hierax said, baring his teeth, 'but since you mentioned it – possibly, yes.'

Castus blinked the sting from his eyes. He was gulping breath, and the smoke caught in his throat. With a grinding rush, one of the larger galleys broke from its cables and rolled down the slipway from the nearest shed. It knifed into the water, bursting spray, and Castus heard screams; several men had been crushed under the warship's ram.

'Go to my residence,' he told Ursio, the words rasping. 'Bring everyone down here – anyone else you can find too. Pass a message: everyone's needed here to fight this. If we don't stop the fire spreading the whole dockyard'll burn, and the city too!'

'We don't have enough buckets, and no siphons,' Hierax said. He was panting for breath, too. Two hundred paces away, Castus could see the ship sheds along the waterfront catching fire. The far end of one of them collapsed, and flames rushed along the hull of the ship inside. It was the *Aquila*, Castus realised; he saw the big gilded eagle on the prow wreathed in smoke. The chains of men hauling water buckets from the harbour were having no effect.

'We need to create a firebreak,' he said to Hierax. 'All the far sheds are gone, but if we clear these nearer ones and pull them down that should do it. Use the ship cables to haul out the supports and collapse the roofs. What's in those warehouses behind the sheds there?'

'Supplies for the expedition, dominus,' Hierax said. 'Vinegar wine and drinking water.'

'Breach the kegs and spill them over the collapsed sheds – do it on my order. Go!'

Hierax nodded, saluting as he staggered away into the smoke. 'You heard the strategos!' he shouted. 'All work gangs! Cables to the ship sheds, axemen to the warehouses – time to fight!'

Over the noise of the blaze came the sound of tormented screams. Castus could see that the fire had reached one of the slave barracks where the Gothic prisoners were confined; many of the slaves had already been freed to fight the fire, but some were still chained inside and now the flames were licking along the roof of the building.

For a few heartbeats he stood poised, indecisive. There were not enough men to fight this new danger. But could they leave the slaves to burn? Sweat filled his eyes, and he coughed and spat.

Then he heard the sound of hoofbeats on the paving, and a group of horsemen came pounding along the quayside. In the lead was a figure in white and gold, flinging off his purple robe as he dismounted.

'Caesar!' Castus cried, breaking into a run. 'Get back from the fire! Don't risk yourself!'

As Crispus bolted towards the burning slave barracks Castus collided with him, grappling the young man to a halt. Saturninus came running up behind them, with a score of his Scutarii troopers.

'Get your hands off me!' Crispus screamed, his voice breaking. 'We need to help those men!'

'They're slaves, majesty, barbarians,' Saturninus cried, his troopers forming a cordon around them. 'Their friends probably started this fire – let them suffer!'

'They're human beings, made in the image of God!' Crispus said in a pained gasp. Castus was still holding him, clasping the young man to his chest, and Crispus was fighting against him.

'Secure the Caesar,' Castus told Saturninus. The cavalry commander gazed at him, open-mouthed.

'Do it! I'll take responsibility. Then I need half your men.'

Cursing through clenched teeth, Castus jogged heavily towards the burning building, a knot of the Scutarii troopers at his heels. He realised that he was still wearing his best court uniform, with his jewelled belts and gilded buckles. Too late to change that now. The strap of his shoe broke as he ran and he kicked it off.

The barracks was already thickly hazed by smoke, the

127

burning remains of a neighbouring building collapsed across the yard in front of it. As Castus leaped across a heap of smouldering timbers he heard the crash of the first ship shed going down, the cheers from the warehouse as the first kegs were smashed open.

His eyes stung, and his whole body felt liquid with sweat in the heat of the fires. As he cleared the last of the debris he saw a group of men crouched along the front of the barracks, flanking the doors. One of them held a long-handled iron mallet, but they were lost to terror.

'Where's the overseer?' Castus yelled, his voice tearing his throat. The men gazed at him, blank and uncomprehending. 'Give me that,' he said, seizing the mallet.

One swinging blow shattered the lock; a second burst the door open.

The wave of heat and noise struck him at once, a black scream bellowing from inside the building. Castus had no idea how many prisoners were chained within. He swallowed one long choking draught of air, then he plunged through the doorway.

Panic in darkness, the flames already ripping along the roof timbers and showering sparks. As his eyes adjusted, Castus saw a mob of men packing one side of the long chamber, most of them naked or dressed in loincloths, all of them struggling and screaming. Their stretched mouths and rolling eyes glared in the smoky gloom.

A soldier came through the door behind him. 'Keep them back from me,' Castus shouted, swinging the mallet at the slaves who pressed towards him. 'Then stand clear.'

The slaves were manacled at the wrist, and every man wore an iron neck ring secured to a chain that ran the length of the building. These, Castus knew, would be the worst of the slaves, those who had tried to fight or escape. Dangerous men; but he could not retreat now.

'Back!' he bellowed, feigning with the mallet. The slaves were yelling at him in their own guttural language, but he understood not a word. Three of the soldiers had drawn their swords and were driving the mob away from Castus. As they moved aside, he made out the big iron bolt securing the chain to the wall timbers.

Burning cinders rained down on him as he raised the mallet. He felt the hair singeing on his arms and the back of his neck. He brought the mallet swinging down, and it slammed against the bolt and rebounded, ringing. Teeth bared, Castus swung again, feeling the shock of impact in his arms and chest. Sparks flew from the iron. Drawing a hot breath through his nose, he set his feet wide, took careful aim and struck again.

With a sharp clang the bolt shattered. At once the mass of slaves heaved towards the door, trailing the slackened chain after them. In the smoke and darkness they were a wave of flesh, of sweat-slicked limbs and fury. Castus gripped the shaft of the mallet, pushing against the surge. One of the soldiers grabbed his arm while the other two lashed out with the flats of their blades, and in the wild tumult they hurled themselves out of the door with the mob charging behind them.

The air outside felt almost clean, and Castus drank it down. He was running, flinging the mallet aside, following the two soldiers back through the maze of debris to the open space of the quayside. He stood, arms braced against his knees, coughing and gasping. His throat was parched, and his mouth tasted as if he had been chewing on a lump of charred wood. Somebody passed him a skin of water; he sucked from it, spat, and poured the rest over his face. Then he slumped down to sit on the worn stones of the quayside.

To his right, the collapsed sheds were holding back the wall of flames, a line of men silhouetted against the glow. Others were bringing up more water from the harbour, flinging the buckets onto the mass of sodden timber and shattered tile that formed the firebreak.

'Brother, are you injured?' Crispus was kneeling beside him, a hand on his shoulder. Castus noticed with dulled surprise that the young man's face was streaming with tears. He thought it was just the smoke, then recognised the anguish in his voice. He shook his head roughly and swabbed at his face.

'The damage – will we survive it?'

'Yes,' Castus said. He gazed out at the dark harbour, the waters crowded now with hulls. 'I'd guess we've lost twenty or thirty of our ships, probably half our stores. But we'll survive.'

Drawing a long breath, he tipped back his head and felt the sting of burns on his neck. The smoke overhead was blotting out the stars. Sitting on the quay, he choked out a mirthless laugh.

The emperor may have banned sacrifices, but the gods had taken their burnt offerings anyway.

PART TWO

PART TWO

CHAPTER IX

Thessalonica, June AD 324

A river of men and horses moved along the broad central avenue of the city. Glittering armour and flashing weapons, bright plumes and standards, freshly painted shield blazons; hour after hour they passed. The noise of horns and trumpets, the cheering of the crowds thronging the porticos, the stamp of marching men filled the air. From a high window of the palace annexe, Luxorius gazed down at the parade passing beneath him. The eunuch had few military inclinations, but even he had to admit it was a breathtaking sight.

'I never would have guessed there were so many soldiers in all the world!' said the man beside him, a minor palace official, peering over the sill in wonder.

'This is only a portion of the full force, I believe,' Luxorius told him. 'The rest have gone via the direct road north, with the baggage train. A show of strength, to awe the provincials.'

Also, he knew, to impress the agents of the enemy who were surely watching the parade, and even now compiling their reports, to be despatched eastwards by the fastest and most confidential messengers.

Leaning from the window, Luxorius tried to identify the different units by their shields and standards. Here were the Moesiaci, with the Divitenses and the Tenth Gemina marching behind them. After the legionaries came a squadron of *cataphractarii*, men and horses alike encased in gleaming armour. Following them, stamping through the dung, came a *numerus* of barbarian auxilia: Franks or Alamanni, it was hard to tell. Interesting, the eunuch thought, to note how quickly the soldiers had accepted the loss of their traditional symbols. Although the legionaries of the Third and Sixth Herculia and the Fifth Iovia still carried the images of Jupiter and Hercules on their shields, it appeared that the signs of the traditional religion had been otherwise successfully banished. How practical were these Sons of Mars!

The fire at the dockyard had, sure enough, been interpreted by many as an omen. Idle wagging mouths, and some not so idle, had spread rumours of divine displeasure, of a curse on the expedition. Sensibly, Luxorius thought, such rumours had been promptly quelled. It had either been an accident or deliberate sabotage; either way, there would be an investigation and no doubt some suitable culprits found, some appropriately severe punishments decreed. The field army stores in the marching camps had not been affected anyway, and only the naval portion of the expedition would suffer.

Just to the eunuch's right, clearly visible from his vantage point, stood the great four-sided arch of the Emperor Galerius. The piers of the arch were covered in carved and painted scenes showing Galerius's victories against the Persians over a quarter of a century before, and the army marched beneath them as they filed steadily towards the eastern gate of the city. Galerius had been one of the fiercest persecutors of the Christians; he had also given the order to destroy the town of Coptos in Egypt, resulting in the deaths of Luxorius's family, and Luxorius himself being enslaved and emasculated. Satisfying, he thought, to see the monument of that hated tyrant now serving as a portal for the vast army of a Christian emperor.

'Surely our enemies cannot hope to resist such a force,' the official beside him said. 'There must be tens of thousands of them...'

'Sixty thousand, supposedly,' Luxorius told him, 'including the men sent aboard the ships. Although that could be an estimate designed to confound the enemy. They say Licinius has more, of course – a hundred thousand? Two hundred thousand? I suspect all these figures are boastful fictions myself.'

Now, finally, the river of marching men was thinning to a stream, then to a trickle. The last few squadrons of light horsemen passed, followed by a mass of beggars and idle spectators trailing in the army's wake. Then the avenue was clear, except for a steaming mire of trampled dung remaining on the paving.

As he made his way back though the palace, Luxorius was conscious of the sudden sense of calm and quiet that pervaded now the emperor and his retinue had departed. For months, and certainly for the last few days, the halls and porticos had been filled with rushing messengers and hurrying officials, the very air charged with military activity. Now there was silence, noonday calm, only a few slaves left to push their brooms along the mosaic floors. As the eunuch passed into the emperor's private wing, he saw the children of the imperial household playing in the garden court, ringed by nurses and discreet guardians.

He climbed the steps from the portico and tapped at one of the tall inlaid doors. A slave admitted him, and he passed through into Fausta's chambers.

'So he's gone then?' Fausta asked as the eunuch entered. She was sitting in a scallop-shaped chair near the far window, eating her midday meal of savoury cheese cakes and boiled eggs. A glass goblet of wine stood on the side table, half drunk. The emperor's wife had not attended his departure; she had claimed a headache.

'Yes, the Augustus left with his vanguard about three hours ago,' Luxorius told her. 'It was a fine sight, domina! His new standard went before him, of course.'

'Ah yes, the Labarum,' Fausta said, waving Niobe away as the girl moved to refill the glass. 'Well, if it terrifies the enemy as much as it dispirits and demoralises our own men, we should have a famous victory!'

'Really, domina,' Luxorius said, lightly fingering his Christian amulet, 'you forget that I, too, am of the faith…'

'Oh, I forget nothing!' Fausta said, and smiled.

Luxorius cleared his throat. 'The domina Helena was there, naturally, to see the expedition depart.' *The emperor's mother, rather than his wife.* Such things, the eunuch knew, would be noted. 'I suppose, with her new position as *Mater Castrorum*, she had to attend.'

'Helena,' Fausta said, spitting the name. 'Well, she's welcome to be the "Mother of the Camp" if she wants, the dry old crow. Where is she now?'

'Retired to her quarters. The early hour tired her unduly.' It was amazing, Luxorius thought, that the two imperial ladies had managed to live in close proximity for several months while contriving never to meet in private. They saw each other at formal events, and managed to appear gracious, but that was all. Their mutual hatred was a palace secret.

'And where is my stepson?' Fausta asked.

'He went with the Augustus, domina. He'll ride as far as Lete, where the army camps tonight, and then return in the morning to join his ships. His excellency Aurelius Castus is currently embarking the troops; they sail tomorrow as soon as the Caesar returns.'

Fausta nodded as Luxorius seated himself on the broad marble bench beside the window. The eunuch glanced out at the view over the garden terrace, across the line of shaggy ornamental palms and the sea walls beyond to the blue waters of the bay.

'Leave us,' Fausta told Niobe. As the girl picked up the dishes of food and made to depart, Luxorius caught her eyes and winked a silent greeting. He was from southern Egypt himself, but as a freed citizen of the empire he still regarded the Aethiopian slave as a lesser being. Nevertheless, he liked her. As she closed the door behind her a thought came to him.

'I always meant to ask you something, domina,' he said. 'You remember that night at the mansio in Dardania, back in February?'

'Of course,' Fausta replied, with a stir of interest.

'Did you... That is to say, when you sent Niobe to sleep with Aurelius Castus, did you intend her to murder him in his sleep?'

Fausta let out a cry of amused outrage. 'Of course not! Why would I do such a thing? And if I wanted to, I'd certainly not send my poor Niobe to do it!'

'I only thought,' Luxorius said, shrugging vaguely, 'that ridding us of Castus might be an expeditious way to accomplish your design with regard to your stepson. If you still had such a design, of course...'

'I have no idea what you mean,' Fausta said, with a pointed glance around the room. *Caution.* But she was intrigued, Luxorius could tell.

'It seems to me,' the eunuch said, sitting forward on the bench and dropping his voice, 'that our young Caesar desires power. He is impatient for it. The incident with the snake, for example...'

'Aha! So you did arrange that?'

'No! As I've told you many times before, I did not. How could I have done, with that Sarmatian oaf dogging my steps? He was practically in bed with me!'

'Wouldn't you have liked that?'

'Domina, please,' Luxorius said, closing his eyes. Fausta's occasionally puerile sense of humour galled him at times. Besides, her words brought other memories, other more shameful impulses...

'You were saying?'

'Yes. As I was saying, the young Caesar desires power, and seems to seek it. Perhaps indeed he wishes to supplant his father sometime soon? He is headstrong, undiplomatic – I don't doubt he's shared these thoughts with our friend Castus, who will certainly have tried to dissuade him. But if Castus's moderating influence were removed, there would no more check to the young Caesar's intent. He might be propelled into some rash statement, even some act. Which, of course, would lead to a rapid fall from favour...'

Perhaps a rapid demise too, Luxorius thought, although he would never say such a thing. Fausta was thinking, biting her ring as she often did.

'And yet you once said that you wished Castus to be protected,' the eunuch said. 'At the time, I didn't know there was...'

'What?' Fausta said sharply, glaring at him.

'Some connection between the two of you?' the eunuch said, tentative. He was on dangerous ground now, and he knew it.

'Your remark is inappropriate,' Fausta said coldly. But Luxorius could see the colour rising to her cheeks, and his suspicions were confirmed. He knew that Fausta had gone to the soldier's room that night at the mansio; he had tried not to think about it since. All these years he had served her, admired her. Jealousy was not possible; it was an obscene idea. And yet he felt it nonetheless. She was the emperor's wife, the mother of his children, but somehow Luxorius had always considered her immaculate, beyond the sordid desires of the flesh. Like a female version of himself, almost. The knowledge that she might have debased herself, even in thought, with feelings for a commoner, a soldier, pained him.

A tapping at the door, and Niobe returned.

'Domina,' she said, keeping her eyes to the floor, 'there are two men here. From the agentes in rebus, they say. They were told that you're unavailable, but they insist on seeing you. They won't leave!'

Fausta glanced quickly at Luxorius; both of them, he knew, were thinking the same thought. But there was no cause for alarm.

'Well,' she said. 'I've finished eating. Let's see what these *men* want.'

Luxorius followed as she walked through into the next chamber. It was a dining room, open windows on two sides with long drapes stirring in the sea breeze. One of the agents was already sitting on the couch, knees spread wide. He was in his thirties, with a broad smiling face and curly blond hair. The other was older, sullen, with a balding scalp and a wiry black beard. He stood beside the couch, like a slave attending his master.

Fausta waited while two of her own slaves carried her chair through from the next room, then sat. Niobe and Luxorius stood flanking her, and the slaves stepped away to stand on either side. A pair of bodyguards and another eunuch waited by the doors.

'Nobilissima femina!' the younger agent said, standing briefly to bow and then sitting down again. 'I do hope we haven't disturbed your meal?'

'No. But your demands for an audience were rather unsavoury.' The agent on the couch had a nervous tic, Luxorius noticed, like a smirk flickering at one side of his mouth. 'I've seen you before,' Fausta said.

'Perhaps so, domina. My name is Flavius Innocentius, and this is my associate Gracilis.'

'Very well. And what business do you have invading my chambers and making demands upon my staff?' Fausta spoke with a tone of controlled severity; Luxorius revelled in it, but he kept his expression blank. The two agents did not appear moved.

'We have a mandate, domina,' Innocentius said. 'A mandate issued by the highest authorities, giving us universal access in investigating potential threats to the security of the state.'

'And you thought to find such threats here, in my dining room? What outlandish ideas you have.'

'We only need to ask a few questions, domina,' the agent said. His smirk flickered. He raised his palms, then clapped them onto his spread knees. The other man, Gracilis, remained completely still.

Fausta sniffed, then made a loose gesture for the man to continue.

'You will remember, domina, that several months ago you and your retinue passed the night at a mansio named Praesidium Pompei?'

Luxorius stiffened, inhaling quickly and silently. Surely it was not possible, he thought, that their conversation of moments before had been overheard? Surely not – it was coincidence. But a chilling one.

Fausta maintained a studied calm. 'Yes. I was there with my children – the emperor's children – and my household. What of it?'

'The most blessed Caesar, Flavius Julius Crispus, also passed the night at that same inn, I believe. Did anything... *unusual* take place?'

Luxorius felt the breath catch in his throat, a prickle of dread run up his spine. He was peering intently at the far wall, struggling not to appear agitated.

'No, not that I recall,' Fausta said.

'Nothing at all, domina? Perhaps your attendants remember something?'

Luxorius glanced down, and caught the agent's eye. He gave a start, shook his head and looked away. Now Innocentius was peering at Niobe.

'As I said, nothing happened,' Fausta told him. 'Is that all you wanted? Your attitude is becoming disconcerting.'

'My apologies, domina,' the agent said, and gave a wide tight-lipped smile.

'You know, I *do* remember you. Spring last year, it would have been. The public burnings in Pannonia. You were both there, I think. You're *torturers*, aren't you?'

Innocentius's face twitched briefly in displeasure; then he was smiling again. 'My associate and I are merely seekers for truth,' he said, angling his head in a show of modesty. 'And penitence, for the guilty.'

'Tell me something I've always wanted to know,' Fausta said, sitting up eagerly, smiling – if her attitude was feigned, Luxorius thought, she was making an excellent job of it. 'When you're, you know, doing your *torturing*,' she went on, 'when you get your little prongs out, and your red-hot pokers and so on, how do you know when your victims are telling the truth? Surely they'd tell you any lie to escape the torment?'

'An interesting question, domina,' Innocentius said with a smug twitch. 'It's really much easier than you might think to tell when someone's lying. But you're right – most people lie under questioning. They believe it will save them, of course. But even a lie can be instructive. It points towards something

141

concealed. So everything we learn goes towards the assembling of truth. Rather like the tiny chips of stone that make up this fine picture here.' He scuffed with his toe at the floor mosaic. 'The death of Hippolytus, if I know my ancient tales,' he said, peering down at it.

'You admire art, then?' Fausta said, not hiding her scorn.

'I admire all beautiful creations, domina. It pains me to see them damaged.' He stared again at Niobe, his gaze unblinking. 'Of course, the human body is the most beautiful creation of all.'

'You really are a very loathsome person, aren't you?' Fausta said, in a tone that made it sound like a compliment. 'But we've answered your questions, so now you can go. I don't expect to be troubled further. If I am, I'll be forced to mention your conduct unfavourably.'

'That will be unnecessary, domina,' Innocentius said as he stood up. 'But also unwise. As I say, our mandate comes from the very *highest* authority.'

He bowed again, rather mockingly, and then he and his associate reversed their steps from the room.

Luxorius exhaled slowly. Was it true? Had the emperor sent these men to investigate his own wife? Surely not. But he knew very well the danger that they posed, whoever they might be working for.

'Luxorius,' Fausta said. 'I want you to make enquiries about those two. If they seem troublesome, arrange something. I don't want to see them again, you understand?'

'Certainly, domina,' the eunuch said. But a cold fear was gathering in the pit of his stomach, and when Fausta rose from her chair he noticed that her hands were trembling. He knew that she felt it too.

CHAPTER X

From the aft deck of the *Artemisia*, Castus looked to windward and saw the sea covered with ships. It had taken them two days to embark and to leave the shelter of Thessalonica's harbour, but now at last they were under way, and a fine northerly breeze was carrying them swiftly down the Thermaic Gulf towards the open Aegean. The sun was warm and bright, the waves sparkled, and the snows of Mount Olympos shone bright in the western sky. Above the deck of the galley the broad white canvas was stretched taut, and the oarsmen and marines sat at their ease on the rowing benches.

'Good sailing weather,' Castus said to Hierax as the shipmaster joined him. 'Let's hope it holds.'

'Not for too long,' Hierax replied. 'As soon as we round the Chalcidice we'll have this right in our faces all the way up to the Strymonian Gulf. Far better to pray for a calm!'

Castus shrugged, unwilling to let the Sicilian's pessimism spoil his mood. A shadow passed across his mind even so: Hierax had been appalled by the order that no sacrifices or prayers could be offered before the fleet sailed. Castus and many of the other commanders had shared his feelings. Surely it was madness to set off on a sea voyage without first asking the blessings of the gods?

The last time he had led an expedition like this, Castus

remembered, he had commanded only a handful of ships and a few hundred men. That had been on the Rhine; now he was on the open sea, with hundreds of vessels and nearly twenty thousand soldiers, marines, sailors and oarsmen under his command. He felt the nervous agitation mass inside him, for the fifth or sixth time that day.

He breathed in, and the fresh racing breeze filled his lungs. So far, there had been no signs of divine disapproval – Castus had not failed to notice Hierax making a swift offering to Neptune as they cleared the harbour mouth. But now the galley was heeling only slightly as she cut through the waves, moving with as steady a motion as he had ever known at sea. If they had been sailing alone they could have doubled the distance they would cover, but the heavy transports that followed them moved at a more sluggish pace, and every few miles the *Artemisia* had to spill her wind to let them catch up.

To the west, keeping pace with her, was Crispus's flagship, the *Virtus Augusta*. With her long white hull and purple strake, she was easily identifiable, the only big bireme to have survived the fire at the docks. Aside from her, all the larger ships were liburnian galleys of fifty oars. Castus scanned the sea, picking them out: the *Lucifer*, *Satura*, *Sol*, *Triumpus*, *Iustitia* and two score others. Between them moved the smaller galleys, the triaconters. Twenty of them had been destroyed in the fire, but the rest had been launched in time and saved. Then came the transports, butting through the waves, carrying stores for the land army and the troops of Castus's expeditionary force. He knew that the men packed in those hulls would not be having such a pleasant cruise. At least the weather was fine. To the east, the first promontory of the Chalcidice peninsula was gliding past, the land sage green and pale grey in the late afternoon sun.

'You see that next headland, strategos?' Hierax said. 'There's a sheltered landing beach with a watering place just to the south of it. We can take up our berths there tonight, I reckon.'

Castus nodded, content to leave the management of the fleet to the experienced seaman. He had seen nothing of Theophilus for several days, but he knew that the naval prefect was aboard Crispus's galley. He could stay there, as far as Castus was concerned.

Two hours later, with the sun dropping to the west, they steered around the low headland into the roadstead, a long curving beach of white sand and a shallow anchorage sheltered from the north wind. The galleys dropped sails and unshipped oars, *Artemisia* keeping her position in the open sea while the smaller vessels backed up to the beach, their crews leaping down into the surf to drag the long hulls onto the sand. The larger transport ships anchored in lines; the luckier men aboard the nearer vessels went ashore to camp above the dunes, while the others bedded down on the open decks.

'Boat coming, dominus,' the lookout called. Castus paced along the gangway as the boat pulled up to the galley's stern and Crispus clambered aboard. The officers on the aft deck dropped to one knee, while the troops and oarsmen raised their hands in salute to their Caesar.

'Everything's going well!' Crispus declared, clapping Castus on the shoulder as he moved to the railing. Land and sea glowed with the colours of sunset, and smoke was already rising from the cooking fires above the dunes. 'Although,' he said, 'I wonder if we might have anchored too early? My prefect, Theophilus, believes we could have rounded the tip of the peninsula before nightfall.'

Castus sucked his teeth. 'The crews needed to rest, majesty,' he said. 'If we get under way before dawn tomorrow we can use the land breezes to carry us right around the southern capes.' He slid a glance at Hierax, who replied with a subtle nod. 'Besides, we need to replace our water if we can. We lost a lot during the fire, and there're springs just above the beach.'

'Ah yes,' Crispus said, his brow knotting. 'Yes, I hadn't considered that... Very good!'

Looking across the waves, Castus could see the crew of one of the larger galleys already heaving the big water kegs and amphorae up and over the side, floating them empty towards the beach to be refilled. He knew that the springs were meagre, and there were only a few hours in which to work; they would not gather much water, but with luck and good judgement it might be enough to last them for the voyage around the Chalcidice to the Strymonian Gulf.

'I haven't had a chance to thank you,' Crispus said, dropping his voice and softening his tone. 'For what you did during the fire, I mean. You were quite right – it was stupid of me to risk myself like that.'

'Not just you,' Castus said, feeling the spur of annoyance. 'You throw yourself into danger and other men have to pull you out – you're risking all of their lives as well as your own.'

Crispus blinked, startled. Castus had spoken more harshly than he had intended. 'I suppose so,' the young man said, chastened. 'Yes, of course you're right... I'm sorry. But, tell me – if I hadn't been there, you wouldn't have gone in and rescued those slaves, would you?'

Castus drew in a long breath and held it, trying to quell his irritation. Thinking of the fire brought bad memories; he still carried the stink of burning in the weave of his clothes, on his skin. 'Maybe,' he said. 'Maybe not. But I, too, regard slaves as human, if that's what you mean.'

Crispus nodded, apparently pleased. He gazed with satisfaction at the anchored fleet a moment more, then turned to depart.

'One more thing, majesty,' Castus said, in a louder voice so the officers gathered at the stern could hear. 'Some of the men are disturbed by the lack of proper sacrifices and prayers. Now that we're away from Thessalonica, I wondered if we could allow it. No need for everyone to join in – but it seems right.'

Crispus frowned, glancing at the men around him. He made a visible effort to compose himself and appear commanding. 'I think not,' he said. 'My father issued strict orders about that. We can't risk the displeasure of the Almighty God with any displays of superstition... any *idolatry*. I think Theophilus is sending a memorandum to all commanders of ships reminding them of that.'

So Theophilus was a Christian too, Castus realised. And presumably that was why he had been appointed to the position: to enforce religious observance, rather than to command the fleet. As Crispus clambered back down into his boat to the wail of trumpets, another thought crossed Castus's mind. Why had Constantine not trusted Crispus himself to do that? Did the emperor doubt his son's piety?

Hours before dawn the fleet had raised anchor and set sail from the beach, and the darkness covered many a private prayer and sacrifice. By the time the sun rose, the cool breezes off the land had carried the mass of ships far around the cape of the western promontory and into the open Aegean. At mid-morning the men aboard the ships could see the snowy peak of Mount Athos above the sea horizon. Noon was blistering, the sea a hot blue reflecting the sun. The breezes died into a fitful calm, and the galleys unshipped their oars and began to row.

'Don't like the feel of the air,' said Hierax. 'Sort of sticky, greasy. Reckon those north winds could pick up once we're past Athos.'

'Are you *never* happy?' Castus asked. He peered at the distant cape, the last promontory of the Chalcidice, growing steadily closer as the oars beat at the waves. Even from this distance he could make out the surf around the rocky coast. No sign of a cove or anchorage. He turned and gazed back over the sea at the white sails that studded the blue of the horizon behind him. The scene looked placid enough now.

'We should get those transports under tow,' Hierax added. 'If the wind picks up they'll be knocked all over the sea.'

Two hours later, and every galley trailed a cable astern, towing a line of transport ships. The sea was rising, long waves coming in from the east, and the *Artemisia* pitched and rolled, her keel spur bursting water. The oarsmen sweated and groaned on their benches, and the lee rail was lined with puking men. Castus gave a silent prayer that he had never been prey to that.

Another hour, and they felt the first headwinds swooping in from the north-east around the cape of Mount Athos. Spume flew from the wave crests, and the ships of the fleet laboured in the heavy swell. Hierax went across to the flagship in a small boat and returned with the news that Crispus was laid low with seasickness and Theophilus was in command.

'He wants us to hold position overnight until the wind drops, then double the cape with the land breeze before dawn.'

'You think the wind'll drop?' Castus asked him.

Hierax sniffed, plucking at his beard. 'Perhaps,' he said. 'Perhaps not.'

But the wind only strengthened, and by nightfall the ships were struggling to keep their positions and avoid being driven back towards the west. The cape was close now, the huge snowy mountain looming tall in the dusk, and Castus could hear the boom and hiss of the surf around the craggy cliffs. No chance

148

of anchoring in such deep water; the fleet would spend the night at sea, rowing constantly just to keep their position.

Darkness had fallen when the first thunder crashed from the north. Lightning split the sky above the mountain, and the men packed in the ships cried out in dread. One by one the stars were blotted out by cloud. Castus remained on deck, fighting off fatigue, his cloak pulled around him. He was trying not to think about the last time he had been on the night sea in a galley, off the mouth of the Rhine. He tried not to think about the shipwreck, the breaking timbers and the slashing waves, the cries of drowning men.

A volley of screams broke his thoughts. Castus glanced up, the fatigue driven from him, and saw the tip of the bare masthead flickering with blue lightning. All along the deck, men stared in horror, lit in ghastly white. The apparition lasted only a moment, then they were plunged into darkness once more.

'Sign from the gods!' Hierax cried, staggering back along the deck past the helmsmen. 'They mean to punish us for our impiety!'

He pulled a knife from his belt, seizing the tip of his beard and sawing at it with the blade. He cut free a chunk of hair and cast it into the wind. 'Father Poseidon, have mercy upon us!' he shouted.

'Quiet, everyone,' Castus growled. He strode forward past the helmsmen, who cursed and prayed as they heaved at the big steering oars. Over the noise of the sea, he could hear the whine and groan of the ship's timbers. Beyond that, the roar of the waves breaking on the rocks. When the clouds shifted, he could make out the cliffs rearing from the sea, mottled with caves.

'Keep pulling,' he called to the oarsmen. 'You can rest each bank at a time, but if we let ourselves drift we could be run ashore.' He hoped his voice carried confidence; he felt little certainty himself, but in the night's darkness, the fury of the thunder and the sea's relentless swell the men needed it. If they had no faith in the gods, at least they should have faith in him.

Dawn came up grey and wet, with a dirty sky and a sea that rolled lines of big waves out of the east like the ramparts of an enemy fortress. Castus awoke from a brief troubled sleep, his limbs aching and his clothing damp from the salt air. When he looked to windward his heart plunged: there was the mountain and the rocky cape, still off the weather quarter. But for all the night's effort, they had been pushed back west and southwards.

'Rowing master reports his men are almost done in,' Diogenes said queasily. 'Half the water's gone too.'

Clambering to his feet and peeling his damp cloak away from his body, Castus stared to the south. Scattered vessels all the way along the horizon, with no sign of formation. The *Artemisia* was pitching heavily, every incoming wave lifting the bows and spraying water along the decks. When he looked at the rowing benches Castus saw the strain on every face; even the experienced seamen looked sick, and wore the unmistakable signs of men at the limits of endurance.

'There he is,' Hierax said, pointing from the stern. Off to the south-east, the big *Virtus Augusta*, Crispus's flagship, had dropped her towing cable and was battling forward against wind and current, her oars threshing the water.

'Can they make it round the cape, d'you think?' Castus asked.

'Like that? No. This headwind isn't slacking, and they'll get it worse the further east they go. If their bow's shoved round parallel with the waves they'll roll and swamp. Interesting. I've never seen a big galley like that go under...'

Castus gave him a pained grimace. Low morning sun was flaring through a gap in the clouds, turning the sea to mottled silver. A signal flag streamed out from the stern of the flagship.

'They want us to follow,' Hierax said. 'The man's howling at the moon if he thinks the whole fleet can do that!'

'Is there a sheltered anchorage anywhere to the west?'

'There's Sarte, dominus, over on the central peninsula. About twenty sea miles, west by north-west. Enough beach to land, and fresh water too.'

Castus stood at the rail, tight-lipped and frowning. Theophilus had senior command over the ships, but Castus outranked him when it came to the men of the expeditionary force. And his men were suffering, he knew that.

'Signal to all ships,' he said. 'We're turning back for Sarte. On my authority.'

Theophilus would notice soon enough that the fleet was heading west. And when he did, Castus thought, he could decide for himself whether to follow.

'You deliberately overruled my explicit order!' the prefect cried as he stamped up the beach. 'An offence to both my dignity and to my status, which comes directly from the emperor himself!'

Castus was sitting on a pile of rocks at the edge of the sand with Ursio and Diogenes, eating his midday meal of bread and olive oil. He chewed slowly, swallowed, then waited a while longer as Theophilus stood before him, red-faced and panting.

'You couldn't have got round that cape,' he said. 'Even if you had, you'd be leaving the transports unprotected. We need to wait until the wind drops.'

'Oh, indeed?' Theophilus declared. 'And what does a mere soldier know of seamanship? Our orders are to take the fleet to join the emperor's army, as soon as possible. He needs the men and supplies we carry – and by your order we shall be delayed!'

'The emperor won't be able to use the supplies if they're at the bottom of the sea,' Castus said, grinding the last bits of gritty bread between his back teeth. 'And he won't have much use for drowned soldiers either. We can use this time to refill our water.'

'Oh, the water again!' Theophilus said, with a bark of laughter. 'And who was responsible for wasting so much of it back at Thessalonica? Pouring it out on the ground, indeed! One might think, strategos, that you're deliberately attempting to sabotage this expedition!'

Castus stood up suddenly, taking a step towards the prefect. Theophilus backed away, stumbling in the dry sand, and almost fell.

'Be careful what you say, fat man,' Castus told him.

With a last narrowed glance of disdain, Theophilus turned and marched away along the beach. Castus did not bother to watch him go.

Instead he scanned the scene before him. The beachfront was packed, lines of galleys pulled up stern-first at the shoreline, a mass of transports anchored beyond them. The headland to the north sheltered the roadstead from the wind's full blast, but even so the ships bobbed and swayed at their moorings, masts swinging. Away to the east across the sea, the peak of Mount Athos was trailing a white streamer of blown snow.

Getting to his feet, Castus walked along the beach, passing the legionary camps. He was glad to see military order reasserting itself after the chaos of disembarkation, although the Frankish auxilia were still straggling all over the shore. He made a note to remind Bonitus that his men were under Roman discipline now.

From the sea, the peninsula had appeared deserted, the land above the beach thick with ragged holm oak and scrub. But already people had appeared from the inland villages, bringing cattle and other provisions to sell. The troops would eat hot food that day. Even so, Castus was troubled. He heard the echo of the prefect's parting threat in his mind. Had he made a mistake turning the fleet back? Would they be trapped here, windbound?

The weather remained the same all that day and through the next, the scout galleys returning to report the headwinds still too strong off the cape to attempt a voyage. 'We're at the mercy of Boreas now, strategos,' Hierax said. Castus took little comfort from that.

After dark, the second night on the beach, Castus was awakened in his tent by the touch of a hand. Even as he tried to make out the shadowy figures in the darkness, he knew what was happening. He realised that he had been expecting it. Eumolpius had woken him; together with Diogenes he led Castus from the tent and up the narrow paths behind the camp. Other figures joined them as they walked, silent men in cloaks, carrying no lights. Castus recognised Hierax among them, and Bonitus; the Frank greeted him with a wordless handclasp. They filed on through the night, climbing the headland to the north of the beach into the thick scrub woodland. Diogenes had said that there was a ruined town here, and Castus made out the pale shapes of broken walls and tumbled columns in the undergrowth. The night air smelled strongly of thyme, and he could hear the noise of the sea on the rocks below the headland.

In a clearing between the bushes the men assembled. A score of them, maybe more, gathered before a rough altar of piled stones. By the wavering light of the altar fire Castus saw the faces of the men around him: most were ship captains, with some of the army tribunes and prefects among them. As the sacrificial animals were led to the altar, Hierax stepped forth and covered his head with a fold of his cloak. The axeman killed each beast, the hot coppery stink of fresh blood filling the night. Then Hierax raised his arms and cried out the prayers in Greek: to Apollo, Lord of Departures, to Zeus and to Poseidon. To the gods and spirits who ruled this land and this sea.

One by one the assembled men stepped around the lake of spilt blood and up to the altar, into the smoke of the fire to pour a libation and eat the sacrificial meat. They touched their brows, touched their lips, and sent their silent prayers to the heavens. As Castus turned from the altar, the flames lit the face of the hooded man behind him; just for a moment he thought he must be mistaken, then he caught the quick forbidding glance, the familiar frown. He said nothing, and moved back into the darkness.

By dawn the next day all could see that the wind had dropped. The surf no longer rushed on the sand, and in the first sun the peak of Mount Athos had lost its streamer of snow. The men boarded their ships quickly and with enthusiasm, the galleys surging off the beach and taking the transport ships under tow as soon as they raised anchor.

Across a placid sea they moved under oars, and before noon they had reached the cape of Athos once more. Well rested and eager, the oarsmen pulled hard, singing on their benches as the galleys powered across the smooth water. Standing on the stern platform, Castus watched the mountain slide past to his left and then fall behind them, the great fleet of ships rounding the cape in formation and turning north towards the Strymonian Gulf. He felt elated, his spirits restored. A faint cool breeze came from the land, refreshing the oarsmen. Another day, maybe two, and they would make their rendezvous with Constantine's army.

Remembering the night before, Castus tried to tell himself that he had been wrong. It had been a trick played by the flickering light. But he knew what he had seen: Crispus, the son of the Augustus, had made sacrifice with them.

CHAPTER XI

'What I don't understand,' said Saturninus as they walked their horses along the sand above the line of beached galleys, 'is why he had to hide his face. If you saw what you claim, that is...'

'I saw him,' Castus said. 'It was Crispus, right enough.'

Saturninus had not been present for the sacrifice at Sarte, although he had heard about it, and wished he had been. Only now, over two weeks later, had Castus decided to tell him about the Caesar's presence there.

'None would have blamed him for attending,' the guard commander said. 'And surely none would have carried word of it to the wrong ears.'

Castus was not so sure about that. 'Maybe he just didn't want anyone to know. Maybe he wants us to think he's a Christian like he pretends? Or maybe he *is* a Christian – I wouldn't mind them so much if they worshipped our gods, too, like we have to worship theirs!'

There had been a parade the day before, all the legion detachments of the army assembled on the broad plain above the mouth of the Hebrus. Constantine's new Christian standard had been solemnly carried before the troops, ringed by an honour guard of fifty soldiers in white uniforms, hand-picked for their loyalty and religious devotion. The Guardians of the Labarum, they were called. The troops had thrown up their hands in salute to the standard, crying out the prayer the tribunes had circulated that morning. Castus had recited the words as well, although they had stuck in his throat.

'Well, it worked anyway,' Saturninus said. 'The sacrifice, I mean. The wind dropped, didn't it?'

'Maybe. Or maybe it was coincidence.' Castus tended to think the gods did not answer requests quite so promptly. Then again, who could know?

They had ridden far down the beach together, all the way to the edge of the marshes at the mouth of the river, and now they were returning to the seaward camp where Crispus's Gallic force was based. Already the land breeze that whipped up the sand carried the stink of men and horses, latrines and damp leather. There were two more camps further inland, even larger than this one, holding the main field army.

Down on the beach, men were gathered in a circle around a wrestling ground marked out on the sand. Saturninus and Castus drew their horses to a halt and watched the men fight. One of them was Gratianus, the muscular young tribune of the Moesiaci, who had come down to the seaward camp to test his strength against the champions of the Gallic army. Castus was tempted to try a bout himself – he had been a keen wrestler when he first joined the legions, thirty years before – but the prospect of being dumped on the sand by a younger, and subordinate, officer did not appeal.

Raising himself in the saddle, Castus peered over the heads of the wrestling throng, past the ships beached above the surf, and out to sea. The transports rode at anchor in the shallows. Beyond them, on the horizon, were the scout galleys patrolling the approaches to the beach. No sign of enemy ships; only a few local fishing boats. The sky was hot and blue, and the empty sea glared under the sun.

The advance so far had taken Constantine's army east along the coast of Macedonia and Thrace. Castus had remained with the fleet, moving offshore in stages as they followed the course of the inland march. Every morning they had sailed with the land breeze, unshipping the oars to row against the current before noon, beaching once more when the Etesian winds set in a few hours later. Hard work in the midsummer heat, but a lot pleasanter than marching: from the sea, the twenty-mile column of troops on the Via Egnatia had appeared only as a vast cloud of dust, rising to obscure the distant hills. And all that time there had been no sign of the enemy. Licinius had not brought his army to oppose them, although they were deep inside his territory now.

'Every time I look out to sea,' Saturninus said. 'I expect they'll appear, there on the horizon.'

'Me too,' Castus said. He sucked his teeth, then swung down from the saddle. Stripping off his tunic, he threw it to one of his orderlies.

'Wrestling?' Saturninus asked with a grin.

'No – swimming!'

He pulled off his boots and breeches, shed his loincloth, then ran naked down the beach and plunged into the sea.

'Messenger for you,' Diogenes said as Castus returned to the little tent enclosure that formed his headquarters. The secretary was sitting at a folding table outside the main tent, and nodded toward a uniformed Protector standing with his horse.

'What is it?' Castus asked. Bending forward, he took a skin of fresh water and sluiced his head, washing the salt from his hair and face.

158

'Excellency,' the Protector said, saluting, 'the most blessed Caesar, Flavius Julius Crispus, requests your presence.'

Castus grunted as he straightened up. The swim had been hard, but he felt refreshed by it. He nodded, then gestured to Eumolpius for a towel. 'Better unpack my best tunic and belts too,' he said.

He found Crispus half an hour later, outside his command tent on the far side of the huge military camp. The young Caesar was exercising with a sword, going through the motions of an exaggerated *armatura* drill under the eye of his trainer. Stripped to the waist, his lean muscles flexing, Crispus stamped the dust and wheeled his blade flashing in the sunlight. Castus could see the angry tension in his stance, the frustration in his every movement.

When he saw Castus waiting, Crispus tossed his sword to one of his orderlies and gestured towards his tent. Inside, the sunlight came through the white linen walls, but it was much cooler. Flies circled in the air.

'I've spoken to my father,' Crispus announced. He stood with his arms spread while two slaves wiped down his torso with a linen cloth and then dressed him in a clean tunic. 'He tells me the scouts have located the enemy. Licinius has his main field force camped at Adrianople, seven days from here up the Hebrus. The army will march the day after tomorrow.'

'Excellent news, majesty!' Castus said. *At last.* But he knew there was more to come.

'We will not be accompanying them,' Crispus said, tense anger in his voice. 'Despite my requests, my father has ordered that I remain here with the ships. That means you remain here too.'

'For how long?'

'For as long as we have to!' Crispus snapped. He slumped down on the couch, elbows braced against his thighs. 'My father believes that Licinius may try and land a force on the coast here and attack him from the rear. We're supposed to guard against that. But he's taking most of our best troops with him. We'll still have Bonitus and his Franks, and I persuaded him to give me the Second Britannica and the Septimani too. But we're reserves, that's all. Left to mind the baggage...'

He broke off, dropping his head into his hands. 'I don't understand it,' he said, his voice muffled. 'We march all the way here from Gaul, with some of the finest soldiers in the empire... I'm twenty-one years old, a grown man! All I want to do is fight at my father's side, and he denies me...'

'He's trying to protect you,' Castus said. He saw the young man flinch, and wished he had not spoken.

'Protect me? Did he tell you that? Why should I need protection? If I'm to rule one day – gods allow it won't be long in coming – then I need to prove myself, in the eyes of everyone!'

Castus noticed the reference. *Gods*, not God. But he merely nodded. Crispus had lapsed into a sullen distracted state. 'And yet,' he said, 'here we are, sitting on a beach staring at the sea, while other men fight the battles...'

Castus thought of his own son, Sabinus. If he were Constantine, would he let his son follow him to war? *Yes*, he thought, *if he asked, I suppose I would.*

'Sometimes, you know,' Crispus said, 'I wish I wasn't the son of the emperor. I wish I was just a common soldier, a tribune or a centurion. Even a legionary in the ranks. Then I could truly feel alive. You'd seen plenty of battles, by my age?'

'Just a few fights, majesty. Against the Carpi and Sarmatians on the Danube. But I was your age when we marched out with Galerius to the Persian war.'

'I saw the pictures on the arch at Thessalonica!' Crispus said with a smile. 'Must have been quite a war... Was your father proud of you, do you think?'

'I don't know,' Castus said, uncomfortable. 'I never saw my father after I left to join the legions. We weren't close.' *And I tried to kill him.* But Castus would say nothing of that.

'I spoke with my stepmother before we left Thessalonica,' Crispus said. 'With Fausta.' Castus noticed the slight catch in his voice as he spoke the name.

'I'm sure all your family are concerned for you.'

Crispus laughed. 'Oh, surely. Far too concerned…! Fausta, though – she told me that my father's a little jealous of me. Can you believe that? He would never admit it, of course, but she knows. She really is quite amazingly perceptive, and so—' He broke off, unable to find the right word. Something new had crept into his attitude, Castus noticed. He was fidgeting, restless, tugging at his fingers as he gazed into the diffuse light. The flies circled above him.

'Do you miss your wife, Castus?'

'Yes,' Castus answered at once. He frowned, angered slightly; Crispus had met Marcellina on several occasions, and Sabinus too. How could he believe that Castus would neglect them? 'Every day I miss them,' he said.

'I don't miss mine at all,' Crispus said in a dazed mumble. 'It's terrible, I know, but days go by when I can barely picture her in my thoughts. Or my child either. My son. Is that wrong of me?'

'War drives tender thoughts from a man's mind,' Castus said quietly. It was no sort of answer, but it was the only one he could give.

Two days later the army marched, the troops forming up and filling the air with thick brown dust. It took them until after nightfall to move out, and the sound of their trumpets seemed to echo long after they were gone.

For eleven more days the fleet lay at the beach. Castus drilled his men aboard the ships, and sent out scouts by land and sea to warn of any enemy approach. But there was no sign of a hostile force. The days were hot and sultry, and Crispus remained sulking in his tent. Then, on the morning of the twelfth day, a rider approached along the valley of the Hebrus, galloping hard with a laurel wreath tipping his spear. As soon as he heard the news, Castus ran to find the Caesar.

Crispus was still in his tent, the tablet that the messenger had brought him gripped in his hands. Even as Castus entered he could see the spring in the young man's pacing step, the energy of excitement flowing through him.

'There's been a battle!' Crispus announced. 'A great battle, at Adrianople. My father has defeated Licinius and driven his army from the field!'

'Glad to hear it. The gods are good. And your god too...'

'My father's been injured,' Crispus said, with a momentary frown. 'Just a minor spear wound to the thigh. He's fine – he assures me he's fine. Licinius has retreated with the remains of his army towards Byzantium.'

Please gods, Castus thought, *don't let this be the end of it*. Twice before Constantine had let Licinius survive after losing a battle.

'And the enemy fleet? Any news of them?'

'Yes!' Crispus declared with a grin. 'The entirety of Licinius's fleet is in the Propontis, guarding the straits of the Hellespont. My father intends to besiege Byzantium by land. As for us – we're to sail tomorrow for the mouth of the Hellespont, force a passage through the enemy ships and blockade Byzantium from the sea!'

Now Castus could see why the young man was so elated. He grinned himself, a crooked snarl of satisfaction. 'I'll ready the troops,' he said.

'Do it!' Crispus took a long step forward, throwing his arms around Castus in a tight embrace. 'My father must have known this would happen – he planned for it all along! This will be my battle!'

He stepped back and spun on his heel, then raised his hands. Spreading his arms wide, tipping back his head, he cried aloud, 'Thanks be to God!'

The *Virtus Augusta*, Crispus's flagship, was a far larger vessel than the *Artemisia*. Castus would rather have sailed aboard the smaller galley, as he had before, but Crispus had requested his presence. That meant sharing a deck with Theophilus, unfortunately, but with the new mood of decisive action Castus found he could endure it. Theophilus himself seemed to find his company less congenial.

'I trust, strategos,' the prefect said, 'that when we reach the Hellespont you will leave the direction of the battle – the *naval* battle – to me? I do have authority in the matter of ships, after all.'

'Of course,' Castus said. 'Don't bother yourself about that.' He had no intention of leaving the direction of anything to this man. He would not trust Theophilus to direct cattle.

'We should make Imbros before dark,' Theophilus said, raising his nose to sniff speculatively at the breeze. 'They do say, you know, that the currents are very strong down the Hellespont, and with this north-east wind blowing so steadily we would be best to remain at Imbros and wait for a change in the weather.'

'Could do,' Castus said, not looking at him. The galley was moving fast under billowing canvas, the sea glittering blue all around and the rest of the fleet spread out behind them, white sails in formation.

Theophilus made a sound of satisfaction. 'Good,' he said, appearing quite surprised. 'Then we are agreed!'

He made his way, stumbling slightly, up the heeling deck towards the cabin beneath the stern. Castus remained sitting by the rail, enjoying the fresh wind and the sunlight. The crew of the galley were relaxing on their benches, oars shipped; the Etesian winds showed no signs of slackening, and they would be safe in harbour on the island of Imbros well before dusk.

A shout from the forward deck, and men leaned from their benches across the lee rail. Castus stood up and followed their gaze. Dolphins were swimming alongside the ship, their sleek grey bodies flashing through the waves. As Castus watched, one of them leaped in an arc from the water. The men on the benches cheered and raised their hands, as if in greeting. The dolphins sported around the ship, racing it, darting ahead and then weaving back alongside.

'They lead us to victory!' Crispus called from the aft deck.

Castus was smiling as he made his way back past the steering position to the little canvas shelter at the stern where the Caesar was sitting. 'A good omen!' he said.

Crispus had a scroll in his lap. 'I suppose it must be!' he said. 'Beautiful creatures, anyway. It does the men good to see them.' He turned and gazed at the fleet, the galleys and the transports, with an expression of deep satisfaction. '*They spread sail for the open sea, their spirits buoyant, their bronze beaks churning the waves to foam!*'

'Hmm?'

'Virgil! The *Aeneid*, of course. Surely you know it? How I wish I'd brought the works of Homer with me, too – we'll be passing the site of ancient Troy, you know. Battleground of gods and heroes! Being here has entirely reawakened my love of poetry... But this is perhaps more useful,' he said, raising the scroll from his lap. 'Marcus Agrippa's account of the battle of Actium. I intend to make a full study of it over the next day or two – I'm sure there are lessons in it for us.'

'No doubt,' Castus said, unconvinced. He lowered himself to squat, braced against the railing. 'I was speaking to Hierax last night,' he said, 'and he told me all he knows about the navigation around the Hellespont. The peninsula that divides it from the sea is shaped like a finger, very narrow at the tip.'

'The Thracian Chersonese,' Crispus said. 'I've seen a plan of it.'

Castus nodded, remembering the sketch that Hierax had drawn in the sand as he described the strength of the current within the straits, the treacherous narrows.

'Once we're at Imbros,' Castus said, 'I want to take a small advance force across to the northern shore of the peninsula. We'll arrive at night, cross to the opposite shore under cover of darkness and take a position overlooking the entrance to the straits. From there we should be able to get a glimpse of the enemy fleet and work out their movements.'

'Good,' Crispus said. The look of inspired glee had left his face; he was all sober concentration now. 'But should you not send a junior officer to lead the expedition?'

Castus avoided his eye; he knew the Caesar was right, but he was impatient. 'I want to see the lie of the land myself, as soon as possible,' he said. 'I'll take two hundred men of the Second Britannica, with the same number of Bonitus's Franks. That should be enough men to take the position and hold it until the fleet can work around the tip of the peninsula. There's an anchorage just inside the mouth of the Hellespont, at Eleus on the north shore. We can gather the ships and men there.'

'Very good,' Crispus said. He turned his head to gaze at the sea, sucking in his cheeks. 'I only wish I could go with you.'

'No,' Castus said firmly. 'You need to stay with the fleet. If we left Theophilus in charge he'd sink every ship.'

Crispus stifled a grin, and made a hushing gesture. The prefect was down in the cabin just below their feet. 'He's not as bad as you think,' he went on in a whisper. 'My father wouldn't have appointed him if he was.'

Castus just shrugged. In the emperor's court, there were more reasons for promotion than mere competence.

'But yes,' Crispus sighed. 'I will remain at Imbros, and bring the fleet into the mouth of the straits once you've established your position. And I'll be praying for your success, brother!'

Thirty-six hours later, a moonless night and a rolling swell, and the squadron of light galleys moved silently out of the bay of Imbros into the open sea. Castus stood on the narrow aft deck of the lead ship, the *Hippocampus*. Ahead of him, the raised gangway between the rowing benches was crowded with armed men crouched with their shields and weapons. The waves rolled past in the darkness.

As they approached the shore of the peninsula the galleys dropped their sails and lowered masts and yards to the deck. Unshipping their oars, the crews pulled onwards towards the low black coastline.

'Won't be long now, strategos,' said the Greek navarch, Dexippus. 'We'll run you as far south as we can, then find a good landing beach. Should have you and your men on the sand in half an hour.'

Castus grunted his thanks. With no moon, the sky above was bright with stars, and when he stared up at them they seemed to spin in the blackness. He could smell the land now, the green scent across the waves. The noise of surf, too. No lights showed on the dark peninsula; if the enemy had lookouts there, they were well hidden. He had left Diogenes, Eumolpius and the rest of his staff back at Imbros, but Ursio sat on the deck wrapped in his cloak. The big taciturn Sarmatian was carefully sharpening his sword with a whetstone; if there was fighting ahead, Castus would be glad of his company.

The motion of the oars changed, the helmsman leaning on the steering bars to bring the *Hippocampus* around in a gentle curve towards the beach. The other ships followed his lead at once, spreading out into an advancing line. In the faint light, Castus saw their hooked prows cutting the water, leaving thin streaks of foam on the black sea. He checked his belts, his sword, then put on his helmet and tied the laces beneath his chin. Beside him, Ursio raised a skin of water. Castus waved it away. His throat was dry, but there was a cold churning nausea in his gut. Not the motion of the sea, but the thought of what lay ahead.

He remembered Crispus's question. *Do you miss your wife?* Marcellina was very close to his thoughts now, her presence almost tangible. He remembered her pleas that he should not throw himself into danger. Over a month of waiting and slow ponderous advancing had wrung that promise from his soul. He reached into the bunched folds of his cloak and touched the silver amulet she had given him. Dolphins, he thought. Like the ones they had seen from the ship. Surely a good omen, but still he was troubled.

Trust in yourself. Trust in the men you command. He always had, but something else stirred in him now. A sense of deep fatigue, a presentiment of disaster ahead. Had he grown too old for war?

For a few long moments he felt lost, indecisive and alone. There was no god he could ask for guidance, no higher power that could aid him. His heart was throbbing in his chest, and his legs felt stiff and cold. He felt very aware of everything around him, his senses sharp. The taste of salt on his lips, the tug of the breeze and the groan of the deck beneath him, the plash of the oar-blades as they bit the waves, the creak of the cables lashing the steering oar: all of it keen and vivid in the darkness.

'Brace yourselves!' Dexippus called in a rasping whisper along the deck. The men on the gangway bunched and shuffled closer together, hefting their shields. The noise of the surf on the beach was loud now.

From deep inside his body, Castus felt the energy of command rushing through him, driving the shadows from his mind and dispelling all doubts.

Then the oarsmen gave a last long pull with the oncoming wave, the surf seethed along both sides of the hull, and the long keel of the galley grated onto the dark sand of the enemy shore.

CHAPTER XII

Boots thudded on the deck planking as the troops moved quickly forward along the gangway to the bows, hefting weapons and shields. Muffled curses as the first men leaped over the side, another incoming wave soaking them to the knees. Castus followed them up the gangway, then waited for the hissing backwash to pass below him before jumping down from the bow onto the wet black sand. The oarsmen were already in the water, primed to heave the galley back off the beach as soon as they heard the order.

'Good hunting, strategos!' Dexippus called. 'We'll stay offshore until we see your signal!'

Castus raised his hand, although he knew the navarch could barely distinguish him in the darkness; the signal would either be a message of success, or a demand for evacuation. Now that he was ashore, he could make out the shape of the land ahead of him. The beach was narrow, and behind it was a steep escarpment thick with dry shaggy vegetation and scored with shallow ravines. He had brought two guides on the expedition, fishermen from Imbros who claimed to know the coast and the tracks that would take them across to the shore of the Hellespont. Between two and four miles, Castus estimated, although it was hard to be sure.

'Everyone is here,' said a voice from the darkness. Bonitus

appeared out of the night, his familiar form altered by the thick cloak piled around his shoulders. 'My men at least. Not sure of yours! Hmm? Maybe they are lost, or drowned in the sea?'

'You got ears, barbarian?' Castus growled, and hoped Bonitus could see his smile. All around them was the familiar low noise of armed men forming up, the hushed voices and the snarls of the centurions, the clatter of shields and spearshafts.

'I suggest to you,' Bonitus said, 'I send my men ahead. They know to move silently in the night. Unlike yours.'

'That's why you're here,' Castus told him, gripping his shoulder. 'Find the guides and have them lead you: they speak enough Latin to make themselves understood. We'll form up and follow close behind. Remember the watchword?'

'*Virtus Augusta*!' Bonitus said, and then he was gone.

As his eyes adjusted to the dark, Castus could make out the troops gathering around their centurions. None of the men wore body armour, and some had short hooded capes to hide the gleam of their helmets. They carried no standards, but many were lugging bundles of entrenching tools, spare javelins and arrows, cooking equipment and big slopping waterskins. Castus had no idea how long they would have to hold their position before the fleet arrived. He moved along the beach, Ursio a silent presence just behind him, and called out in a low growl until he located the tribune heading the detachment.

'We're following the auxilia,' he said. 'I'll take the lead, with Modestus and his century. Have the other centurions lead their men after me. Every man to sling his shield, and keep clear of the thorn thickets. Try not to get lost!'

He caught the movement of a salute, then he went to find Modestus. He found Felix first, almost walking into him. The wiry optio was bent double, retching bile into the tide wrack.

'Still no sailor, I see?'

'Gets better, dominus,' Felix croaked, straightening up and wiping his mouth with the back of his hand. 'That last bit of choppy sea did for me though.'

Modestus appeared, the rest of his men already close behind him. Every man had his shield slung on his back, the leather cover painted with a daub of whitewash. The white streaks were faint in the darkness, but hopefully they would allow each man to keep sight of the soldier ahead of him.

'All present, dominus,' Modestus rumbled.

'Good. Six men in the lead, and we follow. Keep close behind the Franks if you can.'

They began to move, clambering through the wiry scrub above the beach into one of the dry ravines that ran down from the high ground of the escarpment. The track they were following was a scar in the surrounding gloom, and so narrow that the troops had to climb in single file. Noise of boots and breath and crackling bushes filled the night. Castus tried to concentrate on scrambling forward up the track. The thick darkness was unnerving – all the more so, he knew, for the mass of soldiers filing up the ravine behind him. *Just keep everyone moving*, he told himself. If they paused now they would lose sight of the men ahead, and in no time the column would fray and unravel into chaos.

The scrub was dense towards the top of the ravine, thorny shrubs reaching out to grab and to scratch. A couple of the men had drawn their swords to hack through the thickets; others used spears to shove back the thorns as they passed. Then, quite suddenly, the slope levelled and the column emerged onto a flat upland of long grass and scattered trees. In places there were outcrops of rock, still warm from the day's heat. The air smelled strongly of dusty earth and wild herbs, almost overpowering in the dark.

For around half an hour they pushed forward without a pause, scrambling across dry creek beds and stony hill slopes, breaking into a jog to cross the wider open expanses under the bright stars. Then Castus halted, almost blundering into the man ahead of him.

'What's happening?' he hissed. 'Why have you stopped?'

A voice came from just ahead. 'Sorry, dominus. I think we've lost the path. We can't see anyone ahead of us!'

Castus cursed under his breath. They were crouched together beside the gnarled trunk of an old pine tree. Dry stony soil sloped underfoot, rasping with every movement. Craning his head, he tried to make out the pale flash of a painted shield ahead of him, but saw only the mottled grey and black of empty country, a wilderness under the stars.

'Someone's there!' a panicked voice said, one of the soldiers scrabbling back up the slope on his rump. 'Just across that ridge on the far side of the hollow – lots of them!'

Castus reached forward and slapped the man on the side of his helmet, silencing him. Stilling his breath, he listened into the night's quiet. Now they were no longer moving he heard the sounds of the land around them: the steady chirrup of insects in the grass, the creak of the old tree beside him. Narrowing his eyes, he stared into the darkness. Movement, and the dry scrape of stones.

Turning, he found Modestus in the group just behind him. 'Something on the other side of that ridge,' he said, in barely more than a breath. 'Maybe ours, maybe not. I'm going forward.'

'Dominus, let me send my men…'

'No, I need to see for myself, stay here.'

'What, are you a *bat*? Can you see in the *dark*?'

'Stay. Just give me Felix. And Ursio – come with me.'

Pushing himself between the leading soldiers, he began to

pick his way slowly down the slope into the hollow. He placed each foot carefully, trying not to dislodge loose stones, and every few steps he paused to listen. He could sense Felix and Ursio following him silently. Down in the hollow he eased himself forward onto his belly, pulling his sword around behind him, then started to crawl up the far slope on his elbows and knees.

He was certain of it now: just on the far side of the low ridge a mass of men waited in concealment. He paused again, and heard what sounded like the scrape of a hoof. Were they cavalry? His breath was tight in his chest, the blood beating in his skull. Keeping low, he crept up to the top of the ridge and peered through the tufts of long grass.

Shapes moved in the dry creek bed beyond the ridge. A head rose, with what looked like a helmet crest. To his left, Castus made out Felix crawling through the grass. He made a fanning gesture, ordering the man back.

A noise, clear in the darkness. Then another; Castus released his trapped breath in a gasp. He was hearing the dull clank of iron bells. A moment later he heard a deep croaking bleat. Grinning, he shoved himself back off the ridge and ran back to join Modestus.

'Goats!' he said. 'Herd of goats, down in the creek over there. We'll cut around to the left – don't want to panic them.'

They moved off again, with a low mutter of laughter. Now the goats were moving, milling about, it was much easier to hear them. Some of the soldiers let out gargling bleats, and the goats answered them back. Despite all their training, Castus thought, soldiers could never be restrained from making animal noises.

For another hour they picked their way forward, pausing every few hundred paces to scour the darkness ahead and wait for those behind them to catch up. They skirted a small field, edged with a rough palisade fence, and crossed a track. As

Castus reached the bushes on the far side the men ahead of him halted suddenly, dropping to a crouch.

'Somebody there,' the lead man hissed.

A goat noise from behind him, laughter, then the sound of a hand slapping a helmet. 'Quiet!'

This time, Castus thought, he was more certain. In the faint light he could make out the shapes of shields and speartips. The rocky ridge ahead of him was thick with men.

Then a voice from the dark. '*Weertuz!*' The watchword, in a strong Frankish accent.

'*Augusta!*' the lead man called back.

An exhalation of relief from the troops all around him, and Castus heard them stumbling to their feet and beginning to move forward. He picked his way over the rough ground, and a few moments later he heard Bonitus's voice from the darkness up ahead. 'Got lost, Roman?'

Castus just grunted, deep in his throat. He found one of the guides, still keeping close to the Frankish chief, and gripped him by the collar of his tunic. 'Lead me forward,' he said in a hushed voice. 'Slow and steady.'

Together they scrambled up the side of the ridge and across the crest, pushing through the fringe of dry foliage. It was still an hour until daybreak, but there was enough light leaking into the eastern sky to make out the horizon. As Castus emerged from the bushes the guide halted and they crouched down. Before them the land fell steeply, treacherous in the dark. Beyond that was the Hellespont; Castus smelled the sea breeze first, then made out the expanse of water shining slightly in the faint light, mottled with the movement of the heavy current.

The guide was gesturing, explaining the routes down the slope. To the left, where a gulley approached the sea, was a small village. Points of light glimmered among the houses. To the right, beyond a headland, was the broad arc of a bay, the surf showing pale in the night. A half-moon of sand with scrubland behind it, like a great bite taken out of the peninsula's southern tip, large enough to beach a fleet of warships.

No sign of men on the sand, although it was too dark to be sure. They would be billeted in the village, Castus supposed... He was peering down the slope, listening to the guide's instructions, when he heard movement behind him. Ursio had already turned, one hand on his sword hilt. A figure was pushing through the dark scrub along the ridge. For a moment he was visible against the faint light in the western sky: a man with a hood pulled over his helmet, raising a hand in greeting.

'Who's there?' Castus hissed into the darkness. He could hear the man scrambling forward to join him, dislodging small stones from the slope. Ursio's crouch tensed as he slid his sword from his scabbard.

'Forgive me,' a voice said. It took a moment for Castus to realise who had spoken. Then the man was kneeling beside him, pushing the hood back from his head. 'I was with the tribune, but there's not much to see at the back of the column!' He grinned, and in the faint twilight Castus recognised the face behind the nasal bar of the plain infantryman's helmet.

'You're supposed to be back on Imbros,' he said in a tight whisper, his guts clenching as shock and anger filled his chest.

'Well, here I am,' Crispus said. 'And this time, I've brought my own helmet!'

For a few moments Castus struggled to comprehend what had happened. This was a mistake. Or some magical delusion... But it seemed so obvious now that Crispus would have disobeyed his suggestion; easy enough for the young man to attach himself to the tribune's command, to board the ships in the darkness and confusion of departure from Imbros.

'Wouldn't you have done the same?' the young man asked, still smiling. 'Admit it – you're too senior to lead this expedition yourself! And my father once did something similar, I believe – he disguised himself as a soldier and went to scout the Frankish position, did he not…?'

True enough; Castus had heard about that. And Crispus shared his father's love of risk, his lust for glory. Even so, his presence here did no good. It was reckless, irresponsible… He fought back his outrage, and snorted a laugh. Hypocritical of him to criticise. And he could hardly order the young emperor to remain alone on a dark hillside for the rest of the night.

'Stay close to me,' he said, 'and try not to trip over anything. Ursio – make sure you watch *his majesty*…'

He turned back to look at the sea, but another sound caught his attention. With a hiss, he ordered silence. The background noise of the night returned: the insects, the distant wash of the surf. Castus raised his head, listening intently. There – he heard it again: the sound of a man whistling. One of his own men? Surely not – the centurions would have silenced him at once. Then he heard the sound of hooves, the jingle of bridle trappings. Horses were coming along the track behind him.

Muscles locked, he held his crouch, not daring to move as the pulse thudded in his head. Four heartbeats passed, then five. The sound of hooves was distinct now: there were at least ten riders.

A shout broke the quiet of twilight. A horse whinnied, then a man cried out, the scream choked off suddenly. Hooves beat loud on the dry ground, then the night erupted with the sounds of chaotic struggle, cries of panic, hissed orders.

Castus was on his feet at once and stumbling back up the slope through the clinging bushes. Crispus was behind him, and Ursio; he saw the big Sarmatian move to cover the Caesar's flank. His heart was clenched in his chest, his breath coming in short hard stabs. What had happened? An ambush in the darkness?

A black shape loomed suddenly, moving fast, and Castus threw himself to one side as a riderless horse crashed past him. Kicked dust fogged the air. Another rider galloped up the slope from the track; Ursio seized the man's cloak and hauled him from his horse, killing him with one swift sword thrust before vaulting into the saddle. He circled the horse, protecting Crispus.

For a few long panicked heartbeats Castus thought there was a major battle in progress, then he saw things more clearly: there were only a handful of riders, a small night patrol, and they had almost passed through the centre of the stationary column before one of them raised the alarm. Now they were trapped, men appearing from the darkness on all sides, shields closing in. Castus saw one of the riders speared by two of Bonitus's warriors; another fought to control his plunging horse. In the darkness it was impossible to judge distances: he heard steel grating against steel, the clash of blades and shields, the muffled cries of men and horses.

A man came staggering up the slope towards Castus. For a moment he thought it was one of the Franks; then the man snarled and lunged at him with a spear. Castus drove the weapon away with the flat of his blade, seized the shaft with his mutilated hand and dragged it towards him. The man stumbled forward, and Castus drove his sword through him. He glanced around, but could not see Crispus; panic beat at his skull.

A stamp and a clash from his left, and Castus wheeled. Figures were locked in combat in the murky darkness. He saw the flash of a blade, and a body fell. Then Crispus was beside him again, breathing hard, the sword in his hand black with blood.

The dust thinned, and the fighting men peered about them, still keeping to their rough formations. One or two riderless horses were galloping away across the rough ground, the noise of their beating hooves fading into the darkness.

'Tribune!' Castus called. 'Centurions! Form your men and count them off!'

'All present, dominus,' he heard the voices reply. 'All present.'

Only one man had been injured in the brief fight, but there were six dead riders sprawled on the road and in the dry scrub to either side. An injured horse lay in the dust, kicking its legs; Modestus told two men to put it out of its misery. The Franks had taken a prisoner too; the tribune questioned him, then reported back to Castus.

'He says there's only a hundred of them, down in the village by the water. No other enemy at this end of the peninsula, only at some place called Gellybolly, something like that.'

'Callipolis,' Castus said, nodding. It was about forty miles north-east, on rough tracks. The men in the village must have been left to watch over the anchorage in the bay; some of them had escaped the fight on horseback, but they would be summoning no more help tonight.

'Stay close to me,' he told Crispus. The Caesar nodded as he cleaned his sword on his cloak.

'Form up on the track, double column,' Castus called to Modestus and the tribune. 'We'll follow it straight down to the village. Keep quiet till you hear the first sounds of alarm, then we yell like there's an army behind us.'

He waited while the troops assembled. It was getting lighter fast, and already the eastern sky was a bright eggshell blue, fading to yellow at the horizon. A few of the nearest soldiers recognised Crispus; Castus saw their eyes widen briefly. Some of them smiled, raising their hands in salute. Then Bonitus signalled from the vanguard, and Castus waved back to Modestus and the tribune behind him. They set off at a fast pace, a thunder of boots and clashing weapons breaking the dawn hush. Around a curve in the track they began their descent towards the village; already Castus could see the shapes of men running, a horse and rider nearing the perimeter of the settlement. Ten paces further, and the first trumpet wailed.

'*Constantine!*' Castus shouted, and the name was echoed back at once in a roar. The Franks were spilling forward down the slope with wild whooping cries. The Roman infantry doubled their pace, but kept to a jog, holding their formation and conserving their energy. Already the first yells of combat were coming from the village as Bonitus's men cut down the enemy staggering from their billets.

Brightness in the sky above them, but the village was still in deep shade. Castus reached a stone marker at the roadside and slowed; his breath was short, his blood pounding. Modestus moved past him, shouting to his men to follow as he led them up a branching lane. The other units came up in his wake, each one peeling off in formation to block off the routes of escape and destroy anyone who tried to resist them.

Before the rim of the sun had risen from the sea, it was over. The garrison in the village had not put up much of a fight; their sentries had been watching the straits, and none expected an attack from the land behind them. A score or so escaped, scrambling aboard the little skiffs pulled up on the beach and paddling frantically across the dark waves before the attackers could reach them. But many more had died, and more still had surrendered or been taken prisoner.

Castus strode down the dusty main street of the village and out onto the hard wet shingle of the beach. Far across the straits he could see warships, scout galleys with their oars pulling to keep position in the current. Soon enough the enemy would know of what had happened here. They would guess that Constantine's fleet was close by, preparing to haul around the peninsula and into the half-moon bay that was now in their possession. The sun had just broken the horizon, coming up red and fierce over the water.

Behind him, Castus could hear the troops in the narrow street cheering as the young Caesar, bareheaded in the daylight, walked among them. But it was not the emperor's name they chanted now. And it was certainly not Castus's.

'Crispus!' they cried. 'Crispus Caesar! Victor!'

CHAPTER XIII

From the snaking path above the beach, Castus looked down at the galleys pulled up all along the shoreline, the transports moored beyond them and the second line of warships, fully manned and armed, anchored in the open sea to guard the bay. The half-moon of beach and the rising ground behind it had been transformed in the last few days: now the sand was covered with piled supplies and gangs of men working on the ships, the scrubby hollow and the hill slopes turned into a military camp. There was not enough level ground for a regular encampment, but the paths that rose from the beach were lined with tents and shelters all the way up to the line of fortifications along the surrounding summits. Bonitus commanded up there, sending his warriors out on wide-ranging patrols.

Now the only problem was water: the tip of the peninsula had a few springs and small streams, but in the parching heat the thousands of soldiers and marines, oarsmen and slaves would soon be going thirsty.

'Another group of deserters came in last night,' Diogenes said, following Castus as they climbed towards the headland. 'That makes nearly a hundred now.'

'They came by sea?'

'Yes. A small skiff from the north-east, in the early hours. One of them was a centurion of the Second Legion Traiana, all the way from Egypt, if you can credit it! His report confirms what the others told us. The enemy have two hundred ships in the narrows. But they have disease in their camp. So many of their oarsmen have fallen sick that they can only man the lowest benches of some of their ships. They're conscripting local men to fill the places, but they aren't properly trained.'

'Even so,' Castus said quietly. Two hundred ships made a formidable armada, far outnumbering those that Theophilus had managed to bring round the peninsula and into the bay. He cast a last glance over the camp in the glare of the morning sun, then climbed on up the path.

The wind met him as he gained the summit, blowing strongly down the straits. The pines that overlooked the sea bent and creaked, and dust flurried over the new fortifications on the clifftop, where catapults and ballistae were positioned to guard the anchorage below. Beneath the trees a gathering of men stood, ringed by guards. A short distance away, Crispus was staring out to sea, his palms linked to shade his eyes from the low sun. Castus nodded a greeting to several of the assembled officers: Hierax and Dexippus, Saturninus and the other senior tribunes.

'Did you hear the report from the deserters, excellency?' Hierax said as he joined them.

'Just now,' Castus told him. Theophilus was keeping his distance from the others. He gave Castus a sour smile.

'The plain of Troy!' Crispus called, over the steady rush of the wind. He was pointing out to sea. The straits were over three miles wide at this point, the far shore just visible from the elevation of the headland as a dark grey line on the horizon. 'I think that raised mound to the west there must be the tomb of Ajax,' the Caesar said as he rejoined the group.

There was a folding stool beneath the trees, and Crispus seated himself with his commanders standing around him, a cordon of guards, secretaries and attendants beyond them. An imperial war council, but only Castus and Saturninus wore battle gear, their plumed helmets clasped beneath their arms. They waited for a few moments for the last men to arrive. The trees swayed in the wind and the sun glittered on the moving water.

'You've all heard the latest news from the deserters,' Crispus said in a brisk tone. 'They confirm the reports of our scouts. The enemy is holding a position blocking the narrows, ten miles up the straits. We have the current against us, and the wind shows no signs of dropping. I suggest we have waited here long enough, and I would hear your views on our course of action.'

Silence for a few moments, the assembled officers exchanging glances, none wanting to be the first to speak.

'What choice do we have, majesty?' Theophilus said abruptly. 'The enemy outnumbers us nearly two to one, and his ships are bigger than ours. We lack the strength to break his line, and while he holds the narrows we cannot outflank him. In four days we will have run out of water in this exposed place. Our only course of action is to return to Imbros and await a change in the weather, *as I had suggested when we left the Hebrus.*' He directed these last words at Castus, his eyes narrowed with scorn.

Castus held his gaze a moment, until the prefect looked away. But he knew that Theophilus could be right; often over these recent days he had thought that seizing the bay at Eleus may have been a mistake. But he would say nothing of his doubts now.

'Majesty,' said Saturninus, 'the enemy is weakening daily. He has sickness in his camp, and can't fully man his ships. He *needs* to fight a battle soon, before his troops get too weak and demoralised to fight... But bigger ships don't guarantee victory.

Our crews are better than his, our troops are better – he's filled up his ranks with Phrygians and Cappadocians... And the enemy commander knows nothing of fighting fleet battles.'

'Who does?' Theophilus said. 'Nothing of the sort has been attempted for over a hundred years – longer, in fact. Perhaps not since Actium!'

Good point, Castus thought grudgingly. Although he wished that people would stop talking about a battle fought so long ago. It seemed ill omened.

'No,' Theophilus went on, 'I'm afraid it's clear that unless the enemy leaves his position we cannot hope to attack him.'

'*Unless...*' Castus said.

All eyes turned to him, but he waited before speaking. He was gazing at the sea, the movements of the small scouting galleys out in the straits – their own and the enemy's. For days he had been watching the sea. He knew nothing of naval warfare, but this confined stretch of water was familiar to him now. It was possible to regard it as a field of battle, to see the tactical possibilities.

'If your enemy holds a secure position,' he said, slowly and speculatively, 'you either attack him directly or try to draw him out into the open, where he can be outflanked. Like Saturninus says, the enemy commander needs to fight us. Give him an opportunity, and he'll do it. All he needs is a chance at an easy victory.'

'So we challenge him, somehow?' Crispus asked.

Castus was still looking at the sea. 'Hierax, tell them what you told me last night,' he said.

The navarch looked baffled for a moment, then his brow cleared. 'When the enemy scouting vessels come down the straits,' he said, 'they always bear away to the southward when they get opposite our position here. Some of the local fishermen say that there's a wide area of slack water along the southern shore, maybe even a bit of counter-current. Once a ship gets into the slack water, she can row up to the eastwards again and get back to the narrows. Otherwise the force of the stream'd carry her out into the open Aegean.'

'So? What does this mean?' Theophilus said. 'Does this help us at all?'

'This means,' Hierax said with a grimace, 'that if the enemy came down the straits in force, they'd have to turn to the southward once they reached us here. And when they did...'

'They'd be leaving their flank wide open,' Crispus said, with a quick smile. He looked at Castus, with a brief gesture. *Continue.*

'Three squadrons,' Castus said, pointing out over the Hellespont. 'One of light ships, over to the south in the slack water, working up the strait. The second in the centre, trying to get as far to the east as possible against the current. They're a lure, to draw the enemy to attack. Once they do, the central squadron falls back. The enemy would have the wind and current behind them, so they'd have to keep going...'

'Feigned flight,' Crispus said, nodding. Castus could see the dubious glances from a few other commanders.

'The southern squadron harries their flank, stops them from turning too soon,' Castus went on. 'Then, once they're opposite us here, the third squadron – all our bigger ships – puts out from the bay and hits them as they turn.'

Silence stretched uncomfortably. Crispus was fretting, rubbing at his chin. Theophilus looked openly dismissive, but Hierax had a smile on his face.

'Might work,' the navarch said. 'Difficult though. If they don't take the bait, we're wasting our energy. And if they do come, they'll come fast and heavy...'

'They'll come,' Crispus announced. He smacked a fist into his palm. 'They'll come if they see my standard leading the central squadron. I'll command myself, from there; the enemy will think we're attempting a desperate attack with our main strength, and they'll leave the narrows to try and take us. This *will* work...'

His certainty, so sudden, was unnerving. Castus could see Theophilus's accusing glare; he ignored the prefect. 'You only need send your standard, majesty,' he said. 'You could remain here, commanding the northern squadron...'

'No,' Crispus said quietly. 'I command the centre, with Hierax. Theophilus will take the northern squadron, and Dexippus will lead the squadron on the southern flank. We draw them down the straits, then envelop them and hit them with all the strength we possess...'

Castus breathed deeply, filling his chest. Already he was regretting his suggestion. He pictured the battle ahead; the miles-wide gyre of the enemy fleet, the squadrons of smaller ships darting in from the flanks. Any prospect of success relied on chance, on speed and daring. Unfortunately, it also relied on Theophilus.

'Let's do this,' Crispus said as he stood up, flexing his shoulders. 'And meanwhile, we should all pray for a change in the weather!'

The wind was strong down the straits that night, guttering the fires of the men on the beach, spilling sparks across the sand. Foam raced around the prows of the warships drawn up on the shore. Above the sea the new moon hung, thin and yellow as a paring of old cheese.

Castus made his way through the camp, between the piquet fires and the tent ropes. He heard men talking in hushed voices, and the clink and rasp as they sorted their arms and equipment, cleaned straps, sharpened blades. Few would sleep that night. At the entrance to the imperial enclosure he gave the watchword, passed through the sentries, and entered Crispus's tent.

'You keep a late hour, Caesar.'

Crispus smiled ruefully. He was sprawled in a camp chair, a cup of wine in his hand. The lamps in his tent had burned low, and the slackness of his expression suggested that he had been drinking for some time.

'Theophilus doesn't want me to fight,' he said.

'I'm sure he has orders to keep you safe, majesty.'

'As do you?'

'As do I.'

'Theophilus has orders, I think, to prevent me winning too impressive a victory. Or getting myself killed trying for one.'

'You don't have to fight yourself – pull back once the enemy are engaged, use the current to carry you out of their reach, and let the other squadrons do the work.'

Crispus nodded vaguely, whistling to himself. The wind buffeted at the tent fabric, hauling at the guy ropes. The young Caesar was plucking idly at a scroll lying on the side table.

'Herodotus,' he said, rubbing the ivory boss. 'Your old secretary had a copy, it turned out.'

Castus bristled, dropping his chin to his chest. Diogenes was only a couple of years older than him. But Crispus seemed not to have noticed the offence.

'He's a very interesting person, in fact. A treasury of knowledge! He was explaining a theory to me that all of Roman history is dictated by Pythagorean mathematics...'

'You can't have him.'

Crispus laughed. He was nervous, and trying not to let it show. He picked up the scroll again, turning it in his hands. 'I

187

was just reading about the King of the Persians,' he said. 'He built a bridge of boats, you know, right across these straits. Up at the narrows where the enemy are now, I expect. He marched half a million men across the bridge to invade Greece... And yet he was just a man. As all those emperors we call divine were just men. As my father is just a man...'

'What's your point?'

'My point is that you don't need to be a god to fight a campaign, or win a battle.'

'True enough,' Castus said. He had done both, and was far from godlike. 'But even the gods are anxious before a fight.'

Crispus glanced at him, affronted for a moment, then shrugged.

'Even your father,' Castus added. 'I saw him myself, before the battle at Taurinum. His hands were shaking.'

Raising his eyebrows, Crispus smiled. He tossed the scroll back onto the table. Castus had wanted to reassure him, to give him heart for what lay ahead. But something else was troubling the young man.

'Do you remember what we talked about last year, before I left Treveris?' Crispus asked.

Castus frowned, and gave the slightest nod. His jaw was set, and he rubbed at the back of his teeth with his tongue.

'If we win this war,' Crispus went on, 'I mean to speak to my father. I mean to ask that he abdicates at his twentieth anniversary, just as Diocletian did. Handing over supreme power to me.'

He paused, waiting for Castus's response. 'Win tomorrow,' Castus said quietly, 'and you'll be a hero to the troops. They'd have no problem backing you.'

'And you?'

Another shunt of wind against the tent, and the lamps guttered. Castus heard the distant noise of the sea, the muffled voices of the sentries. His heart was beating fast; he had avoided thinking of this question for many months, knowing that it would come. But he knew that the young man before him needed strength and resolve for the battle. There was no room for doubt now.

'If you were Augustus,' he said in a low whisper, unable to meet Crispus's eye, 'would you allow the legions to march behind the standards of the gods? Would you permit sacrifices? Would you restore the temples?'

Crispus took a deep breath. 'I would,' he said. 'I know my father is committed to Christianity. He may well be right – I don't know. But when I read of the ancient days, when I read of Jupiter, Mars, Sol... The great victories won by our ancestors by their blessing... I see that it's madness to deny them. Christianity is virtuous, pure, maybe correct. But when I think of the traditional gods of Rome I feel inspired! Fausta knows this – she has the courage to stand up to my father. If I'm to rule, I hope to be that strong.'

'If that's true,' Castus said. 'Then yes, I'll back you.'

Crispus grinned, all his nervous hesitation falling away. He stood up. 'And if you do, then many of the other officers will follow you, I'm sure of it!'

'But *be careful*,' Castus told him, clapping a heavy hand on the young man's shoulder. 'We have everything to lose.'

Moments later, standing outside the tent once more in the warm night breeze, Castus tipped his head back and inhaled deeply. He realised now that he had made this commitment months before, although he had not known it at the time. A solemn dread ran through him, tempered with joy. *Everything to lose* – he had not exaggerated. But in his mind he heard the words of the loyalty oath he had sworn to Constantine, many years ago when he joined the Corps of Protectores. An oath that still bound him.

... If I should do anything contrary to this oath or fail to do what I have sworn, I impose a curse upon myself encompassing the destruction and total extinction of my body, soul, life, children and my entire family, so neither earth nor sea may receive their bodies nor bear fruit for them.

What were his loyalties now?

Two hours after dawn and the sun was hot upon the open water. Castus stood on the heeling deck of the thirty-oared *Hippocampus*, lead ship of the light squadron, as she hauled across the Hellespont mouth. The slender galley was riding heavily, butting through the foam-streaked water with her oars bending as the men on the benches sweated and heaved. With the wind on her beam, the spray of every wave spattered up across the deck; the dark blue water was muscled with swirling cross-currents, raising short choppy waves that lifted the galley's bows and gave her a sickening twisting motion.

Fanning out across her wake came forty other ships of the squadron, all of them light triaconters. Castus saw the spray bursting up from their prows as they crossed the waves. The rest of the fleet was still back in the bay; they would only put out into the channel once Dexippus had taken the *Hippocampus* and the rest of his squadron well to the east. They would wait until the sun had passed the zenith and begun to drop into the west, where it would glare in the eyes of their enemies.

With the rowers, soldiers and archers, deck crew and officers, there were nearly sixty men crowding the narrow hull. Castus was seated up near the stern, just forward of the helmsman.

He had Ursio with him, and a staff tribune named Ausenius. Eumolpius crouched beside him, holding his spear and helmet. The gangway leading forward was packed with men all the way to the pivot-mounted ballista at the bow. Spare javelins and arrows were bundled beneath the thwarts, while ammunition for the ballista – together with four smoking fire-pots in a wetted canvas shroud – was stacked towards the bows. Modestus was stationed there, heading his small unit of infantrymen, while Felix sat just in front of Castus, head down between his knees, trying not to retch.

Castus took the waterskin from Eumolpius and drank a mouthful.

'You should put a few drops of seawater in there,' Dexippus called from the stern platform. 'You'll need the salt once you start sweating.'

Castus nodded. He was sweating heavily already, and it was not yet noon.

Passing out of the main current and into the slack water was like crossing a threshold. Immediately the motion of the ship steadied, and as the helmsman steered around into the breeze the ship began to run more smoothly. Felix let out a low groan, raised his head, then sank it between his knees again.

By noon the flotilla had gathered just off the southern coast of the Hellespont. Off to their right lay the low olive-green coast of the plain of Troy, with the high land beyond a hazy grey in the sunlight. A slight counter-current carried the ships along the coast, allowing the oarsmen to rest, eat and drink. Castus watched the other galleys assembling around the *Hippocampus*; from one of the nearer ones he saw Bonitus waving, and returned the salute. Castus had allowed the Frankish chief to man ten of the ships entirely with his own warriors, the original Greek oarsmen sent to the bigger vessels.

Many of the other ships also carried Germanic auxilia as marines. The rest carried men of the Second Britannica, Martenses and Septimani legions. It looked an impressive array, every ship bristling with armed troops, spears flashing in the hot sunlight as the oars churned the dark blue water. All had left their yards and sails back on the beach, but every ship had a lookout at the bare masthead, scanning the straits to the north.

'On deck!' came a cry from above. The lookout was waving off to the north-west. 'Central squadron's put to sea!'

The northern shore of the Hellespont was visible as a dark line along the horizon, and a few moments later Castus could make out the uprights of the masts as Crispus's squadron clawed their way up the channel. The Caesar was aboard *Artemisia*; Castus was glad that he had a skilled seaman like Hierax in command.

To the east, the shorelines closed in, the open mouth of the Hellespont narrowing into a throat, then the confined gullet where the enemy fleet lay. The land rose on either side into high bluffs and cliffs, and the current came rushing out of the narrows.

'On deck!' the lookout cried again. He was raising one hand, a fold of cloth in his fist to signal to the other ships. 'Enemy in sight!'

'Gods, they've moved fast,' Dexippus muttered, his lips stretched thin and tight. Every head aboard the galley was craning eastwards now, the oarsmen leaning back in their benches and gazing over their shoulders as they pulled.

'Steady there!' Dexippus roared. He stepped up onto the stern platform, shading his eyes against the reflected sunlight. 'Excellency,' he said, 'you should see this.'

Castus ducked beneath the steering oars and climbed up onto the platform beside the navarch. For a moment he stared, squinting, pushing out his jaw. Then his breath caught. Across the distant sea horizon, between the narrowing cliffs, stretched a black line. As he stared he saw the line taking shape, more hulls appearing above the horizon, stark in the sunlight. A mass of ships, moving fast with the wind and current behind them.

'Best jump down, excellency,' Dexippus said with a taut grimace. 'Things are about to get busy.'

Castus moved forward to his position ahead of the steersman, and as he did so the trumpets carried the signal between the ships. 'Battle formation!' Dexippus cried. The lookout shinned down from his perch, and the deck crew unstepped the mast and swung it down to the deck. All across the squadron masts were dropping, the troops assembling along the gangways as the oarsmen worked to form the galleys into line abreast, prows facing the open straits. The waves chopped at the low hulls as the ships moved out into the strong current once more.

By now, everyone aboard could see the advancing enemy fleet. They could see the other squadron across the straits as well, the *Artemisia* and her flock crawling steadily up the channel along the northern shore, against wind and current. Castus looked at the forty light galleys around him, and they appeared a feeble force to throw in the way of that onrushing armada. Like the little wooden boats his son made, he thought, and launched on the placid waters of the garden pool.

No doubt other men aboard felt the same, but none spoke of it. The enemy ships were in plain view now, most of the leading ones big triremes with their oars thrashing in unison and their heavy bronze rams throwing up a foaming bow wave. They were formed in a mile-wide crescent, but already the larger and faster ships were rushing forward, breaking formation in eagerness to attack the two squadrons facing them. Castus always felt nervous before a battle, but never before had he felt

193

the lurch of stark terror. On land, his feet on the solid earth, he at least felt secure. Here on the open sea there was nowhere to hide, no chance of retreat. Any man who fell overboard would be lost in the churning current. Planting his feet firmly on the deck, Castus fought against the fear. But he felt as if all the blood in his body had drained to his legs, and a cold greasy nausea writhed in his gut.

Hippocampus took a position in the second line. As the command ship of the squadron, with Castus's own purple banner flying from her stern, she was supposed to keep out of the direct fighting, but Castus knew that, with the tactics they had chosen, the coming battle would soon involve every vessel. He remembered the promise he had made to Marcellina, a promise he would once again have to break.

'Now there's a sight no man alive has ever seen, I'd say.' Dexippus had climbed forward of the steersman to join Castus once more. If he was nervous, he was hiding it well. 'They're coming on at some speed! They've got some big cataphract galleys in their first line too. Five times our weight of timber – should be some fight...'

He grinned, and Castus managed to grimace back at him. Then the navarch leaned across the rail and scooped a handful of seawater from a passing wave, dashing it into his face. Castus did the same – the water was surprisingly cold.

'Fresh from the Euxine,' Dexippus said. 'Clears the head, heh?'

Castus nodded. The shock of the cold water, the clean taste of the salt on his lips, had sharpened his senses a little at least. He was glad that the troops massed along the gangway had their backs to him; he would not have liked to look into their faces now. Up in the bow, Modestus was hauling a scale cuirass over his head.

'Armour,' Castus said to his orderly. Eumolpius nodded, and helped Castus strap the bronze muscled cuirass over his linen arming vest. The weight would make it impossible to swim, should he fall overboard, but he did not rate his chances in the water anyway.

'*Sol Invictus,*' he whispered, kissing his fingers and raising them towards the sun. '*Your light between us and darkness...*' Other words crowded his mind, prayers and pleas. But there was nothing more he could ask. Eumolpius passed him his helmet and he put it on, tying the straps beneath his chin.

'Keep the shield up on my left,' Castus said. 'And guard yourself too. Going to be plenty of iron flying about once we get up close to those bastards.'

From over to his right he could hear the hoarse chant of the Frankish oarsmen. *Huor-gah! Huor-gah!* He remembered it from the Rhine. The Franks were moving out on the right of the squadron. Bonitus was standing up in the stern of his boat, his blond hair streaming in the breeze, and Castus saw him pump his spear in the air as he let out a battle cry.

The disordered left of the enemy fleet was closing fast, the galleys of Castus's squadron rowing hard to keep on their flank, forming a smaller crescent of their own. It was hard to tear his eyes from the spectacle of the oncoming ships, but Castus snatched a glance across the straits, and saw Crispus's squadron still moving up. He breathed a curse: they should be holding their position, or falling back by now, to draw the enemy further westwards. Had Crispus decided to fight it out, ship against ship, in the open water?

No time to consider it. Already the catapults and ballistae on the enemy ships were in action, the bolts and stones raising jets of water just ahead of the squadron. They were testing their range, Castus knew. Soon their missiles would find a mark.

He leaned forward and tapped Felix on the side of his helmet. The optio glanced back at him, his face set hard.

'Feeling better now?' Castus yelled.

'Oh, aye, much better. Nothing like the prospect of a scrap to settle the stomach.' Felix grinned, wolfish.

'Good man,' Castus said quietly. The words were drowned out by Dexippus's roaring voice from the stern platform.

'On my command,' the navarch cried, 'full pressure to ramming speed! Those big bastards are coming on fast, but they can't turn as quick as we can. Once we're among them, we'll be spearing fish in a net, boys!'

A cheer from the rowing benches, every man taking a firm grip on his oar.

Castus was fighting to breathe, his chest tight inside his cuirass. *Now*, he thought. *Now – close the distance.*

The *thwack* of the forward ballista reverberated through the deck. All along the front line of the squadron the machines were loosing their missiles. Screams came from a galley to the left as one of the enemy catapult stones struck home. Dexippus called out his command.

'Ready your stroke!' the rowing master roared. 'On three and pull, full pressure – one, two, *three*!'

The galley surged as the oars picked up the rhythm, spray spattering back across the deck. All along the battle line the other ships were gathering pace. Castus felt the hull seem to lift beneath him, the boards of the deck pulsating with the beat of the oars. The breeze was full in his face.

If this was a mistake, he thought, it was a bad one. But it was too late now.

CHAPTER XIV

Across the glittering water, the two lines of ships closed steadily. To his right, Castus saw Bonitus's ships moving fast to outflank the enemy.

'Give the order to evade,' he shouted. The hornblower sounded the call, and the signalling ships along the line repeated it. At once the advancing Constantinian line broke, the galleys bunching together, still surging forward as they steered in columns for the gaps between the oncoming enemy vessels. The powerful impetus of the enemy attack allowed them little chance to alter course, their charge carrying them on straight through the squadron as the smaller galleys dodged aside. Archers were loosing arrows from every deck, the air flickering with missiles.

'Aim for the helmsmen!' Castus shouted. He could see the pivot-mounted ballista in the bow already turning, the mechanism clicking as the crew winched back the slide. Two arrows struck the rail and the deck at his feet, and he flinched. Eumolpius moved around to cover him, raising the shield; another arrow struck it at once.

One of the enemy triremes was coming up fast, passing through the front line with a great wash of foam across her bows. Castus heard the ballista loose a shot; he watched the bolt streak across the sky and narrowly miss the helm of the enemy ship. Then another missile, a catapult stone, came whipping in from the far side and struck the trireme's steering oars. Shattered wood flew, and the helmsman was down. Noise of cheering across the waves.

Most of the light galleys had darted through the front lines of the enemy attack; they turned in formation, rapid and agile, to bear down on the bigger ships from the rear. Castus saw the enemy triremes trying to slow, to back oars, but his own galleys had the current in their favour now. The battle had shifted from a direct confrontation to a swirl of manoeuvre, evasion and ambush.

Over to his left, he saw the lead ship of the enemy centre, a green monster of a trireme with a pair of glaring eyes painted on her bows and a gilded crocodile for a figurehead. As he watched, the ship seemed to slew in the water as one side backed oars; the heavy vessel turned, faster than Castus would have thought possible.

One long pull, and the heavy bronze-plated prow of the green trireme slammed obliquely into the one of the advancing triaconters; she struck the lighter ship on the bow quarter, splitting the hull with a rending crash of timber. Barely slowing, the big ship powered on straight through the wreckage, smashing the galley under her ram. Shattered oars threshed from the water, and Castus saw the screaming men swallowed by the waves. A terrible sight: the shock stilled him for a moment, then his anguish turned to rage.

'The green ship with the crocodile prow,' he shouted to Dexippus.

'We're on it,' the navarch said. The helmsman was already working his oars, turning the *Hippocampus* in a broad arc, white foam in her wake, her deck heeling. To the right, two of the Frankish boats had clashed with an enemy trireme, the oarsmen rushing their narrow keel up against the oar banks of the bigger ship. The trireme's oars rose and thrashed, trying to beat them back; one of the Frankish galleys capsized, spilling men into the water. The other managed to slam her keel spur over the oars, the slim hull rising like a ramp as the oar-shafts shattered beneath it. With a bellowing roar, the Franks hurled grappling hooks, then scrambled forward from their benches to assault the enemy deck.

'Dominus,' Dexippus called, and pointed away to the left. Castus gripped the rail, steadying himself against the heel of the deck. The green trireme had turned further, aiming to cut back between the lines of the Constantinian squadron. Already her bows had raked through the oar banks of a triaconter, smashing the shafts like a handful of dry straw. But her speed had dropped as she turned against the current, and now two more galleys, the triaconters *Alkedo* and *Charybdis*, were closing on her beam, their bow artillery hurling bolts and stones at the men on her deck.

'Closer?' Dexippus asked.

'Closer.'

The archers on the deck of the trireme were pelting arrows down at the two galleys approaching on their beam as *Hippocampus* moved up on the far side. Castus watched the enemy deck; not too many marines up there, but he saw the ballistae mounted at bow and stern pivot in their direction.

'Guard yourselves,' he said. 'Eumolpius – shield!'

Eumolpius dipped past him, swinging the shield around to his far side. He staggered slightly as the deck pitched, and before he could straighten up the back of his head exploded.

Castus heard the scream from behind him, but for a few long heartbeats he was stunned. Pinkish blood and brain matter was sprayed across his chest. The orderly's body had dropped forward against the rail; the catapult stone that had killed him had come in low, skipping off the waves, and missed Castus by a hand's span. When he glanced back, Castus saw the helmsman standing bolt upright, his face white with shock. Just behind him, Dexippus lay across the platform with his blood and viscera covering the timbers of the stern. The same stone that had killed Eumolpius had struck him in the stomach and almost torn him in half.

Kneeling, Castus lifted the body of his orderly. The back of Eumolpius's skull was gone, but his face was intact, still wearing an expression of mild surprise. Castus exhaled in a dull grunt. He had seen men die around him since his youth, but this death had been so sudden, so close... Eumolpius had been his orderly for over ten years. Castus had freed him from slavery; he had become part of the family. Grief blanked his mind.

'Dominus!' the helmsman was crying. 'Dominus – your orders?'

With a shudder, Castus shook himself from his crouch. Felix was beside him now, taking Eumolpius's body from his arms with rough tenderness. But it was the death of the navarch that had thrown the crew into confusion; the *Hippocampus* was wallowing, oars clashing, and the big green trireme was gathering pace again, turning steadily.

Castus wiped a hand across his face, feeling the wet blood smearing across his cheek. All around him the battle had turned into chaos. No order among the milling vessels, no formation remained. Between the hulls the sea was a choppy swell of foam, fragments of floating wreckage and bodies. Smoke was billowing across the waves: several of the ships upwind were on fire.

He stared at the green trireme. He could read the Greek letters gilded on the bow quarter now: *Krokodilos*. One of the two triaconters was keeping up the attack, trying to grapple the bigger ship, but Castus saw that the other had been driven back, her oar benches heaped with dead and injured men. Dark rage boiled inside him, seething through the glaze of grief and shock.

'Helmsman,' he shouted. 'I want that big green fucker!'

The helmsman nodded quickly as Castus pushed his way forward, past Ursio and Felix and onto the central gangway.

'We're going up against the trireme!' he called, in his battlefield voice, his words reaching Modestus at the prow. 'Those bastards killed your navarch – we're taking her and we're slaughtering every last man aboard her! Are you ready?'

'READY!' the shout came back at once.

Castus knelt beside the rowing master at the aft starboard bench. 'I'll need you to direct the other oarsmen,' he said, urgency grating in his voice.

'Can do, strategos,' the rowing master said through his teeth. Castus could see the ferocity in his eyes – all the men on the benches had the same look.

'What's your name?' he asked.

'Epigonus, strategos.'

'Call the strokes, Epigonus: you know the commands better than me. We go in hard and fast against their beam then storm them over the oar banks. I'll need some of your men to follow my marines. Understood?'

'No problem. We'll back oars then rush them. Just give the signal.'

He leaned back and yelled a command over his shoulder, and with a grunt of effort the oarsmen pushed at their oars, sending the galley back in the water and away from the trireme. Castus could see the helmsman holding tight to the steering oars, guiding them.

'Just one thing, strategos,' Epigonus called in a gruff shout as he pulled his oar. 'We need to get those bodies over the side. Custom of the sea.'

Castus nodded, gulping back his dismay. He glanced at Eumolpius's body, but Ursio was already there; one of the deckhands helped him, and within moments the bodies of the orderly and the navarch were gone.

'On my command,' Castus yelled. He could see Modestus at the bow, raising his hand, the artillery crew loading a new bolt onto the ballista slide, all the troops along the gangway with shields raised above them. The oarsmen braced on the benches, oars lifted from the water. All ready.

'Forward!'

The rowing master cried out the stroke, and the backwards drift of the galley halted suddenly and then reversed. A wave burst across the stern, washing the blood from the aft deck, then the narrow hull began gathering speed as the rhythm of the oarsmen's chant increased.

They were drawing closer to the *Krokodilos* once more now. The men on the trireme's deck had seen them, the archers leaning from the rail to shoot down at the approaching galley. Arrows spat into the water, and thudded into the deck planking. Castus saw one of the oarsmen shot through the shoulder, his oar trailing and clashing against the others until it slipped between the tholes. With effort, he took up the shield that Eumolpius had dropped. An awkward grip with the three fingers of his left hand, but he held it tight and lifted it above him. Arrows banged into the shield boards.

A snap from the deck of the trireme as the big stone-throwing catapult released. Castus heard the missile *whoosh* in the air near his head and strike the stern behind him. Then Epigonus gave another shout, the oarsmen bent forward and hauled, and the galley leaped forward in the water.

Javelins and slingshot from the enemy deck. The men on the gangway of the *Hippocampus* were returning the barrage.

Felix stood up, whirled his sling and cast: Castus saw one of the catapult crew knocked sideways as the shot hit him. A second stone, tripped too soon from the machine, spun up into the air. The *Krokodilos* still had all three banks of oars in the water, but as the galley charged for her side Castus could hear the shouts of command from the enclosed rowing deck. The upper bank began to slide inboard, too slowly.

'Brace yourselves!' the helmsman cried. The troops on the gangway were scrambling towards the stern, lifting the bows and the keel spur higher in the water. Castus just had time to fling himself down on his hands and knees before the *Hippocampus* collided with the oar bank of the big trireme. Timbers wailed, shafts shattered; screams of men crushed by their own oar handles or sliced by exploding wood came from inside the hull, and the long keel of the galley rode up over the remaining oars until her spur rammed into the grilles of the rowing deck. No mercy now.

The shock of impact pitched Castus forward. Every man on the gangway had fallen, but they had been ready for it. At once they began clambering up the slope of the deck. Some of the trireme's oars had lifted clear, and now they were swinging, thrashing at the attackers. One oar blade cracked a ballista crewman across the head and knocked him over the bows into the foaming water. But grapnels were flying, the ropes pulled taut. The bow officer had one of the heavy fire-pots lit, and whirled it above his head until flames burst from the smoke. He hurled it, and the earthenware pot shattered against the grilles of the rowing deck, spewing burning tow. Modestus was on his feet, storming up the ramp of the galley's bows and hurling himself across the gap at the enemy deck.

With a roar, the rest of the legionaries followed after him. The enemy troops on the trireme had been thrown off their feet by the impact too, and were slower recovering. Castus saw Modestus vault across the rail, slamming one of the archers aside with his shield. Two more men followed, then a third.

'Everyone forward!' he yelled. 'No quarter!' But his voice was lost in the maddened shouts of the storming party and the screams of the injured oarsmen aboard the trireme. 'Epigonus – first ten benches arm themselves and follow me,' Castus cried.

Then he was running, his boots skating on the tilted deck as he followed Felix and the last of the soldiers. Ursio and Ausenius, the staff tribune, were right behind him. Just for a moment, as he ran, he felt the black energy of his anger propelling him, warding him on all sides, as if some wrathful god shielded him. Then the deck lurched beneath him, and he saw the gulf of churning water and shattered oars right below his feet, and terror punched in his chest.

No time to delay; the rush carried him on. He grabbed for the galley's stem post, got his foot up on the sloping bow timbers and leaped. The gulf veered beneath him, water bursting up between the hulls, then he was down on the enemy deck. His shin caught the low deck rail and he toppled, managing to turn and come down on his back. His cuirass skated on the wet planking; he had dropped the shield but kept his grip on the sword.

'Having a rest?' Modestus shouted. His laugh sounded like a scream.

Castus rolled, got his legs beneath him. Blood slicked the deck; dead men sprawled across the slanting boards. Boots banged and grated around him, then he was up again, sword in hand, surrounded by his own troops.

The enemy marines were making a stand at the bow and stern, and between them the oarsmen were piling up the ladders from the rowing deck below. Smoke gusted from the hatches.

Modestus had his men formed into a wall; with a swing of his shield he drove the oarsmen down the ladders. 'Back into your holes!' he yelled, with another cracked laugh.

'Form on me,' Castus cried, snatching up a fallen spear in his left hand. Men were with him, he could not tell how many. Ursio and Ausenius flanked him. But he could see the knot of enemy marines standing fast around the helm of the trireme. Shields pressed to either side of him, and he bellowed as he broke into a run. An officer in a crested helmet scrambled up from the aft hatch, and Castus hacked down at him without breaking stride.

The group around the helm was falling back now. Only a few of the marines wore armour, padded linen corselets and helmets, and they had the look of recent recruits. They had no experience of battle at all; now they faced opponents in mail and scale, veteran soldiers of the Gallic legions, the toughest fighting men in the Roman Empire bearing down on them at the charge. Terror flayed at them, and they broke.

Castus lashed out with the spear in his left hand, and saw one of the marines dance away from him, skidding on the deck. He was still bellowing, a low roar of rage. With one blow he hacked through a spearshaft, then cut a man down with the backswing. The soldiers to either side of him pressed forward, stamping the deck, battering with their shields. Two enemy marines threw themselves overboard; a third dropped to his knees with arms raised, and died with two spears through his body.

'Smash the rudders,' Castus shouted. 'Disable the ship – throw fire down into the stern cabin.'

Some of the oarsmen who had followed him from the *Hippocampus* were already swinging axes, cutting through the tackles of the steering oars. Another stumbled aft with a fire-pot, and pitched it, smoking and spitting sparks, down the ladder.

Forward, smoke was boiling up from the rowing decks in a thick grey pall. The oarsmen trapped below had retreated to the bows, while many more had scrambled through the wrecked oar ports and into the water. Modestus and his men were finishing off the remaining marines and destroying the bow artillery.

'Excellency,' a voice cried, and Castus stared over the far side of the ship to see another of the galleys, the *Alkedo*, clinging on with grappling lines in a mess of shattered oars. Her commander, an optio of the Septimani, stood in the bow and shouted between cupped palms. 'We almost got aboard them!' the optio called. 'Looks like you were there first!'

Castus raised his fist in the air. He realised now why they had taken the trireme so swiftly; most of her marines had been concentrating on the attack from the opposite beam. 'Sheer off!' he yelled, grinning.

Smoke blew along the deck; Castus got a mouthful of it and coughed. He tasted blood, and spat red onto the deck – he must have bitten his tongue when he leaped aboard. Abruptly the godlike sense of invulnerability that had carried him into the attack was gone. Only a chilled haze of nausea and dread remained. His legs felt unsteady, and he staggered on the pitching deck. Blood ran along the planking and pooled along the rail. *Gods, what a slaughter...* But none of the dead seemed to be his own men – had they taken the ship with no casualties? Then he remembered Eumolpius and Dexippus.

The helmsmen of the *Hippocampus* had brought her up alongside, and as each wave lifted her the troops scrambled back across the rail and dropped down onto the smaller galley's deck. Castus remained aboard the crippled trireme a moment more, gazing over the stern; from this slight elevation he could see out across the water to the far shores of the straits. They were out in midstream now, and the current was bearing the swirling galley fight steadily westwards towards the Hellespont's mouth. As the smoke from the cabin eddied he saw a line of enemy ships, still in formation and cruising fast; beyond them, another mass of vessels locked in combat. *Artemisia* was among them: Crispus had taken his squadron into the battle.

'Back,' Castus shouted to the last men on the trireme, then jumped across the rail and landed on the *Hippocampus*'s stern deck with a crash that left him winded. Ursio came across after him, keeping his footing.

'Ausenius?' Castus gasped.

Ursio scowled, and drew a finger across his throat. So they had taken casualties after all... But already Epigonus and the other oarsmen were sheering off from the burning trireme, pushing oars against her hull and gaining the open water. Wreckage floated around them, corpses washing in the swell, injured men trying to cling to the oar-blades. As soon as the full complement of oarsmen were on the benches Epigonus called the stroke, and the galley turned into the chop of the current.

CHAPTER XV

The battle was still fierce all around them. The lowering sun was lighting the waves with gold and turning the drifting smoke into a glowing fog. Off to his left Castus saw a stricken vessel, another big trireme, half sunk with her hull underwater and only her listing upper deck above the surface, washed by waves and covered in men clinging to the waterlogged timbers. Nearby a triaconter had capsized, the pitch-dark keel rolling in the swells surrounded by broken oars and bobbing corpses.

'Do you have your bearings?' he called to the helmsman.

'More or less. Which direction?'

Castus was crouched on the deck, still feeling cold dread pouring through him. The day was dying, evening coming on; how long had the battle been raging? No way of knowing whether they were defeated or not. He heard warning shouts, and glanced windward to see a black-hulled liburnian galley bearing down on them with foaming ram; the rhythm of the oars picked up, the *Hippocampus* darting forward, and the liburnian crossed their wake, unable to check her speed. Immediately behind them, it rammed into the stern quarter of another enemy ship, with a crack of rending timber. The men on the oar benches cheered.

'Take us north if you can,' Castus called, and the helmsman gave his nod.

Another galley came up beside them, rowing hard. The *Alkedo*: Castus saw the optio of the Septimani still in command. Beyond them, across the waves, two of the Frankish boats were attacking a blue trireme with a Sphinx figurehead, the enemy marines packing the rails and trying to drive the barbarian warriors back and cut their grapnel lines.

A shout from the *Alkedo* caught his attention. The optio was gesturing wildly, pointing back behind him. Castus turned, and saw with a choke of dismay that the black liburnian that had just missed them had managed to turn and was coming up in pursuit of the *Hippocampus*.

Epigonus had seen it too, and already he was shouting at his men to row at full pressure. But it was a straight chase now, and Castus knew that the bigger ship with its powerful double oar banks could close the distance between them fast.

'I'll try and evade when they get close,' the helmsman said, his face bone-white. 'Best grip hard to something!'

The pursuing ship was eating their wake now, gathering speed as her oars thrashed at the waves. A couple of the soldiers threw javelins back over the stern, but her armoured bows appeared impregnable. At the last moment, the helmsman twisted the steering oars to one side, turning the light galley in a sharp evasive move. The deck heeled sharply – but the black liburnian had turned at the same moment.

Three suspended heartbeats, the rush of foam from the enemy ram driving spray up across the stern, and the bows of the warship came smashing through the starboard oar bank of the *Hippocampus*. Wood shattered, bursting splinters the size of daggers, then the liburnian's ram struck a grating blow against the bow.

Castus felt the shock through the timbers of the ship, and fell sprawling, fingers scratching for grip on the wet planks.

The raised oars of the liburnian glided past overhead, then the enemy ship was gone, leaving the battered *Hippocampus* rolling in the wash.

Raising his head, Castus stared along the deck. The starboard oars were all smashed, the benches a mess of blood, of dying and injured men. Epigonus was dead, and the bow quarter of the galley was crushed inwards and taking water fast. Glancing back, Castus saw the helmsman still at his post, his teeth bared in a terrified snarl. A moment of silence, then the screaming started.

'Merciful gods, merciful fucking gods,' somebody was saying. 'We're dead men now... Gods protect us!' It was Felix, hunched against the rail with another man's blood dripping from his face. Ursio grabbed him by the shoulders, silencing him and dragging him across to the gangway.

Modestus was herding his surviving men back from the bows. Water was already slopping between the benches. Breathing hard, Castus forced himself up onto his knees. He glanced around for the *Alkedo*, but the other galley was gone. Across the wilderness of water, the battle was still fierce around the Sphinx trireme.

'Get the oars across,' he shouted, but the words choked in his throat. He gagged, spat blood, his whole body shaking. 'Modestus! Oars across to the broken side! We need to get to that other ship while we're still afloat...'

Modestus stared at him for a moment, open-mouthed, his face red behind the nasal bar of his helmet. Then he understood, grabbing at the remaining men on the oar benches and directing them.

'Lighten ship!' somebody else was shouting. 'Get the bodies over the side, the ballista off the bow – heave the mast over too!'

'Can we make it?' Castus asked the helmsmen. The man appeared paralysed, speechless for a moment; then he managed to nod. 'Perhaps,' he croaked.

Already the hull was settling in the water, timbers groaning and popping, but Modestus had bullied the panicking men on the benches into swinging half the oars over to the damaged side. Taking their places in the swilling blood of their dead comrades, they began to row. The *Hippocampus* was a hulk now, her broken bow almost underwater; any enemy ship could crush her with ease, and at any moment her timbers could part and she could break up completely... But the pressure of the oars was driving her forward. Waves crested over her bow, spilling a flood along the gangway and washing beneath the benches.

Castus plucked at the buckles of his cuirass. He was drenched, and if the sea took him now the armour would drag him down. He let his hands fall. *The will of the gods would be done.* Better a quick plunge into the swirling blackness than hours of thrashing in the water waiting for death to find him.

Beneath his feet he could feel the ship's timbers straining and grinding, the copper nails and mortise pegs that held the hull together close to parting. Air was bubbling up through the cracks in the deck planking; the hull below must be totally waterlogged. The men at the oars were raising a ragged chant, driving the foundering galley onwards, but Castus could see the desperation in their faces. Most of the soldiers on the gangway had dropped shields and weapons and joined the men on the benches. The distance of choppy water separating them from the big trireme seemed immense.

All that I have to lose. Marcellina. His son. The life he had made for them; the life that could have been his... All of it thrown away for nothing, taken by the merciless waters. Remorse choked him, but he set his jaw. He was not dead yet.

'Row for your lives!' he yelled, balling his fists. 'Not far now – *row*!'

The swirling current drove a wave up behind the galley, lifting the stern, and for a few long moments the *Hippocampus* seemed alive again, propelled forward through the water. They could hear the noise of the fighting on the trireme now, the clash of arms and the screams of furious combat. Castus could see rivulets of blood coursing down the hull from the deck and the oar ports. One of the Frankish galleys was wallowing alongside the bigger ship, dead men on her benches, grappling lines still holding the two vessels together.

We could make it. The stern of the Frankish boat was swinging free, loose in the water. Behind Castus, the helmsman was leaning on the steering bars, guiding the galley with the last ebb of the wave in an arc towards the Frankish ship: close, but not close enough.

'Ursio, help me,' Castus cried, scrambling past the helmsman to the stern of the galley. The big Sarmatian joined him, and together they lifted the iron kedge anchor and its reel of cable from beneath the stern platform.

With a wrenching heave, Castus swung the anchor out from the stern, across the gap of water. Ursio grabbed the neck of his cuirass before he toppled overboard, and Castus steadied himself to see the anchor strike the stern planking of the abandoned galley. Together they pulled on the cable until the anchor flukes caught on the other ship's aft rail, then hauled the cable taut and began dragging the sinking *Hippocampus* up to the stern of the other vessel.

Already the men behind them were crowding back down the deck, eager to escape, the remaining soldiers scrambling up from the benches and snatching their shields and weapons from the gangway. Felix kept them back until the two hulls bumped together and Ursio leaped across into the other ship to secure the cable. Castus glanced at the helmsman: he was slumped onto the steering oar, blood soaking his legs, an arrow jutting from the base of his spine. He must have died even as he guided the ship towards safety.

Safety? Castus grinned mirthlessly. Already he could hear the cries of alarm from the deck above him, the crew of the trireme noticing the tide of men pouring across the makeshift bridge of lashed galleys. Ursio kept his grip on the cable, biceps bulging as he held the two hulls close enough for the men to jump the gap. One by one they scrambled across, some of the half-naked oarsmen leaping into the water to swim the distance. One soldier was shot by an arrow and tumbled over the side, his mail dragging him under at once. Felix grabbed a fallen javelin, leaned back and then threw. 'Time to abandon ship!' he said as he followed the last man across.

Another wave lifted the bow of the *Hippocampus*, then rolled up along the gangway. Ursio nodded, keeping his grip tight on the cable until Castus had hurled himself across onto the stern deck. Staggering, Castus got his feet beneath him. Modestus was already clambering forward over the benches of the abandoned galley, over the corpses lolling in the scuppers. The scarred, red-faced centurion stepped up onto the rail, then across onto the broken oars of the trireme. Hanging on the grilles of the enemy rowing deck, he raised his sword and bellowed at the remaining men of his century.

'The gods must love us, boys! Now *follow me*!'

Castus stared in amazement; he had half intended to use the abandoned galley to get clear of the fight. Now he heard the knot of legionaries and oarsmen give a hoarse shout as they rushed forward after Modestus. Survival had made them indomitable; now they were throwing themselves into the storm of battle without a care. Intense pride filled him, intense joy: they might be losing, but they would lose magnificently.

'Everyone forward!' he yelled, dragging his sword free. 'Ursio – with me!'

Arrows thudded into the deck and the rowing benches, but none found a target. Jumping from the rail, Castus seized the stub of a broken oar and hauled himself upwards. A spear jabbed out from an oar port; Castus grabbed the shaft, pulled it clear, then reversed his sword and drove it in through the port like a long dagger. Screams from inside the hull. A body fell from the deck above, dark for a moment against the sky.

The big trireme was rolling heavily in the swell, and the next wave broke over Castus's legs. For a moment he felt his age, the drowning weight of his armour, then Ursio scrambled up beside him and grabbed his belt. The hull rolled back onto the other beam, and Castus kicked his boots against the wet planking until he found a foothold and felt himself propelled upwards. His reaching hand found the rail, then with a last heave he was up onto the enemy deck.

Modestus had already driven the screen of defenders, archers and crewmen back single-handed. Now he was bellowing to his men as they clambered up after him, forming them into a wedge of shields. Few had spears or javelins, but all had swords drawn. Looking down the deck, Castus saw that they had boarded the trireme near the bows; no more than ten paces away, a line of enemy marines and archers formed a bulwark across the waist of the ship, but Modestus and his men had come up behind them. The enemy were facing the stern, where the remaining Frankish warriors held a position around the helm, hedged with shields and bristling with spears. Just for a moment, Castus saw Bonitus through the press of bodies.

He glanced at Modestus, who nodded back at him and grinned. Without a word, the centurion raised his sword, then brought it slashing down. His men hefted their shields and followed him as he charged into the rear of the enemy formation.

At the roar of boots on the deck behind them the enemy marines turned in panic. Modestus let out his battle cry, a wordless howl of killing fury. With a punch of his shield he knocked one marine back off the deck and over the rail; a wheeling slash opened the face of a second. It was six men against twenty, but the speed and surprise of the attack was overwhelming; the enemy line buckled, and the Franks cheered and surged forward in support.

Running in the wake of the charge, Castus came up behind Modestus just as the marines rallied. Oarsmen were piling from the open deck hatch now, armed with knives and hooked falxes, swelling the numbers of the enemy. The noise of studded boots drumming and scraping at the planking was deafening, drowning the howls of the injured, the clash of weapons on shields.

The deck beneath him was rolling wildly with the weight of men; he saw two oarsmen stagger sideways and tumble across the rail into the seething waves. The enemy line surged forward, and Modestus slipped as his heel skidded on a slick of blood. He fell heavily on his back, and at once a young marine dashed forward with a cry of triumph, raised his spear, and stabbed it down at the fallen centurion.

'Bastard! *No!*' Felix yelled, driving his sword into the marine. Modestus was bleeding heavily from the neck; two of the enemy oarsmen had seized his ankles and were trying to drag him back beneath the shields of their marines. With a cry of rage the legionaries pushed forwards; Felix knelt and grabbed Modestus around the shoulders. One of the oarsmen was stabbing at the fallen centurion's legs with a knife, denting his bronze greaves.

Castus ran three steps forward, planting his feet on the deck astride Modestus's body. He swung a blow at one of the oarsmen, then stabbed the man with the knife through the body. Someone crashed against him, and he dropped to one knee. His sword was stuck in the chest of the dead man. Felix was dragging Modestus's body clear, leaving a wash of bright blood. A shield rim cracked against Castus's helmet, then a falx came down on the shoulder of his cuirass. He felt the steel flick against his exposed neck.

Forcing himself upright, he heaved at the hilt of his sword, working it loose. A spear stabbed against his chest, denting his armour; he felt the shock of the blow through his ribs. Then his blade was free, bloody to the hilt, and he slashed it at the men opposing him. Ursio was beside him, cutting down men with methodical fury. Castus could hear Bonitus's Germanic war cry over the screams of combat.

For a moment the enemy hung back, but he could see they were preparing themselves for a last charge to drive the invaders off their deck. He snatched up a fallen shield, trying to hold it steady with his crippled hand. Ursio looked at him and gave a strange half-smile, a shrug. *We did well*, he seemed to say. *Now it ends.*

Something whipped across the deck at head height, and three of the enemy marines died in a spray of blood. Castus glanced to his right, and his heart swelled: there, across a narrowing gap of water, was the liburnian galley *Artemisia*, the ballistae and catapults on her deck aimed at the packed crowd of marines aboard the trireme. A second catapult snapped, and Castus dropped to one knee as the heavy bolt hurtled into the enemy ranks. It punched one marine through the belly, smashed the legs of a second. On the exposed deck there was no shelter, no cover from the incoming missiles; yelling with terror, the enemy troops were scrambling over the ship's side, throwing off their armour and leaping into the sea.

'Are we too late?' a voice yelled from the approaching galley. Saturninus was standing on the aft rail of the *Artemisia*. Castus could see the gore streaking the ship's sides, the arrows jutting from her hull and deck. He flicked a glance towards the helm of the flagship, then at the stern deck behind Saturninus, until with a grunt of relief he picked out Crispus. Alive, unharmed.

'Just in time,' he tried to shout, but the words caught in his throat. He noticed that the light had taken on a strange reddish tint, as if the air was suffused with blood. He blinked, and realised that the sun was setting. The deck of the trireme was streaming with gore, heaped with fallen men, the dead and the injured sprawled together and rolling with the motion of the ship. Bonitus strode forward from the stern, roaring a greeting as he clasped Castus around the shoulders.

'Six of their ships we've killed now!' he bellowed into Castus's ear. 'Are we winning or what?'

They had killed far more than that. But as Castus stared to the west into the glare of the sunset he saw the main division of the enemy fleet running clear, hoisting sail and steering for the southern shore. Nobody opposed them. Not a single ship attacked their open flank as they turned.

Theophilus had kept his squadron in the bay, out of the fight.

The *Artemisia* was close alongside, the deck crew throwing grappling lines across to the trireme. They would burn the captured ship and leave her to founder in the swells. Bonitus and his men were cheering, raising their spears in the ruddy light. But at the centre of the deck, Felix was kneeling over Modestus's body, tears pouring down his face, although his expression was a blank mask.

The red sun burned off Modestus's bronze scale cuirass and greaves, the gold torque he wore at his neck. Felix had pulled off the fallen man's helmet, exposing his face. With one glance

Castus could see that the centurion was dead. *I've known that man for decades.* An instant of remembrance: Modestus the drunk, the shirker, back at the old legion fortress of Eboracum. Modestus the hero, storming onto the enemy deck at the head of his men. *Fuck you, gods; I loved that ugly bastard...*

Castus knelt beside Felix, laying a bloodied hand on his shoulder. The optio nodded, gasped a long breath, then between them they lifted Modestus's body and carried it across to the flagship.

'Bastards,' Felix said, staring towards the distant anchorage of Eleus. 'Left us to die out here – *bastards*!'

Castus could only grunt in agreement. All this killing, all these slain, and they had won nothing. The battle had been a stalemate, and very close to a defeat.

In the last afterglow of sunset, the surviving galleys formed up around the flagship and began to row back towards the shelter of the bay, leaving the wrack of broken timbers, waterlogged or burning wrecks and floating bodies to be carried westwards by the current towards the open sea.

CHAPTER XVI

Darkness had fallen by the time Castus got ashore. Exhausted men were still dragging their battered ships in through the surf, and as he marched up through the camp above the beach Castus heard the groans and cries of the injured and dying from around the glowing fires. Ursio marched behind him, with Saturninus, Hierax and Bonitus. Crispus had remained on the beach, and Castus was glad of that. It would not do the Caesar good to witness what was about to happen.

Ordering aside the sentries around Theophilus's tent, Castus threw open the flap and shoved between the slave attendants. The prefect of the fleet was in his outer chamber, reclining on a couch in the lamplight, wearing an unbelted tunic and dictating a letter to his secretary. He sat up as Castus and the officers entered, setting his cup of wine down on a side table. The men confronting him were still dressed in their bloodstained battle armour. They reeked of sweat, smoke and salt water.

'Get out,' Castus said to the slaves and the secretary. 'All of you, out *now*.'

By the time the attendants had hurried out into the night Theophilus was on his feet, pulling his tunic straight. 'I'm glad to see you escaped the battle unscathed, excellency!' he said, trying to smile. 'Praise be to God. And the most blessed Caesar is unharmed too?'

'No thanks to you,' Castus growled. 'Why did you keep your squadron in the bay? Why did you refuse battle?'

Theophilus let his smile slip, and assumed an affronted air. 'The wind and tide were set far too strongly against us,' he declared. 'My larger ships could not have made headway – ask any of my captains! Besides, too many of the enemy vessels had slipped through your squadrons. We would have been badly mauled if we'd attacked...'

'Your Caesar was in the middle of that fight,' Castus said through clenched teeth. 'It was your clear duty to go to his aid. Why did you refuse to do your duty?'

'I know my duty!' the prefect said. His face was reddening, and he was struggling not to shudder.

'We lost thirty ships. My men fought like heroes out there, and nearly two thousand of them are dead now. Drowned, slain or burned. But we could have won – we could have beaten the enemy if you'd joined the fight. You did not, and now all those men died for nothing.'

He could hear the sound of his own voice, and his words seemed unnaturally calm. But the anger was thundering in his head, charging his body with a lust for violence. Modestus was dead. Eumolpius was dead. Dexippus too, and all those others whose names he would never know.

'Ask him if he's taken money from the enemy himself,' Saturninus hissed. 'Ask him if he's in the pay of Licinius now!'

'You dare to suggest that?' Theophilus said, outraged. 'My allegiances are clear. But you should ask *his excellency* here about treachery, about conspiracies!'

'What are you saying?' Castus felt the words grinding between his teeth.

'I learned of your conversation with the Caesar last night,' Theophilus said, with the smug flicker of a smile. 'The things you discussed regarding our Augustus, and the succession...'

Castus felt the blood rushing to his face, but his body was struck by an icy chill. For a few long heartbeats he could only stare at Theophilus, waves of revulsion, anger and fear coursing through him. He should back away, he should laugh at the man, deny his words...

Instead, with a jarring sense of dislocation, he heard his own roaring cry as he rushed forward. Before he could think, his big hands had seized the prefect by the throat and he was shoving the man back, bearing down on him with all his weight as Theophilus toppled back onto the couch.

Blackness filled his mind as Castus drove his thumbs into the man's windpipe, his fingers crushing the life from him. He was barely aware of the prefect trying to punch at his face and shoulders, trying to rip his hands away as he choked.

'*No*,' he heard, dimly, as if from a great distance. 'No, that's not the way!'

Two men had grabbed him, hauling him back from the body of the prefect. For a moment he fought against them too; his fist smashed back into somebody's face. Then the frenzy left him. Saturninus and Ursio had him by the shoulders, pinning his arms. Blood was flowing from Ursio's nose.

'Sorry,' Castus said, but the Sarmatian just shrugged.

Theophilus had fallen from the couch and was writhing on the floor, gasping for breath.

'You're dismissed from your command,' Castus told him, pulling himself away from the two officers.

'You don't have the authority!' Theophilus managed to croak.

'I have all the authority I need.'

Turning on his heel, Castus stalked out of the tent, the others following him. Outside, they walked in silence through the night camp. He was glad that nobody spoke; he was still too choked with anger to think clearly. All of them had heard Theophilus's accusation. As they neared the beach the officers left him and went to see to their own men. Only Ursio's constant watchful presence remained.

Castus realised that Felix had joined him, the wolfish optio materialising from the darkness. For a score of paces they walked in silence.

'I know you shouldn't blame people,' Felix said, his accent giving a snarl to his voice. 'But sometimes... you just got to blame people.'

Castus looked at him, sensing the unspoken question. A chill ran up his spine. He made a gesture, a shrug and a headshake, that he knew could mean anything. Felix nodded once, and was gone.

Too tired to think, worn down by battle, by rage, Castus stumbled back to his tent, threw off his armour and belts, then dropped onto his bedroll and fell asleep instantly with not a thought in his head.

They found Theophilus in his tent before dawn the next morning. The bruises from Castus's throttling still showed livid on his neck, but it was the four or five vicious knife wounds in his gut that had killed him. The prefect had made little effort to defend himself, it seemed, although he had managed to roll out of bed and die in a pool of blood on the matting floor.

'I've circulated the news already,' Saturninus told Castus as they walked along the beach. The sun was not yet up, and the sand was the colour of wet ash in the half-light, the air hazy with the smoke of cooking fires. 'The story will be that the distinguished Flavius Theophilus took his own life, in shame at failing to come to our aid during the battle. His command will devolve onto Septimius Hierax as acting prefect.'

'Sensible,' Castus said. He had slept badly, and still felt tired. But everyone around him looked worse.

'Although, of course,' Saturninus went on, speaking quietly from the side of his mouth, 'the prefect could hardly have stabbed himself to death! Strange though – he had guards all around his tent, and a slave sleeping in the outer chamber. Perhaps it was a ghost that killed him?'

'It wasn't me, if that's what you're thinking,' Castus said. 'I didn't order it either.' Not exactly, he thought. Although he had a good idea who had carried out the killing. A man with particular skills, a keen grudge, and nothing much to lose.

'Ah well. Plenty of unquiet ghosts in the camp last night, I reckon. Plenty of knives and daggers, too, and angry men to use them. Best think no more about it.'

'I'd say. We've got another battle to fight, after all.'

'What he said last night, when you spoke to him in his tent...'

'Forget it,' Castus said, a little too abruptly.

Saturninus stopped walking and turned to face him. 'That's twice you've asked me to forget things I've heard in your company,' he said. 'You're becoming very interesting, brother!' But he had a wry and knowing smile, and Castus just cuffed him on the shoulder and walked on.

The sun was almost up by the time he found Crispus, The young man was wandering alone through the camp, bareheaded, wrapped in a salt-stained cloak. He looked ragged, and far older than his years, his eyes ringed with dark smudges.

'You haven't slept?' Castus asked him.

'No, I couldn't...' Crispus said, his voice hoarse. 'I spent the night going around the camp, talking to the tent groups and the sentries. I was trying to encourage them, give them heart for today...'

'Good man,' Castus said. Then he remembered to whom he was talking. 'I mean, very wise, majesty!'

Crispus smiled, with a diffident shrug. A few of the men at the cooking fires saluted wearily as they passed, although most of them to Castus himself; the young Caesar was almost unrecognisable.

'I want to leave the wounded on the beach today, with a strong guard,' Crispus said. 'The men who bore the worst of it yesterday, too. We'll embark only the fresher troops.'

Castus grunted his agreement. He had already decided to order Felix to remain ashore. The optio had taken the loss of his friend badly; he could easily make some suicidal foray in the heat of battle. Besides, Castus owed him several favours.

'Another thing,' Crispus said, drawing himself up. 'I think we should make a formal sacrifice before we put out from shore. A purification of the whole fleet, in the traditional manner. I've read of these things... and I think it would help morale, if nothing else.'

'It would, Caesar,' Castus said, too surprised to say more.

An hour after sunrise, all the troops that were to go aboard the ships were assembled on the beach in formation, ready to embark. The slaves had built an altar of piled stones at the edge of the sea, where the incoming waves washed around it. As the horns sounded, soldiers of the Martenses and Septimani led the sacrificial beasts down from the camp. The only animals they had been able to find were a pair of skinny goats and a solitary bullock; Castus hoped that the gods would excuse the meagre offering. Once more Hierax officiated as priest, leading the chant and crying aloud to the sky as the *victimarii* despatched the animals and the blood jetted onto the sand.

Then, as the animals roasted in the fire and the men of the army took the sacrificial meat, a boat rowed out from the shore to circle the anchored fleet in the bay three times. Crispus stood upright in the bow, pouring libations of wine to Neptune the Saviour and the spirits of the four winds. The circuits complete, he threw the golden wine goblet and his own jewelled sword into the waves, costly offerings for a divine blessing.

It was well done. Correctly done, Castus thought, and he felt his spirits lifted and the angry turmoil in his mind stilled. As the Caesar returned to the beach and stepped ashore, the mass of assembled men raised their arms in salute, voices swelling to a massed shout of acclamation.

Two hours later, they were rowing out of the bay in battle formation, into the chop of the current once more. The north wind was still blowing strongly down the straits, and before they had cleared the headland the oarsmen were labouring on their benches. Castus was aboard the flagship, the big bireme galley *Virtus Augusta*. Beside him on the broad aft deck were Saturninus and Hierax, with Crispus seated between them on a folding stool. Despite the breeze, there was a close sticky feel to the air. But if the shade of Theophilus haunted any of the men aboard, they did not show it.

'Here they come, look,' Saturninus said, staring out across the dark blue waters of the straits.

The enemy fleet, unable to work their way back eastwards in the dark, had spent the night on the beaches and in the coves of the southern shore of the Hellespont. Now, as the Licinian ships put out from land, Castus saw how many they had lost in battle the day before. The morning sun showed wreckage all along the coasts, and rafts of debris still floated in mid channel, caught in the eddies. But wind and current were flowing between the two fleets now, favouring neither.

'Reckon they'll work up to the eastward, using the slack water and the whispers of counter-current,' Hierax said. 'We should try and make some way in the same direction. Shadow them up the straits, if we can.'

'Do it,' Crispus said. The young man had been looking unusually grave since conducting the sacrifices, as if he had attained a new level of maturity. Although, Castus thought, he might just be fighting down his fear. The ferocity of the sea battle the day before had marked him deeply.

As the sun climbed the sky and the heat grew, the two fleets moved slowly up the straits, keeping a mile or two of open water between them.

'Why don't they attack?' Crispus asked, frowning. 'It looks like they want to keep their distance.'

'Probably they're wondering where all our extra ships came from!' Saturninus replied with a smile. 'And why we didn't use them yesterday... Maybe they're scared we've got another few squadrons hidden away?'

'They'll make their move soon enough,' Hierax said. 'Once they've worked their way back up to the east they'll swing around and use the current against us.'

Castus caught the slight hesitation in the navarch's voice; he glanced at the man, and saw Hierax studying the sky with his characteristic look of disapproval. Whatever was bothering him, clearly he would say little more for the time being.

Pacing forward, rolling with the motion of the ship, Castus moved between the soldiers seated on the deck, keeping his eyes on the distant enemy fleet. At the bow, he stepped up onto the low platform behind the cathead and studied the motion of the sea. Behind him, the forward ballista crews were checking their machines, oiling the slides and tightening the torsion drums. Bundles of iron-tipped bolts were stacked along the bulwarks on both sides. The ship thumped slowly forward against the sea, oars beating.

'You feel that, dominus?' one of the ballista crewmen said.

Castus glanced back with a questioning grunt. The man was standing in the middle of the deck, head raised. For a few moments Castus could feel nothing; then it came to him. The pressure of the air had changed, the steady whine and tug of the wind falling away. When he glanced out over the sea once more, Castus saw the waves growing smoother, the whitecaps vanishing.

The wind that had tormented them for over ten days had dropped at last.

As the men on the rowing benches felt the change, they let out a roaring cheer that was echoed by all the other ships in the fleet. Castus paced quickly back aft, feeling the ship already gathering speed across the calm sea, the pitching motion of the deck steadying.

Crispus was on his feet, grinning with anticipation. 'The gods have answered us!' he cried, his face alight. 'Now the odds are evened, I'd say. We should go to battle stations immediately!'

The centurion and the two staff tribunes were already calling the orders, the troops on deck shrugging mail shirts over their linen vests, pulling on their helmets. But Hierax was still looking troubled.

'I wouldn't do anything too promptly, majesty,' he said, peering hard to the west. Crispus gave him a scornful glance.

'When a strong wind drops this quick,' the navarch went on, 'it usually means she's veering round. We could get a powerful south-westerly blowing up the straits in no time.'

'All the better!' Crispus said. 'We'll bear up on them with the wind behind us...'

Hierax shook his head. 'You don't want to go driving a fleet into a narrowing strait with a strong wind under your stern.'

Crispus let out a cry of exasperation. He looked at Castus and then Saturninus; neither made a response. Hierax had known the sea and its moods all his life, and this was not a time to contradict his guesses.

But the enemy were forming up now, their ships assembling in a crescent stretching out from the south shore. They were closer, too, the current moving them back westwards. Castus could pick out the men on the decks of the big triremes, the glint of weapons in the noon sunlight.

Another hour passed, the two fleets confronting each other in the still air, only the steady rush of the current beneath the keels moving the decks. The heat was intense, sun burning back off the water, and the troops were suffering in their armour. Then Castus felt the stir of breeze at his back. Out in mid channel, the first whitecaps were appearing; the wind had veered, just as Hierax had said. Now it was beginning to blow up the straits, beating against the oncoming current.

Crispus was pacing, hands locked at the small of his back, obviously chafing at the delay. But the wind was gathering force quickly; the enemy fleet had moved further eastwards, pushed back into the narrows.

'Might I suggest, majesty,' Hierax said, 'that we anchor in mid channel? There's a gale coming on, and we don't want to be anywhere close to land when it hits us.'

The young man nodded, then retreated to the shelter of the awning under the stern. Signals were flashing from ship to ship, the nearer vessels trailing their oars to hold position as the crew readied the anchors. Waves slapped at the stern of the *Virtus Augusta*, and the deck began to pitch and roll in the choppy sea.

With terrifying speed the wind gathered force. Castus staggered as he crossed to the weather rail, reaching out for handholds. The dark surface of the sea was streaked with white, and the sky had taken on a dirty yellow cast. In the distance, the enemy fleet was scattering, the gale shredding their formation.

But now the anchors were down, the ships turning their prows to the west, oarsmen still pulling hard into the wind-driven waves to hold their positions as the blown spray lashed along the hulls. Most of the soldiers were lying on deck, huddled beneath their shields as the wind roared around them.

All through the afternoon the gale increased, and the fleet rode at anchor in the boiling sea. The enemy ships were hull-down on the far horizon, and the spray in the air made the nearer shore appear misty and insubstantial. Castus sat behind the helmsman's position, his cloak pulled around him, trying to ignore the ghastly retching noises coming from beneath the stern awning. There were plenty of other sick men aboard.

Whenever a bigger wave struck, white water burst above the level of the deck rail. A couple of times, wild cries of distress carried across the water. Some of the smaller ships had dragged their anchors and been swept away; others had collided in the thrashing waves. The fear was there inside him, Castus knew, but he felt numbed to it now. Only survival mattered.

He barely noticed the dusk. At least in the darkness he could no longer see the awful raging water all around the ship. But still he could hear the anguished cries from below deck, the wailing of the timbers as the ship laboured. He closed his eyes and tried to sleep, but at once he imagined that the deck was tilting beneath him, the whole vessel capsizing as a monstrous wave loomed over her beam, and he snapped back awake. Gritting his teeth, he tugged the cloak tighter around him and waited.

'Excellency? Dominus?' A hand was shaking his shoulder. Castus woke with a grunt, struggling to sit. He was lying sprawled in the scuppers with his wet cloak bunched around his neck. When he freed himself he saw the grey light all around him. The slave who had woken him had breakfast: a flask of vinegar wine and a hunk of bread.

'The storm?' Castus said.

'The gale blew itself out three hours ago, dominus,' the slave said. 'You slept through it.'

Stumbling to his feet, gripping the rail, Castus gazed around himself. The sea was still white all across the straits, but the wind had slackened to a gentle breeze and the waves no longer broke. Hierax and Saturninus were sitting before the stern shelter, regarding his confusion with wry smiles. Castus took his breakfast and stumbled across to join them.

'How many ships did we lose?' Castus demanded.

'Seven,' Hierax replied. 'Although we rescued the men from two, and two more might have got ashore in the night. The enemy's gone though.'

Sure enough, the eastern horizon was empty. Castus drank wine, and tore off a chunk of bread with his teeth. He felt starved.

Crispus joined them from the stern shelter, still looking queasy. 'We should move up eastwards if we can,' he said, then coughed and spat across the rail. 'Try and find the enemy while they're disordered.'

'For once I agree,' Hierax told him.

The sun was above the horizon by the time the fleet had lifted their anchors and assembled, and the swell was calming. With the breeze behind them they moved slowly up the straits, pulling against the current. Only a couple of miles on, the first wrecked ships appeared.

'Dragged her anchors and capsized,' Hierax said as they passed the floating hull of a trireme. The next wreck was a waterlogged hulk, men still clinging to the upper deck. They waved and cried for rescue, but the fleet rowed steadily past them. And by the time the narrows came into view, the scale of the disaster was plain for all to see.

'Merciful gods,' Saturninus whispered. 'I give thanks we were spared that.'

The rocky shores were covered with wreckage. Broken hulls washed in the shallows, shattered oars and the bodies of men swirling around them. Most of the enemy fleet looked as though it had been driven ashore by the gale. Crispus's fleet coasted through the devastation, every man on deck gazing at the scene in an awed silence.

'They had two hundred ships,' Crispus said quietly. 'How many remain, I wonder?'

'A handful at best,' Hierax told him. 'Not enough to stand against us. I give you congratulations on your victory, Caesar!'

Some victory, Castus thought. It did not feel that way, not now. But it would, soon enough. The Hellespont was open, the passage to Byzantium was clear, and their fleet was intact. They had prevailed. And once the chilling wonder of their survival had passed, they would be celebrating like heroes.

CHAPTER XVII

The city of Byzantium stood at the tip of a tongue of land jutting eastwards into the dark waters of the Bosphorus. It was an old city, a Greek city, and over a century ago it had fallen to the Emperor Severus, who razed it to the ground and then rebuilt it anew. Now another Roman army from the west laid siege to its defences.

West of the regular tent lines of Constantine's bodyguard troops and the legion detachments, the land was stripped bare, every scrap of wood hacked down to build the siege mounds and palisades. Castus had seen Byzantium once before, many years ago, and remembered a green countryside of orchards and villages to the west of it; now there was only a dusty brown wasteland. The aqueduct to the city had been cut, and its stream diverted to the army camp, but Castus knew that there were deep cisterns of fresh water beneath the citadel. With the fleet controlling the Bosphorus, the city was encircled on all sides, but if the walls were not breached, the defenders could hold out a lot longer yet. Diogenes had told him that Byzantium had resisted the Emperor Severus for nearly two years.

Now, after twenty days of siege, the city's landward defences still looked strong: a solid wall of pale grey limestone banded with brick, with a multitude of towers, the ramparts bristling with artillery. But in front of the wall eight vast mounds had risen to almost half its height, packed mud revetted with wood and crested with palisades; on top of them were emplacements for the catapults and archers. The besieging artillery had kept up a steady bombardment, smashing the ramparts in places and pitting the stone facing of the wall.

Constantine had launched his first assault against the city only three days before Castus arrived with Crispus and the fleet. It had been a disaster: the wreckage of broken and part-burned scaling ladders and rams still lay tumbled at the foot of the wall, flocks of black ravens and vultures feasting on the bodies that littered the ground within range of the defenders' arrows.

'It was slaughter, brother,' Gratianus said. 'Sheer bloody slaughter. I'd never been in a storming party before, but we didn't stand a chance. That wall's unbreakable.'

Castus nodded, mumbling his agreement. With the young tribune of the Moesiaci at his side he was making a tour of the siege lines, picking his way along the dirt path that snaked between the palisade walls and the trenches. On all sides were men and weapons, stacks of arrows and javelins and catapult ammunition. Some of the troops looked up as Castus and his party passed; some grinned, and raised their hands in salute. But if they hoped that his appearance among them was a good sign, they hoped in vain.

Losses in the failed assault had been severe. Gratianus himself had his right arm in a sling, and Varro, the commander of Legion VI Herculia, had dark bruises across his temple where a falling rock had almost smashed his skull. Unlike the other officers, Castus had seen cities and fortresses under assault before. At Segusio they had taken the walls in a single rush, but at Massilia he had watched Constantine's men thrown back. This attack was a far greater challenge, and Castus knew how much was at stake; Licinius had been defeated in every battle,

233

but if they failed to take Byzantium he would retain a toehold on the European shore.

Pausing to let his staff officers catch up, Castus leaned on one of the big wicker baskets, filled with rubble, that formed the bulwark of a catapult emplacement. He stared at the city wall, then down at the wreckage in no man's land. In the midsummer heat the bodies of the fallen were already swollen and blackened.

The enemy emperor himself had fled the city as soon as he got word of the destruction of his fleet in the Hellespont. Now Licinius was on the far side of Bosphorus, at Chalcedon, gathering a new army. Constantine needed to take Byzantium soon, before the numbers of the enemy grew too great.

'We'll try again, you think?' Varro asked, with a gloomy resignation. 'Maybe from the sea? Walls are weaker there...'

'Maybe,' Castus said, without enthusiasm. He had surveyed the seaward defences of Byzantium only the day before, rowing around the headland with Hierax in the *Artemisia*. Sure enough, the walls were neither as strong nor as tall, but they stood on rocky bluffs directly above the sea; attacking them would involve bringing ships right up to the rocks and somehow raising towers or ladders from the decks.

'It's maddening,' Gratianus said, scratching at his bandaged arm. 'We beat them at Adrianople! Hooked around their flank and smashed them. And you – you destroyed their fleet in the Hellespont, a magnificent victory! But now here we are, trapped, while Licinius sits over there in Chalcedon gathering his troops once more...'

'He has Goths, I hear,' Varro added. 'Some prince from across the Danube's brought him twenty or thirty thousand warriors! More than twice the number holding out against us here. His name's Alica, something like that.'

Castus had heard that rumour as well. Constantine had an excellent intelligence network, with deserters coming in daily, but it did no good.

The victory in the Hellespont seemed long ago now. When the fleet arrived at Byzantium, after a fast voyage of only four days up the straits and across the Propontis, Crispus had been greeted by his father as a conqueror. The fact that the weather, and not a naval battle, had finally defeated Licinius's squadrons was brushed aside – the wind had been sent by God, Constantine had declared, in answer to all their prayers. There had been one other brief galley fight, against Licinius's reserve ships in the narrows off Callipolis, and that was enough to claim the victory. Now, they had believed, with Crispus's fleet dominating the Bosphorus the resolve of the enemy would surely crumble quickly.

But instead, there was only the slow grinding attrition of the siege. And both sides were being worn down equally. Disease stalked the dusty camps of Constantine's men, and in the midsummer heat the plague of flies and mosquitoes preyed on the nerves.

'Why do we need to take the city?' Castus asked in a musing tone, almost to himself. The two younger officers peered at him, bemused.

'I mean,' Castus went on, flustered, thinking as he spoke, 'if Licinius only has ten thousand men holding it… they can't break out or evacuate with our fleet in the Bosphorus. Why not leave them there? Keep a small force here to guard them and cross over with the rest of the army to fight Licinius on the Asian side of the straits, before he can gather more troops.'

Gratianus raised his eyebrows. 'But the eastern shore's heavily guarded,' he said. 'A landing there would be difficult…'

'So we move up the straits. There must be places towards the Euxine where we could cross. Even if we land on the sea coast. You said the emperor did this at Adrianople? He crossed the Hebrus upstream and outflanked the enemy position. This is the same. What's the Bosphorus but a bigger sort of river?'

Gratianus laughed, but Castus could tell that he liked the plan.

'If you'll permit me, domini,' Diogenes broke in. The secretary was following behind the officers, carrying a stack of tablets. Castus frowned, then nodded.

'I took the liberty of preparing a sketch plan of the Bosphorus,' Diogenes said. 'In case the fleet needed to operate in the northern reaches. I have it back at the camp – it's fully annotated with anything I could draw from ancient sources and the reports of our sea captains.'

'Hmm,' Castus said. He was still peering at the city wall. Gratianus and Varro waited with expectant expressions.

'Perhaps you should tell the Augustus of this scheme?' Gratianus said.

Castus shrugged. 'He wouldn't listen to me.'

'Then tell Crispus. He'd listen. Not to any of us, for sure – but to *you*, he would. He respects your advice, brother, all know it. Anything's better than sitting around like this, dying in the heat.'

The other officer was nodding as well.

'Give me some time,' Castus said, hesitant. If he was going to present the idea to the emperors, he needed to be sure it would work. But he already knew he would do it. The only question was how the stratagem might be carried out.

Back in Castus's campaign tent an hour later, Diogenes found the plan he had prepared. Castus unrolled it with one hand, holding it flat on the boards of the table. He had established his headquarters at the camp of the naval troops, near the

Propontis shore where the galleys were drawn up; the cooler air from the sea was a blessing after the heat of the siege lines.

'I would suggest,' Diogenes said, 'that the place marked as Kalos Agros would be suitable for the embarkation of a force of the size you're suggesting.'

Castus sat for a long time peering at the map, tracing the lines with a thick finger. The transports that had arrived with the fleet were too few to carry all the troops required, and of too deep a draught to land on a hostile shore. Galleys could do it, but there were too few of them. He tapped at the place on the map marked Kalos Agros. *Wooded valley, above deep bay. Good water supply.* It lay about ten miles up the straits, opposite a headland marked *Hieron – Sacred Promontory.* The Asian shore there was steep and heavily forested. Nobody would expect a landing, and it would be madness to attempt one. Further north, though – Castus traced his finger around the jagged line of the coast – there was a beach on the Euxine shore, where the river Rhebas met the sea…

Castus lifted his hand, and the map curled back into a tight roll. Diogenes was studiously appearing disinterested.

'You had this idea a while ago, am I right?' Castus asked with a slow smile.

'It did occur to me a few days ago, yes,' the secretary said. 'I've prepared a few notes, if you're interested. I considered a fleet of landing rafts, built at Kalos Agros, to carry the troops across the straits. Quite an amount of work, perhaps…'

But better than doing nothing, Castus knew. He was glad of the secretary's interest. Since Eumolpius's death Diogenes had seemed morose and withdrawn, given to sighing heavily and gazing into the middle distance. Castus almost suspected that there may have been some sexual connection between the two men; such things were not unknown in the army, and

Diogenes had certainly never appeared interested in women. But could he really not have noticed it, if so?

At least his new orderly, a jug-eared Greek youth named Glycon, seemed unlikely to kindle anyone's desires. He was able enough, if dull-witted and often clumsy. Castus missed Eumolpius's attentive efficiency more every day.

As if summoned by the thought, Glycon appeared at the tent doorway, still holding one of Castus's greaves, which he had been polishing. 'Dominus,' the orderly said. 'A soldier here for you – Felix?'

'Show him in.'

Felix, too, had been suffering from the loss of his friend. He stood silently before Castus, not looking anywhere.

'As you know,' Castus said, in a curt tone that hid his feelings, 'the Second Britannica is to be broken up. The legion took heavy losses at the Hellespont. The remaining men will reinforce other units of the field army, while a cadre of centurions and veterans will be sent back to Gaul to recruit a new legion under the old name.'

Felix nodded very slightly, impassive, showing no expression. He would have heard the news already.

'With the loss of Centurion Modestus, there's a vacancy in the command ranks. I intend to promote you to centurion in his place. Either you can return to Gaul as an *ordinarius* in the new legion, or join my staff as supernumerary. I leave the choice up to you.'

Felix twisted his lips, pondering, although Castus could see by the steadiness of his gaze that the decision had been made as soon as he spoke the words.

'I've been with the old legion twelve years, dominus,' Felix said in his gnarled accent. 'It's like my home now. My family. But it's not the same with Modestus gone, and a lot of other old faces too. Not sure if I'd be much good at staff jobs, though.'

'I'm sure we'd find some uses for you,' Castus said with a brisk nod. He noticed a glance pass between Diogenes and Felix. They were old comrades too, he remembered.

'Be glad of it then,' Felix said. 'Excellency,' he added.

'Just one question,' Castus said. 'I wanted to ask before… The prefect, back at Eleus. How did you get into his tent that night?'

'Don't know what you mean, excellency,' Felix said, stone-faced.

Castus snorted a laugh. 'All right. Let's say *somebody* did – how would this *person* get into his tent?'

Felix paused a while, pretending to think it over. 'Well,' he said. 'Perhaps they could turn themselves into an insect and fly through the air. Excellency.'

Castus blinked slowly, then grinned. 'Fair enough,' he said. 'I should never have asked.'

And Felix gave a slight twitch of a smile in return, as if acknowledging a compliment.

'The Most Sacred Augustus is in the tabernacle,' the old priest declared. 'And the most blessed Caesar is with him.'

'In the what?' Castus asked. He had never heard the word before.

'The *tabernacle*,' the priest repeated, with emphasis. He smiled; Castus knew the man – Hosius, Bishop of Corduba. He had been following Constantine's court around for over a decade, but still appeared full of stern vitality, for all his white hair. 'The tabernacle,' he explained, 'is a tent of prayer and spiritual communion, erected outside the camp as the Holy Scriptures tell us was done by the Ancient Prophet himself. The cloud of God's power descends to earth there.'

'Really?' Castus said. He could see no cloud in the hot blue sky. Only the ever-present haze of dust that hung in a low fog over the main camp of Constantine's army. 'I'll wait then,' he said.

It was midday, and the area around the imperial enclosure was unusually quiet and almost deserted. Castus felt troubled as he made his way to the smaller enclosure of the Caesar's tents, with Ursio pacing silently behind him. He had seen very little of Crispus since their arrival before Byzantium; the young Caesar had spent much of his time with his father, and in the vast network of camps and siege entrenchments there had been few opportunities to meet. But the thought of speaking to him now, outlining the plan that he and Diogenes had devised, made Castus strangely apprehensive. The news about the tabernacle did not ease his mind.

Had Crispus forgotten the pledge he had made, before the Hellespont battle, to return to the old gods? Had he perhaps forgotten Castus's vow to support him in his bid for power? Now that he was back in the presence of the Augustus and the imperial court, Castus was coming to regret his words. It seemed a rash thing to suggest, and possibly dangerous. He had staked so much of his reputation, even his life, on the capricious ambitions of a very young man. But perhaps, Castus thought, the Caesar was only biding his time? Perhaps trying to win his father over to his way of thinking? The prospect made Castus shudder. There was no way, he knew, that the emperor would agree to hand over power to his son. Not without a fight. And where would his own allegiances lie then?

In the outer chamber of Crispus's pavilion, slaves brought a stool and snow-chilled water. Castus had no idea where they had found the snow in this season on the shores of the Propontis, but the refreshment was more than welcome. He sat in silence,

Ursio standing behind him with his thumbs hooked in his belt. Half an hour passed, then a little more, before Castus heard the sound of trumpets, the running feet and cries of acclamation, and guessed the emperors had returned to the camp. It occurred to him that he could just leave now; Crispus would never know that he had come here on this errand, which was already beginning to feel foolish.

But then Crispus was there, sweeping into the tent and hurling his purple cloak at one of the slaves. 'Castus!' he said, surprised and perhaps a little annoyed to find he had company.

Castus stood up quickly, then knelt and raised his hand in salute. By the time he was on his feet again Crispus had paced across the tent and dropped down onto a couch. Castus remained standing. Already he could see that the young man was uncomfortable, aggravated.

'Well?' Crispus said. 'What brings you here? It's been days since I last saw you.'

'It's about the progress of the siege, majesty,' he said. 'I've been discussing it with a number of other officers, and we thought you should hear what we considered.'

'Did you?' Crispus said without warmth. 'So you've devised some plan, eh? Some stratagem?'

'It was my secretary Diogenes who came up with the idea, majesty.'

'Oh yes, that clever old man of yours. What's he discovered in his books now? Are we to emulate the battle plans of the deified Julius, or perhaps Alexander the Great? Well, sit down and tell me.'

Castus bit back his reply. He had seen this mood of petulant sarcasm in Crispus before, but never expressed with this amount of bitterness. He pulled up a stool, took a long breath. *Say what you need to say, then get out.*

Forcing himself to speak calmly, he laid out the plan. He continued speaking even when Crispus gave no impression of comprehending, even of listening. Every few moments the young Caesar's expression would clear, as if some detail had penetrated his mind, then he was frowning and sullen again.

'We think it could work,' Castus concluded. 'Cross the Bosphorus and outflank the enemy with a landing on the Asian shore, take the war to him.'

Crispus sat pondering, his mouth sourly pursed. 'We don't have the ships to carry an army of that size,' he said at last, spreading his palms. 'And if we did, they're of too deep a draught for that sort of work.'

'So we build rafts, or barges. There's plenty of timber in the valley of Kalos Agros, and a voyage from there up the straits to the Euxine shore would only take a few hours, with the galleys towing the troop transports.'

'No, no,' Crispus said, shaking his head. He gave a weary shrug. 'It's impossible. My father is intent on taking Byzantium – he's ordered another assault, ten days from now; the orders are already going out to build new rams and mobile siege towers. Almighty God, you see, has told him in a dream that the city will fall. And so – *it will fall.*'

With a jolt of sudden awareness, Castus realised that the young man must already have made a similar suggestion to Constantine, and been refused. And what more had they discussed? In the tabernacle, no doubt – where else could they converse in private?

'Majesty,' he said in a low voice, leaning closer. 'You remember what we talked about, before the Hellespont battle? Have you spoken to the Augustus about it already?'

The slightest nod from Crispus, and Castus's feeling of apprehension turned to dread. *The fool – the reckless fool.*

Of course Constantine had refused to consider abdication. Of course the suggestion of it had angered him. *It was too soon.*

'How much did you tell him?' he asked, the taste of ash in his mouth.

Crispus flicked a worried glance at Ursio, and Castus nodded. The big Sarmatian could be trusted.

'I merely raised the issue,' Crispus said. 'Don't worry, I mentioned no names, no *conspirators*... But that's why this plan of yours is impossible. If my father suspected that his officers had been discussing things behind his back, questioning his strategy... a *cabal* of soldiers, with some connection to me. It would be... unwise.'

'I see that,' Castus said quietly. He felt the prickle of cold sweat on his brow.

It took only a day for his premonition of danger to be realised. Castus was making his way back through the naval camp after surveying the ships dragged up on the shore, and as he approached his own tents he saw the four horses tethered beside the dusty roadway, two of the riders standing with them, unfamiliar men in dark cloaks who regarded him warily. The other two riders were already waiting for him in the bright sunlight before his command tent. One of them wore a broad-brimmed straw hat, the other was bare-headed, his balding scalp red with burn. Castus recognised them both at once.

'Excellency,' Diogenes said as he moved towards the tent. 'These two officers of the agentes in rebus wish to speak with you.' He gave a wry sniff; clearly he too remembered the evening in Athens, back in the spring, when they had last encountered these men.

Castus paused, his jaw set, then gestured to Glycon to bring stools out into the sun. Flavius Innocentius and his associate must have been waiting for some time already in the heat, but he would not allow them the luxury of shade.

The orderly set out the stools, and Castus sat and nodded for his visitors to do likewise. Innocentius peeled off his hat, fanned himself with it for a moment, a smirk flickering across his face, then shrugged and sat down. The sunburnt man, Gracilis, remained standing.

'Well, what do you want?' Castus asked brusquely.

'Merely a few moments of your busy day,' Innocentius said. He placed the hat across his knees. 'I understand you were one of the last men to see the distinguished Flavius Theophilus before his untimely end. What can you tell me of his death?'

'He stabbed himself. Everyone knows that.' Felix was standing by the tent to his right, and Castus forced himself not to glance in his direction.

'Stabbed himself,' the agent repeated. 'What became of his body?'

'I put all the bodies of those slain in the battle aboard captured ships, towed them out to sea and burned them. The ground was too hard to dig graves, and the bodies were already swelling in the heat. Doubtless Theophilus went with them.'

'A sad end for a *vir perfectissimus*,' Innocentius said, 'a man selected by the emperor himself.' His smirking attitude was probing at Castus's nerves. 'How easy is it, would you say, to stab yourself repeatedly in the belly?'

'Want to find out?' Castus asked. He motioned to Ursio, and the Sarmatian took three steps forward, sweeping out his sword and levelling it at the agent's body. 'Just fall forward.'

Innocentius did not flinch, and his smile did not slip. Ursio stepped away and sheathed his sword. 'I believe his excellency is trying to intimidate us, Gracilis,' the agent said to the balding

244

man behind him. Gracilis said nothing. 'Perhaps he wishes he could strike us down, as he strikes his enemies in battle? Well, there are those who say that Theophilus was a traitor, and had a hand in the blaze at Thessalonica. Perhaps he killed himself from shame?'

'What would you know of shame, torturer?' Castus said. 'Believe it if you like. I'm just a soldier, I don't concern myself with these things.'

'Ah yes, a soldier. And a good one! The emperor thinks most highly of you. But it's odd, Aurelius Castus, how often your name is connected with certain strange and… *unmilitary* events.'

Castus sat still, trying not to frown. The sun was hot on the back of his head, but it was glaring into the eyes of Innocentius and his associate.

'Are you certain we wouldn't like to move into the shade of your tent?' the agent asked. 'Some things are better discussed in private.'

'I have nothing to hide from my men,' Castus told him.

'Very well,' Innocentius said. 'Earlier this year, you were present at a mansio in Dardania, when a possible attempt was made on the life of the Caesar Crispus.'

'It was nothing!' Castus declared. 'Plenty were there and saw it. He was in no danger.'

'Perhaps he was not. But somebody came to your room shortly before the event, I think? And a woman slept in your bed that night. Perhaps the same woman?'

Castus clenched his jaw. He was sweating, and he could feel the colour rise in his face. Obviously the agent had questioned the mansio superintendent and the slaves. 'What business of that of yours?' he asked.

'Anything that pertains to the security of the state is my business,' Innocentius replied. 'I am a seeker of truth, as I told your friend the nobilissima femina Fausta not long ago. Do you deny that she came to your chamber?'

Castus could sense the discomfort of the men around him. They were trying not to look at him. There was a knot in his throat, and he coughed to clear it. 'Yes, I deny it,' he said. He drew himself upright on the stool.

'Ah, then perhaps my source was mistaken. Slaves have been known to lie. But doubtless the truth will emerge in time, with a little prompting.'

Innocentius stood up quickly, swatted the hat against his leg and tugged it back over his head. 'I think we have nothing more to learn here today, Gracilis,' he said. He gave a slight bow towards Castus, then paced back towards his waiting horse.

Castus exhaled, feeling the burn on the back of his neck. Ursio and Felix were watching the agents ride away, hands on the hilts of their swords. *A seeker of truth*, Castus thought. *And may the gods forbid he ever finds it.*

From a dusty brown hilltop half a mile to the west of the city walls, the group of officers squinted into the morning sun. To their left, ringed by guards, the Emperor Constantine and his son Crispus sat beneath a white canopy, surveying the preparations for the second assault on the defences of Byzantium.

A stir went through the assembled men; Constantine had stood up and paced forward into the sunlight. His gilded cuirass and gold-embroidered cape blazed. He gestured, and a moment later the trumpets rang out. Castus heard a multitude of horns echoing the signal.

'Let the games begin!' Saturninus said with a grim smile.

Dust eddied up from the plain as the troops began to advance towards the wall. At the head of each column, gangs of slaves heaved forward a hulking war engine: battering rams in hide-covered wheeled sheds, and tall creaking assault towers. From the mounds, and from the plain behind them, the artillery had begun its barrage. Castus saw the huge arms of the catapults slamming upwards, the slings lobbing boulders at the defences. Peering into the dusty glare of sunlight, he made out the ballista crews on top of the mounds spanning their machines, shooting, reloading. The noise rolled back across the plain to the camp: a steady percussive thud and crack, cut through with trumpet calls.

Saturninus let out a cry, sucking air between his teeth, and Castus saw that one of the ballista emplacements opposite the Thracian Gate had been struck by a stone from an enemy catapult. The dust cloud was filled with falling splinters. Castus could imagine all too well what was happening down there in the sun-shot haze: the volleys of stinging arrows, the screams of the injured and dying. But from the vantage point of the camp, the details were lost in the distance.

'Part of me wishes I was down there with them,' Saturninus said. 'The other part thanks the gods I'm not!'

Castus grunted his agreement. This attack was unnecessary, he knew; if the emperors had followed his advice, they could have outflanked the city entirely. But the pride of the Augustus would not be challenged, and so men must die in the choking dust and the parching heat. Peering closely at the advancing columns, Castus tried to pick out the unit standards. Nearest the Thracian Gate he saw the Moesiaci, with the Tenth Gemina behind them. To their left were the Divitenses, with Bonitus's Salian Franks in support. The dark shapes of the war engines ground slowly and steadily forward, into the barrage of missiles from the wall.

Gritting his teeth, Castus willed the advancing men onwards. The dust was so thick that he could see little of what was happening now. Only the tops of the siege towers showed clearly, each one fifty feet high and covered with damp hides to protect against fire. The defenders on the wall ramparts were directing their artillery against them almost exclusively, the towers shuddering as they took the impact of catapult stones and ballista bolts. Flaming darts shot out from the wall, brief spats of arcing fire in the haze.

A wave of distant cheering came from the north-east, and all the officers on the hilltop craned forward, trying to make out what had happened. A groan ran through them: the cheers came from the enemy. One of the big towers had halted and then toppled sideways, crashing to ruin. As the dust cleared Castus could see the tiny figures of men running forward around the wreckage with scaling ladders. His blood beat fast, and there was a steady ringing in his ears.

He glanced to his left again, at the imperial pavilion. Constantine and Crispus were sitting stiffly upright, their eyes locked on the battle. Around them the dignitaries and attendants of the household stood in nervous silence. Compared to the frenzied action happening down on the plain before the wall, the stillness around the imperial party appeared uncanny.

One of the rams had managed to crawl up to the base of the wall near the Thracian Gate, the archers and ballistae on the nearest mounds keeping the defenders from the ramparts above. Men swirled around it, raising shields, others swarming along the base of the wall towards the gate itself. Flashes of flame showed through the haze: the men on the wall had lit fires, or cauldrons of burning materials. Castus caught his breath, staring hard. A moment later the fire cascaded down, falling in a burning torrent over the ram and the men around it.

Another of the siege towers had caught fire as well, black smoke piling from its upper storeys. Not much chance of saving that one, Castus knew. He was pacing back and forth, fists clenched at his sides. He ran his tongue over his teeth, tasted dust, and spat.

For a long time he could see almost nothing at all, the whole wall wreathed in the fog of battle. The catapult arms still leaped, arcing their stones over at the defences, but it was impossible to see how the assault was faring. A stream of injured men came back out of the fog, most of them carried by the army slaves. The cries of pain and thirst were loud enough to reach the imperial enclosure. Messengers came and went, galloping down onto the plain and returning to bring news. On the hilltop, every ear strained for the cries of victory, the trumpets that would signal a breach in the wall, a successful escalade. Only the chaotic distant roar of battle reached them.

But as the breeze drove away the hanging dust and the swirling smoke, all could see the troops had been driven back in confusion from the wall, abandoning the broken and burning siege engines. When Castus glanced up at the imperial pavilion he saw Constantine on his feet, staring with barely suppressed rage before stalking away towards his tent. Only Crispus remained, still seated stiffly, his jaw locked. Then the trumpets sounded the recall, and a sigh rose from the assembled officers.

Once again, the assault had failed.

The imperial despatch was triple-sealed for confidentiality. Castus knew that copies would have been sent only to the senior army commanders. Ordering everyone but Diogenes from the tent, he told the secretary to break the seals and read.

Diogenes scanned through the tablet, then raised his eyebrows and gave a dry chuckle. Castus stood up, hands clasped at the small of his back.

'Well, what does it say?'

'By the sacred will of the Invincible Augustus Flavius Valerius Constantinus... et cetera... ten thousand select sailors and marines of the naval forces are to be despatched to the valley of Kalos Agros on the Bosphorus strait, there to construct and make ready a fleet of landing barges sufficient to transport forty thousand troops. This operation is to be conducted under terms of the strictest secrecy... Once the barges are ready, his excellency Aurelius Evander will remain in command of the besieging troops before Byzantium, while command of the expeditionary force will pass to his excellency Aurelius Castus... Congratulations, dominus!'*

Castus grunted in satisfaction. 'So he did listen,' he said.

'Maybe so,' Diogenes said, turning the tablet with a frown. 'There's a postscript though. It says that it was the emperor himself who devised the plan for the operation... on the inspiration of Almighty God!'

CHAPTER XVIII

The four men rode up the slope with the dawn sun in their eyes and the purple and gold draco standard hanging limp above them. One of them carried a green branch, the symbol of parley.

Castus sat in his saddle, waiting as they approached. Beside him on the crest of the ridge were his own standard-bearer and herald, Bonitus and Saturninus, and four staff tribunes. None moved as the emissaries of their enemy drew closer and reined to a halt. The herald carrying the green branch urged his horse a few steps onward.

'By order of His Imperial Sacred Majesty, the Emperor Gaius Valerius Licinianus Licinius Augustus,' the herald declared, 'his excellency Valerius Traianus, comes rei militaris, is empowered to speak!'

Traianus would be the slab-faced military commander at the centre of the group, Castus guessed. A soldier, like himself, and one of Licinius's senior officers. A spokesman for his emperor, as Castus was for Constantine.

Behind the group of emissaries, across the plateau above the town of Chrysopolis on the Bosphorus shore, stretched the massed ranks of Licinius's army. Castus could sense Bonitus and Saturninus leaning from their saddles, studying the enemy formations. He tried to keep his gaze locked on the man beneath the draco standard as his own herald called out his rank and title.

Fog still covered the Bosphorus, hiding the city of Byzantium on the far side. The fog had been a blessing: it had cloaked the straits for the last two days, concealing the vast armada of landing barges that had ferried Constantine's army up the narrows and into the Euxine. It had taken over a month to build the barges, four days to move the army, but Licinius's scouts had known nothing of it, until after the troops had disembarked on the beaches at the mouth of the Rhebas. They had marched at once, over the hills and twenty miles south to arrive before dark to the west of Licinius's position. It had all gone smoothly; the gods had been good.

Sitting heavily on his dark gelding, Castus muttered a prayer. *Let our good fortune endure a little longer.*

'Aurelius Castus,' the enemy commander called. 'I know your name. I remember your face too. We met at Mediolanum, I think, when your emperor and mine arranged their alliance.'

Castus kept his expression immobile. 'I remember the day well enough,' he said.

Traianus twitched his mouth into a brief smile. 'Then you remember the oaths they swore that day? Bonds of everlasting brotherhood. A sacred pact, it was, before the gods. Do you remember that too?'

Castus gave no response. He recalled the graffiti he had seen in Thessalonica. *Oathbreaker.* Just a word, he thought. Another weapon in the enemy arsenal. He just angled his head slightly; not quite a nod.

'The Augustus Licinius wishes me to convey his sorrow at the Roman lives lost in your hopeless assault on Byzantium,' Traianus went on. 'Truly a shame, for Romans to die fighting Romans, hmm?'

'So has it ever been,' Castus said.

'The Augustus Licinius wishes to offer a truce to your emperor. He will agree to withdraw his garrison from Byzantium and pull them back across the straits. Your man can have the whole of Thrace. The Bosphorus will be the border between the domains of Licinius and Constantine. And this time, let the pact be honoured in full.'

Castus snorted a laugh. 'Don't joke with me,' he said. 'We've defeated you on land and water. Byzantium means nothing to us – the city'll fall soon enough. And now, as you see – our army is already on your shore!'

'But we outnumber you, brother,' Traianus said. 'Look behind me. You see sixty thousand men assembled for battle. How many do you have with you? How many will die, if we fight? How many more Roman lives must be lost for this madness?'

It was not an argument from a position of strength, and both men knew it. But Castus felt the words strike into his soul; he knew the truth of what Traianus said. But this was war. This was the life he had always led.

'Sure enough, you've got the greater number,' he said. 'But half of them are Goths, Persians and Armenians. The sweepings of the eastern garrisons. We have the veterans of the Gallic and Pannonian armies, the finest soldiers in the empire, beneath our standards!'

'Your standards?' Traianus said, with a cold sneer to his voice that angered Castus. 'What standards are they? Our army marches behind the images of the gods! Jupiter goes before us, and Mars, and the Unconquered Sun! The ancestral gods of Rome. But your Constantine, so I hear, despises the gods. Your troops march under some gimmick of a banner, some *Christian* invention! Is that true, brother? Maybe you're a

Christian yourself, heh? Do you worship at the altar of a dead Jew, like your master?'

Castus hunched forward suddenly, and his movement made Ajax stamp and toss his mane. 'My gods are the same as yours!' he growled. But he felt the anguish in his heart. He could see Traianus's cold quiet amusement as his words struck home.

'Enough of this talk,' Castus said, hauling on the reins to control his horse. 'The Augustus Constantine has an offer for your emperor too. Surrender now, and his life will be spared. He'll be permitted to retire with honour to a place of his choosing. His troops and officers will be permitted to return to their home fortresses with their arms and standards. This war will end, and no more blood will be shed.'

This time it was Traianus's turn to scoff. 'What general with an army of sixty thousand would accept that?' he said. 'You can tell your emperor to eat his offer for breakfast. Or stick it up his rear if he prefers.'

Castus nodded again. He had expected as much. In the open ground behind Traianus and the riders of his party, others were moving forward now. One of them was a big man on a prancing horse, his long hair bound in a topknot. The Gothic chieftain, Castus guessed. He would not be keen on surrendering either, having brought his people all this way to fight a battle.

'So be it,' he said curtly. 'I salute you, brother. May we not meet on the battlefield.'

Just for a moment, as he returned the salute, Traianus's slab of a face softened into an expression of something like regret. Then the emissaries turned and rode back to join their legions.

'So we fight?' Constantine declared, smacking his fist into his palm. 'Good! I'd feared for a moment that the coward Licinius might accept my terms!'

The emperor was in fine spirits, almost ebullient as he strode back and forth in front of his tent, his senior officers gathered around him. Castus recognised the mood. Nervous tension, fear mingled with enthusiasm. But it made him wary all the same.

'What could you make out of their dispositions?'

'They've got between fifty and sixty thousand men on the field,' Castus said. 'Their left's anchored on the town of Chrysopolis and the high ground by the Bosphorus shore. Most of their legionary strength is in the centre. Looks like all the Gothic auxilia are together in a mass flanking the legions. There's a lot of them, but they're milling about down there. Big cavalry force on the enemy right, down in the dip behind the orchards to the south-east. They've got a screen of cataphracts at the front, but most of the rest look to be Gothic light horsemen. Reckon they'll try and flank us up the valley on that side.'

Constantine nodded. 'Our spies report much the same.'

He glanced around the circuit of assembled men. Besides Castus there were all of the senior military officers, the *comites* of the imperial retinue, the Praetorian Prefect Acilius Severus and Rutilius Palladius, Master of Offices, along with Bishop Hosius and a handful of lesser priests.

Constantine drew himself up, head back, and addressed them all. 'Brothers,' he announced, 'this will be the last battle of this long campaign. For nearly ten years I've fought Licinius. I never wanted to – his treachery and duplicity drove me to it. But Almighty God has promised us victory, as I am the instrument of His glory!'

He paused for a moment, eyes closed, fingers flickering to his brow. Castus felt the sweat on his back. He noticed several of the other officers making pious gestures.

'Already God has shown his blessings to us,' the emperor declared, raising one finger to point at the sky. 'My adversary, deceived by the false reports of our spies, has sent a strong division of his army south to the Hellespont, believing we would cross the straits there. Now he stands before us, weakened but still defiant. The hour has come for us to end his unjust rule, and together to avenge his crimes.'

A stir of agreement from the assembly. The emperor called Crispus to his side. He embraced his son, kissing him, then stood with his arm around the young man's shoulders.

'You all know your positions,' he said. 'I myself will command the cavalry on our right, with Polemius leading the infantry. My son here, the Caesar Crispus, will command the left flank. You, Aurelius Castus, will command the centre. Go now to your places, and let us pray for a righteous victory!'

'Augustus! Augustus! May God preserve you! Your salvation is our salvation!'

As the last ringing words of the imperial salute faded, and the assembly broke up, Constantine paced over to Castus and took him by the arm. 'Walk with me a moment,' the emperor said. His voice was quiet, strained.

One of the members of the assembly had lingered behind. A young man Castus had never seen before, with a dark complexion and a large nose, the downy beard on his chin making him look even more youthful.

'Hormisdas!' Constantine called, beckoning the young man closer. 'This is Aurelius Castus, the finest of my commanders.' He gave Castus a slap on the shoulder. 'Castus, this young man Hormisdas is a prince of the Persians. By rights he should be king – perhaps one day he will be!'

The young Persian lowered his head in greeting, and made a fluid gesture of salute. Castus just grunted and nodded.

'You must hear Hormisdas's story some time,' Constantine said, 'about how he escaped from the King of Persia's dungeons.

Quite remarkable! But now I must speak to you alone.'

Hormisdas needed no word of dismissal; he bowed again and departed.

'I wanted to express my gratitude,' the emperor said, the awkward tone returning to his voice now they were alone again. He led Castus a few paces from the tent and paused, gazing at the sky. 'I know it was your suggestion that we cross the straits. A good suggestion! I may have thought of it myself, in time, but I was blinded by anger and pride. By *hubris*, as the Greeks would say. I see that now. I know I should have given you the credit for it.'

Castus made a noncommittal sound. *But*, he thought.

'But,' the emperor said. 'As you know, the course of this war is directed by God. It's important, you know, for the troops to believe that. To see the truth of it. *I* believe it – I feel it *right here*.' He smacked his fist against his chest, and the gilded bronze of his muscled cuirass rang like a muffled bell. 'So you see, I had to give the credit to the divine wisdom. I hope you can appreciate that.'

'I do, majesty,' Castus said, trying not to frown too heavily. In fact, he cared little who took credit for the plan; only that it had worked so far.

'We are – all of us – instruments of God's will,' Constantine said, his voice animated suddenly by an unnerving fervour. 'Even you, brother, though you may not admit it. Not yet, I mean.'

Castus narrowed his eyes, feeling the swelling in his neck, the gathering affront. He forced himself to confront Constantine directly. The emperor had not shaved, and the stubble on his jaw was silver-grey. His hair was the colour of old iron, flecked with rust. But his eyes were clear and bright, shining with certainty.

'How long has it been since we first stood together in battle?' Constantine asked. 'Since Gaul?'

'Since Britain, majesty.'

'That long?' Constantine widened his eyes, then grasped Castus by the shoulder once more. 'I meant what I said to that Persian boy,' he went on. 'You're the best soldier I've known, Aurelius Castus. That's why I'm placing you in command of my centre. Give me victory today,' he said, and the tremor in his voice betrayed him. 'Give me that and I will grant you anything, understand?'

'May the gods guide us to it,' Castus said.

He saw the flicker of doubt cross the emperor's face, then clear. 'Your gods – and mine,' Constantine replied.

The last fog was gone from the straits by the time Castus returned to the battle lines, and the smoke trails from the city of Byzantium were clearly visible on the far shore. Mid September, but the heat of summer had not abated; it would be a long hot day. With the sun well above the hills to the east the expanse of the plain above Chrysopolis was revealed. What Castus had taken to be flat open country in the haze of dawn was actually an undulating plateau, studded with olive groves and orchards, wooded thickets and dry-stone walls. A stream threaded across the centre of the plain, descending towards the Bosphorus. And on the far side, half a mile distant beyond the trees, stood the massed strength of the enemy.

A booming sound was rising from the midst of Licinius's army. The war cries of the Goths, Castus realised. Beside their ragged array, the enemy legions had formed tight regular blocks behind their shields.

'Looks like they're making sacrifice, dominus,' said one of the staff officers as Castus joined the command group behind the lines. Castus caught his meaning. *If only we could do the same.*

Sure enough, smoke was rising from altars to the rear of Licinius's formations. A moment later, and the sound of voices carried across the plain. Castus edged his horse forward until he could make out the words. Licinius's men were crying out acclamations to the gods. To Jupiter, Hercules, Mars and Sol. The tiny figures moving out ahead of their ranks would be carrying the divine images on standards.

But now another party was making its way along the front of Constantine's assembled troops. Above them hung the huge purple banner embroidered with the portraits of the emperor and his sons. And above the banner, the golden emblem of the Christian faith.

The men carrying the Labarum standard halted at the centre of the line, just in front of Castus's position. There were priests with them, carrying incense vessels that wafted smoke into the morning air. At a signal from the tribunes, every man of the army took off his helmet, laid aside his shield and weapons and knelt on the dry brown turf.

'*Almighty God, we beseech You; Holy God, we beseech You.*' The priests cried out the prayer, and in one vast rumbling voice the troops repeated the words. '*By Your favour we gain victory; through You we are mightier than our foe...*'

The voices carried along the ranks, a rumble of noise, the words bleeding together. Castus stood by his horse, helmet clasped beneath his arm. He opened his mouth and breathed words. *Unconquered Sun. Lord of Daybreak. Protector against darkness...*

'*By You we live, to You we commend our souls. Almighty God, hear our prayers and grant us triumph in Your holy name!*'

The last roar of sound died into the stillness. Then a trumpet cried, and the troops rose to their feet, put on helmets and took up weapons and shields as the Labarum with its escort of priests moved along the line. Castus swigged from his canteen, swilled his mouth and spat. Then he pulled the helmet over his head and laced the straps beneath his chin.

'Come on,' he told his escort.

They moved forward through the ranks, and the troops parted before them. Some of the men called out to him, raising their spears in salute. Here and there a voice cried out his old army nickname. *Knucklehead!* Hands brushed against him as he passed, touching his shoulders, his arms. As if, Castus thought, he could bring them luck somehow. Preserve them through the coming storm. He kept his eyes straight ahead, acknowledging nobody.

His officers had already assembled, just in front of the line. For a long moment Castus waited, thumbs hooked in his belt, gazing across the open countryside, so placid in the morning sunlight, towards the vast enemy array. Panic fluttered behind his breastbone. Heaviness in his limbs, a dark heat in his skull. He still felt the touch of the soldiers as he had passed through the ranks. Wanted that touch now. A support, a protection. This was the last battle, the final rush to victory. *Give me that and I will grant you anything.* Nervous dread boiled in his gut. He swallowed, blinked, then turned to face his officers.

Gratianus was there, recovered from his injury and back in command of the Moesiaci. With the Divitenses and Pannoniaci, they would form the front line of the centre. All the tribunes stood with him now, and the commanders of the Tenth Gemina, the Third and Sixth Herculia, the Septimani and the Martenses. Bonitus greeted him with a wry smile, still appearing amused by the Christian pieties. He was leading his own Salii, with the other Frankish auxilia of the Tubantes, the Batavi and the Tungri Sagittarii. Hrodomarus was in command of the Bucinobantes and three more Alamannic contingents. All stood calmly as they waited for Castus to speak.

'You know your orders,' Castus told them, a growl in his voice. 'At the signal we advance, slow and steady. Keep your formations tight – there's broken ground ahead, walls and trees: don't let your lines buckle. I reckon by the time we pass those far orchards we'll be in range of their artillery, so be ready for it. I want light troops out in front, to flush their skirmishers out of the copses. Archers, too. There's a breeze coming up behind us, so tell them to loft their arrows high and shoot fast. We'll see how the rear ranks of our enemy like the rain in their faces!'

A rumble of amusement. Castus could feel the confidence in these men, their trust in him like a solid grip.

'There's nothing more I need to say. Pray to your own gods, in whatever way you know, and let's win this and go home.'

Every man nodded, but still they delayed. Castus moved between them, grasping each officer by the shoulder, clasping him by the hand. Forcing himself to look every one of them in the eye. Let the men in the ranks see this, he thought. Let them see the confidence of the commanders who will lead them.

He stepped back and saluted. As he did so, a cry went up from the assembled troops. Then, as one man, they raised their spears and yelled. '*Victory! Victory! Victory!*' A powerful and mighty roar.

Castus was grinning suddenly, the weight of fear lifting from him, all lingering unease driven away. He swept the sword from his scabbard and raised it above his head, the blade flashing in the sunlight.

They jostled him as he passed back between their ranks, men slapping his back and shoulders, others touching their brows in salute. Castus was still smiling, his back teeth clenched tight. As he reached his command position he could hear the centurions yelling the troops back into formation.

A group of riders passed along the rear of the lines. Crispus was in the lead, heading for his post on the left flank, followed by Saturninus and his guard cavalry. Crispus slowed as he passed Castus, raising his hand in greeting, and for a moment it looked as though the younger man would pause to speak. But there was nothing to say now.

Castus rubbed the nose of his horse; Ajax gave him a baleful stare.

'Well, I can see you're not impressed!' Castus muttered, then swung himself up into the saddle. Around him were the men of his command group: signallers and despatch riders, his mounted escort of archers, Ursio and five other Protectores, Felix, Diogenes and Glycon and half a dozen staff officers, all gathered beneath his personal standard. One of the officers, a young tribune, was grinning nervously. Castus could see the sweat gleaming on his face.

'Were you at Adrianople, lad?' he asked.

'Yes, excellency,' the tribune replied, with a slight stammer. 'But that was different – by the time we got across the Hebrus their main force had withdrawn. Only the flanks engaged.'

Castus nodded. He had heard the same. 'Then pay close attention today,' he said. 'This is likely to be the greatest battle you'll ever see.'

You and me both, he thought. Briefly he felt the fluttering of dread in his gut, the icy breath up his spine. But his blood was flowing, fast and hot, and he began to feel the sense of heightened awareness, the strange focus of battle.

A glance to the right, and then to the left. Despatch riders were galloping along the lines, trailing dust, but the formations were all in place, standards high. Two miles of men and armour and horses, waiting for his word.

Let's do this then, he said under his breath. He turned in the saddle, calling to the tribune behind him in a voice of command. 'We'll move up five hundred paces, to just outside the range of their artillery. Give the signal!'

A moment later the horn notes rang out, repeated along the line in both directions. The mass of troops stirred, the standards dipped then rose, and the advance began.

They covered the ground fast, and before Castus was even aware of it the front ranks were across the stream and through the first open woodland. He followed along behind them on horseback, knees tight against the flanks of his big gelding, and the dust eddied from the thousands of stamping boots and fogged the air around him to a brown haze. Within moments, so it seemed, the horns were sounding again and the formations rolled to a halt.

'Messenger coming!' one of the tribunes cried, and Castus turned to see a staff officer on a lathered horse galloping up behind him and flinging a salute.

'Excellency! Orders from the Augustus – he's shifting flank.'

Castus frowned, uncertain for a moment what the man meant. 'Explain,' he demanded.

The rider gulped air, wiping his face with a sweaty palm. 'The Augustus Constantine will take his full cavalry strength from the right flank to reinforce the left, moving behind your line. He intends to lead a charge into their right, smash through their cavalry and hook around their infantry flank. He orders that you move forward again and raise a lot of dust to cover his redeployment.'

So that was it. Castus nodded slowly, rubbing his jaw. Not a bad stratagem, although it would have been better decided beforehand. And it left the right flank badly exposed, if the enemy noticed the movement and pushed an attack there.

'Messengers, to me,' he called. 'One of you ride to each of the tribunes – entire formation to advance fifty paces further, dead slow. Have the men shuffle their feet and raise dust. You,' he said to one of the men, 'ride to Polemius on the right flank: tell him to bring up his reserve infantry and make a square. *Praetorian Camp* formation. He's to move as we move, but not let anything past him.'

The riders leaped into their saddles at once, galloping along the lines. 'I need a message to Hierax, the fleet prefect,' Castus called, pointing to one of the remaining riders. 'Tell him to bring his ships down the strait, fast as he can. Use the shipboard artillery to harry the enemy left flank along the shore. Go!'

The messenger jumped into the saddle, spun his rearing horse and burst into a gallop away up the trail behind them. Castus knew that he was unlikely to reach Hierax in time; it could be hours before the prefect brought the ships to where they were needed. He cursed himself for not thinking of the idea sooner; cursed Constantine for changing his battle plan at the last moment. But it was too late for regrets now. Already the trumpets were sounding, the lines of men hefting their shields and moving into the advance.

As he rode, chin down against the collar of his cuirass, Castus reflected on the irony of his position. He was in command, but he could see almost nothing of what was happening. Few decisions he could make now would affect what was going to take place. As soon as the infantry lines got close enough to charge, the battle would be decided by the individual unit tribunes, the centurions and the men in the ranks. Spatha and spear, brute strength and endurance would decide the day.

Thunder of hooves from behind him, and Castus turned in the saddle to see the lances and pennants through the whirling dust. Three thousand armoured horsemen of the elite Scholae guard cavalry, supported by the Equites Dalmatae and Catafractarii. Would there be enough of them to break the enemy flank?

'Tribune,' he called to the nervous young officer beside him. 'Follow the cavalry to the left. As soon as the emperor's ready to launch his attack, ride back quick and let me know.'

The tribune saluted and wheeled his horse. Castus gestured to Glycon, and the orderly passed him a waterskin. He tipped it and drank, tasting good wine lacing the water.

'Thanks,' he said.

Screams from the forward ranks, and Castus saw the clearer air above the dust flickering with arrows. There were orchards in front of them, dappled shade beneath the trees, and beyond them an expanse of open ground with the enemy drawn up on the far side.

Castus was trying to breathe slowly, through his nose. Trying to quell the thudding of his heart in his chest. He noticed that he was flexing his right hand, bunching it repeatedly into a fist. Hoping nobody had noticed the sign of nervousness, he took a firm grip on the reins with both hands.

The high brassy wail of a cavalry trumpet came from somewhere far away on the left, and a moment later the young tribune was galloping back towards him, waving his arm. 'The Augustus has redeployed!' he cried. 'He intends to attack at once!'

'So I hear,' Castus said. He raised himself in the saddle, peering intently along the lines. A dense brown plume was rising to the south, and he could make out the distant rumble of massed cavalry moving at speed.

No way of knowing whether Constantine's left-hook charge would succeed or not. No time for further delay either.

'General signal,' he said, speaking quietly to the tribune behind him. 'Battle formation, and advance to fifty paces. Darts and javelins, then we go at them with the steel.'

He barely heard the sound of the trumpets. For a few heartbeats he felt unsteady, disorientated, as if he had swallowed a draught of strong drink. Then the energy surged through him again, the intense and cleansing fury of coming battle. He threw back his head, laughed into the dust, and kicked Ajax forward in the wake of his advancing legions.

Through the trees, stooping beneath the low branches, he rode on into the blaze of sunlight once more. In the air he could feel the pulse of the advance, the steady stamp of men in armour. The enemy line was much closer suddenly, and Castus could make out the shield blazons, the insignia on their standards. Legions I Illyricorum and III Diocletiana held the centre of their line; the Armeniaca and Pontica legions flanking them to either side. Off to his left he saw the sky-blue standards of Legion I Iovia, the proud crimson banners of II and III Isaura and V Parthica. Fine Roman legions, all of them. And now he had to destroy them.

A sharp cry, and Castus turned to see the young tribune slumping from the saddle. One of the hornblowers spurred forward to catch him as he fell, but Castus could see the officer was mortally wounded, blood spouting from the wound where a sling bullet had struck him in the face. Missiles were falling all around them. Ahead of him the front-rank men were hurling javelins and darts. The high clink of steel and the thud of arrows hitting shield boards cut through the fog of noise.

Then the horns again, a single vast yell, and the infantry lines surged together into the bloody mesh of combat.

CHAPTER XIX

Dust was in his eyes, in his mouth, grating between his teeth. Dust like thick brown smoke, cutting visibility to a dozen strides in any direction. Castus felt his frenzy mounting; his horse champed and dragged at the reins, sensing the proximity of battle. The noise of the fighting was unrelenting now, a constant hammering of shields, the scrape and clash of iron, the screams of the wounded and dying. Trumpet calls rose above the din, the same calls for both sides: *rally, hold fast, rotate the ranks.*

Diogenes was slumped forward in his saddle, an arrow jutting from his shoulder. He appeared more perplexed than shocked or pained.

'You're wounded!' Castus yelled. 'Get back to the rear!'

'With respect, dominus,' Diogenes said with a twisted smile, 'I'm not sure I can *find* the rear!'

Steadily more troops were moving into combat, the second line advancing to reinforce the first. *Like feeding meat into a grinder*, Castus thought. And steadily the dead and injured were fed back, their bodies laid on the scuffed turf. Water-bearers dashed into the swirling fog and returned with empty bags. Foot by foot, man by man, with each successive surge and rally the assault was driving the enemy back, but the cost was enormous.

A centurion of the Moesiaci staggered from the battle line, clasping his right arm. The limb was almost hacked through and blood streamed down his side, but the man appeared not to feel it. He was grinning, triumphant.

'We're winning ground, excellency!' he cried to Castus. 'They'll break soon, I can feel it! Gratianus is fighting in the front ranks like a champion – Bonitus too! I saw them...'

'Good man,' Castus said, and gestured to some slaves to help him. 'Now find a surgeon.' He doubted the centurion would live another hour.

'Excellency,' a staff officer called to him, 'you're moving too far forward – you're in peril here, you must move back!'

Castus snarled at the man, kicked his heels and rode further forward, between the ranks of the reserves and into the space directly behind the battlefront. The ground here was thick with dead men: many his own, but many more of the enemy. Who was still with him? Felix, mounted on a tough little pony, Ursio and Glycon, one of his cavalry escort, a single hornblower and his standard-bearer.

Ahead of him the lines surged again, with a volley of yells. Castus knew all too well what was happening, only a score of paces ahead of him. He had fought in the front ranks, endured the punishing attrition of battle many times. He knew the stumbling and the fear, the wild blood-rushing fury. He wanted that now; wanted to spur his horse onwards and crash through into the thick of the fighting.

More men were pouring back from the fight, limbs broken, bodies mauled. Now the rear lines had fed through the gaps and were bearing the brunt of the attack. How long had they fought? An hour – maybe two? There was only so long that humans could continue fighting like gods.

'Follow me,' he called to the few remaining men of his escort, and spurred Ajax to the left along the back of the line. He rode until he found the red and yellow shields of the Septimani, one of the legions formed up in the reserve. The tribune saluted as Castus reined to a halt in a torrent of dust.

'Excellency! Shall I take my men to reinforce the front line?' he shouted. He had a strong Spanish accent, and the men behind him looked fierce and ready for the fight.

'No, form them into column,' Castus called back, the dust in his throat turning his words to a parched rasp. 'I need a wedge attack through the line. When the front phalanx pulls back to rotate the ranks, I want your men to charge forward through the gap and right into the enemy. They're weakest there, right ahead of you. I'll signal with two long horn blasts. Understand?'

The tribune saluted. 'We will do what we are ordered, and at every command we will be ready!'

Castus looked around for a messenger, saw only the remaining escort trooper. 'Ride to the tribune of the Tenth Gemina,' he ordered. 'Give him the same message. Wedge attack through the front line on my signal. Go!'

Blood was hot and dark in his skull, his whole body pouring sweat. As he turned his horse again and rode back for the centre, Castus scanned the rear of the phalanx. There was little order to the ranks now; they were a vast heaving mob of men. But he could sense that they were tiring fast, more of them dropping back. He heard the centurions crying out for their men to regroup; he needed to throw in his attack now.

'Give the signal,' he called to the hornblower.

The notes rang out, long and clear; the man had good lungs. At once cheering came from left and right, as the two columns of reserves pushed forward into the charge. For a few moments the air was so thick with dust that the light grew dim and brown.

Then the dust cleared, and there was chaos.

The centre of the phalanx had buckled and broken, and for three heartbeats Castus could see only a wild confusion of men running or locked in furious struggle. The dirty fog whirled, and he was alone at the centre of a vortex of combat. Through the ache in his head he saw it clearly at last: the enemy had thrown a mass charge at his centre, just as he had sent in his two attack columns to either side, and the lines had frayed and collapsed.

Shouts from his left, and he spun his horse as he dragged his sword free of the scabbard. Figures were rushing out of the dust, bearded men in rough tunics and mail, open mouths howling their barbarian battle cries. Gothic warriors, he realised; then they were all around him.

A spear darted at his face and he slapped it aside with the flat of his blade, then hacked down and felt the sword cut flesh. More spears, stabbing at the flanks of his horse; Ajax backed, then lashed out with front hooves and biting teeth. Castus doubled the reins in his fist. Circling, he leaned from the saddle to slash at one bearded face, then flicked the sword back and cut at another. A blade raked his side, glancing off his cuirass, and he felt Ajax flinch.

Then Ursio was beside him, turning in the saddle with his powerful bow, an arrow pulled back to his ear. His face was set hard as a bronze mask. He shot three times, faster than Castus could draw breath, each arrow finding a mark, then swept out his sword and sheared the head from another Gothic warrior. Felix was spurring his pony into the fight, too, screaming curses as he hacked down at the enemy.

Still the Gothic warriors were coming, pouring forward through the breach in the line in wild disorder. Castus was yelling too, shouting for his men to rally, to form, but his voice was a gasp in the surrounding noise. A rider came crashing though the dust, a big man in scale armour with a raised sword. Castus saw the long hair drawn into a knot, the gleam of gold horse trappings: Alica, the Gothic chieftain.

The barbarian locked eyes with him, turned his horse. 'I kill you, Roman!' he yelled.

The sword swept down, and Castus parried. Steel grated, whined. Alica twisted his grip, slamming his blade down against the hilt of Castus's sword and jolting it from his grip. The weapon fell, and the chieftain sliced his sword up again, cutting at Castus's arm.

Dropping the reins, Castus turned Ajax with the pressure of his knees. Pain exploded through his ribs; the blow that had struck him earlier had been harder than he had thought. He leaned, reaching for the barbarian leader's head. The three fingers of his hand closed on the topknot, clasping hard, and he dragged Alica towards him as he swung his right arm. His fist smashed into the other man's face, and the barbarian screamed, writhing as he tried to stay upright in the saddle. But Ajax was moving, shoving hard against the smaller horse's flank, and Castus's grip did not slacken. Another punching blow, and Alica slid backwards over the saddle horns and toppled into the swarming dust. Castus felt Ajax's hooves kicking at the fallen body.

Wrestling with the reins, he circled the horse once more. A soldier came running up beside him, a legionary of the Pannoniaci, holding his sword with the hilt extended.

'Thanks,' Castus said as he took the weapon. The soldier grinned through broken teeth, then ducked out of sight. When Castus snatched a glance back he saw him looting the body of the fallen chieftain.

For a few moments it seemed the battle had moved on. Ursio was still there, sword in hand as he peered around him, but the surge of Gothic warriors had melted away into the dust. Dead and dying men covered the ground, sprawled in a trampled morass of blood. So many arrows and javelins jutted from the bodies that the scene resembled a rutted field of wheat after a summer rainstorm. Then Castus heard the stamp of marching men, the clash of armour and weapons, and as the dust cloud eddied he saw the disciplined ranks of the reserves advancing in close order, driving back the last of the attackers.

Ursio was pointing, and when Castus stared off to the left he made out another formation moving up into the battle. No legionary array this time: they moved as a solid block of men, with white shields and white uniforms. Above them rose the purple and gold standard of the Labarum, the Christian symbol blazing through the murky air.

Castus stared in amazement. As the standard and its block of guardians advanced, so the enemy fell back. Some of the Goths even threw themselves face down in the dirt, as if struck by terror. The front ranks re-formed on the standard, and as the haze cleared Castus saw even the legionaries of the enemy front line backing away step by step, keeping their shields locked before them.

'That must be what they call a miracle!' a voice said.

Castus turned and saw Acilius Severus, the Praetorian Prefect, incongruous in his gorgeously embroidered court tunic and cape, riding up beside him.

'We couldn't hear your signals from the rear, so I thought I'd come down and order up the reserves myself,' Severus said with an urbane smile. 'It appears that our enemies quail before the holy standard!'

If they did, the respite had been only momentary. Already Castus could see the darts and javelins raining down from the opposing lines, as if the Christian symbol drew them towards it. The men in white were taking casualties, bunching tighter around the Labarum as they shuffled forward. An arrow struck the hanging banner, cutting through the emperor's embroidered portrait, and hung trapped in the cloth.

'But it seems your two column assaults had the desired effect,' the Prefect said, fanning himself with his hand. 'We saw it from the heights: the enemy line is broken in two places, and only half of their centre remains.'

Castus stared at the man, then grinned fiercely. Now was the moment.

'Hornblower!' he rasped, staring through the mill of mounted men that surrounded him now. 'Sound *general advance from the centre* – we need to throw everything at them now!'

'But you're injured,' the Prefect said, touching his own arm. Castus peered down and saw blood spilling from a gash above his elbow, covering his right hand. He had thought it was only sweat, but now he felt the flame of the wound.

'Hazard of the profession!' he said. The signals were blaring out, echoed all down the line, and the men of the reserves were raising a cheer as they doubled their pace. Through the noise, Castus made out the high metal scream of cavalry trumpets to his left. When he raised himself in the saddle, he made out lances through the dust, the banners of the Scholae waving above the milling horde of fighting men.

'The Augustus!' he cried. 'Constantine's broken their flank!'

But it was not Constantine who found him, as the reserves pushed forward into the battle and the enemy flank collapsed into ruin. Instead, charging through the rout on a bloodied horse, came Crispus, with Saturninus and six of his bodyguard troopers riding behind him.

'We did it!' Crispus cried, leaning from the saddle and seizing Castus by the shoulder, grinning in ferocious delight. 'We slaughtered their cavalry and scattered them, then smashed their flank!' His voice cracked as he laughed.

'It's not over yet,' Castus said, pointing to the powerful phalanx of remaining enemy infantry, battered but still unbeaten.

'Oh, but it is!' Crispus yelled. 'Our fleet is in the Bosphorus, and Licinius has fled the field. It's over, brother. We've won!'

They stood in ragged formation, their dead heaped around them. Legionaries mingled with Gothic warriors and dismounted cavalry troopers, all of them gripping their weapons with bloodstained hands. The centre of Licinius's army had been pushed back to the left, their lines collapsing until only this stalwart band remained. Behind them were the walls of Chrysopolis, but the town offered no sanctuary to the defeated. The dark waters of the Bosphorus appeared covered in ships, liburnian galleys pulling close inshore with catapults and ballistae loaded and aimed. Every ship was thronged with troops.

Castus rode forward from the lines of his infantry, Acilius Severus and Crispus flanking him. He saw the faces of the enemy troops, the defiance and the anguish scored deep into every one. On both sides the men leaned on their shields, gulping water.

Reining to a halt, Castus rested his weight on the saddle horns. His right arm was bandaged above the elbow, the wound a burning itch. The remaining men of the Labarum guard had followed him, carrying their Christian standard, but he was content to ignore them. Every muscle in his body ached.

It was a long time before he saw the man he was looking for. The enemy lines shifted and parted, and Traianus strode forward, stepping over the slain. He pulled the helmet from his head and tucked it under his arm. His face was gashed and crusted with dried blood.

'Your emperor has fled,' Castus called.

'So we hear,' Traianus replied. Even now, at the moment of defeat, he stood firm, head back. It had taken all Castus's force of persuasion to bring about this lull in the fighting.

Constantine, in the hour of his greatest triumph, had wanted to press the attack to the very end. Finally it had taken Bishop Hosius to remind the emperor of the Christian virtues of mercy and compassion.

Castus had few such thoughts. He just knew that his troops were exhausted after hours of fighting in the heat. But it was more than that: the prospect of further senseless slaughter turned his stomach.

'We can surround you,' he called to Traianus, 'and shower you with arrows until all of you are dead, or you can submit now.'

'You have plenty of arrows then, I take it?'

'You seem to have sent us plenty of your own.'

Traianus winced, then swiped at his brow. Even from a distance, Castus could see the tears making runnels through the crust of dirt and blood on his face. But the man did not flinch.

'You fought well,' Castus said. 'But you lost.'

'Aye, well, the gods would have it so.'

Traianus glanced at the blood-churned ground before him, the bodies sprawled at his feet. He gripped the hilt of his sword, then raised his hand and drew the blade, reversed. With a contemptuous gesture he flung the weapon down.

'I've seen enough of my good men die today,' he said.

A vast groan rose from the ranks of his men, a gasp and a despairing sigh as the standards dipped in surrender. A moment later, it was drowned out by the cheers of the victors.

Castus was sitting on the ground with his back to an olive tree when Hierax found him, sipping water in the shade as a surgeon attended to the gash in his arm.

'Did my messenger get through to you then?' he asked from the corner of his mouth.

'Messenger? No,' the sailor said with a shrug. 'I took the decision to move down the straits myself. Some of my less scrupulous captains reckoned they might plunder Chalcedon and Chrysopolis while nobody was looking... But then we heard that Byzantium had already opened her gates and surrendered, so I thought perhaps I'd embark a few thousand of Evander's men and ferry them across to give you a hand!'

Castus laughed, then winced as the stitches in his arm tugged. The surgeon made a tutting sound between his teeth.

'You did well.'

'Aye, not bad. Reckon you could've won the battle yourself, eventually. But we saved you a good few hours of it.'

When the surgeon was done Castus eased himself to his feet. The little copse of olive trees had become his headquarters now; all around him were messengers coming and going, secretaries writing reports on the action, bodyguard troopers cleaning their weapons and mending their kit. Diogenes sat on a folding stool, his shoulder wrapped in linen bandages, a dazed look upon his face. Castus felt dazed himself, weary to the bone but still charged with energy, the fury of battle still kicking in his blood. Glycon, who had somehow passed through the fighting uninjured, was polishing Castus's cuirass with ashes and a rag. Flies whirled and whined in the soft late afternoon light.

'How many prisoners did we take?' Hierax asked.

'Close to ten thousand. Twice as many escaped, and nearly three times as many died. Licinius has ridden for Nicomedia, so they say, but he's only got his bodyguard cavalry and a couple of thousand infantry with him. He won't fight another battle.'

'And we follow him there?'

'We follow him.'

'He could flee all the way to Persia if he wanted,' Hierax said with a sigh. 'He could flee to the lands of the Massagetae, wherever they might be. Wouldn't make a difference. Our man's the champion, it seems. Master of the world now!'

'Master of the world,' Castus agreed. They had won, he knew. Surely one of the greatest battles of the age, the culmination of a long and brutal war. They had won, but as he looked out over the field in the last light of the day, the crows and vultures swarming over the bodies of the slain, he felt only tired bitter anguish in his heart.

CHAPTER XX

It was a strange sort of victory banquet. The meal was set out in the triple-apsed dining hall of the imperial palace of Nicomedia, once the chief residence of the emperor Diocletian, greatest of the tetrarchs, and until recently the residence of Licinius. Diocletian's statue, three times life-size and covered in gold, still presided with fierce authority over the hall, but all eyes were on Constantine, Invincible Augustus, the victor of Chrysopolis.

Constantine was dressed in gold-embroidered silk, a jewelled band upon his head. Around him on the semi-circular couch of the central apse were his senior guests, ministers and military officers, and the members of his household. But the place of honour opposite him was occupied by Gaius Valerius Licinius who, until recently, had ruled the east from this very palace, and who, only four days previously, had surrendered at the gates of the city and laid his purple robe in the dust at the feet of the conqueror.

Reclining at the centre of the couch, Castus looked from one man to the other: Constantine in his hour of triumph; Licinius in the ignominy of defeat. And yet here they were, two civilised brothers-in-law eating and drinking together, dressed in perfumed silk and surrounded by splendour. Did it not, Castus wondered, make a mockery of all the years of bloodshed, of all the thousands of other men, who had never known such luxury, who had died in the wars of empire?

One slave refilled the cups with the finest wine of Chios, while another sliced the wild boar and venison. Castus ate the meat, and swallowed it down with the ashes of his resentment. He would have preferred not to be here at all, but as one of the heroes of Chrysopolis his attendance was required. Even so, he would have preferred to have been seated at one of the other couches, with the military men – Saturninus and Polemius – or even with the courtiers and bishops. As it was, he had Crispus to one side of him and the young Persian prince, Hormisdas, to the other. Both kept silent, eating little, and Castus did the same.

And on the far side of the circular table, seated in traditional style on a high-backed chair beside her husband's couch, was Fausta. She had travelled east by fast carriage from Thessalonica, before the final stage of the war had even commenced, and arrived in Nicomedia only the day before. Behind her chair stood her maid, Niobe; the Aethiopian slave glanced in Castus's direction, caught his eye with a quick smile, then looked away.

'I drink to you, brother-in-law!' Licinius declared, raising his cup. Although he had recently shaved, the fleshy wattles of his jaw were blue with stubble. 'Truly the gods must love you, although I can't guess why. I can only hope that, if I'd won the battle, I could have hosted an equally lavish feast!'

'No doubt you could,' Constantine said, laughing as the other guests all raised their cups, 'since it would have come from the same kitchen!'

The Augustus was in a dangerous mood, and everyone in the room knew it. He had been drinking hard ever since the battle. The entire army had done the same, after discovering the stores of wine that Licinius had abandoned in Chalcedon, but in Constantine's case he had not stopped. There was something wild in his attitude now, something cruel, as if his good fortune angered him. Castus remembered what he had said before the battle. *I will grant you anything.* Pointless to remind the emperor of that promise now. The words of the powerful, Castus knew, were smoke upon the wind.

'But you would have won,' Constantine went on in a bullish tone, 'if you hadn't told your troops that my holy standard had magical powers, and would burn out their eyes if they looked at it! You'd be sitting where I'm sitting now...!'

'Not exactly true,' Licinius replied quietly. He at least was managing to appear dignified. 'I never told them that. Besides, by claiming such a thing you demean your own officers, your own son...'

He cast a chubby hand towards Castus and Crispus. 'It was *they* who gave you victory, not some invented symbol on a pole!'

The emperor tightened his mouth into a mirthless smile – the comment had clearly angered him even more – then drained his cup and held it out for a slave to refill. He did not take his eyes off his defeated rival, and Castus was glad of that.

'I know you, don't I?' Licinius said, and with hot unease Castus realised that the former emperor was addressing him directly. 'We met in Sirmium, many years ago, I think?'

'Yes... dominus,' Castus replied. He remembered it well. The desperate winter journey across Alamannic territory, taking Constantine's offer of alliance to Licinius. An offer of marriage, too. And here, sitting opposite Fausta, was the woman whose portrait Castus had carried on that mission, through the barbarian wastes and the frozen waters of the Danube. The emperor's half-sister Constantina was no beauty – she looked too much like Constantine himself – and Licinius was rumoured not to favour women. But he had married her and stuck by her all these years nevertheless.

'Happier times!' Licinius said with a weary smile. 'When we were all friends, heh?'

'Oh, we've been friends for many years, Licinius and me,' Constantine said in a low rumbling voice. 'Oh yes! I remember you at the battle of Oxsa, a quarter century ago, when we faced the Persians!'

Castus frowned. He had been at Oxsa himself, as an infantryman, but had never known that Licinius had been present too.

'Yes!' Constantine went on, with acidic enthusiasm. 'I remember you, Licinius, puking your guts out behind a bush, in terror! You were never much good at battles, were you?'

He laughed again, his face flushed dark red, his grin turning into a snarl. Licinius said nothing, his expression grim as he peered into his empty cup. Fausta was looking away in embarrassment.

'Brother,' Constantina said. 'You promised me that we would be respected and honoured, my husband and I. Not mocked!'

'*Mocked?*' the emperor declared, his voice rising. 'No mockery – just a joke! A joke between friends! Has everyone forgotten how to laugh, heh? Have I abolished *fun*?' He raised himself on the couch until he was sitting upright. The entire hall had fallen silent.

'Licinius should be thankful to me,' he announced. 'We know, he and I, how hard it is to rule! Yes, how weighty is the burden of state... And I've relieved him of the burden! *Ha ha!*'

'Husband...' Fausta said, quietly but clearly.

'Shut up, woman,' Constantine snapped, fury in his eyes. 'No, Licinius here should thank me for defeating him. And he *was* defeated, we all know that. He's knelt before me hasn't he? Or wasn't that clear enough? Perhaps I should have him kneel before me again, right here and now, for all to see?'

'Majesty,' said Severus, the Praetorian Prefect. Castus admired the man's nerve. 'Might I suggest that your good spirits are disconcerting your guests?'

'They are?' Constantine replied, wide-eyed. 'You amaze me! I'm just trying to raise the mood a little...'

Castus gestured to Ursio, who stood with the guard of Protectores behind the couch. 'Get closer to the Augustus,' he whispered. 'You may need to... help him. Understand?'

Ursio nodded, impassive, and stepped away.

'It's all true, I allow it,' Licinius was saying, weariness pouring through his words. 'You have all the power in the world now, brother. But what will you do with it, I wonder? Perhaps you will emulate our deified predecessor here, Diocletian?' He gestured towards the gilded statue at the far end of the room. 'He stepped down after twenty years, I recall. Handed power to younger men. And here I see one who could fill that role – a hero, who resembles the young Apollo!'

He pointed again towards Crispus. Castus stiffened, his throat tightening, and he felt Crispus himself shift nervously on the couch. The anxious silence filling the room grew strained.

'I would be honoured to rule one day, certainly,' Crispus said, his voice catching. Castus could almost feel the heat of the young man's discomfort. 'But my father is emperor, and his will is supreme.'

Licinius coughed a laugh into his wine cup. What, Castus wondered, did the man know? Was his question just a clever guess, or had he learned something of the tensions in Constantine's court?

'It would certainly be pleasant,' Fausta said, in a deliberately casual tone, 'if my husband might one day decide to spend more time with his family. Now his wars are done!'

'I will never hand over power to any man,' Constantine growled. 'Never, while life remains in my body and *God is my protector*!' He was clasping his wine cup tightly, knuckles pale.

Clearing his throat, Licinius stood up slowly and deliberately. He folded his napkin and placed it upon the table. 'If you'll excuse me, friends,' he said, casting a glance around the table, 'I find I've had enough of these... rich pickings. Come, wife.'

With Constantina at his side he turned, stepped down from the apse and walked steadily across the room and out through the doors. Everyone but Constantine watched him go. The silence remained.

'Well,' Fausta said lightly. 'I doubt that was what he'd been expecting!'

Constantine glared at her, the muscle in his jaw twitching.

'Fausta's right, Father,' Crispus said. Castus tensed, willing the young man to be silent. But he would not. 'It's undignified to speak like that to a defeated enemy. And to speak in such a way to your wife, too. It demeans us all.'

'When I want your advice, boy, I'll ask for it,' Constantine said, his voice loaded with quiet menace.

'Perhaps it's time you left us as well, husband,' Fausta said. 'You're clearly *drunk*!'

Constantine roared, swinging his open palm at Fausta. Ursio stepped forward, a moment too late; Fausta flinched, and the blow went wide, but Crispus was already on his feet.

'Don't you dare touch her!' Crispus yelled, his voice high and ringing.

The emperor stared at his son with startled fury. Castus was edging himself forward on the couch, ready to leap up. He expected Constantine to attack Crispus at any moment. But a strange cold glaze was creeping over the emperor's face now.

'If you care so much for your stepmother's wellbeing,' Constantine said, 'you may escort her from the room. And don't bother coming back. Out! Now!'

Fausta's chair toppled as she stood up. Crispus was already edging around the table, keeping his eyes on his father. When both were clear of the couches they paced quickly towards the doors, Niobe trailing after them. Castus made a motion to stand.

'Not you,' the emperor growled, and gestured for him to recline once more.

For a few long moments the taut silence endured. Then the emperor clapped his hands and called for the cups to be refilled.

'Hormisdas!' he said to the Persian youth. 'Why don't you tell us about how you escaped from the King of Persia's dungeons, heh? This is good – you all should hear it! Apparently his dutiful little wife concealed a file inside a *fish*…!'

The palace was in darkness, midnight come and gone. Castus paced heavily along the dim corridors, between the sentries standing in their puddles of lamplight. The banquet had lasted far too long, and he felt tired and aggrieved. Wine swirled in his head, and the rich food felt greasy in his gut. The memory of the emperor's words, Constantine's bizarre vengeful frenzy, weighed upon him even more. He paused, thinking he had lost his way, then doubled back through a domed vestibule and found the doorway to his own chambers. He wanted to sleep, to cast himself into oblivion and forgetting. More than anything he wanted to be away from this place, away from the dangerous charade of imperial power. He longed for Marcellina, for his children, for the certainty of home.

'Dominus?' a voice said. Glycon, waiting for him in the shadow of the doorway. The slave gestured back across the vestibule, where an archway opened onto a broad colonnaded portico.

Frowning, Castus moved through the arch into the cool night air, his footsteps quiet on the marble tiles. Moonlight spilled between the pillars, illuminating the figure that stood waiting there, a cloak wrapping his body.

'Caesar,' Castus said. He moved closer and stood beside Crispus. The portico was raised high above the city, and they looked out over Nicomedia's empty forum and theatre, the ranks of statues that lined the pediments of the public buildings monochrome under the moon.

'I was born here, you know,' Crispus said in a quiet musing tone. 'In Nicomedia. Lived here with my mother until I was five years old. That was when we went west, to join my father.'

Castus made a low sound in his throat. He remembered seeing the boy for the first time in the palace at Treveris. How very long ago that seemed. But he could tell that Crispus had other things on his mind.

'What happens to Licinius now?' Castus asked.

'He'll be sent to Thessalonica, with his family,' Crispus said. 'To live in the palace there for the rest of his days. A luxurious sort of imprisonment, I suppose.'

Castus grunted his agreement. Would Licinius be happy with the arrangement? Perhaps just relieved to have survived…

'That's if my father doesn't decide to have him killed after all!' Crispus added, with a wry grimace.

'You shouldn't have spoken to the emperor like that,' Castus said quietly. 'Though I admire you for it.' True enough – and he felt ashamed that he had not acted himself.

'My father was wrong to say those things.'

'I know it. We *all* know it. But don't pick fights you can't hope to win. Not when so many people have so much to lose.'

Crispus nodded, shuddering slightly inside his cloak. 'I had a dream last night,' he said, after a pause. 'A troubling dream

– it's stayed with me ever since.'

Castus peered at him, unsettled. He had never known anything good come of a dream. 'What was it about?'

'I… don't know. And I need to know. I've made enquiries – there's a man here in the city, an interpreter of these things. I want to go to him.'

'Summon him here!' Castus said. 'You're Caesar – have him brought to the palace…'

'He won't come here. I have to go to him. Tonight. There's a guide who'll lead me.' He turned suddenly to Castus, taking his arm. 'I need you to come too.'

'Just me? You'll need an escort. Saturninus and some of his men.'

'No! No escort – this must stay between us. Do me this favour, please.'

Castus frowned, uneasiness turning to warning in his mind. If there was already a guide then others would know of this errand. It was dangerous. But if he refused, he knew that Crispus would go alone.

'Give me an hour,' he said. 'And wear something dark and inconspicuous.'

Back in his chambers, he threw off his dining robes and pulled on a plain tunic and breeches. A plain cloak to go over them, and a short sword to carry concealed beneath it. Glycon watched him, his face creased with confusion.

'Find Felix,' Castus told the orderly.

Moments later, Felix was there, rubbing the sleep from his eyes. Castus ordered Glycon from the room.

'I'm going visiting with Caesar Crispus,' he told Felix. 'I want you to follow us, there and back, without anybody seeing you. That includes the Caesar. Can you do that?'

Felix nodded, shrugging.

'Make sure nobody else is following us, and if I call, you come running.'

The wiry soldier nodded again. 'And if I meet anybody else on a midnight stroll, dominus, should I send them to bed?'

Castus grinned. 'Do it quietly.'

CHAPTER XXI

The city was ghostly under the moon, a labyrinth of shadows, and the two men moved quickly and silently. The guide went before them, a small anonymous man who had met them at the side gate of the palace baths precinct, and led them without a word.

They skirted the forum, moving between the pillared walkways, and then doubled around the grand façade of the theatre. They were moving uphill now, on stepped streets that grew steadily narrower as they climbed. The large public buildings were soon behind them, tall narrow houses and apartment blocks closing in on either side. Other than the two men and their guide, the streets were deserted. Castus thought of Felix, dogging their steps; he glanced back once or twice, but saw nobody.

After climbing for a few hundred paces the guide turned abruptly and led them along an even narrower street, barely more than an alley, which followed the curve of the hillside. Castus felt his senses prickle, and kept his hand on the hilt of the sword beneath his cloak. The alley twisted, beginning to drop again, and where it branched into two descending lanes the guide halted, pointing at an opening to the left.

'There,' he whispered, then stepped back into the shadows.

Crispus took a coin from his purse and laid it on the

kerbstone, then gestured for Castus to follow him as he moved towards the opening.

A narrow door was set back into the wall. Hesitating only for a moment, Crispus raised his hand and patted on the boards. Twice, then once again. Somewhere inside a latch rattled; then a key grated in the lock and the door swung open. Castus laid a hand on Crispus's shoulder, holding him back, and stepped through the door ahead of him.

Beyond was a low room, the ceiling blackened by smoke, dirty matting on the floor. A clay lamp burned upon the circular table in the centre, and by its light Castus saw the crude drawings scratched with charcoal on the plastered walls, the clutter of strange objects in the corners and the plump waxy-faced man sitting beside the table, wrapped in a blanket.

'Greetings,' he heard the man say to Crispus as he entered. 'I am Tryphonius of Hierapolis. You have come to the right place for what you require.'

Castus had seen dream-diviners before. They tended to hang around in marketplaces, though there were less of them about these days. And this man did not resemble one of them at all. He felt his scalp crawling, his muscles tightening. He had always been superstitious, and the suggestion of magic unnerved him.

'I have what you asked for,' Crispus said, seating himself on a low bench. The scrawny boy who had opened the door closed it again and locked it, then went to sit in the corner, gazing at them with large and frightened eyes.

Crispus took three coins from his purse and placed them upon the table, then a small roll of papyrus with something written on it. Tryphonius reached a hand from beneath his blanket.

'*What's going on?*' Castus hissed as he sat on the bench beside Crispus. 'This man's no diviner.'

'My apologies,' Crispus told him a whisper, laying a hand on Castus's arm. 'If I'd told you the truth, you might have tried to stop me. But the dream, you see – the dream told me to come and find this man!'

Castus dragged the short sword around until it lay across his lap, ready to draw quickly. The man supposedly knew nothing of the true identity of his visitors, only that they came from the palace. But Castus could not believe that. Everything in him was telling him to leave this place now, and drag Crispus with him.

Tryphonius had studied the writing on the papyrus. With lowered eyelids he glanced at Crispus and smiled. 'I see you've noted down the date and time of birth, the exact conjunction of the stars. Good. Now – what would you have me tell you about this person?'

Castus heard Crispus gulp heavily. He knew that the young man was as nervous as he was himself. 'That is my father's birth chart,' Crispus said, blurting the words. 'I need to know... when he will die.'

Castus turned with a sharp grunt, and felt Crispus tug at his arm. Asking to know such a thing was a capital offense; even to read an emperor's horoscope was punishable by death. He should act now – overturn the table and storm out of here, obliterate the scene entirely. But a terrible nervous fear had him in its grip, and he could barely draw breath.

'I see,' Tryphonius said, glancing at the papyrus again. Then he folded it lengthways and held it over the lamp flame until it caught fire.

'Fate is woven of many strands,' he said, with a note of humour in his voice. 'And while, for most of us, tracking the movements of the planets can divine our future without error, some men stand above such things. For some men, fate is a matter for the gods alone to control. I suspect, young man, that your father might be one of those men. And you ask me to commit a very serious crime!'

Crispus made a choking sound. 'You mean... you can't tell me?'

'I did not say that. I mean that I must use other methods. *Costly* methods.'

Reaching into his purse again, Crispus took out another coin and laid it on the table. Gold, Castus noticed. Tryphonius nodded, waiting, and Crispus added one more coin to the pile. The boy scuttled across the floor from the corner and took the money.

'Good,' Tryphonius said again. 'Now, I must ask you to be patient, domini.'

He took a pair of brass incense holders from beneath the table, lighting them with a taper from the lamp, then blowing on them until smoke swirled. Castus smelled burning herbs and spices. Something else too, an acrid odour that caught in his throat and made his eyes smart. He remembered the sorcerer he had seen once, years before, in an abandoned crypt outside the city of Treveris. That same smell, that same sense of otherworldly menace.

'If you're scared,' Crispus whispered, 'you can wait outside.'

'I'm not scared,' Castus replied, his voice rasping.

'You're *shaking*.' But Crispus looked terrified himself, his lips thin and tight and his face grey. The sorcerer had placed a brass bowl between the incense holders, filled with what looked like oil, and was bent low over it, muttering and hissing.

'Did you think this would be *easy*?' Crispus said under his breath. 'You heard what my father said at dinner. I need to know how long his rule will last, and this is the only way to find out!'

But that doesn't make it right, Castus thought. Nausea crawled in his belly, and the stink of the fumes was making his head spin. Then the sorcerer made a movement, and Castus started forward with a cry, drawing the sword partway from his scabbard. Tryphonius had taken a knife with a curved blade from beneath the table, and beckoned the boy to his side.

'Be calm, dominus,' he said with a twisted smile. 'I mean no violence.' He was rolling up the sleeve of the boy's tunic and stretching his bare arm across the table, over the bowl of oil. 'This is merely a small sacrifice, to propitiate the dark spirits so they will allow me to part the veils of the future...'

He lifted the knife and made an incision on the boy's forearm. Blood welled from the cut, black in the lamplight, and dripped down into the bowl. The boy's faced remained glazed, his eyes unblinking. Castus watched it all, perched on the stool with his hand on his sword hilt.

Three drops fell, then Tryphonius dismissed the boy, who crawled away to bind the wound with a dirty rag. Now the sorcerer was bent once more over the bowl, the fumes wreathing his head as he muttered and made popping, kissing sounds with his lips. Castus noticed that Crispus was also leaning forward, watching with his lips drawn back from his teeth. He was conscious of the silence and darkness of the city outside, the empty streets. At any moment he expected the bang on the door, the demands for entry.

Tryphonius fell silent, rocking back on his haunches and drawing in breath. Coughing slightly, he took a wetted pad of cloth and stifled the two incense burners.

'Well?' Crispus said as the smoke cleared. 'Do you have an answer?'

'Oh yes,' Tryphonius said, and gave a weary smile. 'I congratulate you, dominus! Your father will live and be healthy for many years. At least another decade. He will die shortly after that, though, perhaps in connection with water. A drowning? Perhaps shipwreck?'

'*Ten years?*' Crispus whispered. His shoulders sagged, and he stared at the dirty floor. Castus exhaled. Now it was done, he was desperate to be gone.

'Is there... something else that could be done?' Crispus said suddenly. 'Something to... shorten the time?'

'No!' Castus yelled, standing up. The sorcerer already wore a crafty smile, but his face fell slack at once.

Castus grabbed Crispus by the arm and hauled him to his feet. 'You got what you came here for,' he growled. 'And so we're leaving – *now*!'

He shot a glance at the sorcerer, who was quailing behind his table, and dragged Crispus to the door. For a moment the young man tried to struggle, but then the strength left him and he followed without resistance. Throwing the bar across and twisting the key, Castus opened the door and bundled Crispus into the street. For a moment he looked back at the boy – should he take him too? But he knew nothing of the child; he could be the sorcerer's own son as far as he knew.

Out in the street, Castus sucked down clean air in heaving gasps. Crispus was walking fast at his side, and though Castus still gripped him by the arm he seemed just as eager to put the house far behind him. Castus glanced around; no sign of Felix, nor anybody else. They had reached the end of the curving street and the first flight of steps before Crispus halted suddenly and threw himself back against the wall.

'I'm sorry,' he said in a pained voice. 'I shouldn't have taken you there. I shouldn't have gone at all... But if my father will live for ten more years what am I to do?'

Castus turned to him. Now that they were out of the sorcerer's house his dread and nausea had turned to furious disgust. He seized Crispus by the shoulder, pressing him back against the bricks.

'*Nothing!*' he hissed between his teeth. 'Otherwise you endanger us all! Don't you see that? I've supported you because I believed you were better than your father. But now I see you're just as reckless, just as ambitious. You'd risk anything for power. Anything, and anybody! Do you deny it?'

'*Yes!*' Crispus spat back. He tried to struggle, but Castus kept him gripped tight. 'You promised me before the Hellespont battle that you'd back me. If we don't take risks what chance do we have of success?'

'None either way. Unless you want to declare war on your father. Throw the whole empire back into bloodshed. I've seen enough of that to last me!'

Abruptly the fight died in Crispus and he slumped in Castus's grip. He let out a low groan. 'There must be another way,' he said quietly. 'Maybe not now, not yet. But soon. Before the Vicennalia. I can talk to my father again, make him see sense...'

But Castus had been struck by another thought. His brow chilled. They could keep the night's events secret, but if anyone thought to enquire, the truth would soon emerge. The slaves in the baths precinct had seen them, the sentry who had opened the side gate, the guide who had led them to the house, then the magician himself – in a matter of hours it could all be pieced together. In his mind Castus saw the smirking face of Flavius Innocentius, the imperial agent. The seeker of truth. The torturer.

'That man Tryphonius,' he said quietly. 'We can't let him live.'

For a moment Crispus looked appalled. 'But... he had no idea who I was!'

'He knew exactly who you were. And now he has to die for it. You should have thought of that before.'

Castus drew the blade from beneath his cloak and stepped back into the alleyway. 'Wait here,' he said coldly. 'I'll do it myself.'

A shout came from down the street, the clash of a door and the sound of running feet. Castus pressed himself back against the wall, weapon ready. Out of the dimness came the shape of a man in a cloak. Felix.

'Dominus! Three of them – at the house.'

Castus turned to the young man beside him. 'Get back to the palace, quick as you can. Stop for nothing and nobody. *Go!*'

Crispus paused only a moment, open-mouthed in shock. Then he whirled and ran. Castus was already following Felix.

Back down the street, running hard, Castus saw the open door of the sorcerer's house, the three men dragging a huddled figure between them. Tryphonius still had the blanket wrapped around him, and was letting out high breathy cries. One of the men smacked him over the head with the pommel of a short sword.

Outpacing Castus, Felix slammed into the group as they cleared the doorway. His arm lashed out, and one of the three screamed and reeled back, colliding with the wall before he fell. The other two men were gripping Tryphonius between them. As Castus closed in, one of them grabbed the sorcerer by the hair, hauled back his head and cut his throat with one slash. Then they ran.

Two bodies on the ground, spilling blood. Felix quickly silenced the man he had wounded; Castus knelt beside Tryphonius, but the sorcerer was already dead.

'Not such a good fortune-teller,' Felix said, 'if he didn't see that coming!'

The fugitives had separated at the fork in the street, but Castus and Felix were close behind him. The sound of their footsteps was loud between the blank walls and shutters to either side. As they reached the fork, Castus pointed to the left. 'Catch that one,' he gasped, 'I'll get the other!'

Felix nodded, and was gone.

Breath heaving, his chest burning, Castus pounded along the alleyway. He could see the fugitive only a dozen paces ahead of him, but already the chase was lengthening. Castus had no idea where he was – somewhere in the lower slums of Nicomedia – nor where the street was taking him. He was forty-eight years old, heavy and wearied, and the man ahead of him was gaining fast. Teeth clenched, feet hammering the worn paving, Castus willed himself onwards.

The man turned sharply, into a narrower alley. Castus threw himself around the corner in pursuit, and the blackness closed around him. Even through the fury of the chase he felt the chill of danger; at any moment the man ahead could pause, wait in some dark corner until Castus ran onto his outstretched blade... Another corner, the glimpse of a man's form vanishing ahead, the whip of a cloak in the darkness. There was no doubt in Castus's mind who this man must be, or who had sent him on his mission. Snarling, he ran on down the narrow funnel of the alleyway.

Then the buildings fell away to either side, and in the bright sudden moonlight Castus saw an open yard, walled at the rear. A stench in the dusty air, like the spill from a tannery. He paused, heart thumping fast, and gazed around him. Wooden pens to his left. To his right a row of brick arches. Something moved in the shadows, and Castus turned on his heel, raising his sword. The man was over by the arches and trying to edge back around his flank.

He stepped out into the moonlight, and Castus saw him clearly. He had been expecting Innocentius, but this was somebody else, a stranger. The man had flung away his cloak, and wore the sleeveless tunic of a labourer. His flat face was clear in the pale light, and his crooked teeth as he tried to smile. He was still holding the short blade low at his side, in a fighter's grip.

'We don't need to do this,' the man said.

'You know we do,' Castus told him quietly.

For a long moment they stood facing each other. Somewhere a dog whined. All Castus's fatigue was gone now, burned off by the familiar energy of confrontation. Almost without conscious thought he made the slightest feint to his right, then pure instinct took over. His body flowed forward into the strike, a single swift movement. The man tried to raise his sword and parry, too late; Castus smacked it aside, then swung his own blade up and punched it through his opponent's body.

He felt the sigh of breath as the man slumped against him, the wet heat of blood pouring across his hand. The man died without another sound, and Castus eased him down into the dirt and dragged his sword free.

The first light was in the eastern sky by the time Castus found his way back to the palace. He slipped in through the gate to the baths precinct, past the idle sentry and the slaves. Felix was close behind him; he too had got his man, and Castus had already brushed away his apologies for letting the three killers slip past him. 'They knew where we were going,' he said. 'They were probably already waiting for us.'

He left Felix at the bottom of the stairs and climbed through the darkness to the imperial quarters on the upper floor. The soldier in the vestibule recognised him, and Castus returned to his chambers. He was achingly tired, his legs still pulsing from the chase, and his right hand was sticky with congealing blood. Flinging off his cloak and throwing the sword on the bed, he called for Glycon to bring him a basin of water and a cloth.

Sitting on the bed, Castus plunged his hands into the basin, scrubbing at the bloodstains. Gore was spattered all up his right arm as well, dirty brown now as it dried. He rubbed at his hand and arm fiercely until his skin was clean, then he stared down into the murky copper-coloured water. Who was the man he had killed that night? An imperial agent, maybe a soldier, maybe just a hired tough. A man with a duty, ordered to do a job, like Castus himself. Who had sent him, and his two comrades? Was it Innocentius, or the emperor? Perhaps even Fausta – Castus had still not rid himself of the suspicion that she wanted to destroy Crispus. It did not matter. The man was dead; they were all dead.

Suddenly he felt sickened to his core. Sick of war, of blood and killing. He thought again of all the thousands of dead at the Hellespont, all the thousands more at Chrysopolis, and knew that he had had enough of it.

Constantine was emperor; it was the will of the gods. Even if he denied them, it was impossible to deny reality. Madness for Crispus to oppose him now; to do so would only breed new conflicts, fresh battles. And if the plot were exposed, Castus himself would pay with his life. He, and probably his family as well. It was too much to risk, just to further one young man's ambitions.

He lifted his hands from the water and wiped them on the cloth, then screwed it into a ball in his fists. *No*, he thought, *I cannot go on with this*. Whatever Crispus intended to do, he wanted no further part of it. He would have to tell him – and if that meant resigning his position in the Caesar's retinue, so be it. Even if it meant leaving the army altogether. All he wanted now was peace, his wife, his family. An end to death and slaughter.

Throwing down the cloth, he put on his embroidered officer's tunic and cloak, changed his shoes, then marched from the chamber. Only a couple more hours remained until dawn, and already the rooms and porticoes of the palace were filled with a dim grey light. He walked fast, past the sentries and along the broad painted corridor that led to Crispus's own chambers. He must tell him now, before the dawn, before the palace awoke.

The guard at the inlaid doors, one of the Protectores, was half-asleep, sitting on a stool, and leaped up blearily at the sound of Castus's approaching steps. He blinked, baffled.

'I need to speak to the Caesar,' Castus declared.

'Excellency, the Caesar is... sleeping.'

Castus caught the hesitancy in the man's voice. His brow furrowed.

'Then I'll wake him. Let me through.'

Jutting his jaw, he leaned forward on his toes. The Protector flicked a nervous glance towards the doors, then back to Castus. Then he stepped aside.

The antechamber beyond was dim, but lamplight filtered through the drapes from the inner room, illuminating the shapes of peacocks embroidered on the cloth. As Castus approached the far doorway a figure rose from one of the couches. He glanced for just a moment, then stared back again.

'Niobe?' he whispered almost silently.

The Aethiopian girl had been lying on the couch. Now she gazed at Castus, wide-eyed. She raised an open palm – a gesture of warning, or of denial. 'Don't...' she managed to say.

Castus's confused indecision lasted only a heartbeat. Then he marched forward again, sweeping aside the peacock drapes.

A lamp on a tall brass stand illuminated the centre of the chamber, but the margins were in deep shadow and it took a moment for Castus's eyes to pick out the details. He saw a low table set with cups, a pair of couches. On one of the couches, a pair of figures intertwined.

Standing in the doorway, he blinked slowly. He had looked away at once, embarrassed, but now he forced himself to look again. The couple on the couch had stopped moving at the sound of his steps. Amid the rucked clothing, naked flesh gleamed in the lamplight. Crispus had raised an arm to cover his face; the woman with him had pressed herself down between the pillows.

Castus gazed for only a moment; then he stepped back through the drapes into the outer chamber. Niobe was kneeling on the floor beside the couch. She gazed up at him, trembling, and raised a finger to her lips. Castus nodded, stunned, open-mouthed. There was nothing to say.

His mind reeling with shock and confusion, he paced quietly to the door.

He had only had the briefest glimpse of the woman on the couch with Crispus, but he had known her at once.

It was Fausta.

PART THREE

EIGHTEEN MONTHS LATER

CHAPTER XXII

Constantinople, March AD 326

'It's going to be *beautiful*,' Helena said. 'Don't you think, my dear? When it's finished – the most beautiful city on earth!'

Fausta gave only the slightest nod, unwilling to encourage the old woman's enthusiasm further. A cold wind was blowing from the Bosphorus, stirring the dust from around the construction sites and charging the air with powdered brick and ground marble. Stacks of columns and heaps of cut stone lay beside the roads, and the noise of hammering and chipping was a steady percussive assault on her ears. She pulled her fur-trimmed cloak tighter beneath her chin.

In the middle distance, her husband Constantine was talking to his architects and engineers, making wide sweeping gestures with his hands. Behind them, a tall crane of angled wooden beams was lifting pillars into place. This would be a forum one day, or an assembly hall. Maybe a church – Fausta was not sure. For now the whole scene resembled an architectural salvage yard, or the aftermath of an earthquake. The ancient city of Byzantium had been abolished, the walls that had defied Constantine for months dismantled, and most of the other buildings with them. Now a new and far greater city was rising on its foundations. A city named, of course, after the emperor himself. *Constantinople*.

'One day soon, I feel sure,' Helena went on, 'this city could surpass Rome itself in grandeur!'

Fausta hid her smile. She doubted that. Rome was the city of her birth, the place she still thought of as home, although she had not been there in over a decade. The mother city. Mistress of the world. No tawdry new creation on the shores of the Thracian Bosphorus could rival that, however much her husband plundered the monuments of the eastern cities to build it. But she knew how to feign the correct levels of excitement about the project.

'Can we see the new wall from here, do you think?' Helena asked, gazing westwards. The breeze whipped her white silk mantle around her head, but she appeared not to feel the cold. 'I do so want to see it – they've made tremendous progress already. Forty thousand Gothic slaves have been put to work on it, you know! I expect it will be the most beautiful wall in creation!'

'I expect so too,' Fausta said. The new wall stood more than a mile further west than the old defences of Byzantium. She sincerely hoped that Constantine would not insist on dragging them all off to look at it.

'So wonderful that they're putting the barbarians to honest labour,' Helena was saying. 'Turning their hands to the works of peace, rather than war... I must remind myself to show you my new copy of the gospels!'

Fausta frowned, looking at her mother-in-law. What was she talking about now? A brief hope rose in her that Helena might finally have lost her reason; but no, the old woman was still far too sharp.

'I'm having them written out by slaves, you see. Purple ink on gilded vellum! A suitable vehicle for the Word of God, don't you think?'

'I'd love to see them,' Fausta said, with a smile that she hoped appeared genuine. Helena glared back at her, and Fausta sensed the slow relentless blaze of fury behind her eyes.

'Domina,' another voice said. Fausta turned and saw Niobe a short distance away, shivering in her light cloak. 'Domina – the children.'

On the road behind them, between the masonry stacks, stood the line of litters that had brought the imperial party out to view the construction work. Inside one of them, Fausta's two older boys sat miserably huddled. The nine-year-old, Constantius, called out to her. 'Mother! How long must we stay here? It's *cold*!'

'Only a little longer,' Fausta called back. 'We must wait for your father.'

Constantius was proving far more petulant and rebellious than his older brother. Did he get the trait from her, Fausta wondered, or from his grandmother?

Helena was making dry tutting noises. 'You must encourage your children to complain less, my dear!' she said. 'Grumbling about the cold, indeed... You spoil them, I think.' She raised her voice a little, so the children would hear. 'Constantine never grumbled about anything when he was a boy. And think of Crispus, away in Gaul fighting the barbarians once more – we can be sure he was never a grumbler!'

Yes, Fausta said to herself. *Think of Crispus...* She often did, but not in the way that Helena intended. And that was her secret, her closely guarded sin, and her best and most powerful weapon.

Constantine was glancing back towards the litters and the group of women and slaves. Fausta peered at him – perhaps she should wave? Her husband had become entirely possessed by his building project over the last year; since the defeat of Licinius one thing after another had claimed his attentions. He no longer visited Fausta at night, and seldom even spoke to her. That suited Fausta fine, but it also made her nervous. What did her husband think of her? What poison had his mother leached into his mind?

A soldier approached with a message from the emperor. He saluted the two imperial ladies, then dropped to kneel before them.

'Augustae,' he said, 'the Sacred Augustus gives you leave to return to the palace without him. He will be detained another few hours.'

Helena smiled – she enjoyed being addressed like that – but Fausta seethed inside, as she had been doing for many months now. Finally, after all these years of marriage and the birth of four children, her husband had promoted her to the exalted rank of Augusta – a true Empress of Rome. But he had also promoted his mother Helena to the same rank. The insult was unforgivable.

Her hatred of her mother-in-law had only increased with Helena's growing power and influence. The old woman had clambered to the very summit of power since the defeat of Licinius; now she often seemed more powerful than the emperor. Fausta knew – her eunuch Luxorius had discovered – that Helena herself had ordered the imperial agents to question her back at Thessalonica before the campaign. At least Helena's determination to undermine and destroy Fausta, and claim her place as the only senior woman at court, was overt now. But for eighteen months Fausta had hidden her feelings and suppressed her loathing. She too could be clever. She too had her secret designs.

The messenger saluted again and returned to his master, and Helena gathered the windblown mantle around her head. 'Ah well,' she said, 'I'm sure the walls are going nowhere, and doubtless we shall see them another time. If you and your children are feeling the cold so badly, perhaps a return to more comfortable quarters would be best, lest we hear more grumbles!'

As she passed the litter with the two boys inside – both of them Caesars now that Licinius and his son were gone – Helena paused, reached inside her cloak and brought out two large pieces of honeycomb wrapped in linen. She smiled as she presented her gift. The boys smiled too, snatching the sweet morsels from her hands. Helena gave a happy sigh, regarded them fondly as they ate, then walked towards her own litter without another word to Fausta.

'I want to kill her. Can I do that?'

'Time and nature have a way of accomplishing such things, domina,' Luxorius said, pressing his fingertips together.

'In her case, I believe even time and nature would be defeated. And I'd prefer to kill her before she kills me.'

They were sitting in the small marble-lined antechamber of Fausta's private bath suite, the only place in the old palace of Byzantium where she could be sure they would not be overheard. Niobe entered with an enamelled cup full of spiced and heated wine. Fausta drank gladly.

The last year had been hard. First had come the news about Licinius. An imperial investigation had revealed that the former emperor was in illegal communication with the Gothic tribes beyond the Danube; Licinius had been executed in the palace at Thessalonica. Almost as an afterthought, his nine-year-old son had been put to death shortly afterwards. The killings came as no surprise to Fausta; she knew all too well that any man who had worn the purple was liable to die by her husband's orders. But Constantine had vowed to pardon Licinius, to respect him and his family, and this new atrocity chilled Fausta's marrow. Nobody was safe.

Then there was the birth of her child, her second daughter. It had been a difficult labour, a trial of endurance, but worse was to come. Constantine had insisted on naming the girl Helena, after his mother; Fausta had been appalled, but she could not speak against the decision without revealing the depths of her hatred. So she was now the mother of one Helena, just as her husband was the son of a second, and Crispus the husband of a third.

At least Fausta had seen little of the elder Helena the previous summer. Constantine had called a council of bishops and priests at Nicaea, close to Nicomedia, to settle some obscure controversy of Christian doctrine, and the whole court had decamped to the dusty little town while it was in progress. Being surrounded by quarrelling priests, particularly just after giving birth, was not pleasant, and Fausta was still unsure what they had been discussing. *Was Christ made of the same substance as God, or similar substance? Which came first?* That seemed to be the meat of the argument. How could grown men, powerful men, become so passionate about such a meaningless question? But Fausta had been glad that the council had claimed so much of the attentions of her husband and mother-in-law. It had been a temporary respite.

And all that year Crispus had been in Gaul, conducting yet another campaign against the Alamanni. Fausta feared for him. She feared more that he would develop sudden and unexpected feelings for his own wife and child. Sipping the heated wine, Fausta reclined against the marble seat and wondered what Crispus was doing at that moment. When would she see him again? The year of the imperial Vicennalia had already begun; in four months' time it would reach its grand conclusion in the city of Rome. Would Crispus make his bid for power before then? Would he drag his father to the great temple on the

Capitol, as Diocletian was said to have dragged Fausta's own father, and demand that he abdicate...?

Fausta gave a start, and peered at Luxorius. She had the familiar but unnerving sensation that the bald eunuch was reading her mind somehow.

'What is it?' she demanded, lowering her eyelids. 'You look devious. More than usually devious, I mean.'

Luxorius smiled politely. 'Another message has just arrived, domina,' he said. 'From our friend in Treveris.'

A shiver ran through Fausta's body, rippling the wine in her cup, but she concealed it at once. She drew a long breath, composed herself, then put the cup down and extended an open hand. Luxorius had the message with him, of course. He took it from inside his tunic and laid it on her palm: a slim wooden tablet, wrapped around with cord and secured with four wax seals. Luxorius would have opened and read it already; he was certainly not the first to have done so.

Impatiently she ripped aside the seals, opened the tablet and scanned through the words inside. Then she read them more slowly, mumbling beneath her breath. The message supposedly came from an old woman in Treveris, a freed slave who had once been Fausta's nursemaid. Her own replies were sent to the same person. It was close to a foolproof means of communication, and the messages themselves were carefully innocuous, but still it felt charged with danger.

Winter has been long and cold here in the north, she read. *The young Caesar is already preparing for his journey west* – was it unwise for Crispus to refer to himself, even indirectly? Fausta bit her lip and read on – *and will travel via Raetia and the Danube. Perhaps you will see him in Sirmium soon? As for me, I think fondly of your memory, and the times we shared so long ago. Perhaps you could send me something to remind me of them?*

The times they shared had been brief. One night, in the palace of Nicomedia, eighteen months before. Even then they had been disturbed – it could have been the end for them both. But Fausta had no fear that it would ever be discovered now. And the night itself was a revelation. He loved her, so he had said – Fausta had concealed her incredulity, her amusement at the concept. A young man's passion, perhaps, a passing frenzy. But it had endured, it seemed. And how brilliantly her plan had worked. Once she had plotted to have the young Caesar killed, but how much better it felt to seduce him to her allegiance, to encourage his ambitions in secret, to goad him to rebellion?

Laughter was building inside her as Fausta put the tablet down. She leaned back, lips tightly closed, then relented and let it out. The sound of her mirth echoed in the marble chamber. Then she sighed, inhaled, regained her composure.

Perhaps her plan had worked too well? Crispus's declaration of love had shocked her at the time; it shocked her even more now. But she was moved, despite herself. Often she had caught herself thinking about him, not with malice but with affection and desire. She had never, in all her years, felt herself loved by another person. She had never given love to anyone either. The feeling was so novel, so unnerving, mingling with the thrill of danger and the deep greedy satisfaction of revenge.

'Will you send a reply at once?' Luxorius asked. 'The messenger is still here, and will leave for Gaul tomorrow, I believe.'

'Yes,' Fausta said. 'But not a tablet this time.'

She thought for a moment, then grasped the carnelian ring on her smallest finger and worked it free. She had worn it since she was married, and the gold surround bore the marks of her teeth where she had bitten nervously at it so many times. Now she bit the hem of her shawl, then ripped the embroidered silk

310

until a strip of it tore free. Wrapping the ring in the silk, she passed it to the eunuch.

'Send that, with no message.'

Luxorius raised his eyebrows. It was, perhaps, a dangerously peculiar gift to send to an old nursemaid. But Crispus would know what it meant, and Fausta enjoyed the idea of him knowing. All the same, she had often wondered what Luxorius himself made of what was happening. He had served her dutifully and loyally for many years, but she knew well that he guarded a certain impotent affection for her himself. Did he resent the intrusion of the young Crispus? If he did, Fausta thought, he should have made a better effort long before, when she had ordered him to kill the boy.

Taking the ring in its scrap of silk, Luxorius bowed and retreated from the room. Alone, Fausta sat and sipped at the cooling wine as misgivings loomed in her mind. It was true, she thought, despite her laughter: she genuinely wanted to see her stepson, to be with him – wanted it badly.

She had planned to control Crispus. But sometimes she wondered if she was losing control of herself.

CHAPTER XXIII

Castus left his escort at the edge of town and rode alone along the muddy main street towards the river. It was raining, and the cold water dripped down inside his collar. He rode in silence, staring around him. He had expected that this place would seem much smaller than he remembered. He had not expected that it would look so very mean and poor.

How many years since he had last been here? He tried to calculate, but could not. More than thirty, anyway. His journeys had often led him past the town since then – Sirmium was only a day's ride west, and the imperial highway passed right by it – but he had always kept to the road, unwilling even to turn his head. What had he feared to see? Who did he fear might see him? It seemed so senseless now.

He rode along the rutted streets through the centre of the town. He had imagined, when he first steeled himself to return here, that the sight of the place might unlock something in him, some deep well of feeling he had kept closed for many years. But all he saw around him now was a dirty little settlement beside the Danube, brown wooden houses in the rain, moss-grown crumbling brick walls and vacant plots thick with tall weeds. Further east, the last huts straggled along the riverbank; this was where he would find what he was looking for.

His baffled disappointment was so great that he almost

missed the place. He had ridden past it before he realised, and pulled Ajax to a halt in the middle of the street. The horse shivered, dropped its head and began cropping the tired grass along the verge.

Looking back, Castus peered at the scrap of cleared land, the stumps of roof timbers and the more recent building that partly covered it. This was the place, he was sure. But there was little left of it now. He should have known.

'Are you looking for something, dominus?' a voice called. A young woman had emerged from the house across the street. Castus knew that he was watched from every doorway. The woman was dressed in a plain wool tunic and shawl, and carried a baby on her hip.

'There was a house here,' Castus said, pointing to the derelict plot. 'And a blacksmith's workshop. Do you remember it?'

The woman screwed up her face. Clearly she did not, but did not want to give an unacceptable answer. Even with his plain clothing and rain cape, Castus knew that the size of his horse and its gilded trappings would mark him as a man of importance. 'If you need a forge, dominus, there's one closer to the centre,' the woman said. 'My brother's place. Give you good work, whatever you need.'

Her accent caught at something in Castus's memory. Everyone had spoken like that when he was a boy. He shook his head, then dismounted from the saddle and stood in the mud.

'Is there anyone here who might remember the place?' he asked, pushing his hood back. 'Maybe remember the man who lived here?'

'Wait a bit – I'll ask,' the woman said, then returned quickly inside her house.

Castus stood beside his horse, feeling the rain on his head and his face. He looked at the newer building that stood beside him. Whoever owned it must have bought the land, but it too was shuttered and closed now. From the doorway across the street he heard the woman talking to somebody. Hushed nervous voices.

A much older woman emerged, leaning on a stick as she crossed the road. She bobbed her head in a stiff bow. 'My daughter says you were asking about something, dominus?'

Castus asked again. The woman sucked at her teeth, eyes closed to slits, and for a moment he feared that she too would tell him nothing. How old was she? Might he have remembered her once, as a younger woman? Or a child, as he had been himself?

'Yes, there was a blacksmith lived there once,' the woman said. 'But he died. I never knew him myself. Must be twenty years ago now, around the time Diocletian stepped down. May the gods look kindly upon Diocletian!' She touched her brow, and Castus did the same.

'But now we have the blessed Constantine,' the woman went on, a nervous tremor in her voice. 'May all the gods honour him!'

'His salvation is our salvation,' Castus muttered, trying not to appear impatient. 'But about the blacksmith... Do you remember how he died?'

The woman shrugged and widened her eyes. 'As I recall, now you mention it, they said he died from drink! But he was a strange man – a veteran, they say. Bad temper he had; few liked him. A bit cracked in the head, so they say.'

Cracked in the head. Castus felt the wrench inside him. He had struck his father with an ironbound bucket, just before he fled to join the army, and thought he had killed him, until somebody told him otherwise.

Leaning against the saddle, he stared down into the trampled mud of the road. What had he hoped to find here in Taurunum? Certainly not his father – he had known that the old man must surely have died. But he had hoped that something might remain. The house, the forge, or at least some link to that half-forgotten world he had once known.

'Did he have a family?'

'Not that I'd know, dominus. Like I said, he was a stranger here. I do think he had a son, so somebody told me. Ran away to join the legions...'

'What happened to the son?'

'Who knows?' The woman let out a sudden cry of laughter. 'Probably died on some battlefield. So many wars there's been! At least now we have peace under Constantine, may his name be writ in gold in the heavens. No more young men going off to die!'

Castus grunted. War would never be far away on this frontier. Even now he was in the closing stages of an official inspection of the troops of the Danube garrisons. Next year, or the year after, Constantine would be preparing once more to fight the Goths or the Sarmatians.

He felt a great sadness inside him. He had hated his father for so long, but he felt the loss of him now. Pointless even to ask if he had a grave; with no family to mourn him or pay for a funeral, his body would have been burned and the ashes dumped in the river. Castus had seen it happen many times.

'I thank you for your help,' he said. Reaching into his pouch, he took out a gold coin. 'For you and your daughter. And the child.'

The woman hung back, startled, as if she feared some trick. Taking two steps towards her, Castus held out the coin until she took it from him. She stared at it a moment as it lay in her palm, the wink of bright gold so glaring in the surrounding brown and grey. Then she closed her hand and bowed deeply.

Castus did not look back as he rode up the street to join his escort at the highway junction. The woman, he realised, was probably about the same age as him. He had heard what the daughter said, as she summoned her mother: *an old man with a big horse, looks like a soldier, asking questions.*

He was an old man: fifty, and he felt it. But the frightened youth who had fled this place over thirty years ago, fearing himself to be a murderer, was gone now. He was a different man, and had lived a different life. He should feel proud of that fact. As he rode through the rain he thought about fathers and sons. About Constantine and Crispus, and about his own son Sabinus, who would be waiting for him at the villa on the Dalmatian coast, with Marcellina. In just over two months he would be with them again, and he longed for it.

But he was glad he had returned to the town of his birth, even so. Unquiet ghosts had haunted him for too long.

'There was a man here a few days ago, asking questions about you.'

'What sort of man?' Castus asked.

'An imperial agent,' the legion prefect said, curling his lip. 'You know the sort. He said he'd been in Gaul recently. He was asking whether you'd been saying anything to the other officers about the Caesar Crispus. And about the emperor's wife.'

Castus paused as he ate, then swallowed carefully. 'The Augusta Fausta?' he asked. The prefect nodded.

It was a windy night in Singidunum, the fortress a few miles downriver from Taurunum, and rain flurried against the shutters of the praetorium. The lamp flame wavered. Valerius Musonius, prefect of Legion IV Flavia, was a solid, unpretentious officer, and a fellow Pannonian. They talked together like old comrades.

'What did you tell him?'

Musonius snorted a laugh. 'Nothing much that he wanted to hear! There were two of them, in fact, although only one of them did any talking. Didn't like his attitude much – he was... *insolent*. What's it come to when civilians can act like that around soldiers?'

Castus smiled tightly. He was all too aware of this agent's identity.

'But you know what it's like with that sort,' Musonius continued, with a slight note of apology. 'They never let on what they're driving at, do they? You never know who gives them their orders neither, nor who they report to. With the world in the state it's in now, brother, it's best to be careful, heh?'

Castus nodded, fighting to suppress his shudder. 'Where did he go when he left you, this agent?'

'Sirmium, I think. Maybe he's still there now.'

'Then I'll pray I don't cross paths with him.'

Musonius grunted his agreement, but Castus caught the prefect's wary glance. Suspicion was like a curse, he thought: once laid upon you it was very hard to shift, and men became uncomfortable in your presence.

If Flavius Innocentius had been in Gaul, he was surely investigating Crispus. Could he also have guessed at the connection between the Caesar and Fausta? Castus felt a wave of nervous dread tightening his throat. It was nothing to do with him now, he told himself. He had severed his links with Crispus and his retinue over a year before, after the events in Nicomedia. After the shock of what he had seen there, Castus had tried very hard to erase from his mind all that he knew about the affairs of the imperial household. When Crispus had returned to Gaul, Castus had not accompanied him; he had claimed that, with his family now living in Dalmatia, he had no wish to go back west again. The excuse had been accepted without question, and the matter had passed quietly enough at the time. But clearly others were not so keen to forget his old connections.

The rain was still falling the following day as Castus stood on the tribunal before the drill field, but the troops arrayed before him did not appear to feel it. To his left were Musonius's legionaries; to his right, two recently raised units, proud beneath their glinting new standards. Their newly painted shields and polished armour gleamed in the rain. Both were *numeri* of auxilia, part of the restructured army that Constantine had decreed following the final defeat of Licinius. Many of the men in the ranks were of barbarian origin, Franks and Alamanni who had come east in irregular units for the war that had ended at Chrysopolis. Others were Roman citizens, volunteers from Pannonia and Moesia. All of them served together now, their differences forgotten in the pride of their new names and titles. They were devoted to their emperor, too, and to his god. Their shields bore the twinned heads of horned and snarling beasts, with the Christ-sign set between them.

Standing on the tribunal with Musonius and the tribunes of the auxilia, Castus felt more than ever before that the world he had known and loved was slipping quickly away from him. Today was the birthday of Augustus Constantius, of blessed memory, father of the Most Sacred Augustus Constantine. Once the day would have been celebrated with ritual sacrifices to the gods, the altars smoking and the air laden with the rich smells of roasting meat. But now official public sacrifices had been banned by imperial order, and only the droning voices of the Christian priests attached to the military units rose to the heavens. Gladiatorial combat had been banned too; Castus would not miss that, but it seemed a symptom of a greater change, one he could not control and did not like. The old empire, the old traditions, were dying. A new empire was rising in its place.

Unless, Castus thought, as he took the salutes and gave the order to dismiss the troops, *something happened to stop the process*. A revolution, or a mutiny. He thought again about Crispus; did he still intend to supplant his father? Did he still respect the traditional faith of Rome? He remembered what Musonius had told him about the imperial agents and their probing enquiries, and was glad that he did not have answers to those questions.

His current position as superintendent of the troops in the Danube provinces was only temporary; he would have to await the emperor's pleasure with regard to further commissions. He had no idea whether he would ever hold a military command again, or lead men in battle. Strangely, he found that prospect did not trouble him as much as it once had done. All he wanted now was to return to his villa on the coast of Dalmatia, where Marcellina and the family had made their new home; Castus had left them there when he began his tour of the provinces back in February, but already he missed them greatly.

Out of the rain, back in the chambers allotted to him in the praetorium, he dragged off his damp cloak and scrubbed a linen cloth over his head, then went to stand beside the brazier to warm himself.

'When's the emperor due to arrive at Sirmium?' he asked.

'Most likely around the ides of next month,' Diogenes said. The secretary was sitting at the table by the window, sorting documents in the pale grey light. 'Although I believe some of the imperial household and the bodyguard troops will be there already.'

Castus pursed his lips as he thought. His duties would take him eastward down the Danube, and would give him excuse enough not to visit Sirmium again for some time. He had a strong desire to keep his distance from the emperor, and from

Crispus. In July he would have to be in Rome for the celebrations of the Vicennalia – as an imperial *comes* he could not decline – but there was plenty of time before then. Three months; and half that period he could spend with Marcellina at the villa. His stepdaughter Maiana was due to be wed early in July, to the son of a city councillor from Salona, and he had promised to be present for that.

'Dominus,' Diogenes said, with an odd emphasis that broke Castus from his thoughts. The secretary had set aside his documents. 'I would like to speak to you, if I may.'

'Hmm?' Castus grunted. 'You're speaking. Go on.'

'I mean – on a matter of some formality. Perhaps you could sit?'

Frowning, baffled, Castus pulled up a stool and sat down. Diogenes, conversely, had got up and now stood rather stiffly before him.

'Dominus,' he began again. 'As you know, it's been just over twenty years since I joined the legions. I believe I am now eligible for a honourable discharge. With your permission, I would like to apply for one.'

'Discharge?' Castus said. 'You're eligible, yes... But why now? Serve four years more and you can get a meritorious discharge: full veteran's privileges, the rank of an ex-Protector, tax exemptions... Why throw all that away?'

Diogenes cleared his throat; he looked embarrassed. 'To be honest, dominus,' the secretary said, 'it's more a matter of belief.'

Castus let out an exasperated cry. 'By all the gods, sit down!' he said. 'Haven't we known each other long enough to speak openly?'

With a flinch and a nod, Diogenes returned to his stool. He rubbed at his face with the heel of his hand. 'I find, brother,' he said, 'that I can no longer respect the emperor I serve.'

320

A twitch of unease, and Castus glanced around at the door behind him. The sentry could not have heard. Gesturing with a flat hand, he nodded to Diogenes to continue.

'The ban on sacrifice I can endure,' Diogenes said quietly. 'As you know, I doubt the efficacy of it anyway. The gods are surely unmoved by such trifles. But only recently I heard that the writings of Porphyrius have now been banned as well! The very greatest philosopher of our age… And not only banned, but there is an order that his books are to be *burned*!'

'Is that so?' said Castus. Burning a book seemed a thing of little importance – they were just words inked on papyrus – but he could see that Diogenes was deeply aggrieved.

'Certainly Porphyrius wrote against the Christians, but he did so in the spirit of philosophical debate. To consign all of his works to the flames is an act of vile barbarism! And what if I were ordered to participate in such a thing? I would have to refuse, and break my military oath… It would be mutiny. Far better that I leave now, and avoid such a possibility.'

Castus sighed heavily, bracing his chin on his fist. Clearly there was nothing he could say to change the secretary's mind. Had he not felt such things himself? And he had a growing notion that the army would have little use for him in future, anyway.

'Well,' he said at last. 'I can't refuse you. What would you do, once you'd left us?'

Diogenes brightened, visibly relieved. 'I've saved a little, and I had an idea that I might travel to the east, and open a school.'

'Go back to being a teacher?' Castus asked with a half-smile.

'Not a school of grammar, no. Of philosophy. An encouragement to higher thought.'

'Sounds dangerous,' Castus said, still smiling.

'I thought I also might get married.'

'What? To... a *woman*?'

'That is the usual procedure, I believe. It's not illegal, as far as I know.'

Castus could not hide his amazement. In all the years he had known Diogenes, the secretary had never shown any interest in women. Perhaps, Castus thought, he had been wrong about him and Eumolpius? Or maybe not – the world was full of wonders.

'Come with me to Dalmatia at least,' he said. 'You were tutor to Maiana, and she'll be pleased to see you at her wedding. I still get to keep my military staff, for now, or as many as I want. Ursio and Felix. You too, if you can ignore the call of your philosophy for a few months more.'

'I'd be honoured,' Diogenes said.

He left then, with a very correct military salute. Castus was still in good humour as he stood by the window gazing out into the rain. But his smile soon faded. Everything was changing, he thought. And Diogenes' words had reawakened the churning sense of unease in his gut, the quick nervous skip of his heart. He thought of the imperial agent Innocentius and his questions, his enquiries. He remembered the visit to his old home town, the sense that he had made a new life for himself. The army had formed that life; duty had been everything to him. But perhaps it was time to think beyond that. Perhaps, he thought with a pained grimace, it would be wise to get out now? Shut himself away where the world could not make its demands upon him, and nobody questioned his honour or his loyalty?

Squaring his shoulders, setting his jaw, Castus tried to dismiss the idea. He was still a soldier, still an officer of the imperial service. But he knew that the time would come very soon when he would have to decide what his future would hold.

CHAPTER XXIV

'Father!'

Castus heard the cries even before he caught sight of his son; the sound of hoofbeats too. A moment later he reached the crest of the ridge and looked down through the pines to see Sabinus galloping up the track towards him. The boy was mounted on a stout pony, and grinning wildly. As he rode up alongside, Castus leaned from the saddle and gripped his son in a tight embrace.

'We've been expecting you for the last three days!' Sabinus said. 'Everything's prepared for your arrival.' There was a mischievous angle to his smile; clearly some surprise was waiting at the villa.

As he rode on down the slope Castus marvelled at the transformation in his son. Just over four months had passed since he saw him last, but with every separation Sabinus seemed to change visibly. He was fourteen now, nearly as tall as his father, lean and broad-shouldered. His face was tanned, and Castus noticed the downy hair on his upper lip. The boy who had so gravely given him his toy horse, years before in Treveris, seemed long gone.

The trees thinned to either side of the track, and below him Castus saw the bright blue water of the cove, the red tiles of the villa and the white domes of the bathhouse on the shore glowing in the afternoon sun. Smoke was rising from the furnace chamber; he had ridden nearly thirty miles along the coast road from Salona that day, and the thought of a hot bath was delicious.

'Look,' Sabinus said, his voice cracking and warbling, 'everyone's here!'

The track descending from the wooded hills to the villa on the shore passed between terraced olive groves and vineyards, and all along the verges there were people assembled to greet him: tenant farmers and fishermen from the villages on the estate. As Castus rode by they raised their arms in salute and cried out blessings. They looked, Castus thought, genuinely glad to see him.

This villa on the coast of Dalmatia, with its surrounding estate, had come to him as part of his first wife's legacy, but Castus had not visited the place before the previous summer. Marcellina had loved it at once; the villa had stood empty for many years, and Castus had left her to supervise the renovation, cleaning and redecoration. The central courtyard opened onto a pillared exedra that curved around a semi-circular boat harbour, and gave a fine view to the west across the sheltered cove to the sea beyond. Wooded hills rose all around, closing the villa off in a private demesne of its own.

With Sabinus riding ahead, Castus passed through the gateway and dismounted in the dusty yard before the front portico. Behind him rode Diogenes, Felix and Ursio, all that remained of his military staff and escort, with Glycon and four slaves bringing up the baggage mules. He flexed his legs, then stretched to ease the ache in his back. Sabinus had already leaped from his pony and run inside. As the stable slaves took their horses and mules, the new arrivals beat the dust from their cloaks and followed Castus up the front steps.

Marcellina was waiting in the slanting sunlight of the entrance atrium, dressed in a patterned green tunic and shawl, her daughter and her maids arrayed to either side. As Castus entered the whole group welcomed him, very correctly. Slaves removed his boots and cloak and washed his hands and feet. Impatient, he endured their attentions, then stood up and paced across the floor towards his wife. Only then did he notice.

Slowing to a halt, he stood before her in stunned surprise, not daring for a moment to touch her.

'How long?' he managed to say.

'Nearly five months now,' Marcellina told him, her hand moving to her swollen belly.

'You didn't tell me!'

'It seemed better. Bad luck otherwise. And in case something happened...'

But before she could say another word Castus let out a roar of joy and threw his arms around her, clasping her in his embrace. At once, everyone assembled around them cried out in unison, giving their blessings. *'Feliciter! Feliciter!'*

'You want this?' he whispered to her, frowning.

'Yes,' she said, raising her head and kissing him. Her eyes gleamed with tears, but she was grinning.

He kissed her again, and held her tightly, gently, glorying in his good fortune. With his eyes closed he formed a prayer. *Whatever gods exist in this world* – or the Christian god, why not? – *protect this woman and this child...*

An hour later, after he had bathed and changed his clothes, Castus joined Marcellina in the exedra that faced the little harbour basin. The slaves had retreated to leave them alone, and Diogenes and the others were eating in another chamber. Castus sat beside his wife and took her hand, and for a while they were content to gaze out at the blaze of evening sun and bright blue sea. To the right, far beyond the bathhouse that stood at the end of the exedra's curve, Castus could see the two small islands jutting from the water a few hundred paces from the shore; already he was imagining swimming out to them, as he had done the previous summer.

'It'll be strange,' Marcellina said, 'to be pregnant at the wedding.'

'Wedding?' said Castus, widening his eyes.

A moment of outrage, then Marcellina grinned, tugged at his hand and swatted his shoulder. 'Not even you would forget twice!'

Castus laughed, shrugging. They had another month until his stepdaughter Maiana was due to be married. Castus was content to leave the planning to others, but he was glad he would be able to attend this time.

He spoke briefly of his travels over the last months, and of his visit to Taurunum. 'I'm glad you went,' Marcellina said. The sun was lighting the red dye in her hair. 'You've never told me much about it, but I knew your mind wouldn't rest until you went back there and made peace with the past.'

'Peace, yes,' Castus said, and frowned quizzically. It seemed an almost alien concept to him. Was that really what he wanted now? *Yes*, he thought. *Yes, perhaps it is...*

'When do you have to go to Rome for the Vicennalia?'

'I'll leave after the wedding. Sabinus can come with me.' The celebrations of the emperor's twentieth anniversary of rule were due to last for eight days. With the journey time, Castus would be gone for nearly a month. 'If I take the boat across to Ancona, I can return here as soon as possible.'

From where he was sitting he could see the boat, moored down in the little circular dock below the villa. It was named *Phaselus*, and built like a miniature warship with a curving prow and eight oars. Under sail it was fast; Castus had been out in it the previous autumn, around the islands and even down to Salona a couple of times.

'I wish I could go myself,' Marcellina said. 'I've always wanted to see Rome.'

'You will,' Castus told her. 'One day soon, when things are calmer.' He reached across and laid his palm on the smooth mound of her belly.

They sat in silence for a short while, watching the colours of the setting sun dyeing the sea horizon. Castus became aware that his wife was peering at him. 'Something's troubling you, isn't it?' she said. 'Tell me?'

Castus tried to hide his discomfort. He had told Marcellina nothing of what had happened at Nicomedia two years before; nothing about Crispus's plans, or the agent Innocentius. Often he had intended to tell her; she had the wisdom and intelligence to understand the deeper meaning and significance better than he did, and maybe to put his mind at rest. But even to speak about these things felt dangerous, and he had not wanted to involve her in it. Now, the thought of the coming visit to Rome, and his inevitable meetings with the imperial household, had returned all those buried fears to the forefront of his mind.

'Diogenes has asked for his discharge,' he told her instead, with a pinch of guilt at the deception. 'It made me think... perhaps the time's come for me to hang up my belt too.'

'Really?' He could tell she was pleased, but anxious too. 'You want to do that?'

'I'm still not sure. But after Chrysopolis... I feel maybe I've had enough of the army. Enough of wars.' The same thought had been circling in his mind for many days, but it was only now, quite suddenly, that he felt the pressure to choose.

'It feels right,' Marcellina said. 'But you need to be certain. You need to decide this for yourself.'

'Maybe, by the time I get to Rome,' he told her. 'Maybe by then I'll know.' He wanted to sound sincere, but he could not meet her eye as he spoke. He gazed at the sea instead, and felt the squeeze of her hand.

Castus was returning from his morning swim when he first noticed the rider coming along the track that led from the highway. The flicker of movement drew his eye, and then the distant figure was gone again between the trees. For a moment he slowed his steps, perplexed. Then he shrugged and continued along the path that followed the shore. It was a beautiful morning, the air fresh and filled with the scents of the pines, the warm dusty earth and the sea.

As he approached the villa, he caught sight of the white colonnade of the exedra between the trees, the domes of the bathhouse and the tiles of the main building beyond it. Over a month had passed since his arrival here, and the long summer days and the freedom from the routines of military life had lulled him into a sense of deep satisfaction and contentment. All his life, Castus thought, he had moved wherever the army sent him, wherever his duties compelled him to go. This villa, isolated and forgotten, belonged solely to him, and it was solely his choice that had brought him and the family here. As he gazed at it in the beaming sunlight, he felt a great sense of belonging. This, he thought, could truly be home.

Emerging from the trees, he followed the path along the curve of the shore, below the mossy old stones of the bathhouse foundations. Ursio was sitting at the far end of the quay that circled the boat harbour, with Maiana; the girl was sorting different coloured yarn from a basket, looping the strands around Ursio's outstretched fingers. The Sarmatian sat placidly, his face expressionless. Castus remembered Marcellina's comment that she was glad the girl was getting married soon. 'She's becoming altogether too fond of your barbarian!'

'She's just getting used to ordering men about,' Castus had replied with a wry smile.

And tomorrow, he thought, they would all set off on the first leg of the bridal procession to Salona. Doubtless there would be feasting and speechmaking; the groom's father was a wealthy decurion, and he was very keen for all to know of his marriage connection with one of the senior military officers in Constantine's service. The *praeses* governor of Dalmatia would be there too, eager to renew their earlier acquaintance. Castus hoped that neither man would be disappointed with his reduced influence these days.

He was climbing the steps to the quay when he heard the sound of galloping hooves. Glancing towards the road, he saw the horseman, much closer and riding hard, coming down the last slope to the villa gateway. A pinch of apprehension quickened his steps.

Pacing through the exedra, Castus entered the central courtyard just as the rider arrived at the main door of the house. He stood for a moment, waiting, feeling the beat of his heart in his chest. *News that travels at speed is seldom good.*

Then the man was marching in through the entrance hall, trailed by the door slaves. A plainly dressed messenger, brown with the dust of the road, dropping to kneel before him with a tablet extended in one hand.

'Bring him water,' Castus called as he took the message. He did not recognise the seals on the wax. Frowning, he ripped them aside and untied the cord, then opened the slim wooden tablet and read.

His eyes skimmed the words, and he felt shock like a punch in the belly. Ice flowed up his spine. *We are in great danger. You must come at once to Aquileia. Only you can help me now. Fausta Aug.*

'What is it?' Marcellina asked, entering the courtyard from her private chambers.

Castus read through the message again. *We*, he thought. Whom did that mean? He opened his mouth and drew a long breath, feeling the prickle of sweat on his brow.

'I need to go to Aquileia,' he said, and heard the shudder in his voice.

'When?' Marcellina asked, baffled.

'Now. Immediately.'

He turned at once and strode towards the chamber he used as an office. Marcellina came after him, snatching the tablet from his grasp. In the chamber, Diogenes was reclining on the couch, peering at a scroll. He leaped up as Castus entered.

'Call Ursio,' Castus said as he stripped off his tunic. He crossed to the cabinet against the far wall and took out his army tunic, his belts and sword. 'Call the oarsmen too, and have the boat provisioned for three days at sea.' His thoughts were tumbling, scattering; he felt the last month, the last year of peace and stability being roughly stripped from him like an old cloak ripped free by a gale.

'What *is* this?' Marcellina demanded, standing in the doorway. She glanced at the tablet, then back at Castus. 'Husband! *What does this mean?*'

'I can't tell you now,' Castus told her as he buckled his belt. He was trying not to look in her direction. 'I'll explain everything when I get back.'

'When you get back? When will that be? What about the wedding, and...' She glanced again at the tablet, her brow bunching. 'What's this danger? Castus! Talk to me!'

'Please,' Castus said roughly, 'I can't explain now. You have to trust me.'

Fury rose through him, fury and shame. When he looked at his wife he saw tears flowing from her eyes, her face alight as her shock turned to anger.

'*Trust you?*' she said, her voice cracking. 'What have you been hiding from me? What's going on? You're going into danger and you can't even tell me why...'

Castus heard the ringing echo of their raised voices. Others had gathered behind Marcellina: house slaves and porters. Sabinus, too, and Maiana.

'This is duty,' he said through his teeth. 'This is something I have to do – an order I must follow.'

'Duty? *Orders?*' Marcellina shrieked the words, then flung the tablet at him. 'Don't you see they're using you? They don't care about you, or any of us – all your life you've followed their instructions, risked your life for them! What about *us?*'

Castus felt the words strike down through him, piercing him. He heard the echo of something his first wife had said to him, many years ago. He threw the sword baldric over his shoulder, but Marcellina was blocking the doorway, one hand pressed to her belly.

As he moved for the door she launched herself forward, gripping his shoulders and forcing him back. 'For once,' she gasped, sniffing back tears. 'Just for once in your life – *refuse*. Say you never got the message, say you weren't here if you like... But don't go to Aquileia! You're not their slave, Castus. You're your own man now – *rebel*!'

'I'm trying to be my own man,' Castus told her quietly. His jaw was set, but he could hardly breathe. 'I just need to do this one thing – fix the problem – then I'll return.'

'Fix *what* problem?' Marcellina cried. Then her expression changed, a look of cold sickened horror creeping across her features. 'And why is the *emperor's wife* giving you orders now?'

She backed away from him with shuffling steps until she reached the doorway, then pressed herself against the frame. She was breathing fast, visibly shaking. 'What hold does she have over you?' she asked in a stunned whisper. 'What have you *done*?'

Castus moved closer, and Marcellina flinched back from him. As gently as he could, he laid his hands on her shoulders. 'Don't worry,' he said, but the words sounded unconvincing even to him. 'There are things I haven't told you, it's true. I thought it was safer that way. I was wrong. But now I have to go – for all our sakes. I promise you I'll tell you everything when I get back.'

Marcellina sagged back into the doorframe, eyes closed, as the anger and defiance drained from her. She looked nauseated, dazed with shock and disbelief. As Castus moved to pass her she seized him suddenly by the neck of his tunic.

'Remember,' she said in a harsh whisper. '*You are not their slave.*'

He nodded, kissed her on the brow, then strode out into the courtyard. Ursio stood waiting by the doors to the exedra, thumbs hooked in his belt.

'I'm going to Aquileia at once,' Castus told the Sarmatian. 'I'd like you to come with me, but I'm not ordering you. There might be things there...' He halted, unsure how to explain. *Gods, I need to move fast...* 'I might have to do things that conflict with the oath of loyalty that both of us swore. Understand? If you'd rather stay here, you can.'

Ursio's face flickered, as if the thought passing through his mind left a slight ripple. Then he nodded once, and without a word turned and strode from the courtyard. Castus watched him go, puzzled. No time to consider that now.

Already he could hear Diogenes mustering the boat crew down on the quay. Felix was there too, throwing bags of provisions and flasks of water down into the narrow hull of the *Phaselus*. In the exedra Castus found Sabinus and his stepdaughter waiting for him.

'I'm sorry I have to miss your wedding,' Castus told Maiana. The girl was trying not to cry. Sabinus looked almost as distraught.

'Can I come with you?' the boy asked.

Castus shook his head. 'Not this time. You'll have to stay here. Look after the household for me. I'll return as soon as I can.'

From inside the house came loud wails of grief.

Down on the quay in the bright sunlight, Castus checked the provisions in the boat. They could reach Aquileia, he estimated, by tomorrow evening if the wind held and they sailed through the night. How long had Fausta's message taken to reach him? For the first time he was beginning to consider how little he knew of the threat. Cursing, he tried to rid himself of the thought, but it would not leave him. Marcellina's words echoed through his mind.

For once in your life – refuse... rebel.

How easy that would be. But how foolish, when he knew so little.

Maiana's cry came from the exedra, and Castus turned to see Ursio marching along the quay, his sword and military pack slung over his shoulder. The Sarmatian just gave a brief nod as he climbed into the boat. For a moment Castus felt his spirits lift. *At least somebody here trusts me.*

333

'Diogenes,' he said. 'I need you to stay here with Glycon and the family. Make sure they remain safe, and try to explain things to Maiana if you can... To Marcellina as well.'

Tell her I love her, he wanted to say. But no – that would be cowardly. He should have told her himself, and now there was no time. Diogenes dipped his head, eyes closed. Castus took his hand and clasped it tight, then he clambered down into the boat beside Ursio.

Sitting in the stern as the oarsmen pulled out into the cove, Castus stared back over his shoulder at the figures on the quay. Marcellina stood there, Sabinus and Maiana supporting her on either side. She had the hem of her shawl pressed across her mouth. Castus raised himself upright, anguished, lifting his hand towards them. But the figures on the quay made no movement in reply.

Moments later, the boat was clear of the cove and they felt the fresh breeze from the south. The sailors shipped their oars and stepped the mast, dragging up the long yard. The sail canvas bellied out, and the *Phaselus* seemed to lift in the water as the wind took her. Skimming the waves, the boat began to fly northwards.

CHAPTER XXV

All day, all night and all through the following day they sailed. They kept to the open sea, the jagged island-studded coasts of Dalmatia and Istria slipping past to the north-east. When the wind slackened after dark the crew took to their oars and pulled, their rhythmic chant dying to a parched croak as the hours crawled by. Felix sat up in the bows, retching quietly and swigging water from a flask. And all the way, Castus sat silently at the stern, turning over in his mind all that he could imagine of what awaited him. He dared to hope that it was a false alarm, that the danger might have receded by the time he reached Aquileia. But a keen presentiment of threat told him otherwise, and he willed the boat onwards with every sinew in his body.

Evening was coming on by the time they sighted the low marshy coast at the head of the Adriatic. The boat crossed the lagoons and pulled on into the mouth of the Natiso River, and the strong walls and towers of Aquileia appeared on the horizon as the last colours of sunlight flamed in the west. It was fully dark when the *Phaselus* steered between the military galleys riding at anchor in the river and rowed across to the city dock. Castus went ashore at once.

He knew Aquileia well enough, and had tried during the voyage to recall the exact plan of the streets and buildings. With

Ursio and Felix behind him he marched through the gloom of the narrow lanes along the riverfront, past the warehouses and the sailors' taverns, until he reached the wide main street that would take him to the imperial palace. Nobody challenged him, and he could see no signs of crisis or turmoil. There were plenty of soldiers in the streets, men of the field army units billeted in the city, but all of them were off duty and content to ignore him.

The palace of Aquileia was old and small, but Castus knew that Constantine had often favoured it as a residence during his journeys to and from Italy. The emperor was not in residence now – the imperial standards were not displayed above the main gate – but from the number of guard troops at the gateway Castus knew that Constantine must have passed through recently. He announced himself to the sentries, then had to endure a long and frustrating wait while they summoned the tribune of the watch. Standing stiffly, one hand on his sword hilt, he attempted to feign the correct attitude of calm detachment.

He was in luck: the tribune knew his name, and recognised his face. With no further delay, Castus was striding across the barracks courtyard and through the inner gate to the precincts of the imperial household. Now that he was here he wanted to run, but he forced himself to remain wary.

Fausta was in one of the upper chambers off the central courtyard. As Castus was announced she hurried from the window to stand facing him. One glance at her confirmed his worst fears; she already looked like a condemned criminal.

'You're here,' she said, and her voice was hoarse. 'I've waited days…'

'Nobody could have got here sooner.' Castus glanced at the slaves waiting beside the open doors. At a gesture from Fausta they retreated, and the doors thudded closed behind them. Fausta let out a gasping sigh and dropped onto one of the couches. She had lost her ring, Castus noticed, and her knuckles were red where she had been gnawing at them.

Pacing across the room, Castus went to the side table. He poured himself a cup of wine from the jug, unmixed, and drank it back in three long swallows.

'Tell me everything,' he said.

Fausta was still slumped on the couch, shaking her head. She looked dazed, barely able to speak.

'This is about you and Crispus, and your husband,' Castus said. 'Who knows about it, and how much do they know?' He could feel the fury mounting in his body already, all the tension of his desperate journey finding focus.

'They took Niobe, my slave,' Fausta said. 'Five days ago. Snatched her off the street. It was Innocentius, the agent – I know it was. I never thought they'd dare move against me like that. Against my own household!'

'Why? Imperial agents don't kidnap slaves for no reason.'

'To torture her, of course!' Fausta cried. She grabbed at her shawl and ripped the hem between her fists. 'They found out about me and Crispus, who knows how, and they needed proof. They needed dates, witnesses, names.'

It was shocking, Castus thought, to see this woman so unnerved and vulnerable. He had known Fausta for years, and she had always been controlled and composed, effortlessly in charge of herself. Only once had he seen anything different, the face behind the mask, and that had been long ago and far away.

'And that was when you wrote to me?' he said. 'What's happened since?'

'Luxorius, my eunuch,' Fausta said, speaking in a breathless rush. 'He found out where they were keeping her. The night before last he went to investigate – I had nobody else I could turn to! – and he never returned. Either they killed him, or he's their prisoner too.'

Brave, Castus thought, *but foolish*. 'Did he tell you where he was going?'

'He left directions, just in case,' Fausta said, drawing a scrap of papyrus from beneath one of the couch cushions. She held it out, and Castus took it. 'It's a farm, a mile or two west of the city. They have men with them – other agents – six or eight, he thought.'

Castus studied the papyrus. Four lines, and a sketch map. It looked easy enough to find the place. Would Innocentius and his men still be there?

'What can the slave and the eunuch tell them?'

'Oh, everything they need!' Fausta said, despair in her voice. 'Luxorius was passing messages between me and Crispus, Niobe was with me all the time and knows about it all.'

'And what is *all*?' Castus said slowly. He was standing before the couch, thumbs in his belt. 'What did you think you were doing, you and the young Caesar?'

Fausta stared at him, her face empty of everything but remorse. 'I was so stupid,' she said. 'I wanted to use him. I thought I could push him to revolt against his father, and Constantine would destroy him... But it went too far. I never thought...' Her voice caught, and suddenly she sobbed, pressing her face into the ripped shawl. 'I never expected to feel this way about him.'

'You tried to have him killed, once.'

Fausta nodded quickly. 'Yes, yes I did. I didn't know him then. But I allowed it to happen.' She raised her head, her cheeks smudged with kohl. 'We became lovers,' she said. 'And I... I forgot myself. Nobody's ever treated me like that, given me that, wanted me in that way... I *loved it so much*. I loved *him* so much...'

Castus groaned from deep within his chest, and struck his head with the heel of his hand. 'How long?' he asked.

'That night in Nicomedia was the first – and the only one, until recently. When we met again in Sirmium back in March… it became more serious.' She pressed her fingers to her temples, staring at nothing, and for a moment she appeared lost in whirling thoughts.

Scrubbing at her face, Fausta took a deep breath and struggled to regain her composure. 'But it's not Crispus they want,' she said bitterly. 'These agents – they take their orders from Helena, the emperor's mother. She's always wanted to destroy me, and now they're going to give her what she needs. But they'll destroy Crispus in the process. And you, too.'

'What?' Castus tasted ash in his mouth, and his head reeled. This had been his worst fear.

'Oh yes,' Fausta said in a nervous singsong. 'Crispus has gone further than you think in the last year. Further even than he told me! He's been in communication with senators in Rome, and governors and army commanders in Gaul and on the Danube. And he's been telling them that you, Aurelius Castus, are one of his firmest supporters!'

For a few moments Castus could not speak. 'The mad bastard,' he said under his breath. 'The mad, reckless, idiotic…' He lashed out suddenly, smashing his hand down on the table and knocking the jug and cups to the floor. Wine spattered across the mosaic tiles. Fists braced against the tabletop, Castus clenched his teeth and waited for the black fog of rage to clear. He thought of Marcellina, of his son and family: if he was accused of treason he would die, but they too would suffer. They could lose everything, even their lives. When he looked at Fausta again he saw she was hunched over, covering her face. *Yes, be ashamed*, he thought.

Then she raised her head, and lay back on the couch with a sigh. Castus stared at her, frowning. If he had not spent the last month with Marcellina he would never have noticed anything, would never even have suspected. But suddenly he was sure.

'You're carrying his child,' he said coldly.

Fausta sat up with a start. 'You can tell?'

'*Gods*... How? When?'

'Two months ago, in Sirmium. I didn't want it to happen. And now I don't know...' She broke off, unable to say any more. A shudder ran through her, and she began shaking. Castus could see she was on the edge of panic.

He paced towards the couch. Fausta glanced up at him, tears in her eyes, then threw herself forward to kneel on the floor, hands raised. 'Please,' she said. 'Please, only you can help me now.'

For a moment Castus stared in shock. *The emperor's wife*, he thought, *the Augusta, kneeling before me...* Then he remembered how long he had known this woman, how he had mistrusted her, how he had desired her, but how he had always despite everything felt a strange connection with her. Crouching, he took her arms and drew her upright. She fell against him, pressing herself against his chest, and he held her.

'I'll do what I can,' he said. 'Not for you, and not for him. For myself, and for my family.'

'Thank you,' she said quietly. Expensive scent surrounded him, mingled with the acidic tang of her sweat.

'Where's the emperor now, and where's Crispus?'

'Constantine's gone to Mediolanum,' Fausta said, mumbling. She was still clinging to him tightly. 'I'm to meet him at Ravenna, five days before the ides, so we can travel on to Rome together. Crispus is travelling down from Carnuntum. He should be here in four days, maybe five; I was going to wait for him.'

'Don't. You need to get out of here now. Leave tonight. Go to Ravenna and wait for the emperor there. I'll send a message before dawn if I've managed to stop this.'

'You will?' Fausta said, glancing up at him. Just for a moment Castus saw the young woman she had once been, the naive and rather petulant girl who had married the emperor back in Treveris, nearly twenty years before. Then she closed her eyes, and was herself once more.

'I always knew that you were the one I could trust,' she said.

Felix and Ursio were waiting in the pool of lamplight just inside the gateway of the barracks court. Another man was with them, but until he turned Castus did not recognise him. *Thank the gods*, he thought. At least something tonight was in his favour.

'Brother!' Bonitus declared. 'I meet you in a strange place!'

'Likewise,' Castus said, and grabbed the Frankish chief in a tight embrace. He had not seen him for over a year; Bonitus had been with the imperial retinue for many months. 'What are you doing in Aquileia?' he asked.

'Going home!' Bonitus cried, with a happy shrug. 'Too long I've been adventuring under these foreign skies. I saw Antioch! Even Egypt! But now I'm away home to my own lands, my own people. My wife and son!'

'Do you have anyone with you?' Castus said quietly, still gripping Bonitus by the shoulders. He drew him aside, into the shadow behind the gates.

'A handful of men. My bodyguard warriors, those who didn't want to join the new auxilia. Why?'

'I need your help,' Castus told him. 'Just for one night. There's somebody I need to find, and it won't be easy. It's a lot to ask, I know. Could be tough work…'

Bonitus shoved away from him with a growl of annoyance. 'How long are we friends?' he said, scowling. 'You want help, I give it. We're brothers. No?'

Grinning, Castus dragged him back and clasped his hand.

'Meet me outside the Concordia gate, just after the change of watch. I'll need six men, good with a blade and fully armed.'

Bonitus raised his eyebrows. 'Oh,' he said with a smile. 'So this is fighting work?'

Castus smiled too, and felt the warmth returning to his limbs. It was good to be back in the company of warriors. '*Fighting work*,' he said.

In the pale moonlight it was hard to make out the men waiting by the road. Tombs lined the verges on either side, big old masonry structures half consumed by scrub, and the figures formed out of the darkness. Castus picked out Bonitus; the men with him had thick hair and heavy moustaches, and all wore cloaks and belted swords.

'I told the sentries,' Bonitus said with a quiet laugh, 'that we were going out hunting. They thought – ha! – barbarians do strange things at night!'

Felix had drawn horses from the palace stables, enough for them all with two spare. There was still a chance, Castus thought, that the captives might be alive. Once all were mounted, he gave the signal and led them off along the straight causeway heading west from the city. As they rode, he told them what was going to happen.

'All this for a slave and a eunuch?' Bonitus said. He shrugged. 'Surely you have your reasons! But I remember that man, Innocentius.' He spat from the saddle. 'No trouble to put my blade through him.'

The country around Aquileia was dead flat to the horizon

in every direction. Fields of tall wheat lay on either side of the road, pale under the moon and waving in the breeze, like a shifting grey sea. The riders broke into a gallop, the hooves of the horses kicking up dust. Across a canal on a plank bridge, boards drumming beneath them, they approached a crossroads.

Castus slowed his horse, gazing at the dark country around him. He had memorised the instructions that the eunuch had left, but now he was out here in the open he mistrusted his sense of direction. There were farms all around them, buildings jutting up like islands in the sea of wheat. All of them dark, all of them quiet. He rode on a little way past the crossroads, then slowed again. To his left, a smaller path branched from the road and slanted away across the fields. A glance back, then another glance forward. He was sure this was the place.

The riders slowed as they crossed the fields, the sound of the hooves muffled in the dust. Ahead of them was a solitary clutch of farm buildings, a large house with a walled yard, surrounded by tall black poplars. As he drew nearer, Castus saw a wink of light from one of the upper windows. Nervous tension flowed through him.

'Bonitus,' he called in a hushed voice. 'Four of your men circle the perimeter. Stay mounted – they need to stop anyone trying to get away.'

Bonitus gave the order, and the riders separated. Castus and the rest of the group rode a little further, then dismounted and tethered the horses beside the first of the poplars. The air was damp and close, muddy-smelling. As they crept closer, an agonised scream cut the stillness. Castus already had his sword in his hand, his body in a fighting crouch. But the scream had come from inside the house.

'Sounds like this is the right place,' said Felix, with a grim smile.

They moved up fast between the trees to the wall of the yard. There was a gate ten paces to the left, but it was surely barred. Wrapping his cloak around his left arm, Castus crouched with his back to the wall and gestured to Felix. The wiry soldier needed no explanation; he ran at the wall, slapped his foot into Castus's cupped hands and boosted himself up onto the crest. Castus turned at once, gazing upwards, but Felix was already gone. A dry scuffling sound came from the far side of the wall, a scrape of heels and a muffled thud. Four heartbeats later, the gate creaked as the bar was lifted free, and swung open.

A body lay in the dirt of the yard, just inside the gate. Felix wiped his knife on the dead man's cloak, then slipped it back into his belt sheath. Castus was already moving, crossing the yard towards the main building on the far side with Ursio, Bonitus and his warriors close behind him.

Another shriek from inside the house. The sound chilled Castus's blood. Only extreme pain dragged sounds like that from a human being. Then a dark shape exploded from the far corner of the yard, a mastiff, barking furiously as it charged. Ursio bent his bow, loosed, and the barking choked abruptly into a dying whine. No time for stealthy approaches now. The house had a single door, shuttered windows above. Castus gave a quick signal to the men behind him, then he ran at the door.

The boards exploded inward, old wood shattering from the locks.

Castus crashed through the doorway into the narrow passage beyond, staggering as his shoulder collided with a plastered wall. Light at the end of the passage, a lamplit atrium at the heart of the house. He threw himself forward, screwing up his eyes as he charged. Two men in grey tunics stumbling up from a table, snatching for their weapons; Castus took two running

344

strides and cut the first man down. Behind him, Ursio shot his bow from the passageway. The arrow pinned the second man through the throat and he toppled backwards into the basin of water at the centre of the atrium.

Wooden stairs led up to a balcony circling the chamber. Castus stared up and saw faces at the railing, men peering down. His eyes locked with one of them: Innocentius. The torturer blanched, mouth open to shout, then ran into one of the upper doorways. Castus was already on the stairs, charging upward.

Ursio shot another of the guards from the balcony and the man fell, crashing through the railing. Another crouched at the head of the stairs, shield braced and sword ready. Castus lashed at him as he reached the top step, his blade smacking against the shield and sliding to strike the sword and knock it aside. He threw his shoulder up, slamming into the shield and shoving hard, but his opponent kept his footing and struck back. Castus parried the blow but, with the guard still holding the top of the stairs, he could not drive an attack. Bonitus, coming up behind him, reached between his legs and seized the man's ankle, pulling him down. The man fell on his back, yelling, and the Frankish chief jabbed a spear into his chest.

Leaping over the body, Castus ran along the balcony towards the far doorway. He burst through it with sword raised, breathing hard, then paused in shock. The chamber beyond held a scene of horror.

In the smoky light of the oil lamps Castus saw a naked captive seated on a wooden bench, his arms bound to a frame above his head. The captive's body was running with blood, mauled with scars and burns. A hot brazier stood in one corner, and the floor was littered with crude implements, iron bars and blades. The air stank of blood, vomit and burnt flesh. For a heartbeat Castus stood and stared, his fist tight on his sword grip. Then the bound figure raised his head. His eyes rolled in their bloodied sockets, and he nodded once to the left.

Castus turned, just in time. He arched his back and threw himself against the attacker who had been hiding just inside the door. The knife slashed above him and struck the plaster of the wall, then Castus rammed himself against the man, smashing him backwards with all his weight. The man twisted, trying to free his arm to strike again, and Castus punched him in the face with the pommel of his sword.

Others were behind him now, Bonitus and two of his warriors crowding into the room. 'Hold this one!' Castus cried. The man was still writhing, but Castus recognised the balding head and bristly black beard. Gracilis, he remembered. 'Where's Innocentius?' he snarled.

'Back room,' the bound captive said in a ghastly liquid croak.

Bonitus had already seen the far door from the chamber, and ran for it. He returned a moment later. 'Window's open,' he said with a sneer of frustration. 'Nobody else back there. Don't worry – if he jumped my men outside will catch him!' He was gazing at the contents of the chamber in disgust.

'They'd better,' Castus said. 'Search the rest of the house.'

Bonitus took charge of Gracilis, holding him pressed to the wall with a forearm across his neck. Castus noticed that the bearded man was wearing a bloodied leather apron, like a butcher or a surgeon. His stomach clenched. He remembered the torture chamber he had been shown in the cellars beneath the town of Arelate; that had been brutal enough, but it seemed sophisticated in comparison with this room.

The bound captive was struggling to speak, his ruined mouth trying to shape words. Castus forced himself to look at him. The torturers had ripped his flesh, burned his armpits and groin, mangled his hands and feet. He stepped closer, lifting the captive's head. For a moment he did not recognise him, the face was so beaten and swollen. Then his vision cleared. It was the eunuch, Luxorius.

'Bring water,' he said in a hoarse grunt. 'And cut him free of this thing – gently!'

'Dominus?' Castus turned and saw Felix in the doorway. 'You'd better come and see this.' The flatness of his voice told Castus everything.

Felix led him to another chamber that opened off the balcony, then stood aside with a lamp raised. Peering past him, Castus saw the dingy room, the scratched and pitted walls. Then he saw the straw mattress on the floor, and the naked body of the Aethiopian woman lying upon in.

With a low groan he dropped to kneel beside her. He pressed his fingers to her neck, then held them above her parted lips. The flesh was cold, and he felt no breath.

Felix waited in the doorway, cursing under his breath. 'What have the bastards done to her?' he said.

'Everything,' Castus told him. He dropped his head, eyes closed as the bitterness of remorse washed through him. Fausta had been guilty of her plots and schemes; Luxorius too, for aiding her. But this girl had done nothing. She had followed orders, and had died a hideous death, alone and terrified in the grip of the tormenters. For a few long heartbeats Castus could only kneel there, head hanging, lost in anguish. Then he opened his eyes, blinking away the tears. He snatched up a blanket from the floor and draped it carefully across Niobe's body. He stalked from the room with ferocious murder in his heart.

The Franks had captured the two remaining guards, holding them pinned against the wall. Castus glared at them. They were lumpish men, stunned and terrified, but he had no pity for them. They were worse than beasts.

'Kill them both,' he ordered.

He went back into the torture room, where Luxorius was lying on the bench, freed of his bonds. The eunuch was shaking uncontrollably, his ruined hands clasped to his belly and his shaved head running with sweat. Castus crouched, and helped him to drink water.

'What did you tell them?' he asked.

For a moment the eunuch could not speak. He sucked a gargling breath, weakly spat blood. 'They know... it all,' he managed to say. 'The girl... she held out for days. But when they took me too... they told her I'd confessed everything. And she told them... what they wanted to hear.'

'No doubt they played the same trick on you both,' Castus said quietly. He got to his feet, feeling the first nauseating swells of dread rising through his anger. When he glanced at Gracilis, he was astonished to see that the man was grinning.

'You're too late,' the torturer said, his voice metallic with scorn. 'We sent a messenger to Mediolanum at dawn yesterday! The emperor will know everything by now – his wife's treason, and his son's – and yours!'

A moment of shocked silence. Castus heard Bonitus draw a sharp breath; now everyone knew what was at stake. He looked back at Luxorius. The eunuch raised his head and gave a pained nod. Clearly Innocentius and Gracilis had been prolonging their tortures for pleasure alone. *Too late – and now everything's lost...*

'You've condemned yourself anyway!' Gracilis hissed. 'Attacking imperial agents, conspiring with traitors... you're all dead men!'

With a roar of fury Castus stamped across the room and punched his fist into the torturer's belly. Gracilis grunted, but Bonitus was still holding him pressed against the wall.

A shout from the atrium, and the sound of running feet on the stairs. One of the Franks appeared in the doorway, shouting. 'Suandicco is killed! The agent took his horse!'

Bonitus cried out, lurching towards the door, and as he moved Gracilis shoved himself away from the wall, breaking free of the Frankish chief's grip. Castus snatched at him, but the torturer had flung himself across the room to a side table covered with bottles and blades. He grabbed one of the bottles, then seized the leg of the table and sent it crashing to the floor.

Castus kicked the table aside, stumbling. Gracilis was crouched against the far wall, tugging at the stopper of the bottle. Castus kicked again, catching the man on the wrist and knocking the bottle from his grasp. It fell to the floor and spun. Seizing the man by the neck Castus hauled him upright and threw him back into the middle of the room. Bonitus and Felix fell on him at once. The bottle was still spinning, and Castus snatched it up. A small earthenware flask, glazed red, no larger than a child's fist.

'What's this?'

Gracilis lay on his back, pinned to the floor by three men. He glared at Castus, lips drawn back from his teeth. His face was grey and sheened with sweat.

'Poison,' Luxorius croaked, struggling to sit upright on the bench. 'Easy way out. He thinks… you'll torture him.'

Castus gave a nervous shudder as he clasped the bottle. For a moment he wanted to hurl it against the wall. Then he pushed it down into a fold of his waistband and took one of the knives that had fallen from the table.

'Bind him and gag him,' he told Felix.

For a moment he stood with the knife in his hand. Gracilis was still thrashing on the floor, letting out strangled gasps. Two of the Franks held him while Felix knotted a rag around his jaws and tied him hand and foot. Flipping the knife, Castus held out the handle towards Luxorius. He recalled that the eunuch did not like blades.

'Can you use this?'

The eunuch lifted his mangled hands towards the knife, his face contorting into a ghastly expression of vengeful relish.

'See he doesn't leave here alive.'

Outside the house the night air was cool and damp with mist, and all of them sucked down great lungfuls of it. Castus still felt shaken and slightly sick. Felix had wrapped Niobe's body in the blanket and carried it with him; he tied it across the saddle of one of the spare horses, while two of the Franks carried the body of their murdered comrade. They moved silently up the track between the poplars, pretending not to hear the muffled shrieks from the house behind them.

The countryside was open in all directions; in daylight they might have had a chance of tracking the fleeing imperial agent, but dawn was hours away and there was no time to waste in pursuit. Castus felt the hard globe of the poison bottle digging into his side. He drew it carefully from his waistband, intending to throw it away from him into the darkness. Then he thought again about what might lie ahead. With a quick shiver, he slipped the bottle into the leather satchel hanging from his saddle.

As they reached the junction with the main highway, he swung himself up onto his horse and gazed towards the distant sentry fires of Aquileia.

'So,' said Bonitus. 'What will you do now?'

Castus could not answer; he had been turning the same question over in his mind since they left the house. He knew what he should do: ride at once for Mediolanum and surrender himself to the emperor. Hope for Constantine's mercy, if he offered to confess everything. But how could he do that, when he knew so little of the accusations against him? He knew also what he wanted to do: walk away from all of this, sail home to Marcellina and hope that he would be spared the consequences of what would surely happen next.

Yet he could do neither. He needed to think clearly, take a decision, but his mind was blurred with shock and fatigue, and a terrible sense that events were spinning far beyond his control.

'Crispus,' he said. 'He's on the road from Carnuntum. Should be here in four or five days…' He was thinking as he spoke. Bonitus mounted his horse and nudged it closer.

'You intend something,' the Frank said quietly, and whistled under his breath. 'Be very careful! Maybe this is not your fight?'

'It's not a fight I want. But it's coming to me, whether I like it or not.' Suddenly he was certain. There were no good plans, no ideal outcomes. But he knew what he needed to do.

'I'm riding east,' he said. 'I'm going to find Crispus and warn him, before the emperor makes a decision.'

'Warn him?' Bonitus asked, stroking his moustache with his thumb. 'Or take him prisoner yourself?'

Castus had not wanted even to consider that option. 'I'll know when I find him,' he said. 'I'm not asking any of you to come with me.'

Bonitus gave a low chuckle, then turned to the five Frankish warriors who remained with him. Each nodded gravely. Castus looked at Felix and Ursio – both men nodded as well.

'We're already with you, brother,' Bonitus said.

CHAPTER XXVI

By noon they had reached the Frigidus River, and they rested and watered their horses beneath the walls of the fortress that guarded the crossing. All of them were weary and saddle-sore. Castus had not slept properly since leaving his villa two days before, and whenever he closed his eyes he felt a vertiginous rush of exhaustion threatening to overwhelm him. The temptation to lie down in the grass of the riverbank and let the warm midsummer sun lull him into sleep was compelling, but he forced himself to refuse it.

They moved on, and the road carried them steadily upwards through the forested lower slopes of the Julian Alps. As they climbed the temperature dropped, and the riders pulled their cloaks around them, peering up at the cloud-wreathed mountain peaks barring the eastern horizon. Castus prayed that Crispus was still travelling towards them, somewhere on the road ahead, that he had not delayed his journey far to the north, or taken a different route. He still did know what he would do or say when he met the Caesar.

As evening came on the party turned off the mountain road and made camp in a wooded dell ringed by pines. It was still a few miles to Ad Pirum, the fortification that guarded the pass between Italy and Pannonia, but Castus did not want to risk passing through there after dark. It would arouse too many suspicions; so far Bonitus alone had spoken to anyone they met on the road, and Castus and his two companions had blended into the Frankish entourage. Nobody would know that the comes rei militaris Aurelius Castus had passed that way. Already he was beginning to think like a fugitive.

'Why do you take this risk?' Bonitus asked him. They were sitting beside the flickering fire, the shapes of the men watching the road almost lost in the blackness, the others already asleep in their blankets near the tethered horses. Castus took his time before replying.

'Because if I didn't, I'd be living in fear the rest of my days,' he said. 'Anyway, it's instinct. Always take action. Like in a battle – if you hang back or pause, the other man strikes first.'

Bonitus laughed quietly, probing at the fire with a stick to rouse a bit more warmth from the embers.

'What about you?' Castus asked him. 'You must have guessed something of what's happening. But you aren't involved. You could've gone home to Gaul in peace, you and your men.'

The Frank shrugged, raising his eyebrows. 'True enough!' he said. 'For my men, they follow me where I go, same as yours. For me… You remember, years ago, when we met on the Rhine?'

Castus frowned, nodding. His head felt weighted with sleep.

'You remember when we all attended the audience with Crispus for the first time? Me and the other chiefs. I said then – with *this man* as Caesar, and *this man* as commander, I am at peace with Rome.' He pointed at Castus. 'Because of you, and Crispus, my life has been different. I have seen incredible things! Now there's some trouble – I don't fully know what and I don't want to know, but it involves you both. So, I reckon, it involves me. Anyway, these are lonely mountains. Not a place to travel without friends, heh?'

Castus glanced around at the blackness beyond the firelight, the looming pines and the steep rocky slopes. He shivered, and tugged the cloak tighter around his shoulders. Somewhere out in the night a wolf howled.

They met Crispus at the town of Emona on the evening of the following day. Castus had pushed the pace for the last ten miles, leading his riders at a canter along the straight tree-lined road that ran from the mountain foothills. The sentries at the town gates told him what he needed to know: the Caesar and his military escort were lodging in a large townhouse on the far side of the forum. As he rode on along the main street, Castus tried to temper his feelings of relief; after two days of rapid travel, he had found his quarry, but the hardest part was yet to come.

Crispus was just finishing his dinner as the men entered his rooms. He sat up, smiling as he called out a greeting; then he saw their grim expressions, their clothing stained with sweat and dust, and his face fell. Leading them into a side chamber, he seated himself in a high-backed chair and dismissed the slaves. When only Castus, Bonitus and his guard commander Saturninus remained with him, he nodded for them to speak. Briefly, in a curt monotone, Castus told him what had happened at Aquileia.

When he had finished speaking, Crispus sat in silence, his eyes unfocused. Castus could see him struggling to draw breath, his fingers clasped tight on the arms of the chair.

'Do you blame me?' the young man asked quietly.

'This is not the moment for blame!' Castus snapped. 'This is the moment for clear thinking and prompt action.'

Crispus stammered something, clearly unable to do either, unable even to look at the three men confronting him. He blushed, and shivered quickly. 'Where's Fausta now?' he asked.

'Gone to meet the emperor at Ravenna, as he travels down to Rome,' Castus told him. 'She'll try and save herself as best she can, I reckon.'

'She should have come to me!' Crispus cried in sudden anger. 'Why didn't you bring her here?'

'Forget about Fausta,' Castus growled. 'Hasn't she brought you enough trouble already?'

'I have no choice. I'm in love with her...'

Castus choked a curse. 'She's your stepmother!'

'That matters nothing! There's no blood connection between us... We don't choose whom we love – surely you know that?'

'You have a wife and child, back in Treveris,' Castus said, his words grating.

'I care nothing for them,' Crispus replied with a shrug. 'How can I help that? The gods compel us to certain feelings – and they have made me love Fausta...'

'She tried to have you *killed*. Back in Gaul, years ago. She sent her eunuch to murder you.'

Crispus stared, his jaw slack. 'That's not true,' he gasped.

'It is true, and you need to hear it,' Castus said, cold and hard. He saw Saturninus's startled expression. 'Whatever you think you're doing, you've been led down a bad path. And now we're all in danger.'

Rubbing at his face with both hands, Crispus struggled to gather his thoughts. Castus glanced at Saturninus; the other officer was the commander of the Caesar's bodyguard, but Castus was still his senior in rank. Saturninus evaded his eye. The tension in the room drew taut.

'It's my guess that the imperial agents weren't acting on direct orders,' Castus said. 'If they were, they'd have taken their captives to Mediolanum. They wanted to gather enough evidence to make their case before they presented it to the emperor. That might give us time...'

'Time for what?' Crispus asked vaguely, and let out a bleak laugh. Castus could see the contrary emotions pouring through him: anger and terror, grief and guilt. Confusion above all.

'We have to act quickly,' Castus said. 'As soon as the emperor makes a decision, he'll send out men to block the roads and seize you. He may even order your immediate execution.'

'Execution?' Crispus said, unable to hide his gulp of anguish.

'*Of course!*' Castus yelled in sudden fury. 'What do you think? You plotted treason against the emperor and committed adultery with his wife! If Constantine finds you guilty, you'll be hunted down and killed like a rabid dog!'

'But he's my father...' Crispus hunched in the chair, crushed. Castus could almost feel sorry for him, but the young man had brought this on himself with his vain and reckless actions. All they could hope for now was to limit the damage he had caused.

'We could return north, majesty,' Saturninus said. 'The garrisons on the Danube would favour you, and there's a whole army in Gaul devoted to you. Reach them, and you'd be safe.'

'And then what?' Castus said, his hand going to his sword hilt. 'Start another war, against Constantine? Romans killing Romans all over again?'

For a long moment Saturninus glared back at him, and Castus could see the calculation in his eyes, the hostility in his stance. The executioner's sword was poised above them all, and they knew it. Then Bonitus cleared his throat quietly and took a step closer to Castus. The bodyguard commander shrugged and dropped his gaze.

'You promised once you'd back me, brother,' Crispus said quietly.

Castus clenched his teeth, fury seething inside him. Yes, he thought, once he had promised that. To give this young man some heart and some courage. He had meant it too, back then, when success seemed possible. But now it was madness.

'At this moment,' he said, slow and harsh, 'I'm just trying to keep you alive.'

'What would you have me do?' Crispus said, with a shrug of surrender.

They moved out at first light, heading towards the mountains on the Aquileia road once more. Saturninus had chosen sixteen of his most dependable men as an escort, and Crispus rode with them, dressed in a soldier's uniform and a plain military cloak. Every man had a second horse as a remount, taken from the stables at Emona. Moving at a fast pace, resting at intervals, they passed through Nauportus by mid-morning and were climbing the twisting road into the mountains by noon.

Crispus had agreed to Castus's plan readily enough. The only other option was open rebellion, and with the odds of even reaching Gaul ahead of the emperor's messengers so slim only a fool would chance that. As he rode, Castus tried not to think too much about what lay ahead. But he knew that he was riding directly into danger, perhaps the greatest danger of his life. His best hope was to try and slip through the guarded posts in the mountains, evade the imperial messengers and meet Constantine somewhere on the road towards Rome. Then – if the gods were good – Crispus might be able to reconcile himself with his father. How he would do that Castus did not care. He had told the young man that he should be ready to prostrate himself at the emperor's feet if necessary. The thought that he might have to do the same brought a churn of anguish and shame. But he needed to protect his family and he would do that by any means necessary. Even if it meant Crispus's death, his own death, so be it.

Four days had passed since he had left the villa, and he had sent no word to Marcellina. He tried not to imagine what she must be feeling now. Spurring his horse onwards up the rocky mountain road, he concentrated only on the demands of the immediate present, and the urgency of his mission.

Two miles short of Ad Pirum, they met a cart and a group of riders coming down the hill in the opposite direction. A merchant, travelling with his slaves and a shipment of Italian wine. The military escort rode to the verge to let the cart pass, and Castus saw the merchant eyeing them warily. He raised his hand in greeting as the rider drew level with him.

'How are things up at the fort?' he called, nodding up the road.

'Very busy, dominus!' the merchant replied. He was a Syrian by the look of him, with a short black beard and a nervous catch to his voice. 'Quite a few wagons held up by the checks – but you must know all about that?'

'We've just come from Emona,' Castus said. He tried not to glance in Crispus's direction; the young man had pulled the hood of his cloak up to hide his face. 'What are they checking for?'

The merchant raised his palms, shrugging. 'My apologies, dominus, I thought you were patrolling the road… It seems they're searching for somebody – but I couldn't say who! Is there some danger, do you think?'

Castus shook his head. 'We've seen nothing today. Road behind us is clear. But you'd best hurry on.'

With a brief bow from the saddle, the merchant shook his reins and moved off at a trot, the cart groaning after him. As the travellers passed around the lower bend in the road Bonitus joined Castus at the head of the column of riders.

'You think like me?' he asked quietly.

'Yes,' Castus said. He could feel the weight of despair sinking through him. The emperor's messengers had already reached Ad Pirum, with their orders that Crispus was to be stopped on the road. *Gods, they were quick.*

'We can fight through them, perhaps, or work around?'

Castus shook his head. 'The whole pass is blocked with a palisade, and there are over a hundred men normally stationed in the fort – could be more than that now. And less than thirty of us – not a chance.'

For a few moments they sat in silence, their horses cropping grass from the verge. Crispus and Saturninus joined them, both of them stone-faced. Already they looked like beaten men. Castus could hardly bear to glance at them. Instead he rubbed his brow, staring at the steep forested mountain slopes.

'There was a side road, a mile or two back,' he said. 'Any idea where it leads?'

'It's a quarrying trail, I think,' Saturninus said, turning in the saddle. 'But it probably links up with the main road to Pola, down at the end of the Istrian peninsula.'

Castus nodded, sucking his teeth, an idea forming in his mind. 'And there's a harbour at Pola? The Ravenna fleet keeps ships there?'

Saturninus frowned, catching the direction of Castus's thoughts. 'It's a hard road,' he said. 'Two or three days' travel. And how do we know the troops at Pola won't be waiting for us?'

'Nobody's expecting us to travel that way – they're watching the mountain passes. If we can reach Pola we can take ship across the Adriatic to Italy, and wait for the emperor on the Flaminian Way.'

The bodyguard commander still looked sceptical. Castus remembered his suggestion that they head north, to raise a rebellion. Saturninus had never been happy with this plan.

'Caesar?' Castus asked.

Crispus jerked his head up, blinking, as if he had been lost in sombre thoughts of his own. He took a moment to gather his wits once more. 'Yes,' he said, without much enthusiasm. 'Yes... I agree. It's the only way.'

It was unnerving, Castus thought, to see the extent to which the young man was relying on him now. All Crispus's clarity of mind, his daring and spirit, had deserted him. *And I could well be leading you to your death...*

While Saturninus marshalled his troop of cavalry, Castus drew Bonitus to one side. 'You can leave us here if you want,' he said. 'I've asked enough of you already.'

'Who says I'm here because you asked me?' the Frank replied with a grin. Then his expression darkened, and he leaned closer. 'But think for yourself,' he said. 'We both have sons, you and me. I want my son Silvanus to have all that I have, and more. To serve Rome, as a loyal soldier. You want the same for yours, yes?'

Castus nodded curtly.

'Then we must think about their future too. I will help you, and Crispus, because you are my friend and Crispus is my Caesar. I took my oath to him, and I'll honour it. But I'm wondering if he is already a dead man. I don't want to follow him into Hades, you understand? If the moment comes when I must sacrifice him, then I will do what I must.'

'I understand,' Castus said. 'Just be sure and warn me first!'

Bonitus left him, and Castus summoned Felix with a wave. 'I want you to ride on up the road, to Ad Pirum,' he said. 'Tell them the road's clear, then ride on to Aquileia as fast as you can. Find the *Phaselus* at the docks, and tell the boat crew to bring her down to Pola. Got it?'

'Got it,' Felix said. He gave a quick salute, then turned and rode on up the road, flapping his legs at his horse's flanks.

Castus watched him go; if there was trouble at Pola, he wanted another means of escape. A last glance to the west, and he pulled on the reins and followed Saturninus towards the front of the column.

The quarry road led them southward, around the flank of a mountain spur thick with tall pines and studded with high outcrops of pale grey stone. It was narrow, and the column of horsemen spread out into single file as the trees closed in around them. At the summit of the next ridge Castus glanced back, half expecting to see riders coming in pursuit. The road was clear in their wake; they changed mounts, then rode on. But Castus knew that it would not be long before the net tightened around them. He wondered whether Flavius Innocentius would be leading the search – doubtless he would want the glory of capturing the renegade Caesar himself. Was he already back at Aquileia, or perhaps even at Ad Pirum? And if he tracked them down, would Saturninus's small body of cavalry troopers protect their Caesar against agents with an imperial warrant?

Shaking the thoughts from his mind, Castus spurred his horse onwards. But with every turn in the road, every looming forested mountainside, he sensed the threat gathering, like the terrible premonition of impending defeat.

By evening they had moved out of the mountains and into the rolling forested uplands of Istria. Both horses and men had reached the limits of their endurance, and Castus called a halt for the night. The party made camp in a grove of trees, the ground carpeted with soft pine needles, and in the lowering light the smoke of the cooking fires was a golden haze. After countless hours in the saddle, Castus felt as if his legs had become permanently bowed. His thigh muscles burned, and there was a hard ache in the small of his back. Making a circuit of the camp perimeter, he watched the troopers rubbing down their horses and watering them beside the stream that tumbled below the grove. Something seemed wrong; he counted the riders, then went to find Saturninus.

'One of your men's missing,' he said.

Saturninus just nodded. 'Faventius,' he said. 'He was at the rear of the column. Maybe his horse went lame, or he lost the track... hopefully he'll catch up with us by nightfall.'

But Castus noticed the way the commander evaded his eye. 'If he's not found us by morning, we can't wait,' he said.

He unrolled his sleeping mat under one of the larger trees, and a soldier brought him bread and oatmeal porridge with a cup of vinegar wine. Crispus was sitting alone, a short distance away; Castus had seen the way that the soldiers pretended not to notice the young man. He had thought it was just the confusion of rank, but now he realised that they were nervous of him, perhaps even ashamed of his presence. They must have guessed what was happening. The thought only doubled his anxiety, and he was glad that he had Ursio with him, and that Bonitus and his warriors still accompanied them.

As the light faded, the soldiers kicked ash over the cooking fires and stretched out in their bedrolls, leaving eight men to stand sentry around the camp perimeter. Castus pulled his cloak around him, and within moments exhaustion had stilled the turmoil of his mind and eased him down into sleep. Scraps of dreams tormented him: visions of his wife and son, the twisted memory of Fausta begging for his help... He woke, cold and stiff-limbed, then rolled, grunting, and slept again.

'Dominus?' The hushed voice was insistent, breaking into his slumber and bringing him back to wakefulness with a start. One of the soldiers knelt beside him. Castus sat up, rubbing his face, and hissed a question.

'The Caesar, dominus…' The soldier pointed away into the darkness, towards the sleeping form of Crispus.

Castus threw off his cloak and stretched, winging his shoulders as sleep poured out of him. As he grunted upright he could hear the breathy cries, the mumbled half-words. Two more soldiers were standing nearby, and he could tell that several of the others were awake. Cursing quietly, he ordered the sentries back to their positions, then paced across the bed of pine needles and knelt beside Crispus.

The young man had thrown off his cloak and lay rigid, his neck tense, muttering and gasping in the grip of his nightmares. In the pale gleam of the moon Castus could see the sheen of sweat covering his face. He reached out, taking the man by the shoulder and shaking him.

Crispus woke with a start. 'Father?' he cried, lurching up.

'Quiet,' Castus whispered. 'You were talking in your sleep. Bad dreams.' He suppressed a shiver, thinking of the evils that dreams brought, the messages from other worlds.

Crispus exhaled, then shuddered, his eyes rolling. He sat upright, trembling as he felt the cool night air. Away in the darkness a horse blew and stamped.

'I… I thought I was talking to my father,' Crispus said in a tight whisper. 'Others were there – guards and agents. Fausta, too. They were… hurting her. I tried to stop them…'

'Don't think about her now,' Castus told him. Several times he had considered telling Crispus that Fausta was pregnant, but decided against it. The young man had enough to worry about already. 'Put it out of your mind. You need to sleep.'

He noticed that Crispus's right hand was clenched tight. As the Caesar slackened his fist, Castus saw the small dark object in his palm. Frowning, he leaned closer.

'She sent me this,' Crispus said. 'A token.'

It was Fausta's ring, Castus realised, the small carnelian one she used to wear on her smallest finger. Crispus held it between finger and thumb, then tried to slip it on. 'Too tight!' he said, and breathed a laugh.

'Listen to me.' Castus shook the young man by the shoulder. 'Don't think any more about Fausta – just yourself, and all the others you've dragged into this. When we find your father, you're going to need to make a good case. If you can't do that, we're wasting our time.'

'I can do it,' Crispus said with a quick nod. 'I think I can... Do you think it's possible?'

Castus pondered a moment, sucking his cheek. In truth, he had no idea. 'The emperor's impulsive,' he said. 'He makes decisions quickly, especially when he's angry. He listens too readily to flatterers and spies. But we both know he can change his mind. If you confront him, face to face, and beg his forgiveness, there's a good chance he'll be merciful.'

'Merciful,' Crispus repeated bleakly. 'Is that the best I can hope for? My father's *mercy*?'

'Yes. And not just for you and Fausta – remember that.'

For a moment Castus saw Crispus's eyes gleam in the moonlight as the young man looked at him. A flash of defiance, then it was gone. As Castus straightened, the young man seized his arm.

'Promise me something,' Crispus said. 'If, for some reason, I can't speak to my father... Promise me you'll speak to him for me. Tell him that I take full responsibility for everything, and beg his forgiveness, as a son to a father. Tell him that Fausta is innocent, as are you and the others. I, and nobody else, must take the blame. Can you do that?'

'I will,' Castus told him. 'But let's keep praying that you have the chance to tell him yourself.'

They broke camp before dawn, and were back on the road before sunrise, after a brief meal of stale bread and olive oil washed down with water. The road they were following broadened, and they rode two abreast, the sea appearing at times in gaps between the hills and the trees. Pausing at intervals to rest and change horses, they kept up the pace through the long summer hours, keeping clear of towns and passing the isolated villages along the way without stopping. By noon of the following day Castus saw the first roadside milestone: another twenty-eight miles to Pola.

It was nearing dusk once more, after two days of as hard travel as Castus had ever known, when the column crested a ridge and the riders saw the walled town below them, the tiered arches of the amphitheatre rising proudly against a sea coloured by the blush of sunset. They waited in an abandoned building while Ursio and two men went ahead to scout the town; when the men returned and reported all was clear, they moved on. As the last daylight faded they rode in through the triple-arched eastern gate and down the main avenue to the mansio set aside as official lodgings.

They were in luck; there were no other travellers staying that night. While the soldiers stabled the horses, Castus accompanied Crispus to the upper chambers of the mansio. They would pass the night there, he decided, and find a ship to carry them across the sea the following morning. Saturninus went down to the harbour with two of his men to make enquiries; Castus sent Ursio with him, to seek out Felix and the *Phaselus*. He needed to send a message to Marcellina, before they set off the following morning; he would tell her everything. He knew he should have done it sooner.

With their baggage stowed in the upper rooms, the two men returned to the dining chamber and joined Bonitus. The superintendent had not been expecting such a large party; dinner would be delayed, he explained hesitantly, while he rounded up his kitchen slaves and set them to work. But there would be hot baths soon enough, he promised, and wine to refresh them while they waited.

Reclining on the couches, the three men sipped their wine in silence, too weary and travel-worn to speak. Each had a sword laid beside him; they carried weapons everywhere now. Two of Bonitus's warriors stood guard at the doors, while the other three waited in the yard leaning on their spears. Insects whirled around the lamps on the table.

Helping himself to another handful of nuts and dried dates – all the supervisor had been able to provide at short notice – Castus chewed slowly and tried not to consider the days ahead and what they might bring. He had got Crispus this far at least; the plan was going well. He took another draught of wine, and made a sour face as he swallowed. There was a tall water clock in one corner of the room, and Castus noticed that a quarter hour had dripped by already. He waited as another quarter passed. Where was Saturninus?

Suddenly he was alert, awakened from his tired daze. He felt his scalp prickling as he glanced towards the open doors and the yard outside. A gate banged, and he heard the scrape of studded boots on flagstones. Immediately he was up on his feet, drawing the long spatha from his scabbard as Crispus and Bonitus peered at him, baffled.

A moment later, torchlight flared in the yard, throwing the long shadows of men. Bonitus's three warriors were retreating towards the dining-room doors, their spears levelled. Bonitus, too, was on his feet, weapon in hand, his back pressed against the far wall. As the Franks retreated the men outside advanced into the light: four of Saturninus's Scutarii troopers, helmeted and dressed in scale corselets, the rest of their comrades gathered behind them.

'What's this?' Castus demanded. 'Where's your commander?'

But now he could see Saturninus pushing his way forward between his men. There was another officer with him, a centurion with a blue naval cloak flung around his shoulders. They halted in the doorway, flanked by their armed guards. For a few long moments Saturninus just stared at the three men gathered around the couches, his jaw set hard, shameful resolve burning in his eyes.

'Put down your weapons,' he said. He raised his hand, showing the slim tablet he was carrying. 'This arrived only two hours ago, by fast boat from Aquileia. An order for the immediate seizure and confinement of Flavius Julius Crispus, former Caesar. It's signed by the emperor himself, and bears the imperial seal.'

Castus felt his chest tighten. He could see that the yard was crowded with men – bodyguard troopers and marines from the harbour. Bonitus's warriors had already moved back from the doors, but kept their weapons levelled. Castus glanced at the Frankish chief; Bonitus exhaled slowly, then shook his head. He lifted his hand, opened his fingers, and his sword fell with an iron clang to the floor. At a gesture, his warriors lowered their spears. Crispus was still lying on the couch, gazing blearily at the scene before him.

'You warned them,' Castus said to Saturninus. 'You sent a man to Aquileia and told them where we were going...' Rage was massing in his head, narrowing his vision; he saw only Saturninus now, the man's shrug and blink as he slipped the tablet into his waistband. 'You've been passing information to Innocentius all along, haven't you?'

'Some of us haven't forgotten how to follow orders, brother,' Saturninus said, colour rising to his face. 'I had no choice. I'm a loyal soldier of the emperor.'

'You dare speak of loyalty?' Castus yelled. He gripped the sword tight in his fist. The troopers were edging nervously forward, moving with shuffling steps along the walls to surround him, their shields held before them.

Saturninus opened his mouth to speak, but before he could make a sound Castus let out a bellowing roar and charged across the room with his sword raised to strike. From the corner of his eye Castus saw Bonitus snatching up the heavy wine jug from the table. He saw Saturninus flinching back with a cry of terror, the shields rushing in from all sides.

Then pain exploded through his skull, his legs folded beneath him, and he dropped senseless to the tiled floor as the sword fell from his hand.

CHAPTER XXVII

Flavius Innocentius arrived at Pola by ship the following day. Bonitus came to tell Castus the news, then sat with him in the chamber where he was confined.

'You didn't have to hit me so hard with that jug,' Castus mumbled. His head still pulsed with pain, and he kept probing at the back of his skull with his fingertips, wincing as he touched the swollen bruise.

Bonitus shrugged. 'Sorry, brother,' he said. 'But you were about to get yourself killed. It was the only way to stop you!'

Castus grunted. He had already discovered that his sword and knife had been taken from him.

'What are you now, then? My jailor?'

'No!' Bonitus said. 'To be true, I don't know what I am. Alive is good enough, for today. You too, eh?'

'And Crispus?'

'Under guard. He's following Saturninus's orders like a meek child.' He paused to spit on the floor, then rubbed at the spatter of saliva with his toe.

Castus could not blame Saturninus for what he had done, although he despised him for it all the same. The guard commander had decided to save his own skin. Natural enough; sensible even, in the circumstances. But Castus had known the man for years, and had believed him to be a friend. The thought of that betrayal ached in his soul. Voices came from the yard outside, and the sound of running feet; Innocentius and his party must have arrived from the harbour. Castus stood up, glancing towards the two guards who waited under the portico outside the open door. 'Am I free to greet our friends, then?' he asked.

Bonitus raised an eyebrow. 'I'll come with you.'

Wincing at the throb of pain in his head, the ache in his limbs, Castus left the room and walked out into the portico. The clear daylight hurt his eyes, and he blinked away the sting, but the guards made no move to stop him. He saw Innocentius at once; the imperial agent stood in the middle of the yard, flanked by four of his grey-clad quaestionarii. He had a staff tribune with him, and two other men in full armour. Innocentius had clearly seen Castus too, but was pretending to ignore him. Bonitus strolled over to join his small band of warriors, who were idling beneath the far portico with a look of careful disinterest. Castus had the sudden unnerving sensation that he and Innocentius were the only men present who knew clearly what they were doing, and which side they were on.

The feeling of tensed uncertainty was palpable. The soldiers gathered in the yard had a sullen look, obviously confused by the night's strange events. Even the officers appeared wary; there was a mood of something like mutiny in the air, and for a moment Castus felt hopeful. But he knew that none here would attempt anything now. There was too much to lose, and nothing to gain.

Two men crouched against the wall of the yard, heads down and hands tied behind their backs. Castus's heart clenched as he recognised Ursio and Felix. Both of them were bruised, their faces bloody.

'Release them,' he growled to Saturninus. 'They were only following my orders.'

The guard commander stood in the shade of the wall, thumbs hooked in his belt. He jutted his jaw, then nodded. 'If they give their word to stay calm,' he said. 'And not try to leave this place. The big Sarmatian almost killed two of my boys with his bare hands last night.'

As the two men were freed of their bonds, Castus stared around at the guards stationed at every exit. More armed men lined the balcony above him. Breathing slowly, he stood upright, unflinching, and waited for Innocentius to speak.

At last the agent glanced in his direction. He gave a brief sickly sneer, then turned to Saturninus. 'Where is the other prisoner?' he demanded.

'In the largest of the chambers upstairs. He's been searched for weapons, and two of my men are guarding the door.' At least there was no trace of deference in his voice; Innocentius might hold an imperial mandate, but several of the officers present outranked him.

'Good,' Innocentius said. He smiled again, and appeared to be enjoying himself immensely. 'I have with me,' he called, addressing everyone gathered in the yard, 'an epistle from the emperor, his Sacred Majesty Flavius Valerius Constantinus!' He reached into his belt pouch and withdrew a slim tablet, similar to the one that Saturninus had received the previous evening. Holding it up for all to see, he continued.

'Six days ago, at the city of Mediolanum, the emperor and his consistorium met in closed session to discuss the evidence laid before them regarding the crimes of the former Caesar. After long debate, the court agreed unanimously that Flavius Julius Crispus was guilty of treasonous conspiracy against the emperor, and also of committing foul and incestuous adultery with the Augusta Flavia Maxima Fausta, his own stepmother!'

Castus heard the gasps from the men all around him. He kept his teeth clenched, breathing slowly. The stillness in the yard was uncanny, nobody wanting to move or make a sound. Somewhere outside the walls a dog was barking.

'The sentence ordained by the Sacred Will of the emperor,' Innocentius went on, 'is *death*. This sentence will be carried out immediately, and the name of the former Caesar erased from the annals of history. Let his memory be damned to infamy for all eternity!'

Silence followed his words. From the corner of his eye Castus could see the soldiers shifting nervously. Innocentius signalled to one of the agents behind him, and the man stepped forward and drew his sword. 'Bring out the prisoner,' Innocentius said coldly.

'Wait!'

It was Saturninus who had spoken, taking a stride forward. The imperial agent glared at him, tight-lipped. 'The prisoner is under my guard,' Saturninus went on. 'I insist that sentence be deferred until noon tomorrow, in case a countermanding order arrives. Such things have been known...'

Castus snorted a laugh. Saturninus was still trying to keep himself out of trouble. But he was glad all the same; Innocentius gave a sniff of pique, but he had no authority to insist on his order, and everyone knew it.

'Very well,' the agent said. 'Until noon. But no one is to leave this place until then.'

What was he afraid of? Castus wondered how much power the man really possessed. Was there truly a possibility that Constantine might change his mind and lift the guilty verdict? Hope swam in his mind, then faded.

'Aurelius Castus,' Innocentius said, drawing himself upright with his shoulders back. 'I believe you are responsible for the murder of my associate, Sergius Gracilis, and several of my men. They were acting under my orders, on imperial business.'

Castus said nothing. He fixed the agent with a fierce stare. In his mind he saw the rooms of the torture house outside Aquileia, the eunuch bound to the trestle, Niobe's mauled and mistreated body dumped naked on a filthy mattress. There was no limit to his loathing for this man.

'The emperor has also considered certain allegations against you,' Innocentius went on, the smirk flickering across his face. He was making a show of self-control, but Castus could hear the scornful hatred in his voice. 'It seems you were conspiring with the former Caesar! Perhaps, indeed, you hoped to set him on the throne in his father's place, and then act as his chief advisor, heh? Perhaps in time you might have hoped to overthrow him as well, and become emperor yourself with the support of the troops? Was that what you had in mind?'

Castus snarled, baring his teeth as the fury mounted through him. He knew the agent was trying to goad him, trying to coax some outburst, some violence that would give him the excuse to have him killed. He willed himself to remain calm. Sweat was pouring down his back, and his muscles were rigid. Then he realised: if Innocentius was trying to provoke him then the agent must have no power to order his death otherwise. The allegations against him had not been proven. Not yet.

'Make no mistake,' Innocentius went on, snarling as he spoke. 'Once the prisoner has been executed, there *will* be a full investigation of your part in these treasons.' He jutted out a finger, pointing at Castus. 'You, your family, all of your household will be questioned, and when the truth is found you will be punished, I'll see to that! You'll be stripped of your rank, branded with infamy and put to death like a common criminal, your family reduced to slavery—'

'Enough,' Saturninus broke in, his voice thick. 'Aurelius Castus is not on trial here. He'll remain under guard until we get some clarification of the emperor's decision.' There was a note of warning in his words, and Castus was glad of it. Innocentius closed his eyes for a moment, obviously restraining his urge to protest, then smiled again.

'Very well. We will all remain here together and see what happens – or *does not* happen – by noon tomorrow. But now,' he said with a grin, clapping his hands, 'I'm hungry!'

In the gloom of his shuttered chamber Castus sat on the edge of the bed with his head in his hands. There was nothing he could do now to save Crispus. Nothing, it seemed, that he could do to save himself. The agent's taunting words echoed in his mind. His family would suffer. Marcellina and the girls, Sabinus, even his unborn child. There was no justice, no meaning to it, only the pitiless working of fate, of slow vengeance. He wanted to throw himself on the bed and surrender, give in to exhaustion, but a furious energy still beat in his chest, charging his blood. Fantasies of escape reeled through his mind.

A knock at the door and Castus stood up quickly, reaching instinctively for a sword that was not there. The door opened, and a figure stood in the spill of light. The centurion commanding the marine detachment that had come from the harbour with Saturninus the night before.

'Excellency,' the centurion said with a stiff nod. 'I just wanted to say I'm sorry how things have turned out. I served under your command at the Hellespont two years back, aboard the *Lucifer*. You and the Caesar, I mean.'

'It's not what any of us would have chosen, eh?' Castus replied quietly.

'Is it true what the agent said? About Crispus and... you know?'

Castus just shrugged heavily. 'Don't ask me!' he said, and managed a grim half-smile.

'If there's anything you need, dominus – anything I can get you...'

'A blade? Or how about a mutiny, or a sudden Gothic invasion?'

The centurion stifled a laugh, then shook his head.

'A quart of wine then?'

Once the man had gone and the door was locked again, Castus dragged his blanket roll and leather satchel from beneath the bed. Nobody had thought to search it, or take it from him; there was nothing in it he could obviously use as a weapon. Opening the satchel, he thrust his hand deep inside until his fingers closed around the smooth globe of the bottle he had taken from the torture house. The poison that Gracilis had wanted to use. Castus had been carrying it with him ever since.

Drawing the bottle from the bag he sat with it in his hand. It felt cold, as if it were packed with ice, and shudders ran up his arms as he held it. This was death, he thought. Not an honourable death, not a soldier's death. He remembered seeing Marcellina's father take poison, twenty years before in a Pictish prison. Not painless either, he thought. But quick, and simple. If he killed himself now, would Innocentius be content? Would the threats to his family end?

Lowering his head, Castus squeezed his eyes shut. His neck ached, his head throbbed, and he breathed in short tight gasps. The thought of never seeing his wife again, never seeing his son, or the child Marcellina was carrying, agonised him. Was it better to die, if it might guarantee their safety?

But there were no guarantees, he knew that.

Another bang on the door, and Castus just had time to conceal the poison bottle before the sentry entered with the quart flask and set it down on the low table. Left alone once more in darkness, Castus poured himself a cup of wine and drank. How easy it would be to die. But he would not.

Taking the poison bottle, he levered out the grimy waxed plug. Very carefully, he tipped the bottle over the neck of the flask. It was too dark in the chamber to see the liquid that poured from the bottle, but Castus could hear it trickling and then dripping into the wine. The bottle was empty; he gave it a tap, set it aside, and swirled the flask to mix the fluids. Then he jammed the stopper back in the wine flask, picked it up and banged on the door.

'I want to speak with the Caesar Crispus,' he demanded.

One of the sentries went to check with Saturninus, but he returned quickly. A single nod, and the two soldiers led him along the dark inner passageway and up the steps to the upper floor. Two more Scutarii troopers waited outside the room where Crispus was confined. One roughly patted at Castus's tunic, searching for concealed weapons. The other pulled the stopper from the flask and sniffed. Castus could not breathe. The soldier made a face.

'Not exactly the finest Falernian!' he said. 'But if that's all you got…' He replaced the stopper and handed the flask back to Castus, then unlocked the door.

'Leave us alone,' Castus said, passing the sentry a gold solidus. It was the only thing of value that remained to him. The soldier took it smartly, smiling, and it vanished into his belt.

Light cut across the gloom of the chamber from a crack in the shutters, and for a moment Castus could not make out the figure crouched in the far corner. There was a dense, sweetish reek in the air. The smell of fear, Castus thought. He waited until he heard the guards locking the door behind him, then he stepped forward into the beam of light.

'Caesar,' he said.

Crispus was wrapped in a blanket, his knees drawn up to his chest. He released a long shuddering breath as he recognised Castus. 'Gods, I thought they'd sent a man to kill me,' he said. 'I wondered if they might force you to do it...'

'Never,' Castus said, setting the flask and cup down on the floor. 'They wouldn't trust me with a sword in my hand, not now.'

As his eyes adjusted, he saw the young man's wasted expression, the darkness beneath his eyes, fatigue and grief scored into his features.

'It'll be soon though, won't it?' Crispus said, his voice hoarse. 'That worm Innocentius came to see me. To gloat. He said... he said he could lift the sentence if I testified against Fausta! Against you as well – he really wants you dead, it seems, for killing his friend. If I swore that the plot was all the work of you and her, I'd be spared.'

Castus drew a long breath. The news did not surprise him. 'What did you say?'

'What do you think? They might accuse me, but they can't murder my honour! I don't desert my friends. I deny nothing. And I'll always be true to Fausta... But I'm afraid, brother. If they torture me... I don't know if I can hold out.'

Exhaling slowly, Castus knelt beside Crispus. He took the flask and placed it between them. Suddenly he found he could not speak. His mouth was dry, his throat tight, and he felt the dread crawling up his spine. In his mind he heard the words of the old woman's prophecy. *And you also will kill your own king...*

'Is that...?' Crispus asked. He reached out and picked up the flask.

'It's not great wine. And I doubt I've made it taste any better.'

Crispus held the flask to his chest, dropping his head with a groan of anguish. 'Thank you,' he said quietly.

377

'There's enough for both of us, if you want.'

'No!' Crispus said, his voice cracking. 'No... I need to do this alone. Remember your promise, brother. Speak to my father for me – tell him that I take all responsibility, and beg his forgiveness... And there's something else.' He reached into his waistband and withdrew the small carnelian ring. 'If you can, see that this is returned to Fausta. So that she knows... I never deserted her... I always —'

His voice broke off in a stifled sob, and he turned his face away. Castus took the ring and put in his belt pouch. 'I'll do what I can,' he said.

'When I'm gone,' Crispus said, almost choking, 'don't let them dishonour my body. They do that, don't they, to traitors? Mutilate the face...' He raised his hand and brushed lightly at his cheeks, his eyes. 'They throw the flesh to the dogs...'

'Don't worry about that.'

For a few long heartbeats they sat together in the hot darkness. Castus could hear the sentries shuffling on the landing outside the door.

'I'm sorry,' Crispus said, his face wet with tears. 'Sorry I caused all this.'

'We did the best we could,' Castus said.

He stretched out his hand, and Crispus seized it and clasped tightly. Then Castus pulled him into an embrace.

'Goodbye, friend,' Crispus said.

It was not a grand funeral. No sarcophagus of carved purple marble, no trains of mourners wailing to the skies in the swirl of incense. Flavius Julius Crispus went to the gods in the traditional way, the old simple way of soldiers in enemy country, in the smoke of a burning pyre.

The flames rose into the night, throwing shadows that

danced around the stone walls of the yard behind the mansio. Castus had ordered the pyre constructed of wood from the bathhouse furnace rooms, the body of the dead Caesar laid on top, wrapped in clean white linen. None had challenged him, or refused him; his towering rage was its own authority.

Now he stood before the blaze, the hem of his cloak draped across his head, and felt the heat of the fire drying the tears on his face. Around him in the glow of the flames stood Ursio and Felix, Bonitus and his warriors, and the marine centurion with his helmet clasped beneath his arm. Solemnly they called the dead man's name to the four directions. In the shadows around the margins of the yard, Saturninus's Scutarii waited, impassive. The smoke swirled around them all.

Finally, when the flames had died to a heap of glowing embers, Bonitus stepped up beside Castus and laid a heavy palm on his shoulder. 'Here,' he said. 'You'd best take this.'

He passed a bundle, wrapped in an old army cloak. Castus felt the weight of it, then saw the glint of silver in the fire's last glow. The eagle hilt of his spatha.

'They've gone then?' he asked.

Bonitus nodded. 'Saturninus and the bastard Innocentius. They left by galley just before dusk. Reckon they'll get across to Ancona and hurry on to Rome. Report to the emperor, and get their reward.'

Castus gave a scornful grunt. He knew that Saturninus would be eager to accompany the imperial agent down to Rome, and rid himself of the last taint of involvement in the conspiracy. He had been quick to seize Crispus's imperial insignia and the purple cape he carried in his baggage, almost as soon as the death was discovered. Innocentius had only managed to steal the dead man's shoes.

'You'll give me your word that you'll remain here,' Saturninus had said before he left. 'Until the emperor makes a decision about your fate?'

'Oh, sure,' Castus had told him. His word meant nothing to a man without honour. Although there was still no formal charge against him, all knew that Castus had given the prisoner poison. Killing a man condemned to death by imperial order was not exactly a crime, but Saturninus had left twelve of his troopers behind as guards anyway.

As they moved away from the smoking ruin of the pyre, Castus glanced appraisingly at the soldiers. They had a biarchus to command them, but none appeared very resolute.

Bonitus cleared his throat quietly. 'With your two and my warriors, there's nine of us against their dozen.'

'You'd do that?'

'Not willingly!' Bonitus said. 'But if you need it, we could scare them a little, maybe...'

Castus shook his head. He had taken Bonitus and his men far enough down a dark road. But he realised now what should have been obvious to him; Saturninus had left him this chance to escape. The guard officer would have known that Innocentius would depart for Rome at once, and that Castus would be left behind. His men had no intention of trying to stop him if he slipped away.

Castus summoned the naval centurion. The complement of marines that he had brought from the harbour still occupied the mansio, guarding the gates.

'How long will it take Saturninus and the imperial agent to reach Rome?' he asked.

'If they get across to Ancona tonight and take the Via Flaminia,' the centurion said, 'they could be there in seven or eight days. The emperor's ahead of them on the road. He's travelling fast...' The man rubbed his jaw, frowning as he thought.

'But?' Castus asked.

'But there's a faster way. If, maybe, you took a boat down the Italian coast to Aternum, you could follow the Via Valeria straight across the mountains. It's a rough road, but you could get to Rome ahead of them, perhaps...'

'Brother,' said Bonitus, seizing Castus by the shoulders. 'What are you thinking? If you have the chance now to flee then take it! Go to your villa, to your family. Get away from this madness while there's time!'

His warriors had gathered around him, still looking casual but with weapons ready. Castus could see the Scutarii troopers shifting back into the gloom around the walls of the yard. The gates were clear. Over by the pyre, Ursio and Felix were pouring wine on the last smoking embers. The *Phaselus* was in the harbour, Felix had said, the crew ready to sail. Tempting, Castus admitted, to think of steering for Salona, for Marcellina and his family.

'I can't run,' he told the Frankish leader. 'This storm's not dying down, and I need to confront it, alone. But you must go – you and your men. Go back to Gaul, to your wife and your son. Your own skies.'

Bonitus stared at him, his brow lowered. Then he gave a curt nod and a laugh. 'I can never argue with you,' he said.

Castus turned to the centurion. 'I'm walking out of this place at dawn,' he said. 'Are you or your men going to try and stop me?'

The centurion dropped his gaze for a moment, then shook his head. 'What are you intending to do?' he asked.

'I'm going to Rome,' Castus told him, slinging the sword belt over his shoulder. 'I'm going to see the emperor.'

CHAPTER XXVIII

Station to station, changing mounts regularly, he had crossed the mountainous spine of Italy from the tiny seaport of Aternum on the Adriatic coast to the rolling hills of Latium. The road across the Apennines was old and poorly maintained, rough with stones and overgrown for stretches, but he had kept up the pace with only the briefest pauses. Through narrow valleys and over steep wooded ridges, he had passed through Corfinium and then Alba Fucens. Now, on the morning of his seventh day since he sailed from Pola, Castus was leaving Tibur and riding on down the wide valley that led to Rome.

He rested for a moment beside the old stone bridge that crossed the river, letting his horse drink. The first rays of the sun cast his shadow across the road, and on the far verge a huge old tomb rose like a fortified tower, capped with scrubby foliage. By now, he knew, Ursio and Felix would have returned to the villa in Dalmatia. Both men had wanted to accompany him on this journey, but he had refused; this was a task he needed to do alone. He had sent them by road from Pola, carrying the message to Marcellina that he had composed in the early hours before his departure. It had been a hard message to write, frowning over the wax tablet in the light of a flickering lamp, his hands still smutty from the ashes of the pyre. Writing was hard enough at the best of times, but trying to trap the meaning of what he wanted to say that night was harder than ever, the stylus slipping in his hands. He hoped he had been sincere. Hoped that she would hear his voice through the imperfection of his words.

Tugging at the reins, he drew the horse back onto the highway and rode onward, passing the streams of other travellers making their way towards the city. The celebrations of the Vicennalia were due to begin that day, and Rome would be crowded for the festivities.

By noon, Castus was passing through the Tiburtina Gate in the eastern wall of the city. He had dressed that morning in his finest embroidered tunic and cloak, and with his eagle-hilted sword and golden neck torque clearly visible a path opened before him as he rode. Only the grimy leather sack slung on his saddle horn drew questioning glances, but the stern fury in his eyes deterred any challenge. It was hot, the July sun burning down over the rooftops, the heat reverberating in the packed streets. Forcing his way through the swelling crowds, Castus rode westwards along the road that crossed the Esquiline slope, through the Arch of Gallienus and down towards the Subura.

In the heart of the city the great public buildings were already decked out for the celebrations, the statues freshly painted and gilded, laurel wreathing the door lintels. Garlands hung across the main streets. As he passed the Porticus of Livia Castus glanced up and saw a line of imperial portrait roundels displayed along the façade. Constantine, and his sons – Castus caught his breath as he recognised the face of Crispus among them. The Roman people, he realised, had not yet been told of the Caesar's condemnation.

Shortening his reins as the crowd grew thicker, Castus turned off the main street and rode up across the hill beside the Baths of Trajan. There was a unit of horse guardsmen stationed in the open area surrounding the huge Flavian Amphitheatre. More troops in the porticoes of the larger temples. The people thronging the streets appeared in good humour, but Castus knew how quickly the mood of the city mob could turn. How would they react when they learned that the beloved Caesar Crispus was dead by his father's order? And what about Fausta – she was a daughter of the city, more popular here than anywhere. Would the people accept that she, too, was a criminal?

Up the slope past the Temple of Rome, Castus turned onto the street that climbed towards the imperial palace on the Palatine. He could already see the standards displayed proudly above the main portico: Constantine was in residence. He left his horse in one of the old arcades beneath the wall of Jupiter's temple, paying a boy to watch over it from the purse of coins that Bonitus had insisted on giving him before he left Pola. Pulling his cloak around him, he slung the leather bag from the saddle horn and marched across the paved square in front of the palace. The doors of the smaller audience chamber stood open, a crowd of petitioners waiting in the portico outside. Castus pushed his way between them, marched straight past the doorkeepers and entered the hall.

Grey marble gloom surrounded him, and his footsteps echoed on the polychrome pavement. More men stood at the far end of the hall, awaiting admittance, dressed in brightly patterned cloaks and tunics. They glanced at Castus as he approached, then moved aside with expressions of startled pique as he marched on through the midst of them. A line of soldiers blocked the far doorway, long-haired Germanic guardsmen of the Schola Gentilium. They straightened to attention, raising their spears to bar the way. Castus stamped to a halt before them.

'I am Aurelius Castus, Imperial Companion, and I have an urgent message for the emperor from the Caesar Flavius Crispus,' he declared.

The guardsmen stared at him, unmoving. Did they even understand Latin? Castus's words had echoed in the vast chamber, and several of the waiting petitioners edged closer and peered at him. A long moment passed, then one of the guardsmen gestured towards the open doorway behind him. Another man appeared from the far room, a court *admissionalis* in a long white tunic and black cape.

'Did you hear me?' Castus growled, throwing back his cloak to show his eagle-hilted sword and the insignia on his tunic. 'Or do I need to repeat myself?'

The courtier studied him, frowning. Castus could hear whispered voices echoing through from the next chamber. A white-uniformed Protector stepped into the doorway, glanced at him, then signalled to the guards to stand aside.

'Excellency,' the Protector said, 'come this way please.'

Two of the Germanic guards fell into step behind Castus as he followed the officer through the next chamber and out into a sun-filled courtyard. A fountain sent arcing jets splashing into the central pool, the water flowing around a maze-pattern of channels. Castus realised how thirsty he was; he had drunk nothing since leaving Tibur. Palace officials and slaves stepped aside to let them pass.

Castus had only been inside the imperial palace of Rome on a few occasions, and just once had he entered the inner precincts. Back then, Maxentius was master here, and Castus had been his prisoner. As he followed the Protector through the pillared halls and antechambers, Castus tried to keep his sense of direction, but the palace was a vast complex, covering the entire southern plateau of the Palatine Hill, and he was soon bewildered.

Word of his arrival had been sent on ahead; as they entered the second great courtyard a further guard of four Protectores

385

took over from the Germanic troops. Escorted on all sides, Castus advanced through a pair of tall inlaid doors, then through a chamber lined with dazzling mosaics and into a smaller anteroom beyond.

'Wait here,' the man leading him said, turning on his heel. 'The emperor is currently in council, but I'll send word of your arrival.'

Another of the Protectores took a pace forwards, gesturing for Castus's sword. Castus drew his lips back in a snarl. 'See this?' he said, jerking a thumb at the gold torque around his neck. 'That means I get to keep my weapon.'

The Protector drew back, neck stiff and eyes narrowed. He glanced towards his comrade, who nodded.

'The bag?' one of the other guards said.

Castus hefted the leather sack in his left hand. 'This is for the emperor's eyes only,' he said. 'And I've travelled all the way here from Pola to bring it to him. I doubt he'll want me to be kept waiting by you!'

Two of the guards withdrew, leaving the others to stand sentry before the inner doors of the anteroom. A pair of silentiaries entered, taking positions by the outer doors. Castus stood for a while, feeling the exhaustion massing in his head, his legs beginning to ache. He had not had a chance to bathe in many days; he stank of sweat and dust and old smoke. Drawing a long breath, he paced to the padded bench along one wall and sank down to sit. He lowered the leather sack to the floor with a muffled thud.

Light fell from the arched windows high overhead, and Castus tracked it as it moved across the painted plaster. Half an hour passed in silence. The entire vast palace seemed motionless, poised. Closing his eyes for a moment, he lulled himself into a state of glazed calm; then he remembered the danger he was in and woke again with a start. Nervous tension jumped in the pit of his chest. At any moment he expected to hear the tread of nailed boots approaching, the armed men who would seize him and lead him away. Perhaps, he thought, they would confine him in the same basement cell he had occupied when he was a prisoner of Maxentius? All too easy to fall into imagined terrors. He forced himself to remain alert and awake, to keep his head up and show no sign of apprehension.

He had waited for almost an hour when the inner doors creaked back. A small round-faced man in a gorgeously patterned robe appeared in the opening, smiling nervously. 'I am Arcadius,' he said, 'Master of Admissions. The Most Sacred Emperor will grant you a brief audience now, excellency.'

Castus got up quickly, grabbed the sack, and followed Arcadius through the doors and along a broad corridor. At the far end, another set of portals, inlaid with gold and flanked by Protectores and doorkeepers. Another brief wait; Castus felt his mind clear and focus. His blood was flowing fast, as it did before he went into battle. The doors swung open without a sound.

'This way, excellency.'

The chamber beyond was not large, but it glittered with gold and intricate mosaics. The pavement was a depiction of the continents of the earth, surrounded by the constellations of the heavens. At the far end, on a low dais, Constantine was seated on an ivory throne. His chief ministers stood in a half-circle to either side of him. Arcadius called for the room to be cleared, and the guards and attendants retreated. Castus heard the doors sigh closed behind them.

'Constantine Augustus, your salvation is our salvation!' he cried. 'In truth I speak, on my oath I speak!'

'Approach the Sacred Presence,' Arcadius murmured.

Castus took five marching steps forward, then set the leather bag down on the low table in the centre of the room. The emperor sat stiffly upright on his throne, glaring at Castus, saying nothing. His face was pale, but his jaw was set hard.

'What is the meaning of your unannounced appearance?' said one of the ministers. Castus knew the man: Rutilius Palladius. 'And what's that?' He pointed at the bag on the table.

'Majesty,' Castus said, the words grinding in his throat. 'I come to tell you that your son, the Caesar Flavius Julius Crispus, is dead.'

A collective intake of breath circled the room, but nobody moved; many of these men would have been among those who agreed the Caesar's death sentence. For three heartbeats there was only tensed silence. Constantine was as still as an ivory statue, but Castus could see the pained fury gathering in his eyes.

'Do not speak that name in the Sacred Presence!' Palladius snapped. 'That name no longer exists!'

But everyone was turning to the emperor now. Slowly Constantine raised a hand to his face. His jewelled fingers shook slightly as he brushed his brow.

'I have no son of that name,' he said, his voice grating as cold and hard as the rasp of an iron file.

Castus met his furious gaze and held it. He took one step forward, and loosed the ties that sealed the top of the leather bag. The assembled officials drew back at once, muttering in consternation. He pulled the leather aside, exposing what the bag contained.

The object on the table was a sealed urn, the cheap glazed ceramic looking almost uncouth in the gilded surroundings of the council chamber.

'Your son's ashes,' he said.

'This is infamous!' Palladius declared. Castus stepped back from the table and hooked his thumbs in his belt. He had intended, through all the days of his journey here, to do the sensible thing. He had meant to kneel before the emperor, to show respect and contrition, to plead his innocence and to beg for mercy. He had been ready for that. But now, seeing the bitter outrage on the faces around him, the inflexible severity of the emperor's scorn, a surge of angry pride rose through him. He would not yield; he could not.

'Before he took his own life,' he declared, 'Crispus asked that you consider him solely responsible for the charges against him. Fausta is innocent, as are the other accused. He asked that you forgive him, as a loving father forgives his son.'

For a long moment there was silence. Castus held the emperor's stare, seeing the harrowed torment burning in his eyes. Then Constantine let out a low groan and covered his face with one hand.

'Take it away,' the emperor said quietly, flicking his fingers at the urn on the table. 'Get it out of my sight. Take it to the Via Appia and smash it between the old tombs, scatter the contents – go!'

Palladius himself rushed over to the table, lifting the urn gingerly in both hands as if it might burst open and spray the ashes across the room.

'As for you,' the emperor said, dropping his hand to gaze at Castus once more. 'You can get out as well. Surrender yourself to my guards. You are not to leave the palace until...' His voice faltered, and he glanced away. Just for a moment he appeared to be struggling to breathe. Colour rose in his cheeks. Castus saw him swallow heavily, then the emperor raised a hand and pointed towards the doors.

'This way, excellency,' Arcadius said, his voice drained of all warmth as he took Castus's arm.

The guards were waiting outside the doors, but they had not yet heard the order and Castus marched straight through their cordon. Arcadius's outraged cries followed him as he crossed the anteroom and strode out into the colonnade of the garden courtyard. He took a swift right, pacing fast. Running steps behind him, shouts. In only moments he would be cut off and surrounded.

Had he really expected the emperor to react any differently? No, but he had done what he had to do. He had looked Constantine in the eye and seen the truth of his anguish, his deadly resolve. Blood hammered in his head, and he gripped the hilt of his sword, trying not to break into a run. Men were behind him now, dogging his steps, calling out to him to stop. He did not pause. The possibility of violence flickered all around him, and he choked a laugh. He could barely breathe, let alone fight.

'Halt,' a voice commanded, and a figure barred his way. Castus blinked, and recognised the man before him. He was wearing the white uniform of a tribune of Protectores now, but Castus broke into a grin. 'Gratianus!' he said. 'Have you come to arrest me?'

'*What have you done, brother?*' Gratianus hissed between his teeth. From the corner of his eye Castus could see other men running along the colonnades, Protectores and Germanic bodyguards. The soldiers at his heels had halted too, looking to Gratianus for instruction.

'Two of you, come with me,' Gratianus ordered. 'The rest, back to your positions! What do you think this is, a gymnasium?' He gestured curtly to Castus, and then led the way along the colonnade walk and through the doorway at the end. In the chamber beyond he turned suddenly and grabbed Castus by the shoulder.

'Is it true?' he demanded. 'Is the Caesar dead?'

'He's dead by his own hand,' Castus told him.

Gratianus closed his eyes, breathing a curse. Still gripping Castus by the shoulder, he led him quickly out of the chamber by the far door and into the sunlight again. They were in a raised portico above a long sunken garden, shaped like a hippodrome. A few scattered figures strolled along the garden walks, but none glanced up. Gratianus nodded to the two Protectores, and they hung back inside the chamber doors.

'Where's Fausta?' Castus said.

'The Augusta? She's not here. I heard she's being kept at the Sessorian Palace, in the custody of the Augusta Helena.'

Castus knew the place: an old imperial residence out on the far eastern corner of the city, just inside the walls. He glanced around the circuit of the colonnaded garden; all seemed quiet, tranquil even, but he knew he was surrounded by guards.

'You can't escape, brother!' Gratianus said in an urgent whisper. 'They'd catch up with you, wherever you went.'

'I don't mean to escape. There's something I need to do. A matter of honour.' Yes, he thought, an oath to a man on the threshold of death was nothing less than sacred. And there was still a chance to fulfil it.

Gratianus sucked a breath between his teeth. His brow was bunched tight. The word *honour* hung in the air between them. Both knew its power.

'You know I can't let you leave here,' Gratianus said.

'You're not *supposed* to let me leave, no.'

The tribune grimaced, rubbed his forehead with the heel of his hand, then glanced behind him. 'The gateway at the far end, on the left,' he muttered quickly. 'There are stairs, dropping down to the slope above the Circus Maximus. They won't try and stop you if you're on the way out... I can only give you a few moments before I raise the alarm...'

With only the briefest nod of thanks, Castus gathered his cloak around his body and ran. Along the portico above the garden, the sunlight flashing between the pillars, he reached the gateway and swerved, nailed boots skating on the tiled floor. In the sudden gloom he plunged down the narrow stairway, remembering to slow as he reached the bottom and passed the sentries guarding the lower gate. One of them called after him, but he was already crashing down the steps that dropped into the shadowed ravine below the massive arches of the circus, breaking into a run once more as he hit the cobbled street.

Breath burned in his chest, and with every step he felt the pain in his legs and back. He had left his horse on the far side of the Palatine Hill; no time to go and find it now. Somebody stepped from a shop doorway and Castus slammed them aside, hearing the yell of abuse as he ran onward. The street followed the lower arches of the circus all along the southern flank of the Palatine; there were stalls in the arches, selling hot pastries, sausages and wine by the cup, and mobs of people swirled around them. A few glanced as Castus as he ran, some of them calling out jokes.

At one of the exits from the stalls, a group of covered litters stood waiting, the bearers idling in the shade of the arches waiting for custom. As Castus approached, a skinny man in a conical cap stepped from the shade and waved his arm, grinning through broken teeth. 'Late for dinner, dominus?' he cried. 'For only two *nummi* we'll get you there quicker than a good lawyer can get a rich man off a bribery charge!'

Castus checked his pace, stumbled over to the nearest litter and slapped his palm down on the box. 'You know the Sessorian Palace?' he gasped.

The man's grin slipped as he noticed Castus's sword and the torque at his neck. 'Make it double?' he said.

'Make it *fast*,' Castus told him, scrabbling in his purse for coins, then swung himself down into the box of the litter. Heaving breath as he dropped onto the worn horsehair padding, he dragged the curtain across. Sitting awkwardly with his knees drawn up, he felt the beams creak beneath him as the bearers lifted his weight. How, he wondered, did people travel comfortably in these things? Then, with a lurch and a swing, they were moving.

Sunlight filtered through the threadbare red curtain, and Castus closed his eyes and dropped his head back against the padding of the seat. The bearers were moving at a jog, the man in the cap striding before them to clear a path through the throng. Very soon, Castus felt the angle of the litter change; they were moving uphill now, climbing the slope of the Caelian. When he glanced through the gap in the curtain he saw the tall brick piers and arches of an aqueduct above him. They passed through a district of gloomy apartment blocks, then the buildings fell away and the litter was jogging along a broad paved road between garden walls and orchards. Castus let the curtain drop. He pressed his hands to his face, muttering prayers. *Fortuna the Homebringer, let me see my wife and family again in this world...*

CHAPTER XXIX

'The Augusta Helena is sleeping, excellency,' the eunuch said with an ingratiating smile. 'She often does, during the hottest part of the day. But you may pass your message to me.'

The eunuch was named Olympiodorus, Castus had learned, and was the procurator of the *domus augustae*; his pattered crimson robes and the massive jewelled brooch at his shoulder proclaimed his status. He was also very nervous, and failing to hide it.

'My message is not for the Augusta Helena,' Castus told him. 'I'm here to see Fausta, the emperor's wife.'

'Fausta, ah!' the eunuch said, the agitation jumping in his voice. 'I'm very sorry, excellency, but that will not be possible either...!'

Something was not right at the Sessorian Palace, and Castus had noticed it the moment he strode through the main vestibule and into the atrium. The palace stood in a tract of gardens just inside the city wall, and resembled a country villa built on a lavish scale, the halls and porticos gleaming with polished marble and colourful mosaics. The perfect retreat for an emperor's elderly mother, or an emperor's condemned wife. The cordon of guards at the main gate had shown no signs of agitation, and allowed him to pass without challenge when he told them he was carrying an important message from the Palatine. But inside the building the mood of tension was palpable; at the margins of his vision Castus could make out the slaves and attendants peering at him from the doorways with fear in their eyes. Had news of his approach reached them already? He was sweating heavily, red-faced from the heat and the exertion of the last few hours, but that was not the cause. No, he thought – this was something else.

'Where is she?' he demanded, taking a step towards the eunuch. 'Take me to her now and I won't trouble you any further.'

Olympiodorus raised his hands, beseeching. 'Dominus, please, I cannot...! The domina Fausta is... bathing!'

Castus frowned, peering past the eunuch into the sunlight of the central garden court. A figure drew his eye: a slave girl, hunched between the pillars of the garden portico. She was weeping, covering her face with her hands. Olympiodorus had noticed the direction of Castus's stare. He gulped visibly, and took a quick sidestep to block his view.

With one fast movement Castus drew his sword, reaching out with his left hand to seize the eunuch's jewelled brooch. He dragged and twisted, pulling the cape tight around the eunuch's neck, then levelled his blade at his throat.

'Take me, now,' he said quietly.

He could hear the shrieks of dismay from the adjoining halls, the sound of running feet on marble, but the Augusta Helena kept no armed guards inside her residence. Four smooth-faced Syrian youths with curled hair and silver-tipped staves had accompanied Castus from the vestibule, but they did not appear willing to put up a fight. Castus gave the brooch another twist, and the eunuch gasped, his eyes on the polished steel blade.

'This way, excellency!' he croaked.

From the entrance atrium they paced rapidly out into the garden portico. Castus kept a fierce grip on the eunuch, shoving him stumbling ahead of him. The four Syrian youths, and a crowd of other palace servants and slaves, followed warily behind. Castus noticed that the weeping girl had vanished.

'Send word to the Augusta!' the eunuch managed to gasp as they walked. One of the Syrians nodded and jogged away in the other direction. Castus prodded at the eunuch's back with his sword tip, hurrying him on.

Leaving the garden court, they passed through a smaller pillared atrium, then into the vestibule of the baths. The group of female bath attendants waiting in the vestibule shrieked at their appearance, pressing themselves back against the walls.

'Which bath?' Castus demanded. One of the attendants pointed, and he shoved Olympiodorus forward again.

'Really, dominus, this is... ah! Most irregular!' the eunuch gasped.

Castus grunted, prodding him again with the sword. As they passed through the cold baths, between the plunge pools, he could feel the damp heat in the air. The tiles beneath his feet were unusually warm. Shoving the eunuch ahead of him, he paced on into the octagonal hall that led to the hot baths. The heavy doors at the far end were closed, a bar laid across them, and at either side stood a fat man in a loincloth. Eunuchs, but they had the bulk of gladiators. Both of them were gleaming with sweat.

'What's happening here?' Castus hissed, dragging Olympiodorus closer. 'Why are the doors barred?'

'The orders of the Augusta Helena, dominus!' the eunuch said. 'The doors must remain closed, and no one is to enter – or to leave!'

Castus felt the heat on his face, the heat of the tiled floor burning up through the soles of his boots. For a moment he stared at the doors, utterly baffled. A chill breeze rushed across the nape of his neck, and fresh sweat broke on his brow. Behind him, the crowd of slaves and attendants that had followed him through from the garden were gathered in the doorway of the cold chamber, staring in frightened anticipation.

With a roar of fury, Castus grabbed the eunuch by the hair and shoved him to his knees. 'Open the doors at once!' he bellowed, his voice resounding from the domed ceiling. 'Open, or I'll kill every one of you and paint the walls with your blood!'

He flourished the sword at the crowd of onlookers, then brought the blade down against the eunuch's neck. Olympiodorus let out a shriek, cowering.

'Open the doors!' the eunuch cried. 'Open them – God protect us!'

Without a word, the two doorkeepers threw the bar from the doors and hauled them open, stepping away quickly. Heat blasted from the opening, then a rolling wave of steam. Castus turned away, raising his arm to cover his face as perspiration washed his whole body. Olympiodorus had pulled free of his grip and slid away across the floor as the crowd behind them fell back.

Coughing the hot wet air from his lungs as he sheathed his sword, Castus stumbled into the fog cloud. He snatched up the bar from the floor – the wood was hot to his touch – and hurled it forward into the chamber, so the doors could not be sealed behind him. Then he pulled a fold of his cloak up over his nose and mouth and stepped across the threshold.

He was in a small circular chamber, a *sudatorium* with a mosaic pavement and a stone basin in the centre, although for a few moments Castus could make out nothing more through the dense steam. The floor burned like the embers of a pyre, and the walls of the chamber radiated a fierce heat. Fanning his hands before him, he blinked and stared into the hot white fog. To his left was an apse, with white marble steps down into a semi-circular pool. The surface of the water was seething, steam curling upwards into the saturated air. With the heat pressing on him, it took several moments for Castus to notice the body sprawled on the steps.

Fausta was naked, lying on her side with her unbound hair flowing black over the marble. Gasping, Castus dropped to kneel beside her. She must have crawled from the hot pool and then fallen onto the steps, overwhelmed. Impossible to tell if she still lived. Clenching his teeth, he got an arm beneath her, and the hot tiles scalded the back of his hand. Her body was limp, her soft flesh burning, slippery with sweat. He lifted her to his chest and struggled upright, carrying her in his arms as he stumbled back out of the chamber.

Gasps and cries from the crowd in the octagon hall as he emerged from the steam. Castus kept moving, carrying the body on through to the chamber of the cold baths. 'Take her!' he shouted to Olympiodorus. The eunuch quailed, stammering, but Castus shoved the woman's body into his arms. He ripped his cloak from his shoulder and spread it over the tiled floor, then took Fausta from the eunuch's cringing grasp and laid her down upon it.

'Bring water!' he cried, kneeling beside her again. 'Cold water – and salve!'

She lay on her back, and he covered her lower body with the hem of the cloak. Now he could see her face, the blood flowing from her nostrils, her mouth opening as she struggled to draw breath.

'Domina,' he said, taking her hand and leaning closer. 'Domina, can you hear me?'

Her eyes opened, unfocused for a moment. Then she recognised him, and he felt her grip tighten on his hand. A cough racked her body. Castus could see the livid red marks of scalding on her skin, the blood staining her teeth as she tried to smile.

'You,' she said in a faint pained croak.

Trembling, Castus reached into his belt pouch and took out the small carnelian ring that Crispus had given him. Fausta's eyes widened as she saw it. A long breath sighed from her. Castus eased her hand from his grip, then slid the ring back onto her smallest finger. Her chest was still, her eyes blank. He stooped over her and lightly kissed her brow, then covered her face with the cloak.

'She's gone, then,' a voice said. 'I did not intend it.'

Raising his head, Castus saw the woman standing in the far doorway. She was old, with a dry brown face, and dressed all in white silk with a golden Christian amulet around her neck. It took only a moment for him to recognise the woman he had last seen two years before in Thessalonica. The emperor's mother, Helena Augusta.

The slaves had returned with cups and flasks of water, and Castus waved them angrily aside. Too late for that now. Kneeling beside the dead woman, he stared at the figure in the doorway.

'You did this,' he said. 'You ordered this! You told them to bar the doors and heat the bath beyond human endurance. You murdered her!'

The old woman made a tutting sound, curtly shaking her head. She appeared entirely without remorse, entirely in possession of herself. 'She entered the baths of her own free will,' Helena said in a crisply accented voice. 'Intending, I believe, to purge the child she carried inside her. You're quite correct that I ordered the chamber sealed and the furnaces stoked higher. I wanted her to suffer, yes. I wanted her to experience the consequences of her sinful ways. But the heat alone would not have killed her. I suspect she took certain herbs or potions to induce the purge, and the combination proved fatal.'

'Say what you like,' Castus growled, getting to his feet. 'You murdered Fausta, just as your actions, your agents, caused the death of your own grandson!'

Helena merely shrugged. 'That, too, I did not intend,' she said. 'I loved my grandson, naturally, before that woman's perversions turned him to evil. But my agent Innocentius went too far with his investigation. He exceeded his mandate most grievously.'

She already knew. Castus gaped at her as the last traces of steam wreathed the air around him. And if she knew, the emperor himself must already have known that Crispus was dead. Fausta as well. Was that why she had tried to kill her child?

'How?' he managed to ask.

'Innocentius caught up with us two days ago,' Helena said. 'At Ocriculum, on the road towards Rome. He gave his report in confidence, of course. Fausta only learned of the death a few hours ago.'

Of course. And doubtless the emperor had concealed the news from all but the closest circle of his court. Clearly he had planned to wait until after the Vicennalia was concluded before making a public announcement.

'She claimed, you know,' Helena went on, nodding towards the body under the cloak, 'that my grandson forced himself upon her. As if he would do such a thing! She hoped it would save her from her husband's wrath, but she was wrong.'

Castus glanced down at the body, holding the pain gripped inside him. He could not blame Fausta; if she knew that Crispus was already condemned, she would have been desperate for any way to escape punishment herself. Jutting his jaw, he drew himself upright and faced the old woman again.

'Whatever you say,' he told her, his voice booming from the walls, 'it makes no difference. You're responsible for both their deaths. And if you're really a Christian, you'll burn in their fiery hell for this.'

Helena narrowed her eyes. 'Strong words,' she said. 'But I know my God better than that. And I know you, Aurelius Castus. You are a soldier; you understand duty, as do I. As a mother, I have a duty to protect my son. Constantine has a soft heart. But I do not, and I will take action when he hesitates.'

A man came running through the halls, one of the Syrian youths. Dropping to his knees, he slid to a halt before Helena. 'Augusta!' he cried, lowering his forehead to the tiles. 'There are soldiers at the gate, demanding admittance!'

'Tell them they must wait,' Helena said. 'As you can see, we have suffered a domestic tragedy here.'

For all his fierce loathing for this woman, Castus could not help admiring her cool composure. Helena, too, wore the mask of command. And with Fausta gone, her authority was absolute.

'Speaking of Innocentius,' she said, 'he has displeased me with his recent actions. He becomes impertinent in his demands, and knows too much about our affairs. I would be happy if he were silenced.'

'I'll silence him gladly,' Castus said. 'But not for your sake. Where do I find him?'

'Oh, no need for that,' Helena said with a thin smile. 'I understand he's intending to find *you*. When last I heard from him, he was on the way to Salona. I believe you have a villa near there?'

Castus's heart clenched, blackness pressing in his skull. He scrubbed his fingers across his scalp as the wave of nausea and dread flowed through him. 'When?' he gasped.

'As I say, he has two days' start on you, by the Flaminian Way. But you seem a tenacious man indeed – if you travel with the same speed as you arrived here, you may outpace him.'

How was it possible? Castus had left the *Phaselus* at Aternum, ordering the crew to wait for him there. But he was still in Rome, and the emperor's men were at the gates. Already another messenger was running from the entrance hall.

'Olympiodorus,' Helena said to the eunuch procurator. 'Conduct his excellency Aurelius Castus to the stables, via the cryptoporticus. Provide him with a horse, and see that he reaches the Praenestine Gate without hindrance. Do it on my authority.'

She turned back to Castus, regarding him with a cold clear eye. 'This matter has gone far enough,' she said. 'Say nothing of what has happened here to anybody. Track down Innocentius and rid me of him, and I will speak favourably of you to my son. I *may* be able to influence his judgement of you.'

Castus took a long breath, and shuddered as he exhaled. He glanced down once more at Fausta's covered body. Then he strode from the hall, brushing past Helena. The eunuch was already moving ahead of him, beckoning.

As he passed through the baths vestibule, Castus broke into a run.

CHAPTER XXX

With a fresh southerly breeze on her quarter, the little *Phaselus* had made a fast crossing of the Adriatic. Putting out from Aternum the previous evening, the helmsman had sailed her through the night, navigating by the stars, and by late afternoon the high coast of Dalmatia was visible on the far horizon. As the islands off the bay of Salona slipped by, the boat turned north and ran up around the forested cape that hid the cove and the villa. Castus sat stiffly on the stern bench as the oarsmen guided the little vessel in towards land. He laid his sword across his knees, and felt the renewed swells of fear in his chest.

The journey from Rome to the coast had taken him only two and a half days, riding post horses across the Apennines, pausing only occasionally at the way stations for a few hours' sleep, risking his life on the mountain roads in darkness. He had managed to rest during the voyage, at least, lulled by the sound of the waves washing the hull and the creak of the sail. Now, as the boat rounded the headland and pulled into the cove, he was tense with anticipation. He had seen no other ships during the crossing, only a few fishing boats around the islands. Could he really have beaten Innocentius?

There was the villa, lit by the early evening sun. As the boat pulled closer, Castus saw a figure running from the quay into the house; a moment later he heard the sound of voices. He stared, eyes narrowed, his breath held tight. Then, as the boat nosed into the harbour, he picked out the figure of his wife, running down the steps from the portico with her hair loose. Ursio and Felix came after her, and Sabinus. All of them safe. Bracing himself against the pitch of the boat's hull, Castus stood upright and raised his arms, crying out his thanks to the protecting gods.

As soon as the *Phaselus* touched the jetty, Castus sprang ashore. He was still dressed in his best uniform tunic, stained now with dust and sweat. He had lost his cloak, his gold brooch and all his baggage, but he cared nothing about that. He strode along the stone jetty, then dropped to his knees before Marcellina, embracing her with his face pressed to her swollen belly. He could hear her sobbing as she clasped his head in both hands.

Then she pulled away from him, swung her arm and slapped him hard across the face. 'Never leave me like that again!' she cried. 'Never!'

'I won't,' Castus said, grinning as he felt the pain of the slap lighting his face. He got to his feet, kissed her and threw his arms around her. 'I promise you, I won't.' He meant it more than she could know.

Back up the steps to the house, all of them thronged around him, taking his hands to guide him. *Like I'm an invalid*, he thought. And he felt like an invalid, twisted in mind and body, worn to the bone. A sob choked in his throat, and his eyes burned with tears, but he was still smiling.

Sitting in the seaward portico in the evening light, while the slaves ran to fetch wine and food, Castus told the household what had happened in Rome. Marcellina had already heard the news of Crispus's death from Felix, but as Castus told her about the emperor, about Fausta, and about what Helena had said, she covered her mouth with her hand to stifle a cry.

'And he's coming here, this man Innocentius?' she asked.

Castus nodded. 'I'm sure of it. He wants revenge, and he's not one to give in easily. Whether by land or by sea though, I don't know.'

'Then we must be prepared for him,' Marcellina said. She sat upright, turning to give orders. 'Felix – ride up to the junction with the highway from Salona and watch for anyone approaching by road. Ursio – remain here in the portico and watch the cove. Send slaves out to the headland to warn us of any vessels coming in.'

Castus smiled, surprised for a moment to hear his wife giving orders. But she was a soldier's daughter; she knew what needed to be done.

'And you need to rest, husband,' she said, taking his hand. 'Eat, bathe, then sleep.'

That night the villa was an armed camp. Felix kept his sentry watch at the highway junction three miles away, while Ursio guarded the seaward portico. Slaves were stationed at every door, armed with cudgels and shortswords. Castus knew that he would be warned if anything happened, but still he could not sleep. He lay flat on his back, Marcellina lying beside him with her belly pressed against his flank.

'I know how you feel,' she whispered. 'I've hardly slept more than a few hours, all the time you were gone.'

'The baby?' Castus asked, touching her belly.

'No! The baby's fine.' She rapped him on the brow. 'I was worrying about you! *Knucklehead.*'

He could not help smiling, feeling the warmth of her body beside him easing him towards sleep.

'I was angry with you a lot of the time,' she said. 'Furious. I couldn't believe that you'd go off without telling me and throw your life away on some matter of honour.'

'Honour,' Castus said drowsily. 'I don't have much of that left.'

She kissed him. 'You have all you'll ever need,' she said. 'I'm proud of what you did, despite everything. Standing up to the emperor like that – it was a noble thing. He needs to understand that all our decisions have consequences.'

'It's the consequences for us that I'm worried about.'

'Shh,' she told him, and kissed him again. 'Sleep – and tomorrow we'll know.'

At dawn Castus found Felix sitting outside the kitchen, breakfasting on bread and boiled eggs. Two of the house slaves had relieved him at the junction.

'No sign?' Castus asked.

'Nothing. You think they'll come today?'

Castus nodded. 'Get some rest,' he said.

By midday, there was still no word from the sentries. In his own chamber Castus sat at the window and cleaned his sword, oiling and polishing the blade, then sharpening the edge with a whetstone. The familiar tasks eased his mind a little. A light tap on the doorframe, and he turned.

'Father,' Sabinus said.

Castus nodded a greeting. 'You did well while I was away,' he said. 'Keeping the house safe.'

The boy just inclined his head, looking bashful. 'I cried when I heard about Crispus,' he said. 'I'm sorry.'

Smiling, Castus got up and clasped his son's shoulder, then rubbed his head. 'Don't worry about that. I did too, when it happened.'

'I made a vow, to God,' Sabinus said. Castus frowned; he had already noticed the small Christian amulet that his son wore at his neck. 'I vowed that I would help to destroy the man responsible. Is that wrong?'

'Be careful of vows,' Castus said, nudging the boy lightly. 'It was the emperor who ordered Crispus's death, and me that gave him the poison.'

'I mean the other man, the one who's coming here.'

'Listen. Things could be hard today. You've got to follow my orders, and do exactly what I say. Understand?'

'Yes,' Sabinus said, downcast, and Castus embraced him tightly.

When the boy was gone, he changed his tunic and dressed himself in a padded linen arming doublet. Taking an old mail shirt from his chest, he pulled it on over his head, put a looser tunic of drab wool over the top and tightened his belt. There were three helmets in the smaller chest beneath the table; Castus selected the plainest one, an infantryman's helmet of polished iron, with no crest. With the helmet slung over his arm he paced out onto the seaward portico.

Ursio was still there, dressed in a scale corselet and sitting in a cane chair with a sheaf of arrows laid on the table beside him. He was cutting new fletchings, then lifting each shaft to his eye to check the alignment.

'Won't be long now,' Castus said. 'I feel it, do you?'

The Sarmatian nodded his agreement.

Standing in the shade between the pillars, Castus listened to the sound of the sea washing against the harbour stones. Between every wave he heard the chirrup of insects from the surrounding land. His belt was tight, and he adjusted the fit. Then, as he turned to enter the house, he heard the sound of hooves.

The rider was coming down the track fast, throwing a plume of dust behind him. Castus thought it was one of his own slaves, but as the horse approached he saw that it was a boy in the saddle, barely older than his son. Drawing the horse to a staggering halt, the boy leaped down and ran to the front steps. He was one of Maiana's new husband's slaves, Castus realised, from Salona.

'My master sent me,' the boy said, rushing the words. 'There's an agent at Salona, an imperial agent with a mandate from the emperor so he said, he's got orders to seize you, he said, and he wanted the governor to give him men but the governor refused...'

'Slow down,' Castus said. He knew the governor, Octavianus. Not a bold man, but a stubborn one, and he had granted Castus time he needed badly. With a silent prayer of thanks, he led the boy through into the central courtyard and sat him down on the low wall between the pillars. 'Bring water,' he called, then gestured for the boy to continue.

'So the agent,' the boy said, 'the agent, he went down to Spalatum, and ordered the prefect there to give him men instead... and the prefect gave him half a troop of cavalry, and now he's on his way here, the agent I mean... My master ordered me to ride like the wind, but the soldiers are only an hour or so behind me.'

'You did well, lad,' Castus told him. Spalatum was an imperial villa on the coast, once the home of the retired emperor Diocletian. Now it was used as an arsenal, with a small military garrison of barbarian irregulars from the Equites Taifali. Clearly Innocentius was taking no chances.

'Diogenes,' Castus called. 'I need you back up at the junction. Soon as you see them, ride back here.'

The secretary saluted, like the soldier he had once been, and set off at a jog for the stables. At least, Castus thought, they knew that the imperial agent was coming by road. He felt a touch on his shoulder; Marcellina stood beside him.

'Half a troop,' she said. 'That's, what, fifteen men?'

'Fifteen or sixteen. If we stay here they could surround the house. I'll take Felix and Ursio up the track to the top of the ridge. We'll wait for them there – they've had a hard ride all the way from Salona, and it's a steep slope, with the stream to cross as well.'

Marcellina groaned, and dropped her forehead against his chest. Behind her, Castus saw Felix emerge from his chamber with a tired grin. Then Sabinus appeared, his bow in his hand.

'I'm coming with you, Father.'

'No you're not. I need you here at the house. Keep watch all around, and if anyone you don't recognise gets close, feel free to stick an arrow in him.'

The boy opened his mouth, about to protest, then recognised the note of command in his father's voice and nodded.

Out in the yard, the horses were already waiting. Castus was glad to be reunited with his big gelding, Ajax. The horse even appeared to recognise him, and consented to a nose-rub. Then Castus swung himself up into the saddle. Felix and Ursio were already mounted.

'Remember, we only have to kill Innocentius,' he told them. 'But don't let anyone past us.'

Up the track, they rode in silence until they reached the brow of the hill. The trees grew close on either side here, tall dark reaching pines. On the far side, the track dropped down the slope, with a rough plank bridge spanning a stream that rushed in a narrow crevasse towards the sea. Halting his horse, Castus sat still and listened. Birds sang, and the pines creaked in the breeze.

'Ursio,' he said. 'You know the Taifali language? Climb up onto those rocks over there. When you see them coming, call out to them that the man leading them's a traitor. Got it?'

The Sarmatian dismounted and moved off without a word, scrambling up onto the rocky spur that stood above the slope of the hillside.

They waited in stillness. Felix had dismounted, too, and positioned himself behind a tree up the slope to the left. He had his sling coiled around his fist, a heap of shot at his feet. An hour passed, maybe more, then they heard the hooves on the slope. Diogenes appeared, riding hard, with the two slaves that had been watching the junction galloping behind him on their ponies.

'Right behind us,' Diogenes gasped as he reached the top of the slope. 'Sixteen troopers, a biarchus and your man Innocentius.'

'Good,' Castus said. At least the waiting was over. 'Now get back to the house with the others.'

'I'm staying,' Diogenes told him, drawing his sword, then waved the two slaves on towards the villa. Castus shrugged; no time to argue about it now.

Already they could hear the sound of the riders climbing the slope towards them, the heavy beat of hooves and the clink of harness. Two of the troopers appeared first, unarmoured men in cloaks and fur caps with spears, carrying bows cased on their saddles. Ursio stood up from the summit of the rocky spur, cupped his hands around his mouth, and cried out in the guttural Taifali language. It was so long since Castus had heard the Sarmatian speak, he had forgotten how deep his voice was.

The approaching riders halted, gazing about them into the trees. Ursio cried out again, then cackled loudly and raised his fist. An angry yell from down the slope, and the riders kicked their horses forward again.

'They didn't believe you?' Castus called. Ursio had dropped down onto the flank of the spur, and was readying his bow. He shrugged, raising his eyebrows.

Can't say we didn't try, Castus told himself.

Now the war cries came from down the track, the lead troopers pushing their sweating horses into a gallop across the plank bridge and up towards the ridge. Ursio aimed, held for a moment, then released. The first trooper went down, toppling back off the saddle. As the second reached for his bow Ursio shot again, the arrow striking the man through the leg.

From behind the tree to the left Felix whirled his sling, a quick whip and a snap. The third rider screamed, struck in the head, and dropped. Castus felt his face locking into a savage grin, the big horse stamping and shifting beneath him. Down at the bend in the track he could see the Taifali bunching together, the biarchus who led them yelling orders. For the first time, he spotted Innocentius among them, and his jaw clenched hard. The agent was dressed in a thick grey cloak, but his blond curls were distinct in the shadows of the trees. He was screaming at the troopers, directing them. Castus saw six of the Taifali slide from the saddle, cross the stream and advance up the verges of the track on foot, readying their bows. Another three rode into the trees flanking the path. A stratagem, Castus thought. But he could play the same game.

'Diogenes,' he called. 'They're trying to outflank us while the archers keep us pinned down. Get into the cover of the trees, but stay close to the track and stop anyone who tries to get past you.'

Pulling on the reins, he turned Ajax and spurred the gelding through the bushes edging the track. The ground rose, and the trees were thick, but the big horse easily forged a path through the dense scrub. Castus dipped his head, keeping clear of the low branches; he knew this ground well, and knew how to fight here. At a break in the trees he caught a glimpse of two Taifali riders coming up the slope towards him, the horses picking their way through the tangles of fallen wood and undergrowth. Keeping very still in the cover of the trees, he waited until they entered a clearing below him, one of them turning aside towards the track, then he kicked Ajax into motion.

The big horse burst from cover and crashed down the slope towards the second rider. Castus already had his sword raised. The Taifali had time to scream a warning and jab with his spear, then Castus seized the spearshaft and wrenched it, dragging him halfway from the saddle. A sweeping slash, and his blade chopped down into the man's shoulder. Blood sprayed as he fell, but Castus was already turning to confront the other rider.

The second Taifali was a big man, heavily bearded, his fur cap pulled down low. He flicked back his cloak, reaching for the bow case behind his saddle; but Castus was closing on him fast, screaming as he came. With a snarling cry the rider snatched the spear he carried slung across his shoulder, couching it beneath his arm like a lance, then spurred his horse into a charge.

They met at the gallop, the spearpoint driving straight for Castus's chest. At the last moment Castus tugged at the reins and Ajax shied, then reared. Swinging the flat of his blade, Castus drove the spear aside. Then he cut down at the rider, missing and striking the horse. The Taifali had kept his grip on the spear; reversing it, he stabbed with the butt-spike. But his horse was injured, bucking and shying. Castus felt the spike jab against the small of his back, stopped by the mail. The Taifali roared, his teeth gleaming in his beard, then Castus leaned in the saddle, aimed, and drove his sword through the man's neck.

No sign of the third rider. Castus shoved the dead man from the saddle, shook the blood from his sword, then spurred Ajax into the gloom beneath the trees. From the track he could hear shouts, and the cries of wounded men. An arrow struck a tree close to him, thrumming. Cursing between his teeth, he hauled the reins and turned Ajax back up the slope.

Through the trees at a hard canter, he scaled the ridge and then turned again, towards the track. As he broke from the cover of the bushes he saw bodies sprawled on the road, injured men crouched in the cover of the trees. Ursio was still standing on the rocky spur, aiming and shooting, but the crop of arrows stuck in the ground at his feet was thinning fast. No sign of Felix, nor of Diogenes.

A sudden rattle of branches, and two of the Taifali riders burst from the trees on the far side of the track. They must have climbed around the flank on that side, Castus realised, and now they were behind Ursio. He yelled a warning to the Sarmatian as he spurred his horse forward. To his left, Felix stood up from behind a tree and whirled his sling.

Ursio turned, staggering on the rocky slope. He swung his bow, drawing back the string, but the rider was too close. With a scream of triumph the Taifali hurled his spear, and the iron head sank into Ursio's neck just above the collar of his scale cuirass. A moment later, Felix's slingshot knocked the rider from the saddle.

Castus was already on the road, driving Ajax forward into the bushes. The other rider had a bow, and shot from the saddle. The arrow went wide, and before he could draw another Ajax slammed into his horse's flank. Roaring, Castus lifted his sword, stabbing the point down and through the bowman's shoulder.

When he glanced back, he saw confusion. Dead men and wounded horses all down the slope below the ridge, half a dozen riderless horses circling in wild panic. Below them, the remaining Taifali were advancing again, some mounted and the rest on foot. Castus saw Innocentius riding at their rear, still crying out orders. Felix snapped a last shot from his sling, then drew his sword as Diogenes came cantering back up the slope, hunched in the saddle, blood streaking his face.

The biarchus commanding the troopers whirled his arm, shouting, then pointed up the slope at Castus. With a ragged cry, the handful of riders behind him bunched closer and pushed their horses into a heavy trot. Only three of them remained in the saddle, at least three more on foot with bows.

'Out of slingstones,' Felix said, back on his horse and riding up beside Castus. 'Charge them, you think?'

'May as well,' Castus said. They had the advantage of the slope at least. The wiry soldier grinned at him, and Castus smiled back. Then they both screamed and, with Diogenes behind them, they burst into a downhill gallop.

Hooves battered the dust from the track, and the leading Taifali riders slowed in shock as the charging men came down at them. One tried to turn, too slow. Ajax crashed against the man's horse, teeth snapping, and he tumbled from the saddle. Veering, Castus saw the biarchus staring at him, white-faced, sword in hand. He swung Ajax to the left, then feinted with his sword at the head of the biarchus's horse. The animal flinched, the rider wrestling with the reins, and Castus slashed the officer across the face. A heartbeat later, Felix's sword struck the biarchus in the side, and he fell.

'Almost got to him first!' Felix laughed. Then an arrow hit his chest, another pinning him through the neck.

Castus wheeled, his horse rearing. He could not see Innocentius. Diogenes was still mounted, slashing furiously at one of the surviving Taifali. Castus rode to help him, then felt a sudden shock through his horse's body. Ajax stumbled,

414

an arrow jutting from his straining neck. The big gelding raised his head, dragging on the reins, then blew bloody froth. Castus threw himself clear as the horse collapsed into the dust.

Rolling, keeping his grip on his sword, he forced himself back to his feet. The man fighting Diogenes had broken free and was galloping fast back down the slope, the last of the Taifali riding with him. Both of them carried wounded comrades clinging to their saddles. Dust milled in the air, and Castus stared around him, the violence of battle powering his blood. One of the archers, the one that had shot Ajax, bolted from the bushes and Diogenes rode after him, sword raised.

Castus turned, heaving breath. His horse was dying, legs still weakly kicking. Ursio was dead, and so was Felix. Where was Innocentius?

With a cry of anguish, he saw the imperial agent riding through the trees to his left. He had been keeping clear of the fight on the track, but now he was behind Castus, pushing back through the bushes. With a smirking glance over his shoulder, Innocentius kicked at his horse, riding up towards the ridge. Diogenes was still far back down the slope. The road was clear all the way to the villa.

Sucking in air, Castus broke into a run. His legs burned, muscles aching from the horseback fight and the hard fall. The base of his spine felt bruised where the spear-butt had struck him. But he stumbled on up the slope, feeling nothing but anguished despair.

Innocentius was almost at the crest of the ridge, riding fast with his cloak swirling behind him. A figure appeared at the top of the track, against the narrow gap of sky between the pines. Sabinus, bow in hand. Castus tried to shout, but his breath was caught in his chest and all he could do was run.

The boy raised his bow, aimed calmly, then loosed.

415

The agent flinched in the saddle; for a moment Castus thought the arrow had hit him, then he sat upright again and seemed to laugh. A heartbeat, and his horse shuddered beneath him, blood flowing from its flank where Sabinus's arrow had grazed it.

Innocentius sawed at the reins, but he was off balance, and as the horse screamed and stumbled forward onto its knees he was flung from the saddle. He fell heavily, the reins slipping from his hand, and the wounded animal cantered free. Castus was still running, his last breath bursting from his lungs as he yelled.

Staggering, Innocentius lurched back upright. He glanced at the horse; too far away. Sabinus was already aiming a second arrow. The boy loosed, and the shaft struck the ground close to Innocentius's feet. With a shout of frustration, the agent limped off the track and into the bushes.

Sabinus was already running down the slope, but Castus raised a hand to keep him back. He paused for a moment to draw breath, then plunged into the bushes after Innocentius. Briars caught and dragged at his clothes, but he hacked his way through them. The ground rose, rocky under his feet; ahead of him he could hear the sounds of Innocentius crashing through the undergrowth beneath the trees. Then Castus was out in the open, clear ground between the pines, and the shape of the fleeing agent was stark against the sunlight.

Ten more running strides, and the trees fell away. They were on a bare grassy summit, the ground dropping on all sides to rock-strewn slopes, the broad blue sea below them. Innocentius had come to a halt, panting. His cloak was gone, but he still held his sword. For a moment he leaned and peered over the brink, and Castus thought he might try to jump. Then he turned, and Castus advanced towards him.

The agent's face was gashed, and smeared with dirt. His blond curls were sweated flat across his skull, but the nervous

416

smirk was still flickering around his lips.

'You can't kill me!' he declared. 'I'm an imperial agent, with a mandate from the emperor himself!'

'Hasn't stopped me before,' Castus said, still advancing. 'It won't now.'

Innocentius raised his sword, and for one satisfying moment Castus thought he would fight. Then he dropped the weapon and fell to his knees, palms spread.

'Please,' he said, a sick tremor running through him. 'I'm surrendering. You can't kill me.' The smirk flashed back across his face. 'I was only following orders.'

'You were writing your own orders,' Castus said, halting before him. 'Now you can die on your knees like a coward if you want.'

He raised his sword. Innocentius let out a low whining sound.

'This is for Niobe,' Castus said.

The agent's face fell blank, and his brow creased into a frown.

'You didn't even know her name, did you?'

Then he brought the sword down, hacking the agent's head from his shoulders with a single slashing blow.

The bodies were lying on the track, Diogenes and Sabinus kneeling beside them. Castus stood and gazed down at their faces. Ursio, the big Sarmatian who had fought loyally at his side for so long. Felix, the wiry soldier from the slums of Rome, whom Castus had promoted to centurion only two years before. He too had died as he had lived, fighting.

Sabinus was weeping openly, and Diogenes had tears in his eyes.

'He taught me how to shoot,' the boy said, brushing the Sarmatian's brow with his fingertips. Castus felt nothing now but a deep drowning sadness.

'Let's get them up,' he said. 'Find some horses and put them across the saddles, and we'll take them home.'

They mounted, Castus riding one of the troopers' horses. He knew that several of the Taifali had escaped, and guessed they would ride back to Salona to report what had happened. With any luck they would not return.

Up to the brow of the hill they rode slowly, leading the horses bearing their fallen comrades behind them. Diogenes was wounded, though not gravely. Sabinus was sniffing back tears, still too stunned to speak. With a shock of sad pride, Castus realised that his son had become a man now.

As they crossed the ridge and the trees parted, he glanced down towards the villa. He frowned, and turned his gaze to the sea. A despairing cry burst from him, and without a word he kicked his horse into a gallop.

Down in the cove, an imperial liburnian galley lay at anchor, a boat packed with armed men already pulling towards the quay.

Dragging his horse to a halt in the gravelled forecourt, Castus flung himself from the saddle, stumbled, then ran towards the front steps. He knew that the boat had already reached the harbour; he had seen the marines advancing along the quay towards the house as he came down the last slope. Up the steps and across the front portico, he shoved open the main doors and strode through the entrance vestibule.

Marcellina was on the far side of the central courtyard, seated in the pillared doorway of the main reception hall. Beside her stood Aelius Saturninus. Half a dozen marines rested on their spears in the vestibule of the seaward portico.

'Greetings, brother,' Saturninus said as Castus approached. 'I see you're keeping yourself amused out here in the countryside! Good hunting?'

Castus realised that his tunic and right arm were spattered with blood. 'I got what I wanted,' he said through his teeth. His sword was sheathed, but he was gripping the hilt. Marcellina stared at him, pale with shock and fear. He came to a halt, a few strides from Saturninus.

The officer smiled tightly, clasping his hands behind his back. 'I've got something for you,' he said. 'Hot from Rome.' He took a slim scroll tube from his belt and tossed it onto the table beside Marcellina.

'An imperial rescript,' he said. 'Stating that Flavius Aurelius Castus, by the order of the Sacred Wisdom, is hereby cleared of all charges laid against him. I don't know how you did it, but it was the emperor's own decision. You still have friends in the palace, it seems.'

'That's all?' Castus said. The blood was beating loud in his head, and his legs felt unsteady.

'Not all, no,' Saturninus said. 'The emperor is also glad to agree to your... *request*... for discharge from the army. You will give up your rank, but keep your status as a retired military commander. However, the note adds that you will no longer be expected at court, nor will you be permitted to enter the Sacred Presence.'

No hardship there, Castus thought. He dipped his head, eyes closed, then gazed at Saturninus again.

'Seems you're free, brother,' the officer said with a shrug. 'Free to spend your days slaughtering things in the woods, hm?'

Marcellina pressed her hand to her brow. She looked sick. Freedom, Castus thought: he had wanted this, prayed for it. But now it was here he felt suddenly bereft.

'I'd stay for dinner,' Saturninus said, 'but I'm due at Salona before sundown. Message for the governor there. Apparently there's a renegade imperial agent somewhere around here. If

419

you happen to see him, you can tell him his mandate's been revoked.' He shot a wry glance at Castus's bloody tunic. Castus just nodded.

Saturninus gave a quick bow to Marcellina, then paced out towards the portico. Castus touched his wife lightly on the cheek, then followed him. As the marines filed back along the quay towards the boat, Saturninus paused and stood with Castus, gazing at the sea.

'You should tell the prefect at Spalatum there are some of his men up in the woods,' Castus said. 'He can come and get them any time he wants, unless you want to load them aboard your galley.'

'Oh no,' Saturninus said. 'Can't carry dead men aboard a ship. Bad luck!' He smiled, and just for a moment Castus caught a flash of the man he used to know, the brother officer he had commanded back in Gaul.

'I should thank you,' Castus said, forcing the words out. 'You could have ordered your men to stop me leaving Pola.'

Saturninus just inclined his head in acknowledgement. 'I expected you to come straight back here,' he said. 'That would have been the wise thing. But Rome... that was audacious. Seems to have worked in your favour somehow though.'

'What about Fausta, and Crispus?'

Saturninus flinched deliberately, kissing his teeth. 'Officially,' he said, 'there are no Fausta and Crispus. Their images have been destroyed, their memory abolished. They never existed, brother, and their names must never be spoken. You'd do well to remember that.'

Castus nodded. It pained him, but he knew how these things were done.

'The mob in Rome weren't happy, when they found out,' Saturninus went on. 'There were riots. They stoned the emperor's

420

statues, smashed the face off one of them. Palladius wanted to set the Germanic guards on them, but Constantine refused. Strange, he just seemed to shrug it off. Like he felt he deserved the punishment.'

'You don't think he did?' Castus said in a low voice.

'As a loyal officer of Rome,' Saturninus replied stiffly, 'I would never criticise the decisions of the Invincible Augustus.' Castus could not tell whether he was joking. This was the new world, he thought. A new empire. Best ask no questions. But he could not resist.

'What happened to Helena? Did the crowd turn on her, too?'

'The Augusta Helena? No, of course not. She kept herself well out of it. Although the emperor's not happy with her. She's going on a pilgrimage, apparently, to the Holy Land. She worries about sin, so they say. Doubtless she'll be gone many years, and at her age she may never see Rome again.'

Castus nodded slowly. He wondered if he would ever see the city again, either.

'Goodbye, brother,' Saturninus said, stretching out his hand. Castus paused, frowning at him, then clasped his palm. Just for a moment he had forgotten that he hated the man.

Then, without another word, Saturninus turned and jogged down the steps to the quay and the waiting boat.

Back inside the house, Marcellina was waiting. Diogenes and Sabinus had joined her, the same question in all their eyes. Castus forced himself to smile. With a groan of relief Marcellina ran to him, and he wrapped her in his arms.

'Is it over?' she asked.

'Yes,' Castus said, holding her tightly. 'Yes. It's done.'

EPILOGUE

The sun was low over the sea as the three men traced the path along the shore. Diogenes was in the lead, with Castus following him and Sabinus bringing up the rear, a heavy basket clasped in both hands. They passed the first of the trees, and paused before the two rough earthen mounds in the clearing above the path. Both were piled with smooth stones from the shore; in time, Castus would have proper headstones cut in Salona, and flat slabs to cover each grave. He would have the names of the men who had died in his service carved in marble. Valerius Felix, Flavius Ursio. Dedicated to the gods below. *May the earth lie lightly upon them.*

A reverent pause, the three men standing with bowed heads and touching their brows. Then they moved on along the path. It was only a short distance to the next clearing, set back a little from the shore and screened by pines. The slaves had already dug the pit and prepared the stones that would cover it. There would be no headstone this time, but all Castus's household would know who had been laid to rest here, and they would guard the secret well.

Sabinus set the basket down on the turf and opened the lid. From inside he lifted the pottery urn, and together they lowered it into the pit. They stepped back, raising their hands to the sky, and Castus spoke the words.

'Immortal gods, we commend to the earth the remains of Flavius Julius Crispus, Caesar. If his shade still wanders the realms below, we ask that you raise him up to a seat in your heavens, and unite him with the divine.'

Don't let them dishonour my body. The pyre had taken Crispus's flesh, but the urn that Castus had taken to Rome and presented to the emperor contained only the remains of a burnt pig, mixed with ash from the bath furnaces. Ursio and Felix had taken the Caesar's ashes, and carried them here to the villa when they left Pola. Now they would lie undisturbed.

Diogenes took up a shovel and filled the pit with earth, and the three of them piled the stones over the mound. Castus poured a libation of wine onto the grave, and set a brass dish of smoking incense on the highest stone. In silence they stood and gave their prayers, while the low sun stretched the long shadows of the pines between them.

As the red disk sank below the horizon, they faced the sea with arms raised and cried out a salute. '*Sol Invictus, Unconquered Sun. Return this world to light again, and to hope.*' His son might call himself a Christian now, Castus thought, but he still understood the power of the old ways.

The sky was still glowing, the sea reflecting the sunset's gleam. Diogenes and Sabinus had already begun picking their way back along the path, but Castus lingered a while, until the brightness had slipped from the sky. Behind him, the incense still burned on the grave mound, the smoke twisting between the trees, scenting the twilight. Castus sent a last silent prayer to Crispus's shade, but soon the words in his mind thinned to nothing, and he remembered only the man himself. The man, and the emperor he might one day have become.

Along the curve of the shore, he could see the lamps glowing from the portico of the villa, glimmering points of light against the vast gloom of the darkening land. The sight gladdened his soul. Diogenes and Sabinus had almost reached the house. A last glance across the waves, then Castus turned and followed them home.

AUTHOR'S NOTE

The fates of Crispus Caesar and Fausta Augusta are among the most mysterious episodes in later Roman history. Just as the deaths of these two prominent individuals were immediately hushed up by the imperial authorities, so the details of their lives were also erased, quite literally: their names were chiselled from monuments, and the church historian Eusebius rewrote his major work to omit the glowing references to Crispus in the first edition.

In the absence of an official story, rumours bred, and many of these are mentioned by later writers. Byzantine historians allude to a sexual connection between the pair; Zonaras agrees with the fifth-century churchman Philostorgius that Fausta falsely accused Crispus of raping her, and was put to death in turn when the truth emerged. Many recent commentators have followed this line, but it does not explain why neither victim was ever pardoned, nor their reputation restored. Whatever crime Fausta and Crispus were alleged to have committed, Constantine must have believed it to be heinous, and never forgave either of them. Clearly the deaths were connected, and unusual: Ammianus Marcellinus tells us that Crispus was killed at Pola, and Sidonius Apollinaris gives poison as the cause; he and several others mention that Fausta died in an overheated bath. There are strong hints of conspiracy and treason, and suggestions that the emperor's mother had some influence over events, but beyond that all is conjecture.

Modern scholars have little more to go on, and have been able to offer only tentative theories about what might really have happened. It was Jacob Burckhardt who first proposed that Crispus had wanted his father to abdicate, while N. J. E. Austin and Timothy Barnes have both suggested a possible connection to the illegal practice of divination. But, as Jan Willem Drijvers puts it, 'in the case of the executions of Crispus and Fausta, historians should admit that they have a mystery which will never be solved'.

In composing this story, I have tried to make the best sense of the scraps of evidence we do possess, and to devise a scenario both historically plausible and dramatically engaging. Two recent scholarly papers have been particularly useful. David Woods's 'On the Death of the Empress Fausta' (1998) presents the best summary of the ancient sources and also suggests an attempted abortion as a likely cause for Fausta's end, while Lars Ramskold, in 'Constantine's Vicennalia and the Death of Crispus' (2012), uses the evidence of imperial mints and legal rescripts to reconstruct a much clearer chronology of the events of AD 326.

The course of the war between Constantine and Licinius two years previously is only slightly better known. Both Zosimus and the anonymous *Origo Constantini Imperatoris* provide brief descriptions of the campaign, although, characteristically, neither agrees with the other. I've chosen largely to follow Zosimus's account, as it is the more detailed of the two. No source mentions a fire at Thessalonica, but it might explain the disparity in the size of Constantine's fleet between the preparations for the campaign and its conclusion.

The clash in the Hellespont was the last great naval battle of classical antiquity and, if we can trust Zosimus, the last time that the venerable trireme, mainstay of the ancient fleets of Greece and Rome for centuries, appeared in combat. Zosimus, however, is a notoriously unreliable writer, and while I've retained the triremes, I've opted for a cautious reduction in the numbers involved in the various battles. Edwin Pears' 'The Campaign Against Paganism' (in *The English Historical Review* of 1909) remains the only attempt at a detailed narrative reconstruction of the war to date, and, although Pears probably overstates the religious aspects, I've adopted many of his suggestions.

While there is plenty of modern scholarship on the Roman navy and ancient seamanship, little of it covers the later period of the empire. Alongside several excellent works on the earlier Greek and Roman navies, I've drawn much from John H. Pryor and Elizabeth M. Jeffries's *Age of the Dromon: The Byzantine Navy ca 500–1204*; this covers a much later era, but is an invaluable source of information on galley construction and warfare, naval tactics and logistics, and the handling of the ancient oared war vessel.

The composition of Constantine's army is largely unknown, but many of the units I've mentioned appear in slightly later sources and almost certainly existed at the time. Gratianus 'Funarius' was probably one of Constantine's senior officers; he was the father of the future emperors Valentinian and Valens. Ammianus Marcellinus mentions Bonitus the Frank, who 'in the civil war fought vigorously on the side of Constantine against the soldiers of Licinius'. We don't know in what capacity Bonitus served, but making him leader of an irregular Frankish auxilia unit seems plausible. His son Silvanus went on to a glorious career in the Roman army, and an inglorious end after his troops on the Rhine acclaimed him emperor; he was assassinated on the orders of imperial agents in AD 355.

The speech given by Constantine in Chapter V is loosely based on passages from the *Oration to the Saints*, reputedly composed by the emperor himself at around this time and recorded by Eusebius. The authenticity of aspects of the oration has been questioned, but I think it gives a good idea of the state of Constantine's religious beliefs during this period, and the way he might have expressed them. His mother did indeed make a pilgrimage to the Holy Land c. AD 326: she allegedly discovered the site of the crucifixion in Jerusalem, and the fragments of the True Cross. Soon after her return to Rome she died, and was canonised as St Helena.

As with my previous books, I'm immensely grateful to my editor, Rosie de Courcy, and to the production team at Head of Zeus for their enthusiastic support and encouragement. I must also thank, once again, my agent Will Francis and everyone at Janklow & Nesbit, and my tireless copy editor Richenda Todd, who has exercised her extraordinary attention to detail in all the books in this series, and saved me from many an embarrassing error. I'm most grateful to Professor Boris Rankov and to Dr Philip de Souza, and to the Polish historian Damian Waszak, for their enlightening discussions of the Hellespont battle, and the difficulties of interpreting dubious ancient sources. As always, I claim full responsibility for any imaginative excesses.

CLAIM A FREE
TWILIGHT OF EMPIRE EBOOK

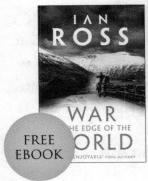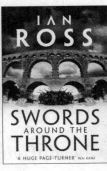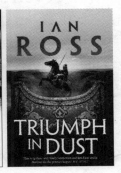

FREE EBOOK

TO CLAIM YOUR FREE EBOOK OF
WAR AT THE EDGE OF THE WORLD

1. FIND THE CODE

   This is the last word on page 299 of this book, preceded by
   HOZ-, for example HOZ-code

2. GO TO HEADOFZEUS.COM/FREEBOOK

   Enter your code when prompted

3. FOLLOW THE INSTRUCTIONS

   Enjoy your free eBook of
   WAR AT THE EDGE OF THE WORLD

A letter from the publisher

We hope you enjoyed this book. We are an independent publisher dedicated to discovering brilliant books, new authors and great storytelling. If you want to hear more, why not join our community of book-lovers at:

www.headofzeus.com

We'll keep you up-to-date with our latest books, author blogs, tempting offers, chances to win signed editions, events across the UK and much more.

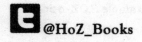 @HoZ_Books

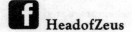 HeadofZeus

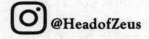 @HeadofZeus

HEAD *of* ZEUS